THE BEST IS YET TO COME

KATY COLINS

ONE PLACE. MANY STORIES

HQ
An imprint of HarperCollins*Publishers* Ltd
1 London Bridge Street
London SE1 9GF

www.harpercollins.co.uk

HarperCollins*Publishers*
1st Floor, Watermarque Building,
Ringsend Road, Dublin 4, Ireland

This edition 2021

1

First published in Great Britain by
HQ, an imprint of HarperCollins*Publishers* Ltd 2021

Copyright © Katy Colins 2021

Katy Colins asserts the moral right to be identified
as the author of this work. A catalogue record for this book
is available from the British Library.

ISBN: 978-0-00-820225-5

MIX
Paper from
responsible sources
FSC™ C007454

This book is produced from independently certified FSC™ paper
to ensure responsible forest management.

For more information visit: www.harpercollins.co.uk/green

This book is set in 10.8/15.5 pt. Sabon

Printed and bound in Great Britain by
CPI Group (UK) Ltd, Croydon, CR0 4YY

Praise for *The Best is Yet to Come*

'The kind of emotional and heartwarming read that do not disturb signs were made for. This is Colins at her best' **Mike Gayle,** *Half a World Away*

'Uplifting, warm and full of heart. I loved it!' **Cathy Bramley,** *A Patchwork Family*

'A gorgeous warm novel about finding hope and friendship in the most unexpected places' **Paige Toon,** *The Minute I Saw You*

'I can't remember the last time I related to a character as much as Izzy! A warm and touching read about identity and friendship and all that's in-between' **The Unmumsy Mum**

'Will break your heart and put it back together again. A touching, emotional, uplifting and life-affirming tale about the importance of love and friendship' **Isabelle Broom,** *Hello, Again*

'Heartwarming and full of hope, I fell in love with Arthur and Izzy as they fell in love with each other' **Clare Pooley,** *The Authenticity Project*

'Absolutely gorgeous – heartwarming and emotional. I loved it!' **Rachael Lucas,** *The Telephone Box Library*

'Warm, wonderful and life-affirming' **Cressida McLaughlin,** *The Cornish Cream Tea Summer*

'A proper feel-good story about an unexpected friendship that brought a happy tear to my eye' **Josie Lloyd,** *The Cancer Ladies' Running Club*

'Joyful, uplifting and wise. Just the tonic for our times – a love song to kindness and connection. I loved it' **Katie Marsh,** *My Everything*

'Te

Katy Colins learned there is always a second chance in life. Jilted before her wedding, she sold all she owned, filled a backpack and booked a one-way ticket to the other side of the world.

Her solo travels inspired her to pen 'The Lonely Hearts Travel Club' series and saw her dubbed the 'Backpacking Bridget Jones' by the global media. And, in a stunning twist of fate, Katy found her happy-ever-after by marrying the journalist who shared her story with the world.

She now lives in the middle of England with her husband, John, and two young children.

You can find out more about Katy, her writing and her travels at www.katycolins.com or @notwedordead on social media platforms.

Also by Katy Colins

Chasing the Sun
How to Say Goodbye

The Lonely Heart Travel Club series:

Destination: Thailand
Destination: India
Destination: Chile

E & A. I'm so proud to call you mine.

CHAPTER I

Izzy

Izzy wished she could stop crying. She sniffed loudly and glanced at her phone – there were still six hours until Andrew came home. Six hours until she would be rescued. Three hundred and sixty long minutes left to endure, unless he called to say he was going to be late, again. That may tip her over the edge. She had been proud of herself this morning for managing to hold back the tears until his car had left the drive. He had been too busy connecting his phone to the car's Bluetooth to see her stare out of the rain-splattered window at him, visibly overwhelmed by the prospect of another day with no purpose other than to survive. The cold, grey February day loomed long, not helped by the swollen sky and determined rain clouds to scupper any plans she might have had to brace the outdoors.

She grabbed a tissue, the last in the box, and blew her nose. Some days she couldn't exactly remember *why* she was crying but right now it was because she had reached her limit. This bone-aching exhaustion was certainly slowly killing her. Grit rested in her eyes, her limbs constantly ached and pounding headaches were never far away. If she could just get more than three hours of sleep in one go then she was sure she could take on anything the world threw at her. She cupped her hands over her ears to drown out her newborn daughter's cries. The torturous sound made her heart feel like it was being stabbed with a thousand jagged pieces of glass.

Izzy had decided to try the 'cry it out' method, one that her mother-in-law had suggested – among many other snippets of *advice* – in a bid to get Evie to sleep. It had seemed so simple. You made sure your baby was fed, clean and winded – then you laid them in their cot to sleep. You checked on them when they cried, after three minutes, but never picked them up in the hope that they would eventually settle themselves.

Anything was worth a shot at this desperate stage. In the five weeks since bringing Evie home from the hospital Izzy had tried everything – from using stuffed animals that played lullabies on a loop, to rocking her, to blasting white noise from her iPhone. Nothing worked. She was 'lucky' if her daughter managed to settle for a couple of hours each night.

According to her phone timer, it had only been forty-two seconds since she last checked on her. Izzy bit down on her bottom lip as the steady cries grew in volume from upstairs. All she wanted was five minutes of peace, downstairs, on her own. Enough time to enjoy a hot cup of tea, or even take a super-quick shower and wash her greasy hair instead of constantly relying on dry shampoo. Enough time to sit in silence and clear her head. If she was really honest with herself, what she wanted was to have her old life back. She could never ever say this out loud to anyone. Even just thinking it made her feel a little bit sick. But it was true. She had imagined maternity leave to feel like one long, lovely weekend with idyllic family outings discovering local hidden gems that she'd never had the time to explore before. Or long, lazy pub lunches as her peaceful baby napped, or even time to dedicate to a new hobby, but it wasn't like that at all. Right now Izzy longed to have a purpose; some place to be, something that fulfilled her, as she clearly wasn't cut out to be a mother.

Izzy glanced around the messy lounge to find the remote control. Perhaps she could turn the volume up really loud to block the crying out. The room had been taken over by gaudy plastic and stuffed toys. 'Welcome to the world' new baby cards in every possible shade of pink you could imagine cluttered the surfaces, she should probably get round to taking them down. A once shiny helium balloon in the shape of a baby bottle was slowly deflating in the corner. Four bunches of flowers, all way past their best, were shedding brown petals across the carpet that needed a decent hoover. Damp, sicky muslins were discarded across the sofa. Half drunk, cold cups of tea and snotty, balled-up tissues from her last big cry lined the side table. She couldn't see the remote anywhere in amongst this chaos. She began flinging cushions to the floor, her exasperation growing in sync with the volume of Evie's cries.

Sleep training was hell. How did other mums do it? How did they let their babies cry and cry and cry? It was taking all her willpower to stick it out until her phone alarm went off. She glanced at her screen, it had been one minute and seven seconds – she wasn't even halfway. Just then the chime of her doorbell startled her. Who the hell was that? The postman had already been and she certainly wasn't expecting visitors this time in the afternoon. She wiped her wet eyes with her sleeve and shuffled in her slippers to the front door, flinging it open.

Izzy stared at the delivery man standing on her doorstep holding a parcel. He was in his mid-eighties, with neatly combed baby-fine white hair, much older than the usual Amazon delivery guy. She couldn't remember what *life-changing* gadget she'd ordered this time that promised to fix everything. Desperate to get through another night feed she had taken to scouring the internet for anything that guaranteed a decent chunk of sleep. One-click ordering and next-day delivery was both a blessing and a curse.

'Hello.' The many wrinkles on his face reminded her of an overcooked jacket potato. 'I'm Arthur. From number thirty-nine.' His voice was deep and low. The kind of voice used to being spoken over. That was the house opposite, the one on the corner of the cul-de-sac. Perhaps the parcel wasn't for her and had he actually come to complain about the noise. He probably presumed something terrible was taking place inside, thanks to Evie's ear-splitting screams.

'I'm sorry to bother you but I've had this delivered to me by mistake,' he said, clearing his throat, holding out the slim brown cardboard box. It was the exact same shade of brown as his trousers and his thick overcoat that was missing a button.

'It's been labelled correctly, but it's been left at my door by accident. I'm sorry if it was anything urgent. I did try and call over yesterday but you must have been out.'

Izzy had been in all day but she'd ignored the doorbell. Yesterday had been a rough day, even worse than today, if that was possible.

She eventually found her voice. 'Thanks.'

Evie's cries were getting louder, shooting down the stairs, under her skin and into her bones.

4

'Oh,' The old man looked as if he had only just heard the terrible noise. 'I'm sorry to have disturbed you. I hope I didn't wake—'

'No, she wasn't asleep. She's allergic to it,' Izzy said.

'Oh, oh dear. I—'

'She's not! It was a joke, a poor one,' Izzy explained hurriedly. 'She's fine, just fighting a much-needed nap.'

'Ah, OK…' He shifted on his feet as if waiting for something. 'Shall I just leave it here or…?'

The package! She took it from his large veiny hands, the movement making her dressing gown flutter open. The old man's gaze fell on her pink faded unicorn slippers that matched the pyjama set she was still wearing at ten past two in the afternoon. He kindly turned away as Izzy quickly grabbed the dressing gown tie and pulled it tight. *Great*, she cringed, she had just exposed the large wet patch around her right boob where her breast pad had leaked. She was suddenly aware of her own body odour, a heady mix of sweat and puked-up breast milk. It was days like this when she felt like she was in someone else's body, living someone else's life.

'Thanks for dropping it round,' she coughed, swallowing back tears of mortification.

'You're welcome, dear,' he said softly, a sort of worried look dancing across his large hazel-coloured eyes behind his thick glasses. 'Take care now.'

Izzy closed the door, letting out a weary sigh. She tore open the cardboard and pulled out *101 Ways to Mother Like a Boss*. Another baby how-to book from her mother-in-law. This must be the fourth one she had sent her in as many weeks. Izzy knew she meant well, clearly wanting to do *something* to help, but it was so far off the mark. When did she have time to sit and read an entire book? What was wrong with sending a stonking box of posh chocolates or a gift basket filled with fancy smellies? She tossed the book on the stairs where it would remain, unread, until she next did a clear-out for the charity shop.

'Why not sort out your own problems instead of getting involved in mine?!' she grumbled, fully aware that talking to yourself was the first sign of madness. Her phone alarm began to beep, the three minutes were up. *Thank God.* Her nerves couldn't handle the cry-it-out method ever again.

Izzy raced to pick up a red-faced Evie from her cot and bring her back downstairs. She fell to the sofa, aware of the tingling sensation in her boobs. It didn't seem possible but perhaps she was still hungry. Izzy unhooked her feeding bra and momentarily winced as Evie latched. She may never sleep again but at least she had cracked breastfeeding, that counted for something, didn't it? Within seconds her daughter was calmer. Izzy wished she could say the same about herself. Her ears were still ringing from the traumatic experience. She lolled her head back on the sofa to ignore the state of the lounge. She had literally achieved nothing today apart from tend to Evie and re-boil the kettle but never actually make that cup of tea she longed for. Did other mums feel this way or was she the only one? Her Instagram feed was full of perfectly made-up new mums celebrating the wonders of motherhood and how they hashtag cherished every minute. Izzy did not cherish every minute.

She looked around for the remote; the only way to blot out the self-doubting thoughts was to fill her tired mind with rubbish telly. Reality TV shows had become her lifeline, her escapism from the monotony of newborn life. Sure, it was probably frying what little of her brain cells she had left that hadn't been eradicated from the torture of sleep deprivation, but it wasn't like she had to be up on current affairs for any office discussions. The last person she had spoken to, bar Evie and Andrew, was that old man, she was sure he'd said his name was Arthur. The realisation troubled her. She tried to cast her mind back to when she'd had a conversation that wasn't mindless small talk with a supermarket cashier. Apart from the congratulatory messages from colleagues and friends she hadn't heard from anyone properly in weeks, but then everyone was so busy with their own lives. She realised that the last adult interaction outside of her home was probably with the midwife who had discharged them from her care.

Izzy was convinced that appointment had been a mistake, she wasn't ready to be booted out into the big wide world with a baby. Couldn't they see how white her knuckles had turned from tightly clinging on to the sides of the straight-backed chair in the clinic? Didn't they – the qualified professionals – not have doubts that they were handing the most precious thing in the world to someone clearly so incompetent? But no, apparently not. She had been left in charge of this tiny, unhappy, demanding baby all on her own once Andrew returned to work after his paternity leave ended. Not that he was much help whilst he was off but it was better than fending for herself. Back then happy adrenalin raced around her body, shielding her from the devastating hormonal rollercoaster she was about to ride solo.

Surely there should be some advanced level of training required for keeping a human alive? It was a big deal.

Everything she'd learnt at her antenatal classes had vanished the moment she was handed her tightly swaddled daughter after a 'textbook' labour and birth. She'd nodded dazedly as beaming midwives congratulated her and clucked around before leaving her leaking, sore and bone-tired. It felt like she had gone into battle, but instead of time to recuperate she was then sent straight back into another war zone, this one without any troops for support.

Izzy was convinced Andrew was working longer hours to avoid spending time in the bombsite of their home with a sobbing irrational wife and a frustrated pink-faced daughter. He didn't know what to do with either of these demanding women.

'Oh give me strength!' she groaned as her eyes finally fell on where the remote control was – hidden behind an empty family bag of Kettle Chips, way out of her reach. Her frustrated cry startled Evie, who tugged at Izzy's cracked nipple.

'Owww!'

Izzy began to cry once more. No one told her it was going to be this hard.

CHAPTER 2

Arthur

They say time flies when you're having fun but when you're waiting to die the opposite is true. No one understood this more than Arthur Winter. He also conceded that a bout of insomnia only highlighted how arduous everything was. He had had another rough night tossing and turning, chasing sleep that never came. When he'd finally dozed off, around 3 a.m., the sound of the bin lorries trundling into the cul-de-sac had jolted him from this superficial slumber. He must have drifted back to sleep as he now woke to the sounds of car doors slamming and people chatting below his bedroom window. The morning school run.

There was a time when Arthur had leisurely embraced the lack of a commute but now he knew better; he needed to get up and get out of bed. No good came from lying there thinking. If he had learnt anything since living alone, it was that he had to keep his mind and body as active as possible to avoid the dark clouds that were never far on his horizon. Instead of succumbing to the lure of another hour or so wrapped under the warm duvet, he slowly forced himself up. He winced at his aching joints, scrambled a hand on the bedside table for his glasses and let out a deep yawn.

'Let's get it over with,' he muttered to himself.

He pulled open his curtains to be greeted with a dull sky, as if the sun was matching his lack of energy to shine any brighter. At least it had stopped raining for the first morning in what felt like a very long time. Arthur slipped on his worn dressing gown that had once been a brilliant royal blue and mentally ran through his to-do list. Wake up. Well, that had been ticked off, accompanied by the daily sense of disappointment.

Get up – tick. He headed to the bathroom. Take a shower – tick.

He preferred to have baths but found he was struggling to get in and out of the tub. Once he'd even nodded off and had woken with a gasp and a coughing fit as water trickled down his nostrils. That was not the way he'd planned to go, so had taken showers ever since.

Get dressed – tick.

Arthur had a uniform of a shirt, pullover, slacks and comfortable lace-up leather shoes that he still made sure to polish, even if he wasn't exactly sure why. All in the muted palette of biscuit brown. No trends to follow, no patterns to match, no umming and ahhing over what to wear; it was the same each and every day. In the height of summer he would swap the pullover for a sleeveless one. A jerkin, that's what Pearl called it. Fastening the shirt buttons was growing trickier but he persevered.

Give the house a quick once-over – tick. By that he meant plump the dark green velvet sofa cushions and squirt some furniture polish on a cloth and give the set of framed photographs that stood proudly on the mantelpiece a brisk wipe.

'Good morning, my darling.' The butter yellow cloth danced over Pearl's smiling face. His own smile faltered. 'I'm still here.'

The black-and-white one was from their wedding day, they looked so alarmingly young. Next to that was a shot of the pair of them on a beach in Benidorm. He could count on one hand the number of times they had been abroad, it was all very overrated. He wasn't even sure why Pearl had bothered to frame this photo that a particularly dull couple from the same hotel had offered to take as they all waited for the nightly entertainment. As an out of tune Frank Sinatra tribute act had warbled, they'd raised their overpriced ice cream cones and smiled for the camera. It hadn't particularly felt like a moment worth capturing.

The most recent one was taken at a church dance that Arthur had grudgingly agreed to go to. His tight, barely there smile was eclipsed by Pearl's broad and beautiful grin. He had stared at that photo every day since, surprised by how terribly old he looked and how oblivious they had both been to what lay ahead just months later. It had been one year and ten months since he'd lost Pearl. He didn't much like that expression, you lost your house keys or an odd sock, not a person, not the other half of you. He was the one who was lost without her.

Have breakfast – tick. A bowl of cornflakes, a cup of tea and a banana to keep him regular. Sometimes he would have toast. A slice of white bread with a generous scraping of real butter, an indulgence that he knew his doctor would raise an eyebrow at. He would leave the dishes until later, to give him something to fill his afternoon with.

'Oi!' he shouted, banging a fist against the kitchen window that overlooked his small back garden. 'Gerroff!'

That pesky pigeon was back. Every morning he would find it messing about in his borders, landing on his rose bushes and clawing at the soil on his neat lawn. His loud noise did nothing to move the stubborn bird away. He grumbled under his breath and grabbed a baking tray and a wooden spoon. This usually did the trick. He padded outside and banged the utensils loudly together.

'I said, get off. Get away with you!'

This time the sudden noise and movement forced the bird to flap its grey speckled wings and fly over to his neighbour's roof. Arthur kept one eye on it as if baiting it to return. The bird thankfully stayed where it was. Arthur gave his rose bushes the once over and plodded back indoors.

Go and get the paper – tick. Errands equate existence, he'd read that somewhere. His daily walks were the only thing that loosely resembled a fitness regime. It was quite terrifying just how frail he had become without realising. It was as if old age had sprung up on him like an unexpected utility bill. To look at him now, no one would believe the hours he used to spend keeping in tip-top physical condition. Back then his athletic abilities had been the key to a wonderful new career. He tried his hardest not to think of that time, for plenty of reasons it was easier not to go there.

The newsagents was a short walk away, past the common and along to the small row of shops. It was next to a hairdressers, a Chinese takeaway and a new shop that sold these funny looking things called e-cigarettes. Great plumes of fruity smoke would billow out of the door like a cabaret act was about to walk onto a stage. He stepped to one side to let a man in a suit stride past, a jogger almost careered into him. Everyone was always in a hurry nowadays. Rushing from here to there. Must dash, busy busy busy. Arthur couldn't remember the last time he'd had to rush anywhere. Time was all he had and he had it in bucket-loads.

As he strolled back home with his paper under his arm, he noticed some activity further down his street. He sighed. Pearl had been the one who would happily stand on the edge of their driveway and have a chinwag with the neighbours. Cooing over any new addition to the street, whether it be animal or human, genuinely interested in the welfare of those geographically close to her. She would offer a cheery wave, a pleasant good morning and some little quip about the weather that was often reciprocated. This then led to a lengthy chat that always precluded Arthur from getting where he needed to be.

After Pearl had passed away, Arthur had suffered the well-meaning interest in how he was getting on. But truthfully, Arthur couldn't be doing with all that nonsense. He never knew what to say. Trying to make small talk with people he had absolutely nothing in common with was exhausting. He didn't know how his wife had done it. Arthur just wanted to keep himself to himself, what was so wrong with that? He was used to being invisible and, for the most part, it suited him fine. He spent his days waiting until he could go to bed, hoping he wouldn't wake up, hoping to finally be reunited with Pearl.

'Hello! Thank goodness it's cleared up for once, hey?'

The less than dulcet tones of his neighbour Mrs Peterson from number forty-three rang out. She was the one who owned three dogs; a dozy lurcher, a shaggy-haired collie and a fluffy poodle-type thing. He'd almost spat out his tea when he'd seen her pushing the latter about in a special pooch pushchair one time. The dog seemed perfectly comfortable being treated like a baby or a dolly. It was absurd; the woman was clearly losing her marbles.

'Hellooooo!' she shouted louder to get his attention.

Arthur pretended not to see her. If only his feet would move as quick as they once had, he could be inside his front door within seconds. Unfortunately, he couldn't seem to walk any faster without his joints screaming in pain. There was nothing for it. He was going to have to make eye contact.

'Morning,' he replied formally and raised his right hand in what could be considered a greeting.

'Isn't it nice to be able to get outside without getting soaked? I was just about to take Pebbles out for her walk to make the most of it. They're saying that it's not going to last, you see, more rain is on its way.'

Arthur was still moving in the direction of his house, which somehow felt like it was being moved further away. He was already running late for the quiz show he quite liked to listen to on Radio 4 as he prepared his lunch.

'It reminds me of something your Pearl used to say. What was it now?' She paused, tapping a chubby finger to her pursed lips.

Arthur stopped walking at the mention of his wife's name.

'Oh yes! She used to say make hay whilst the sun shines! That was it. She always did have a saying for every moment, didn't she?'

Arthur nodded tightly. He was forever remembering Pearlisms, or as he put it, Pearls of Wisdom. She'd glance out of the window on a bright summer's morning and say things like 'it's a lovely day for the race'. Arthur was then meant to

14

ask which race, she'd reply with a chuckle 'the human race!' It never got old that one.

'She really was a wonderful woman. I'll never forget her kindness when Fluffy went missing. Our late cat,' she added at Arthur's blank look.

Oh yes, he remembered now. Mrs Peterson had been beside herself in near hysterics when her cat had gone missing a few years ago. She'd raced from house to house asking everyone to be vigilant. Arthur had found the ball of silver fluff hiding at the back of his shed a few days later when he'd gone to store the antifreeze he'd bought on offer. The damn thing had scratched his lawnmower cover to shreds. Pearl had scooped it up and nestled her face in its fur, chiding Arthur for being so rude towards the wretched creature. Mrs Peterson had cried with relief when they had been reunited. Arthur was still waiting for her to replace his lawnmower cover.

'She would do anything for anyone, wouldn't she? Do you know what, I've still got some bits and bobs from her last round-up of donations for the church. There are some tins of food that must be past their sell-by date by now.'

'Yes. Right, well... I really need to be getting on—'

Mrs Peterson acted as if she hadn't heard him. 'Oh Arthur, I wanted to have a word with you actually. The thing is, I had hoped that I could rally the troops and get the whole of the cul-de-sac involved in a fun project.' She waddled over to him. Her dog was on a lead and not in a pram this time. 'It's called wheelie bin art.'

Arthur stopped shuffling and turned to face her.

'Wheelie bin art?' he repeated, sure he had misheard her.

'Yes!' She grinned, pleased to finally have caught his

attention. 'I was thinking the other day how dull it is on an evening when the bins go out. It's a sea of grubby grey soldiers all lined up waiting for the bin men, sorry, bin people, to come and collect them. So what I thought would be rather fun,' she winked, 'is if every house prettied their bins up a bit. You can buy these decorative stickers that you just stick on. I've seen them in Poundland. I'd be happy to get you some and you can reimburse me.'

Arthur had never heard of anything so ridiculous. A bin was a bin, it wasn't a piece of art.

'I don't—'

'You can get all sorts of designs, from flowers to colourful abstract sort of swirls to a complete beach scene. You could look out of your window and be forgiven for thinking you were on the shore of Torremolinos!' Mrs Peterson laughed, making her chins dance. 'I've spoken to next door and they're keen. Like I said, I'm happy to buy the stickers and everyone can pay me back later. I just think it would be a bit of fun.'

Arthur had to turn his scoff into a long cough at the look she gave him.

'I imagine you're a keen fisherman. I can see if I can get you the koi carp one, if you like? Or is gardening more your thing? There's one with adorable spades and trowels!'

'Neither. Thanks,' Arthur found his voice as soon as he realised she wasn't winding him up.

'Oh, come on.' She nudged his arm. He was taken aback by the unexpected physical contact. 'You can't be the only bin left out. It would ruin the whole effect!'

There were only seven houses in the cul-de-sac.

'I'm sorry but I think…'

They were suddenly interrupted by the mewling cries of a newborn baby and the harassed shushing of its mother. Arthur glanced up to see the young lady from the house opposite struggling to heave a bulky car seat from her car.

'Oh Lordy, someone's got a good set of lungs on them!' Mrs Peterson called out with a chirpy laugh.

Izzy Carter flushed with colour. Arthur remembered her name from delivering that parcel to her the other day. She had looked utterly exhausted when he'd briefly spoken to her on the doorstep. She must only be in her late twenties or early thirties but her eyes had been worryingly lifeless. He'd been thinking of her since then and keeping watch on her house, as if sending her supportive thoughts out of his window. Her husband, the tall man who drove a nice Renault, pulled up on their drive at half past seven, like most evenings. Arthur wished Pearl was here, she would have known what to do. She probably would have baked her a cake or delivered a casserole but Arthur didn't know how to do either of these things, and even if he did it he worried he would be overstepping the mark.

'Oh, yes. She certainly likes to make an entrance,' Izzy laughed weakly, dropping her keys and flashing a tight smile.

'I'd best be off,' Arthur said, sensing his chance to escape.

'Oh, alright then, dear,' Mrs Peterson said. 'Have a think about what design you'd like. I can drop round some examples in the week? See you soon, love!'

Arthur turned and plodded with as much pace as he could muster down his front path. He couldn't care less what colour, shape or design his wheelie bin was, just that it was collected on time and with as little noise as possible.

*

The day trundled forward, as it tended to do, in an unmemorable fashion. Arthur had read the paper, paused for lunch, washed his dishes, and had had a snooze. He switched on the television and turned up the volume. Perhaps there would be a decent film or a documentary that could fill a bit of time until he decided which tin to open and heat up for his dinner. He flicked through the channels, skipping past a chat show with heavily made-up middle-aged women discussing the menopause, an antiques specialist rummaging through someone's junk, and a talk show where two men with a full set of teeth between them, shouted at one another about sleeping with the same woman.

'Can you believe this nonsense?' Arthur said to the empty spot on the sofa where Pearl would sit. Sometimes he liked to imagine she was just in another room, her seat cushion still warm, her knitting balled up to the side and her favourite mug on the coffee table.

'Right, I may as well make another cup of tea.'

Didn't someone once say that the first sign of madness was talking to yourself? he mused. As he rose to his feet something caught his eye from the lounge window, temporarily distracting him from the pain in his joints and the empty spot on the sofa.

Mrs Peterson had found her next victim. She was talking to the mother of teenagers who lived at number forty-one, on her way home from the school run. Her car was like a taxi to those girls who filed out, slamming the doors, carrying various bags, gym kits and sports equipment, and not a word of thanks or a smile between them. He watched as the woman politely nodded along, listening to this ridiculous bin art idea. Arthur started to make his way to the kitchen, chuckling to himself.

He was too busy thinking about wheelie bins that he wasn't concentrating on where he was going. He didn't see that the edge of the rug had lifted near the coffee table. His slipper caught in the unexpected obstacle. And, as if in slow-motion, he realised what was coming next. He shot forwards. He wasn't as quick to find his balance as he once had been. He was unable to stop himself from falling. His arms reflexively sprang out as his whole body slammed onto the carpet, his glasses shot off somewhere. Thankfully his head narrowly missed the edge of the fireplace, he would certainly be a goner if that had made contact. He was too dazed and trying to make sense of his narrow escape from smashing his skull on the cold stone surround that it took him a second or two to acknowledge the unnatural way his left leg was lying. A flame-like heat tore through his body, followed by the unmistakable urge to vomit. With a deep breath he pushed with all his strength to lift himself up.

'Oww!' he roared, the sound shocking him.

He blinked rapidly, trying to hold back the tears that stung his wide eyes. He'd had slight falls before but nothing to this level. *Stay calm*, he told himself, he needed to call for help but there was no way he could get to his phone. The landline was sat on the windowsill nearest his armchair, in view but out of reach. He hadn't the foggiest where his mobile telephone was, he hadn't used it since Jeremy bought it for him a year ago. He could really do with an unexpected visit from his nephew right now.

'Help. Help! Heeeellllppppp!'

He shouted so much that his throat grew hoarse, pausing only to listen if he could hear his neighbours rushing to his aid. But Arthur knew it was wishful thinking. Irritating theme music blared from the TV, masking any noises he was making. He tried desperately not to succumb to the throbbing pain in his ankle but it was too difficult. Blackness caved in around his eyes, the lounge growing smaller under the unstoppable encroaching darkness. The last thing Arthur remembered was wondering how long it would be until help came – if help came at all.

CHAPTER 3

Izzy

Izzy had come to the supermarket to pick up a few bits for dinner. She knew that she'd needed to get out when the four walls of her lounge felt like they were closing in on her but she hadn't been prepared for this sensory overload. Everything was so loud and bright. Weeks of sleep deprivation was making her feel like she was walking through treacle. Her brain had been replaced with cotton wool, her gritty tired eyes struggled to focus on the items on the shelves. Apparently this was normal – every new mum said they felt tired in the early days but Izzy hadn't quite anticipated this level of crippling, disorientating exhaustion. She couldn't shake the constant nausea or the dizzying headaches that came from weeks of broken sleep. She was clumsy, absent-minded and her emotions swung on a knife-edge. At least she didn't need to rush around the aisles, Evie had finally fallen asleep in the special baby-friendly trolley so Izzy could take her time, a blessing given her current indecisiveness.

'Shit,' she muttered under her breath, turning the corner. It was all going so well.

Standing in the chilled desserts section near the cream horns and profiteroles, was Pauline, her boss's PA. It must be someone's birthday. They usually sent Pauline out to buy a selection of chocolate eclairs if there was a celebration in the office. Izzy had promised she would bring Evie in to meet her colleagues but she hadn't felt up to socialising. It wasn't just surviving the well-meaning pleasantries but the fear of Evie screaming down the whole office and Izzy being unable to soothe her that stopped her from fixing a date in the diary.

She didn't want her colleagues to see just how badly she was handling everything. Before having a baby, she was in control, organised and well turned out. This new Izzy felt, and looked, an utter mess. Her hair, that managed to somehow be greasy and matted at the same time, was permanently pulled into a high messy bun. She never had time to put make-up on and she couldn't even remember if she'd brushed her teeth most mornings.

It wasn't just surviving idle chit-chat, and Pauline was a chatterer at the best of times, but the anxiety that followed. Izzy knew she would only pick apart and analyse whatever conversation they were about to have for days after. There was only one choice – she had to get out of there as quickly as possible. She spun her trolley around and jogged to the checkouts, praying that Pauline would take her time deciding between an apple turnover or a custard tart.

Thankfully the checkouts were quiet. Izzy hurriedly began shoving her shopping, she wasn't even sure what she was buying, onto the conveyor belt. The young lad on the till smiled hello and slowly began scanning the items. She noticed he glanced up at her a couple more times, his mouth pursed as if looking briefly amused at something, as he slid the conveyor belt forwards. Izzy self-consciously rubbed her chin in case she had some crumbs there from the biscuits she'd scoffed on the drive to the shops.

'Sorry. This one's not coming up right.' He pressed a button that lit up a call bell.

'Do you know what... I'll just leave them,' Izzy said, nodding to the box of extra-thick sanitary towels he was dramatically waving in front of the scanner.

'Ah, you can but it's buggered up the machine. It'll take as long to clear them from the system. I still need my line manager's approval to do that too.'

'Fine, but can you please hurry up?'

'Oi! Mike, where's Dave at?' the lad shouted across to another young guy working on the checkout in front. He shrugged and also pressed a call bell. Izzy felt the queue of disgruntled shoppers growing behind her. She dared not turn to see if Pauline had joined it.

'Sorry about this.'

'It's fine,' Izzy said tightly. It wasn't fine, it was a world away from fine but she was British and in a public place.

'Having a pj day are we?' he asked with a smirk.

'Sorry?'

'Your pyjamas. I wasn't sure if it was for some charity thing or...'

She looked down. She was still wearing her fluffy pyjama bottoms, the ones with cartoon sleeping sheep. The man in the queue behind her chuckled. A wave of heat spread across her cheeks.

'We sometimes have fancy dress days here too...' he trailed

off, taking in the horrified look on Izzy's face. 'Ah, great, here's Dave now.'

He swiftly moved out of the way as the manager leaned across and swiped his card to correct the system. Izzy felt tears pushing at the back of her eyes, *keep it together*, she willed herself.

'So, er, do you still want these?' He nodded to the box of sanitary towels.

'No.' Izzy's throat was tight. 'No, I don't.'

'OK. Cool, so that's… nine pounds fifteen. Have you got a loyalty card?'

Izzy blinked, trying with all her might to keep herself together. She tapped her debit card on the machine and quickly threw her shopping into her trolley. Mercifully, Evie had slept through the whole thing. She flew out of the shop and over to her car without looking back.

'Izzy?' a familiar voice called out.

Izzy debated for a moment whether she could leap into the driver's seat and accelerate quickly, pretending like she hadn't seen her but it was too late. Pauline was strolling towards her, waving an arm in the air.

'I thought that was you!' Pauline's smile faltered as she grew closer, taking in Izzy's sleeping sheep pyjama bottoms.

'Pauline!' Izzy said, her voice high-pitched and unrecognisable. 'I'd love to chat but—'

'Oh my God.' Pauline ignored Izzy and zoned in on Evie nestled cosily in the built-in baby seat of the trolley. 'She is just gorgeous! Well doesn't she look like her mummy? She's the spit of you!' Pauline said in a baby voice. 'Look at her all wrapped up sleeping like an angel. Is she good?'

'Some days,' Izzy said as light-heartedly as she could, pushing her trolley onto the pavement next to her car and opening the boot. If she kept moving then Pauline would realise she didn't have time to chat. 'Sleep is for the weak, isn't that right?' Izzy joked, chucking her shopping bags in as quickly as possible.

Izzy felt like the only person awake in the whole world most nights. Except for last night, she suddenly remembered. As she'd made her way to the bathroom at some godforsaken hour, her heavy lids had noticed a flickering blue light from her neighbour's front room. All the other houses in the cul-de-sac were in darkness, even the street lights had been turned off as part of some council initiative to save energy, which only illuminated number thirty-nine's light even more. The house belonged to the old man, Arthur, the one who she had unwittingly flashed yesterday morning when he'd delivered that parcel. Izzy had never seen anyone else coming or going from his house, so she presumed that he lived alone. She'd thought it was strange for him to be awake at that time; if he was anything like her grandparents had been then he'd be paranoid about the cost of his electricity bill after leaving the television on all night. She'd been so stressed trying to get out of the house that she'd forgotten all about it.

'It's nice to see you but we really had better make a move.'

Izzy closed her boot and clapped her hands together but Pauline was oblivious.

'My Billy would only sleep on his back, that's what they tell you to do nowadays, isn't it? But back then everyone put their babies to sleep on their front and...'

I don't care! Izzy wanted to scream as Pauline tilted her

head and took a trip down memory lane. Izzy didn't care about how her colleague's son was a thumb-sucker, she was more concerned about what Pauline would say to the rest of the team about how Izzy Carter was falling apart.

'Mmm hmm...'

'And then we made the mistake of giving him a blankie. It seemed like a good idea at the time but boy! Talk about a meltdown when he lost it one day in the park.' Pauline shook her head, lost in some memory.

Izzy smiled politely. By the end of the day everyone in the office would know about her wardrobe malfunction, she'd be the talk of the water cooler. If she couldn't even dress herself then how was she capable of looking after a baby?! She imagined them laughing. They wouldn't be able to believe that Izzy, usually so well turned out, was caught shopping in her scruffy pjs in the middle of the day.

'It's all just a phase.' Izzy tried to follow what Pauline was saying and not catastrophise about being office gossip. 'I remember when my Billy was Evie's age, when he was really, really young, he would just cry and cry. I thought I was losing the plot.' She stopped suddenly as if catching herself from saying anything more. 'It was the hormones, I suspect. Anyway, I'd better get back.'

Without warning, Pauline leaned in for an unexpected hug. Izzy found she held on to her for a second too long. She wanted to go back to the office with her colleague. She wanted clean hair and ironed clothes. She wanted to escape the never-ending routine of feeding, nappy changes, battling for longer naps, and wiping up milky sick.

I can't do this anymore! A voice roared in Izzy's head.

She was so close to admitting what she knew she couldn't admit. Tears pricked her eyes as she forced the truth back down. She just wanted someone to know how she felt, not that anyone would understand. How could you say such a taboo out loud – that you weren't cut out to be a mother? No one said it was going to be this hard. No one else struggled this much.

'You take care of yourself, love,' Pauline said, with a sympathetic head tilt.

Izzy could only bite the inside of her cheek and nod in reply. She watched Pauline walk away and felt her heart fall and spirit crumple. She slammed her boot shut and jumped into the driver's seat, a fresh wave of embarassment washing over her as she tugged the seatbelt across her, catching sight of her fluffy sheep pyjamas once more. She turned the engine on and thrust the car into reverse, desperate to get back to the safety of her messy house. If she needed proof that she was failing so spectacularly the look on Pauline's face had said it all. Izzy turned the radio up trying to forget what had just happened. She drove down the main street with Pauline's sad expression scorched in her mind. It had been a long time since anyone had looked at her like that. The car in front began to brake, Izzy slowed down and looked out of the window, catching sight of two mums pushing their pushchairs and laughing together. *What was their secret?*

The DJ was playing a dance track from some band she'd never heard of. The song was too loud and upbeat for how she felt. She pinched the bridge of her nose to try and relieve the tension headache that was coming on and turned the radio off. Silence filled the car.

Evie must have fallen back to sleep. Perhaps Izzy would have enough time to unload the shopping before her daughter woke demanding her next feed. She momentarily caught sight of her bloodshot eyes and heavy eye bags in the rear-view mirror. She barely recognised herself, God only knew what Pauline must have thought. It was then that she felt her heart stop. It wasn't the sight of her haunting face staring back at her that alarmed her but what she could see in the backseat. Evie's car seat was empty.

'Shit! Evie!'

Izzy had been so busy fretting about Pauline and what she was going to tell the team that she'd forgotten to lift Evie from the trolley and strap her into the car. She was still in the supermarket car park! Saliva rushed to her mouth, she felt like she'd been slapped. Izzy beeped her horn aggressively hoping someone would let her pull out. But she was trapped in a queue of cars, unable to turn around or even nudge forward. The driver in front stuck two fingers up at her.

'Hurry up, hurry up!'

Finally there was a break in the traffic. She somehow managed to inch through an extremely tight gap. Her hands shook as she slammed on the indicator and shot around the corner. If she took the next right she could swing back on herself and race into the supermarket car park, although she was forgetting that there were temporary traffic lights on this road.

'Nooooo!' She screamed as the lights turned to red just as she approached and a stream of people crossed the road. She was trying to think straight. Should she call someone to check that Evie was still there? Get someone to wait with her? Her shaking fingers dialled Andrew's number but she hung up before it connected. She would be back at the supermarket in thirty seconds once these lights turned green. What would she even say to him? *Sorry, babe, I forgot our baby as I was too preoccupied with being judged by someone I work with.*

Izzy tried to control her erratic breathing. Should she call the police? What if the police were already there? What if another shopper had seen an abandoned baby and called them?

The lights finally turned green. Izzy screeched into the Tesco car park. She felt hot and sick and terrified. If something had happened to her baby, if someone had taken her, she—

'Oh thank God!'

Izzy soared over the speed bumps, she could see the trolley that was partially blocked behind a pillar – exactly where she had left it no more than two minutes ago. Evie was peacefully gazing up at the clouds, still tightly strapped in. Izzy had her seatbelt off and the door flung open within seconds. She scooped Evie out of the trolley baby seat and showered her with kisses, her salty tears falling on her daughter's milky soft cheeks.

'I'm so sorry. I'm so sorry. Mummy's here.'

It was official. She was the worst mum in the world.

CHAPTER 4

Arthur

It had been almost twenty-four hours since his agonising fall and still no sign of help. Arthur knew this because the six o'clock news had just aired on his television. He must have drifted in and out of consciousness as he couldn't remember seeing the lunchtime news. He cursed his luck that he had been awake to suffer through *Loose Women* and coverage of the British Swimming Championships. He had found the latter particularly hard to stomach. It may have been decades but he could still feel a ball of tension in the pit of his stomach and a pounding in his head when he was reminded of his dream that had been snatched away. The pain this memory brought on was not helped by the blinding headaches his accident had caused.

Jeremy would definitely be moving him into a care home after this, Arthur thought, *if* he survived. He had used up the last of his lifelines. His nephew's patience following Arthur's previous bumps and trips – minor scrapes compared to this – had already worn thin. This time there was no excuse. However, his future felt very uncertain right now. As every hour passed he was growing more dehydrated, his stomach rumbled with hunger and his head throbbed. It was looking more and more likely that Arthur was going to die like this. Despite this he felt surprisingly calm. He wondered how his obituary would read, or if his passing would even make a line in the local newspaper.

Man discovered weeks after a swarm of house flies seeped out of the downstairs window.

The neighbours complained of the smell without realising what horrific reason was behind it.

You often hear of people being found that way, don't you? Arthur thought. Their bodies accidentally 'discovered', rotting away to pulp and larvae, by some poor unsuspecting sod. He shuddered at the image. Usually a neighbour or dog walker or jogger. In his case, Arthur hoped it wouldn't be Mrs Peterson and her three dogs. She was probably his best bet as she was often half dragged down the street by that giant lurcher of hers. Could dogs sense death? Sniff out the smell of decay? Possibly. Probably not her dog though, it certainly hadn't been first in the queue when intelligence was handed out. Pearl had been near hysterical with laughter at the sight of the dog scampering on the common as it chased a plastic bag that kept dropping with the wind. It had been a mere pup then. But, then again, he didn't want Izzy to find him. He often spotted her doing that motherly bounce-step, willing her baby to sleep as she stared dead-eyed out of the upstairs window. Perhaps she would happen to look across at his house during her next late-night routine and raise the alarm. No, he wanted her to stay as far away from his problems as possible, she had enough on her plate with her little one.

Maybe it would be Jeremy that would discover Arthur when he popped over next. His nephew liked to unexpectedly turn up unannounced. Despite himself, Arthur's heart would sink when he saw his perfectly polished white Skoda pull up outside, wondering what on earth he had come to request this time. Jeremy would shuffle in, prattling on about something and nothing. Arthur would struggle to politely follow along, mentally calculating how long it would be until he cleared his throat with an awkward cough and enquired about 'borrowing' something of Arthur's, promising to return the last thing he 'borrowed'. He was still waiting for the electric drill Jeremy had taken nearly five weeks ago now to make a reappearance. As the sole family he had left, Jeremy was the only other person who had a key – 'for emergencies'. Arthur had grudgingly got one cut after his last accident when he'd slipped on the wet bathroom tiles and skidded into the door. He was left with a juicy black eye, a bruised ego and the cost of getting a spare key cut to put a stop to the unsubtle hints of 'home help' and 'carers'. That was nothing compared to the pain he was in now. A rush of searing heat shot up his left hip, halting his thoughts. He thought he might vomit again, it was the disconcerting angle of his foot that threatened to shift the bile in the base of his stomach.

The haze of consciousness seeped around the edges of his exhausted eyes. His glasses had shot from his face as he'd dropped like a dead weight to the floor and he couldn't stretch far enough to reach them, his blurred vision was not helping with his persistent headache. How had he missed the ridge in the rug? It must have inched out from where it usually rested when he'd last dragged the vacuum cleaner around. This was why he detested housework. That was another topic Jeremy liked to discuss during his visits – the state of Arthur's house. Since Pearl had died Arthur hadn't quite relished fixing things as he once had. What exactly was he future-proofing for?

Jeremy was keen for Arthur to get himself a cleaner, some Polish or Eastern European woman like his nephew and his fiancée, Elaine, had. He'd pay for it, he offered, as if that was the issue. There was no way Arthur would let someone into his house to whip around a feather duster. What would Pearl say? No, Arthur was perfectly capable of keeping this place to a reasonable standard. Granted things had slipped since his wife last worked her magic. The windows could do with a squirt of Windolene and she certainly mopped a lot more often than he ever did but he wasn't living in squalor. He'd tried his best to keep up appearances, not that he cared about things like that, he just didn't want to let Pearl down. In all honesty he found it bordering on offensive the way Jeremy droned on about getting some help in. Arthur was coping just fine, or at least he was, before this happened.

It was getting dark now. He'd given up shouting for attention hours ago. It had only succeeded in making his dry throat even more hoarse. Once, he thought he could make out the repetitive shrieks of a baby, but perhaps not. If he was honest, as time went on, he was growing a little bit frightened. He wondered if Pearl had felt like this. That thought made his stomach lurch as if he was going to be sick again. He never wanted to imagine her feeling scared or alone. In all the pain he had experienced since she'd left him he had always told himself it was better this way, that he would rather *he* was feeling these overwhelming pangs of grief and not her. He wouldn't have wished those intense and very dark early days on his worst enemy.

As strange as it seemed, given his current circumstances, he thought about the unfinished jobs that he had meant to get round to. It wasn't just the odd spot of DIY that Pearl would have once nagged him about, such as fix the toilet roll holder back to the wall or replace the batteries in the smoke alarm, that now niggled him. As time was running out he became keenly aware that he hadn't touched Pearl's things since she'd passed. It had felt too overwhelming. Getting rid of Pearl's possessions had felt like he would be losing her all over again. But right now, when every breath could be his last, he wished he'd been braver. He didn't want anyone to go through his or his wife's belongings once he was gone.

Not that there was anything particularly valuable in the house but he could have made sure that things went to the right people or that a charity of his choice benefitted. With no children of their own, Arthur assumed it would be Jeremy, who would inherit it all. He was sure his nephew would simply agree to a house clearance service who would gut the place to get it over with as quickly and efficiently as possible, he would be ruthless over things that Arthur had felt paralysed with indecision over. It was this train of thought that spurred him on to try one last attempt to call for help.

He needed to focus on getting across the carpet to his telephone. On the count of three he held his breath, bracing for the shock to course up his body as he tried to heave himself towards the windowsill where his landline was. Clenching his teeth and using all his strength he managed to inch ever so slightly forward. He could see the tightly coiled wires of the grubby receiver, if he managed to move closer he should be able to give it a good tug so it would land on the floor.

With one great roar he dropped flat onto the carpet. There was no way he could get any closer, his pathetic efforts were completely fruitless. The tiny gap between him and the receiver was laughable, it felt like an abyss. He pictured himself as a younger, stronger version of himself, looking down at this shrivelled, feeble form. He was once so fit, he never could have comprehended that getting old would be so terrifyingly debilitating.

The pain was too much. He was going to pass out again, perhaps this time he wouldn't wake up. The pounding migraine was threatening to take over once more. Blackness encroached on his vision and the thud of his temples increased in force. He forced himself to take some deep breaths. If this was how his final hand was to be played then he had to accept it.

Another wave of nausea shuddered across him. It was too late now to do anything else. Arthur had to accept what he was leaving behind. None of his shouts had been heard, he was unable to move even an inch to get to the telephone, let alone the door. He simply had to wait and accept his fate. He took another deep breath, suddenly aware of how shaky and rattly it felt and told himself not to be frightened. If this was how it ended it would be OK. He was ready to see his Pearl again. He didn't need to be scared anymore.

CHAPTER 5

Izzy

'Babe, what are these?' Andrew dropped his work bag on the floor and held up a packet of large, bright butterfly stickers he'd picked up from the hallway.

'They're for our bin. Apparently there's some sort of street art project or something,' Izzy explained, carefully laying down their milk-drunk baby in her Moses basket. She hadn't been properly listening when Mrs Peterson had collared her. In a bid to leave the conversation she'd agreed to join in. She'd have to get round to actually sticking them on at some point.

'Right...' Andrew tossed the stickers in their shiny plastic packaging on the cluttered dining room table. He gave them both a quick kiss, tugged at his tie and flopped on the sofa with a satisfied sigh. 'So, how are my two best girls? What have you done today?'

'Nothing,' Izzy replied quickly, fastening the straps on her feeding bra. 'Why?'

'Nothing?' he repeated, picking up the remote control.

'Oh, well just a quick trip to pick up some bits from the shops but that was all really.'

Izzy had left the supermarket a complete trembling mess. She drove with one eye on the road and one repeatedly checking the rear-view mirror for signs that Evie was OK and not suffering from PTSD after being abandoned like that. Her baby had mercifully appeared nonplussed by the whole adventure and fallen asleep in her car seat, ferociously sucking on her dummy. Once back home Izzy had wasted no time googling to see how much damage her negligence had caused. It was the most shameful thing she had ever done.

'Did you have fun?' Andrew's question jolted her from her self-loathing thoughts.

'Why? What do you mean?'

Andrew's smile faltered. 'Nothing. I just mean that sounds really boring.'

Izzy turned away to begin picking up the collection of Cadbury Heroes wrappers scattered across the sofa cushion. She hadn't realised she'd gotten through so many. She'd absent-mindedly scoffed the lot as she spent the rest of the afternoon feeding Evie whilst binge-watching some American dating show. It hadn't succeeded in trying to distract herself from the nightmare scenarios racing in her mind. What if there had been a paedophile doing his weekly shop? What if another car had mounted the pavement and hit Evie in her trolley? What if a bird had swooped down and carried her away? What if a huge gust of wind had blown the trolley onto the road and in front of—

'Babe?'

Izzy looked up to see Andrew staring at her.

'Are you sure you're OK? You were miles away then!'

Izzy rubbed her eyes, they felt gritty and tight. 'Sorry, did you ask me something?'

'I said, what's for dinner?'

Dinner. In the chaos of the doomed supermarket trip she hadn't actually picked up any of the ingredients she had planned. 'We've probably got something in the freezer.'

Andrew flicked on the TV. 'Great. Thanks. The game's about to start.'

Izzy sighed and got to her feet, she was too tired to start an argument about gender roles despite the rising bubble of irritation that cooking was now her domain as she was 'off' on maternity leave. She picked up the butterfly stickers on the way to the kitchen. Admittedly, the colourful design would brighten up the bin. She shook her head. What had her life become?

'There's chicken Kievs or fish fingers? Which do you want?' Izzy called through from the kitchen.

'Ooof.' Andrew winced at an overpaid and over-styled footballer rolling about on the grass as if auditioning for an amateur dramatics play.

'Andrew?' Izzy walked into the lounge.

'Yep?'

'I'm trying to have a conversation with you. Can you not just pause it or something?'

He threw her a quick apologetic glance. 'Sorry, babe, it's the semi-finals though.'

'Oh, well, don't mind me then,' she muttered under her breath. 'I said... do you want Kievs or fish fingers?'

'Kievs, please.'

Izzy plodded back into the kitchen and turned the oven on. She scattered a healthy portion of oven chips on a baking tray too.

'Right, the oven is pre-heating. Are you OK to put it in in about five minutes? I'm going to go for a quick shower,' Izzy asked.

'Mmm,' Andrew replied, without taking his eyes off the screen.

She had one hand on the lounge door when, as if on cue, Evie let out a well-timed squelchy fart that made Izzy's heart sink. She'd lost count of the number of nappy and outfit changes she'd gone through today. She wasn't sure she could face another one. Andrew appeared not to have heard the explosion in the nappy region. Izzy wondered how long she could feign ignorance too, until the smell hit.

'Jesus. Is that you?' Andrew gasped, pulling the sleeve of his jumper down over his hands and up to cover his nose. Evie began crying in protest.

'Course not! She needs a nappy change…'

Andrew began dramatically wafting an arm in their daughter's direction, keeping his eyes glued to the screen. Evie's shrieks grew louder. Every part of Izzy wanted to react and make her daughter happy but another, more stubborn part, wanted to see if Andrew would step in and help. She knew it was childish, an immature test, but it mattered all the same. He still made no effort to move.

'Fine. I guess I'll be the one to change her then,' she snapped, picking Evie up. Izzy gagged at the smell catching at the back of her throat. 'It's not like I've done this all bloody day.'

'I was just about to,' Andrew protested limply. 'I just wanted to wait until they took the next corner.'

'Oh really? Funny that. Well come on then,' Izzy had Evie on the changing mat and was popping open her baby-gro. There was actual mustard-coloured seepage.

'I've been at work all day, babe, I'm sure you forget about that sometimes. I know it's hard for you but it's not like I sit there relaxing all day.'

'At least you have adult conversations and someone making you a hot cup of tea every so often! I'm serious. Keeping a small person alive is a full-time job but when do I get to clock off?' Izzy gritted her teeth, wanting to suppress the anger rising in her chest.

'I know you're tired, don't take it out on me please.'

She'd managed to ease off her daughter's soiled vest and clean the mess up. Evie was still crying. Izzy's fingers fumbled trying to fasten the new nappy.

'Come on,' she hissed, pulling at the fabric tabs that tore in her hands. 'Oh, give me strength!' She grabbed another nappy from the pack and tried again.

'Jeez, someone's not happy.' Andrew turned up the volume on the television.

'Do you want to get off your arse and help me?' Izzy shouted. She'd had enough. Her head felt like it was going to explode. 'What is with this stupid nappy!'

'Babe, chill out. You're stressing her out.'

'You try doing this on zero sleep! I can't get it to work!'

She had never been so quick to lose her shit before. Now it felt like a switch could be flicked to turn her from sleepy to shouty to hysterical within seconds. It was all too much.

'I give up!' Izzy surrendered at the exact moment she realised she was putting it on back to front. But it was too late. 'You take over.'

She handed the half-dressed still crying baby to Andrew and stomped out.

'Babe?! What's the matter?'

'Everything!'

Izzy roughly shoved her feet into her trainers.

'Where are you going? Iz, don't be like this. I didn't mean it. I—'

Izzy slammed the front door shut before she could hear the end of his apology. Tears streamed down her warm cheeks. Her heart raced. What did *he* know? Izzy stormed down their path, she didn't know where she was going. She'd not picked up her phone or purse or coat. She would go for a walk, get some air and try and calm down, hopefully when she returned Andrew would have the TV off, dinner cooked, the baby asleep and an apology. She could dream.

As she strode past Arthur's house, she wondered what her own grandparents, God rest their souls, would have made of Evie. Izzy knew that Evie was lucky to have grandparents in her in-laws and her own dad when he would bother to visit, but she couldn't help imagining her own grandad who would have been besotted by Evie. They would have made excellent great-grandparents. A wave of nostalgia replaced the ebb of her anger. She wished they'd been able to meet her daughter. Her grandma would probably be telling her to not take any stick from Andrew, that she was tired and emotional but a good night's sleep would cure it all. Izzy stopped stomping.

She felt a little foolish being out on the street at this hour. She shouldn't have flown off the handle like that. Andrew worked really hard and it wasn't easy for him, he was sacrificing spending time with his daughter, time he could never get back. Izzy shivered and tightly wrapped her arms around her chest. It was much too cold to be out on a night like this in just a thin hoody and leggings. The shock of the winter air had at least helped to clear her head. Izzy turned on her heels ready to head back home, but something stopped her. A chill danced up her arms that had nothing to do with the temperature. She suddenly felt this funny sort of feeling, as if someone was watching her.

The cul-de-sac was empty, even that group of teenagers who sometimes hung out by the entrance to the common had gone home. It was the light from Arthur's lounge that was bothering her. There had been something niggling her when she'd spotted it earlier. She'd been so traumatised after forgetting Evie at the supermarket that she'd forgotten all about it. Perhaps there was nothing to it, people left their lights on as some sort of burglar deterrent all the time, but something didn't feel right.

She slowly walked up his gravelled path. All the houses on the cul-de-sac had similar style layouts. She knew it was his lounge at the front, like hers, but his window frames were the old style, single glazing probably. Stepping closer to the window she raised a hand to her forehead and leaned nearer to the thin glass, trying to see through the fussy net curtains.

That's when she saw it. A wrinkled hand peeping out of a dark brown bobbled jumper. Izzy gasped. Her eyes took in the lifeless form of the old man lay at a disturbing angle on the floor, his foot looked trapped by a chair leg. The light that she had seen was from the chunky box television, still on, illuminating the terrible scene before her. His head was turned away from her. She couldn't see any blood but the retro carpet was full of dark green and plum coloured swirls, so it was hard to be certain. Her heart began to race, instinctively she pounded a fist on the pane of glass. The sound echoed down the silent street. She was sure she saw his sleeve flickering at the noise she was making. He was still alive!

'Don't worry, Arthur! Help is on the way!' she shouted through the window, the panic obvious in her voice, unsure if he was able to hear her or not.

Izzy was suddenly overcome with guilt. Why hadn't she checked up on him earlier? She knew that the flickering light she'd noticed the previous night had been odd. He hadn't simply fallen asleep in front of the television like she'd presumed. How long had he been lying there? She flew down the street to call an ambulance, cursing herself for forgetting her phone, praying that help would arrive in time.

CHAPTER 6

Arthur

If this was the afterlife then Arthur wanted his money back. He must have done something terrible in a past life as purgatory was lying in a stiflingly hot six-bed hospital ward next to a gentleman who hacked up phlegm every seven and a half minutes – Arthur had timed him – opposite a man who didn't seem to care that his pyjamas had holes in very unfortunate places. If Arthur was fed up at not being reunited with Pearl then his mood fell even more at being trapped here. Who knew God's waiting room was so noisy? The nightly snoring competition was bad enough, not to mention the constant interruptions from nurses, doctors, tea ladies and medical students all coming in to consult some forms, take some blood, change his dressings, or give him a prod.

'Morning, Mr Winter, what a lovely day. You should see how sunny it is out there for a change,' a nurse with very large bosoms straining under her pale blue uniform said in a thick Jamaican accent. She had tiny black plaits in neat, uniform rows running down her skull and spoke at an unnecessarily loud volume as she dramatically opened the blinds by his bed.

Everyone kept telling him how lucky he was to have been given a spot near a window. He hadn't yet worked out why a view of the concrete car park roof was so enviable. It didn't even provide any fresh air, it could only be cracked open an inch or two so the occasional cool breeze that made it through was more of an irritating whisper.

Fate had decided that he was to remain on this planet a little longer and be subject to this penance. It had been two nights and Arthur was more than ready to go home. He'd had his nastiest fall yet, he'd managed to badly sprain his left ankle – the medics were amazed it wasn't broken – as well as sustain some impressive bruises all up the left-hand side of his body.

'That lovely nephew of yours is waiting outside. He's even bought some fudge for the nurses. Shame I'm watching me figure.' The nurse patted her round stomach and laughed heartily. 'Well, no one else will, hey! Anyway, young man, I just wanted to see how you were doing before I let him in. That OK?'

Arthur nodded reluctantly.

'Alright then, also the doctor is doing his rounds so he'll be over shortly. Let's hope he gives you some good news to help turn that frown upside down!'

She padded off, squeaking on her navy plastic pumps. A few seconds later he had company in his small cubicle.

'Hello, Uncle Arthur, how are you holding up?' Jeremy had his hands in the pockets of his nylon bomber jacket, bouncing on the balls of his pearly white trainers. 'I'm sorry Elaine couldn't make it again but she sends her regards.'

Arthur was grateful for her absence, it meant he didn't have to force a smile with another person. However, even despite the awkwardness between them, it had taken Arthur by surprise just how much he had missed seeing his nephew on a regular basis. Jeremy had visited every day despite Arthur insisting he didn't need to – he struggled with making small talk at the best of times. Yes, Jeremy couldn't make a decent cup of tea if his life depended on it and he liked to talk about cricket too much, a sport Arthur had no interest in whatsoever, but it was comforting knowing he had someone thinking of him, someone who cared enough to visit.

'Excuse me, gentlemen, Doctor Khalid is here to see you, Arthur.' The nurse poked her head around the bed.

In strode a man who, in Arthur's opinion, looked much too young to be in charge of Arthur's freedom from this place.

'Morning, Mr… Winter. I hope all is well today?' He scanned his tired eyes over the clipboard at the foot of Arthur's bed. 'Ah yes, badly sprained ankle. Are you finding the painkillers are doing the job? I'm loath to prescribe you something stronger but we want to make sure you're comfortable.'

Arthur nodded his head slowly. Whatever pills he was taking were quite miraculous. It wasn't so much that he was in physical pain, more that he was mentally frustrated.

'I'm feeling a lot better. When can I go home?' he repeated the same question every time he saw anyone with an NHS lanyard.

'Well…' The young doctor glanced down at his notes and frowned. 'I think, judging from this, ideally we need to do some more tests before we send you on your way.'

'Tests on what? Apart from a gammy ankle I'm perfectly fit and healthy.' Arthur didn't like the expression on the doctor's face as he reread his notes. He noticed the doctor pause for a second too long, enough time for him to pass a look to Jeremy.

'What's going on? I know about the NHS bed crisis, it's ridiculous that I'm taking up a space here when I can recover perfectly adequately at home.'

'The thing is, Uncle Arthur,' Jeremy piped up. 'This is the third time you've had a fall.'

'Pfft. The other ones don't count.'

'Well, if you think getting a concussion and a split lip doesn't count then you need to think again. They were serious accidents—'

'They weren't serious enough to warrant a stay in hospital though,' Arthur disputed.

'We need to work out why you're having these falls, Mr Winter,' the young doctor interjected.

'I already told you,' Arthur sighed. 'I must have forgotten to straighten the rug. I wasn't paying enough attention and I tripped,' Arthur repeated for the umpteenth time. Why would no one listen to him? 'That's all, nothing else to it apart from a dose of clumsiness and I don't think even the NHS can prescribe anything for that,' Arthur added, trying to lighten the mood. He couldn't work out why both men in front of him looked so serious. They weren't the ones who had been forced to stay here next to the nasal warriors and suffer sloppy macaroni cheese that apparently passed as a meal.

'Mr Winter, please let me try and explain.' The doctor cleared his throat. 'We did some routine examinations when you were brought in.' Arthur couldn't remember the ambulance journey. He had quite a fright when he woke up in a strange single bed to the cacophony of snorers, with no idea where he was or how he'd gotten here. 'And the results from your brain scan have given us cause for concern.'

A baby crying. He remembered that in the fuzzy fog. This was a ward for senior gentlemen, the birth centre was in a separate part of the hospital but he was certain he had heard a baby wailing. It was as if he was trying to pin down the trail of this memory but it kept slipping away like a billowing bed sheet hung on the washing line on a windy day. Pearl used to love glancing out of the window in the morning, declaring it was the perfect weather for washing, a satisfied smile on her lips. She'd hang things out with a uniform neatness, pegging trousers and shirts just so, explaining that, 'The things you wear on top you hang from the bottom and those you wear on the bottom you hang from the top.'

'Uncle, are you listening?' Jeremy sat forward earnestly, squeaking loudly on the vinyl chair squashed next to the bed.

Arthur blinked back the memory of his wife hanging out the washing, humming a tune to herself with the pegs clutched in her small hands. He would give anything to be able to watch her do this mundane task just one more time.

'I've told you I'm fine. I'd like to go home now.' Arthur was unable to hide the gruffness in his voice.

'We would like to do some more tests, Mr Winter. We need to figure out what is causing you to lose your balance so regularly.'

'I'm fine. I just need to get home and recuperate there.'

Jeremy passed a look to the doctor. 'I told you he was adamant.'

Clearly these two had been in cahoots without him knowing about it, Arthur noted.

'Mr Winter.' The doctor cleared his throat. 'I don't think you'll be leaving us just yet, not until we can do some more assessments and get to the bottom of this.'

Arthur met the young doctor's eye. He looked dog-tired. His bushy black hair needed a decent trim. When did people stop making such an effort?

'It was just an accident. I promise I'll try to take better care in the future.'

The doctor wasn't convinced at this plea. He did a little scribble at the bottom of the clipboard and put it back at the foot of his bed.

'I'll come round and see you when we've got the rest of the results back,' the doctor said, glancing at his wristwatch. 'Chin up, Arthur.'

Chin up indeed. Clearly, he hadn't ever spent a night sharing a ward with such animals, Arthur grumbled under his breath as the doctor slipped out from behind the closed curtain.

'Perhaps you should see this as an unexpected break?' Jeremy said. 'A holiday of sorts! All you need to do is rest and recover whilst someone else brings you dinner and takes care of you.' His nephew's voice raised in the way you'd speak to a child trying to distract them into doing something you knew they wouldn't like. He then began pointlessly faffing with the bedspread, tucking in a loose edge, before launching into a very detailed update on the latest test cricket match.

Yes, Arthur thought, sinking back against the pillow. This was definitely hell on earth.

Another day, another cheery wake-up call from the big-bosomed nurse Arthur now knew was called Monique. She had five children, smoked Lambert & Butler cigarettes on her break and spoke to everyone she cared for as if they were a deaf baby. Of course, most of the old boys did have a hearing aid, but not Arthur. Monique also liked to loudly offer her suggestions as he quietly tried to do the crossword puzzle.

'Two down, Agatha Christie. Three across, Stratford or is that Shetland?'

She hadn't got one right yet.

'Knock, knock, can I come in?'

'Oh hello my love,' Monique smiled as Jeremy walked in, pretending to rap his knuckles against the bed frame. 'We're just doing the crossword, aren't we, Arthur? It's a little tricky but we're getting there!'

'Lovely,' Jeremy smiled broadly and dropped some magazines on the bed next to Arthur's legs.

'I'll leave you to it and will have a think about seven down…' She shuffled out.

'Alright, Uncle Arthur?'

'I will be when I get out of here.'

'Well, about that.' Jeremy picked up one of the thick magazines. Arthur realised it wasn't a magazine but a glossy brochure. 'You know we're all concerned about you. The last thing we want is another fall.'

'I'm just a little clumsy, that's all. The tests were inconclusive…' Arthur had clung onto this word as if it would make a jot of difference.

'Yes, well, thankfully they haven't revealed anything sinister but it's still a worry that you could have another accident, and what if this time you're not so lucky? You know you can't rely on random neighbours happening to just wander past and spot you through the window!'

His neighbour. He'd been meaning to ask Jeremy about that.

'How are they?'

'Who?'

'The person who… *found* me?'

'Well, she was a little shook up as you can imagine.' Jeremy poured himself a cup of water from the jug on Arthur's bedside that seemed to magically refill.

'The one with the dogs?'

'I don't know if she's got a dog.' Jeremy frowned. 'She lives at number forty-five. I'm not sure what her name is, I just got a call from the hospital as I'm on your records as your next of kin.'

Number forty-five – that was the young mother, Izzy. Arthur felt a funny sort of drop in his stomach, he didn't want it to have been her who had discovered him.

'She's got a little one. Cries a lot.'

Jeremy nodded. 'Well that's what babies tend to do.'

Arthur wasn't sure, this baby seemed to cry rather a lot. The mother looked permanently exhausted. He remembered the vomit, the loosening of his bowels. Had she seen him in that awful state? How had she even known to check on him? He wished he could remember the events that brought him here but there was just a fuzzy blankness where that lost time should have been.

'Anyway, we need to focus on you right now.' Jeremy cleared his throat and shifted in the uncomfortable-looking chair. 'Like I said, Elaine and I are concerned about something else happening to you and I'm not sure home is the best place for you anymore. I've been doing some research and found some lovely retirement villages that offer as much, or as little, support as you want so you can still keep your independence but help is on hand if you need it.'

Here it was – the real reason for this visit. Arthur wasn't surprised Jeremy had brought this up, only that it had taken him this long to do so. Still, Arthur was glad he was lying down.

'I know we said the first time you fell that if you had another accident that we would look into your options. Then you got that shiny black eye. You promised me that if it happened again you wouldn't fight it. So, it's third time unlucky, I suppose,' Jeremy said, smiling weakly. Arthur had reached the end of his nine lives. 'I think it's time for you to move to a retirement village.' Jeremy pointed to an image of a modern-looking brick building. Two people, around Arthur's age, were manically laughing at something one of them said. The sky was cornflower blue, the sun shone and people acted like grinning simpletons... apparently.

'You've coped so well without Aunty Pearl but I think you need to admit that it's time to look after yourself. I'm afraid they won't let you leave here unless we have a plan in place. The alternative is that we look at getting you a carer, a home help, someone who pops in every day and helps you out or even a live-in companion?'

'Someone who treats me like some bloody invalid, you mean?' Arthur said, through gritted teeth.

'No, someone who helps you with the chores and—'

'I manage perfectly fine.'

He ignored his nephew's raised eyebrow.

'I don't want to speak out of turn, but your house could do with a bit of TLC. The maintenance alone is a full-time job. If you move to sheltered housing, then you don't have to worry about that. Plus, I'm sure you'll agree that a three-bed really is too large for you on your own, perhaps downsizing is the best thing to do. I mean, wouldn't it be nicer if you could move somewhere and not have to worry about the upkeep or trying to keep it clean?'

'A house move is an enormous upheaval!' Arthur interjected.

'It's not ideal, yes, but nor is the fact that you keep having falls. In my opinion, the sooner we move you to a safe and secure new home the better.'

Arthur didn't know what to say.

'I'm sure you must get a little lonely not having someone to talk to all the time?' Arthur shuddered at the thought of having Monique perched on the sofa next to him, settling her wide bottom in Pearl's chair, booming across incorrect crossword answers. No, that would not do.

'Of course I'll try and visit more often but you know how it is with Elaine and her allergies.'

Elaine had many allergies and the one and only time she'd visited Arthur's house had broken out in hives, so had been advised to stay away. It was no loss to Arthur, he thought she had a funny smell about her, but it had meant that Jeremy's visits were more and more infrequent.

'In the meantime we could think about adapting your home? Maybe move your bed downstairs or get a stairlift? We will probably have to think about modernising your downstairs toilet with grab rails and even, in the future, possibly widening door frames for a wheelchair but…' Jeremy paused and rubbed his thumb and forefinger together. 'Very pricey and it's not a long-term solution. It won't solve the worry of you being completely alone and having another accident.'

Arthur turned his head away in response.

'Come on. Please, I feel like I've been fair enough. You agreed that if anything else happened to you then we would have to rethink your situation. And, well, I'm afraid that means things are going to have to change. You have to see that? Think about it from my perspective? I could never live with the guilt if something else happened to you. I feel terrible as it is that I let it get this far. What would Aunty Pearl want? She would be devastated if she knew the danger you were putting yourself in.'

Jeremy handed Arthur the brochure with the couple of simpletons on the front cover. Arthur stared out of the window past the smear of bird poo on the grubby glass. Jeremy had to play the Pearl card, didn't he? Arthur knew exactly what his late wife would say.

'I'm sorry, Uncle Arthur. It's not easy for any of us. I'm only doing this because I, well, Elaine and I, care about you. So I've made us an appointment to go and look at a new home for you.'

'What?!'

'It's the only way I can get you out of here. We need to have a care plan in place.' Jeremy raised his hands in defence. 'RoseWood Lodge comes highly recommended and there's even a cinema room, I mean, imagine that!'

Arthur let Jeremy prattle on about the fancy mod cons, the safety features and regular social events. There was no way he'd be partaking in such organised fun. He kept his eyes fixed on the filthy window and out at the grey sky. He refused to take his last breath in hospital or in some godforsaken care home. Pearl had died at home, why couldn't he?

'I can help with the paperwork side of things, selling your house and all that. You don't have to do anything except pack a bag and look forward to making some new friends. It'll be like going back to boarding school, if you ever went there? So… what do you think?'

'I think you've lost your marbles. There's no way I'm going to spend whatever time I have left trapped in some sterile home being fed soup by a kid on minimum wage who couldn't give two hoots about me!'

A rush of colour swam to Jeremy's cheeks, he flicked his eyes to the gap in the curtain onto the ward. Arthur knew what he had promised his nephew following his previous accidents but he had no intention of actually going through with it – not then and not now.

'Arthur, please, it's not like that—'

'I said no. Now, if you don't mind I would like to take a nap.'

Jeremy let out a deep sigh. He nodded before he tightly closed his mouth, stopping himself from saying whatever he was about to say next.

'Fine, why don't you have some rest? Perhaps all you need is a good night's sleep. You might feel differently about things in the morning?' his voice rose expectantly. 'I'll pop by tomorrow and see how you're getting on.' He got to his feet and placed the brochure on the side table. 'I'll just leave this here in case you want to have a look yourself.'

Arthur remained silent.

'Alright then.' Jeremy shuffled on his feet. 'Well, rest up.'

He drew the thin curtain open, about to leave then stopped and looked back.

'You know you're allowed to ask for help, Uncle Arthur. There's no shame in that.'

He walked away leaving Arthur alone once more. It was the first time he envied Pearl's sudden death when his own appeared to be so drawn out.

CHAPTER 7

Izzy

Izzy was running late. She was frantically racing around the house to pack a changing bag with enough of everything to survive the short trip to see the health visitor for Evie's weigh-in, accompanied by the ear-piercing shrieks of a grumpy newborn. There was no time to tidy up the breakfast dishes, deal with the soggy, milky muslins crumpled on the floor or try and make it look like she hadn't been burgled.

'Right! I think we're good to go. Ha, see, Mummy can do this.'

Thankfully the rain clouds had held off as she ran between her house and her car with the baby and the bags. Izzy was determined to get out before this storm that the media were getting very excited over, hit. Despite another rough night she promised herself to try and get through at least one day without breaking down in tears. Today was a fresh start. She was going to get them both out of the door, ignoring the bone-heavy weight of tiredness, if it killed her. She took the house keys from her mouth and quickly locked up. Evie began crying loudly.

'It's OK, sweetheart. You'll be fine once we get going!' Izzy sang.

'Morning!' Izzy waved to her neighbour who was hurrying her school uniform-wearing teens into the car. They were both glued to their phone screens oblivious to their mum's growing exasperation. Izzy had lived here for almost a year and a brief but friendly 'morning' was the extent of their relationship. She really must go over and properly introduce herself one of these days. Her eyes flicked across to Arthur's empty house. It had been three days since she'd watched serious-faced paramedics whisk him away in an ambulance. A wave of guilt washed over her as she fastened Evie's car seat straps. She was sure she'd read that 'baby brain' was scientifically proven to exist but that didn't ease the burden of blame she carried around with her for not checking on him sooner.

'Come on, pudding,' Izzy said through gritted teeth, the sound of Evie's wailing managing to get under her skin and scratch against her bones. 'Where's it gone?'

She quickly tried to locate a dummy, most likely wedged down the side of the car seat, not noticing that Evie's screams had stopped. Izzy glanced down at her daughter to check she was OK. Just at that moment, Evie projectile vomited over them both.

'Shit.' Izzy grabbed a half-dry muslin from the enormous change bag as milky sick trailed down her chest, puddling into her maternity bra. She took a deep breath and fixed on a tight smile as she unbuckled Evie from her car seat.

'Alright, darling, come here.' Each movement brought a fresh waft of vomit. 'Let's go back inside, get us both dressed and try again, shall we?'

Now she was definitely going to be late.

*

'So, how's she getting on?' Judy, the health visitor, asked after calling Izzy to the front of the community hall where the local clinic was being held. She was a no-nonsense-type woman, with a severe cropped haircut and thick black plastic glasses that she wore at the end of her pinched nose. She'd kept Izzy waiting for half an hour, much to Evie's impatience, because she'd missed her original time slot.

There were a couple of tables pushed against a wall with changing mats on. Izzy gently placed Evie down under some interesting artwork made from recycled bottle tops and shiny sweet wrappers.

'Good, well, I mean she does seem to cry a lot. My mother-in-law said my husband was quite the crier as a baby, so perhaps it's a genetic thing,' Izzy said with forced cheerfulness, all the other babies in the room were a lot more docile than her daughter.

'She seems pretty happy to me,' Judy noted.

Annoyingly, right now, Evie was being a model student as she lay peacefully on the padded changing mat.

'And how's Mum?'

'Surviving,' Izzy tried to laugh it off. Judy looked at her with a raised eyebrow, waiting for an honest answer. 'I'm doing OK. It's all a learning curve, I guess.'

'How about sleep? It's a bit of a shock to the system, right?'

'You can say that again.'

'And feeding going OK? You're still breastfeeding, right?'

'Yep, for now. I mean, she's a hungry baby and there are days when it's like she is never satisfied but—'

'Is she weeing and pooing regularly?' Judy nodded to the plastic scales, without waiting for a response. 'Can you take her clothes off and place her on there?'

Izzy began fumbling with Evie's cardigan, suddenly forgetting how to change her daughter now she was being observed. The poppers on the small white vest were refusing to open, Izzy was all fingers and thumbs. Evie was losing her patience and began to cry.

'Sorry, it's just… ah, there we go.'

'And the nappy off too please,' Judy said, peering up from the red book that Izzy had been told to bring to every doctor visit and weigh-in.

'Oh, right. Sorry.' Izzy tore off the nappy and placed her naked, pink squirming baby onto scales that resembled an extra-large mixing bowl. The shock of the cold hard seat made Evie cry even more.

Izzy was loudly shushing, willing her daughter to calm down. Judy pressed a button on the scales, jotted down the reading and nodded for Izzy to pick Evie up. Despite being cradled in her mother's arms Evie was still screaming.

'Oh, let me just find her dummy, that usually does the trick…' Izzy held Evie in one arm, whilst she frantically rummaged in her changing bag. 'You can never find anything in here when you need it!'

Nappies, soft toys and clean baby-gros were chucked onto the table. A tub of Sudocrem dropped to the floor and skittered away somewhere. Evie was still crying. Izzy felt eyes on the back of her head from the other mums waiting on the row of chairs behind her, their impatience growing at the hold-up. After what was an eternity, she managed to find the dummy. It was like magic. Evie took some ferocious sucks and stopped crying. Sweat beaded down Izzy's forehead. Why was it that wherever they went it had to be such a testing ordeal, she thought, biting her lip so as not to cry.

'Here you are.' Judy handed Izzy her health-tracker book, seemingly oblivious to the last painful few minutes. 'She's following her weight curve perfectly. Pop back if you feel there are any other problems. Next!'

Izzy grabbed everything she had thrown onto the table and stuffed it back into the changing bag. She cradled a much calmer Evie and stepped aside to let another mum come up to the table. She had never felt so exposed yet so invisible before. The other mothers ignored her, could they not see how badly she was coping? With her proverbial stiff upper lip jutted out, Izzy knew she would never ask for help. Asking for help meant admitting failure. *If you get in a mess then it's up to you to get yourself out of it. This family never gives up, Isabel.* She'd learnt that from her dad, his ominous words echoing in her ears as clear as if he was standing over her shoulder, dishing out this stern advice after angrily scrunching up another letter with her primary school crest in the corner. Izzy didn't need to unravel the ball to read what it contained. Being the third one she'd received in as many months, she could recite it word for word: Following concern from teachers, offers of help that were available and information on counselling, special grants for uniforms and free school meals for families like yours etc. The letter had been met with the same reaction from her dad each time. 'We don't need handouts, we don't need special attention and we don't need stuck-up jobsworths sticking their noses into our family business.' Her dad had thumped a fist on the table making the dinner plates judder. 'Do they not understand what we've been through?'

'Excuse me!' a soft voice interrupted Izzy's painful memories. 'Sorry, but do you have a minute?'

Izzy turned to face a woman wearing a name badge, Nina, pinned to her burnt orange mohair jumper, the type that you instinctively wanted to stroke. Nina had shiny blonde hair neatly tied in a low plait and perfectly shaped eyebrows that framed large, kind brown eyes.

'Did I forget something?' Izzy automatically glanced behind her. Forgetfulness was certainly a side effect of sleep exhaustion. She'd left twenty pounds in an ATM a few days ago, simply walked off without picking it up.

'No, no, I just wondered if I could have a quick chat with you before you went? I'm fairly new to the team and just wanted to meet as many mums here as possible.'

'Oh, OK.'

The thought of her much-longed-for sofa was growing further away.

Nina picked up on her hesitation. 'It won't take long.'

She duly followed her into a side room that had two low sofas and a coffee table. There were pamphlets on child benefits and girl guiding posters stuck to the magnolia walls. It smelt overwhelmingly of synthetic vanilla from a large reed diffuser plonked on the windowsill.

'I'm sorry, I didn't catch your names?'

'I'm Izzy and this is Evie.'

'Well it's lovely to meet you both. Do you want to pop Evie on the playmat so we can have a little chat? I remember that feeling of needing a minute without them being on you. The baby cuddles are amazing but it's also nice to feel like you're not just a permanent pillow for someone,' Nina suggested.

Izzy couldn't have agreed more. She gently placed Evie onto a playmat near a selection of cushions and soft toys; she was immediately entranced by the colourful plastic monkeys hanging near her head. Izzy perched on the sofa opposite.

'She seems to like that.'

'We've got a similar one at home.' Izzy replied, still unsure why she had been pulled in here. She'd not noticed any of the other mums being asked into the small room. Immediately a trickle of panic rolled across her body. What if Nina had picked up on something from Judy? Was there some sort of health visitor secret signal that meant Izzy needed to be pulled aside from the other mums?

'So, my name is Nina and I'm usually based at the children's centre in Leek Green.'

Izzy listened, feeling warmer as time went on, convincing herself that Nina was somehow about to deliver some terrible news related to her baby or about Izzy's failing as a mother.

'Like I was saying, I'm fairly new here so for the moment my role is to observe and be an added pair of helping hands. This means that I'm able to pick up on things that the other health visitors might have missed.'

Oh God. This was it.

Things finally clicked into place in Izzy's brain, she felt like she might be sick. Had someone seen her abandon Evie at the supermarket and reported her? Her heart raced. They were going to take her baby away, she was sure of it.

'Is this about what happened last week? It was completely my fault!' The confession started to tumble out of Izzy's mouth. 'Thank God she was OK but—'

'Sorry?' Nina frowned.

'I swear it was an—'

'Are you OK?' Nina asked. 'Take a breath.'

Izzy did as she said and gulped at the air, Nina's concerned eyes never strayed from her clammy face.

'I didn't mean to alarm you, Izzy. I just wanted to have a little chat, that was all. You seemed, well you seemed like you could do with a sit-down after what happened in there.'

She was talking about Evie's meltdown as she waited for Izzy to find her dummy. Nina didn't know about what happened at the supermarket, if she was in serious trouble the police would have already turned up on her doorstep.

'Thanks,' Izzy sniffed, trying to calm down. 'Sorry, I'm just very tired.'

Nina nodded gently. 'I remember it well and it's totally normal. Have you got much support? You know, parents or in-laws you can count on to help out? It takes a village to raise a child after all.'

'No, not nearby anyway.'

'What about any friends you could call? I think sometimes we worry what others will say but many times they would be horrified to think of us struggling without asking for help.'

Izzy had a limited social network, her university friends were scattered around the country and, if she was honest, she had grown apart from them due to putting work first and cancelling one too many times when they were supposed to meet.

'Or work colleagues?'

She thought of her colleague Joanna as her closest friend, but she didn't have children or any immediate plans to join Izzy in this new unfamiliar world of motherhood. Izzy had been rubbish at replying to Joanna's messages and even guilty of ignoring her calls. She simply didn't have the energy to pretend that everything was wonderful. She had replied on the odd occasion, so Joanna wouldn't send out a search party, with a short but positive:

I'm fine. Mad busy with baby life. Must catch up soon!

Joanna had replied that she was sure Izzy was nailing it. Izzy couldn't tell Joanna just how much she was struggling. Where would she even begin with explaining what was going on in her head? Despite always having Evie for company, Izzy was actually very lonely.

'How about any neighbours? Someone you trust who could watch Evie and give you a break?' Nina asked.

Izzy didn't know any of her neighbours well enough to impose herself like that or indeed leave her daughter with. But there was one neighbour she had struggled to get out of her mind. Perhaps if she knew that Arthur was doing OK she would at least be able to sleep when Evie slept instead of lying awake worrying.

'I had a bit of a fright with a neighbour recently. He's an old man who had a nasty fall and well, I was the one who discovered him.'

Nina's eyes widened.

'I've called the hospital every day for an update but, as I'm not family, they won't give me any information. So I've just got to wait until he comes home.' *If he comes home.*

'Gosh, that must have been terrifying for you.'

Izzy nodded, taking a tissue that Nina offered her.

'I feel so guilty. I should have checked on him sooner. He

had no one looking out for him. Can you imagine that? No one. I just keep thinking of all the what ifs.'

'You shouldn't beat yourself up, Izzy. I'm sure he understands that you've got a lot on your plate. Thank goodness you were there to help him in the first place! Let's hope he makes a speedy recovery, he's in the right place now.' Nina pressed her hands together and smiled at Evie. 'How about Evie's daddy? Does he help?'

'He does when he's around.' It didn't help that Andrew was out from seven till seven most days, plus a busy workload that rolled into their weekends eating into any plans she had for them. If she'd hoped that once Evie came along he would take his foot off the gas in order to support her more, then she was sorely mistaken. 'He works long hours.'

'Have you spoken to him about how you're feeling?'

'No. I mean, I just feel like every other new mum I guess.' Izzy was tired of feeling like this. Tired of being tired. 'It's been a big adjustment for both of us.'

'I understand but it might be a good idea to try and tell him exactly how you feel. Something else that can help is to make sure you're prioritising self-care too, you know, taking a bath, getting some exercise, reading a book, that type of thing. Do you go to any mother and baby groups?'

Izzy shook her head.

'They're a great way to meet other mums, allow you to spend some quality time with Evie, and an excuse to get out of the house as I know it can feel claustrophobic at times. What do you do with your days? Sometimes things can feel a lot more manageable if you have a routine. It doesn't have to be anything too demanding but it's good to try and get out of the house at least once a day. Fresh air helps to lift your mood too even if it feels like the last thing you want to do.' She paused and rummaged around in a bag at her feet.

'You need to take care of yourself before you can take care of others. Why don't you take this away with you and maybe have a read.'

Nina handed over a pamphlet titled 'Ways to Help With PND'. The front cover was a gurgling smiley baby wrapped up in a fluffy white towel.

'Have you heard of postnatal depression, Izzy?' Nina asked, her voice lowering slightly.

Izzy looked up at her. Is that what Nina thought she had? A chill rolled across her. Is that what others thought too? She suddenly remembered the funny look Pauline had given her in the supermarket car park.

'One in seven new mums experience some level of PND. Babies are hard work and the first three months are especially tough, that's why they call it the fourth trimester. It should be a time of rest, recovery and relaxation as you get to know one another.' She paused. 'There's a list of numbers for a couple of fantastic charities on the back of the leaflet offering plenty of support for new mums. I don't want you to feel like you're going through this on your own.'

'Thanks but I'm fine, just a bit tired.' Izzy plastered on a bright smile and tucked the pamphlet into her changing bag. She didn't have postnatal depression. Nina was wrong, Izzy didn't need help back then and she didn't need it now. She leaned down to pick up Evie.

'I just wondered if perhaps you ever feel overwhelmed with it all? Like you're drowning all the time?'

Izzy had a hand on the door frame. Since she'd got home from the hospital she felt like she was constantly treading water, with more than the occasional slip under the surface. She looked back and nodded reluctantly.

'Maybe have a read of the leaflet, Izzy. If you ever just need to talk, I'm here.'

Izzy strode out feeling like she was on the verge of tears yet again for no reason. She would be fine on her own. Izzy Carter was made of strong stuff, or so her dad always told her. She had coped with bigger things before so surely she would get through this too.

CHAPTER 8

Arthur

'Guess what, Uncle Arthur!' Jeremy did this funny drum roll with his index fingers. 'The doctor says you're fit to leave.'

'Thank goodness for that.' Arthur's spirits soared. He was more than ready to say farewell to this place. 'When? Right now?'

'Hang on, there is a caveat to this.' Jeremy fidgeted with his sleeve. 'Before they discharge you we need to have a care plan in place like we talked about before.'

'You mean shipping me off to a home.'

'No one is shipping you off anywhere. It's called a retirement village,' Jeremy corrected him. 'A place where you keep your independence but have help on hand when you need it. I know you're not overjoyed with the prospect but I think it's the best option for you.' He paused. 'Otherwise, the alternative is… and I know you weren't keen on this… but we look at getting you a live-in carer.'

Arthur didn't feel like he was able to respond without saying something he might regret. He was eighty-four years old, he didn't need babysitting.

'I understand you're not happy about leaving your home so getting you a carer may be the only way I can prove that you're able to stay living independently for the foreseeable future. We'll make sure we choose someone really lovely. You never know, you may become friends! We will need to give your place a complete home safety evaluation too, I think there's a team at the council who look after that. Depending on the results we could be looking at a large refurbishment project as we bring your bedroom downstairs... but whilst that's taking place you can always stay with Elaine and me. Temporarily of course.'

There was a moment of silence as Arthur ran through the bleak options he had just been presented with.

'Let's take a look at the retirement home,' Arthur said eventually, through gritted teeth.

He decided that if he grunted in the right places and looked vaguely interested then it would work to his advantage. The sooner he agreed to go along with Jeremy's ridiculous plan the sooner he could be off this ward and back where he belonged, in his own home, just the way it was. Arthur would show Jeremy just how capable he still was without needing to hire a carer. Being here for the past few days was the incentive he needed to take things a little slower and be less clumsy.

Jeremy's face lit up. 'Great! That's brilliant, I can breathe a sigh of relief now.' He dramatically wiped his brow. 'I know it's a change but I truly think it's for the best and you never know, it might give you a new lease of life!'

It was late evening by the time Arthur had been discharged from the hospital and Jeremy had dropped him off home.

He had gingerly tried to assist Arthur up the step to his door before being barked at that he could do it himself. Arthur had shooed him away and spent the time before bed making sure everything was as he had left it. He had never been so relieved to be home.

The next day was Sunday and, despite his injury, he couldn't bear to miss another week without seeing Pearl, which is why he clenched his teeth to make the short but painful journey to church. The hospital had issued him a pair of ugly crutches to aid his recovery, Arthur had reluctantly taken them as they were marginally better than the Zimmer frame he'd been offered; he hadn't planned on actually using them but he'd needed the support. The temporary support, he vowed, hating every moment of being forced to use them. If looking like a victim was the price to pay for getting out of that stuffy ward and into the chilly sunshine then Arthur would suffer it. He could imagine both his doctor and Jeremy's concerned faces that he was doing too much too soon but, if anything, the thought of defying their orders only spurred Arthur on. His slower pace meant it had taken double the time to get here, stopping whenever he saw an available bench and also to pick up a newspaper from the corner shop, but it had meant that he could sneak in the back of the church halfway through the service.

'We are all God's children. He embraces each and every one of you, loving you for your flaws. You can do no wrong in the eyes of our saviour, which, I guess, is something to bring you comfort when you're having a bad day,' said the vicar.

He was one of these 'cool' vicars, in his mid- forties, with a bushy brown beard and trendy spectacles. He liked to add jokes to his sermons and make references to TV shows that Arthur had never heard of. He had a small silver earring in his left ear, wore Dr. Martens and rode here on a scooter. Clearly the church had to do something to try and bring in a younger crowd, Arthur thought as he glanced around the half-empty pews that were mainly filled with his generation.

Arthur huffed loudly, ignoring the looks from the couple sat in front of him. He stretched out his arms and gave a slight shake of the paper to open it fully. He used to bring his small portable radio with him but others complained that the service was being ruined by the horse racing playing from the tinny speakers – not very Christian-like of them, he'd retorted as the vicar meekly asked him not to bring it again. Arthur had picked up the Sunday papers to entertain him as he sat through this load of garbage and drivel.

'And now for our next hymn. If you all turn to page 302 in your hymn books for one of my favourites… "How Great Thou Art".'

The silence of the draughty church was broken by the collective sound of people getting to their feet, the odd crack of joints and sigh of effort. Arthur stayed seated. It was times like these that he was envious of those with a hearing aid. He'd love to switch off from the long-winded sermons and the out of tune singing, instead, he had to make do with focusing on the badly written article about the latest with the rail scheme. Finally the congregation returned to their bottoms and the vicar summed things up with one of his irritating 'do good-isms' as Arthur called them. Small snippets of advice meant to motivate them until they were all sat in their same spots next Sunday.

'Have a great week!' the vicar grinned, snapping his bible shut.

'Finally,' Arthur muttered, struggling to his feet and tucking the paper under his arm. He could now go and get on with his day. He only came and persevered through the tedious service because of Pearl. She'd been a keen churchgoer, forever offering to help out at the summer fair or bake for the bring-and-buy sale or even clean up after the playgroup in the church hall. Arthur didn't know where she found the energy but that was his Pearl, always helping others. He'd come and sit on an uncomfortable pew every week with her, grumbling under his breath as the vicar rattled on about whatever psalm he was reading. She would tut that Arthur needed to be more present but he couldn't help it, this wasn't his thing.

'Arthur! Lovely to see you, sir. Oh dear, have you hurt yourself?' The vicar nodded to Arthur's crutches, turning his bright smile into a concerned frown. Arthur didn't want to make small talk; he wanted to slip out without being accosted but the crutches put paid to that idea.

'Nothing serious. I'm on the mend now.' He would get rid of the mobility aid as soon as he could put his full weight on his ankle. Not a moment too soon. They were a beacon for pity and sad sympathetic smiles that Arthur didn't appreciate being on the receiving end of.

'I'm glad to hear that. It's great to see you. Oh, before you escape I think you missed the announcements at the start when I mentioned our Golden Oldies group? You're more than welcome to come.'

'The what now?'

'Every other Tuesday evening we get some of the old boys

together at the Lion's Head, you know, the one on the corner of the old high street? It's a chance for you to catch up with some of the congregation over a pint. We've got a fantastic group of gents who are similar to you, they've lost their wives and, well, they know how isolating it can be.' He paused, tilting his head. 'What do you say? It starts at 6.30 p.m. so you'll be back in time for *EastEnders*, if you're into that!'

'I'll... er... think about it.'

'Great! Please do, we'd love to see you. We also have our Monday Walkers group. We meet at the war memorial at midday and enjoy a gentle stroll around town. Afterwards we have a biscuit and a cuppa back at the church hall. It's a lovely way to meet new people and a chance to get your daily steps in, well, perhaps that's one to think about for when everything has healed? Anyway, I'll let you go. Hopefully we'll see you soon, Arthur!'

Arthur nodded politely and made his way out of the gloom of the church into the sunshine. The path to the cemetery was full of pebbles of different sizes so he needed to pay close attention to his footing. He'd almost taken a tumble here once before. Pearl's grave was in the far corner, away from the small headstones, colourful teddies and occasional balloons that danced in the air; the ones that broke Arthur's heart. Pearl had been lucky to get a plot that was close to one of the few bins so Arthur didn't have far to walk when he did the weeding. Her grave was also near a memorial bench, every time he sat on it he hoped the family of a Mr Kenneth Black would appreciate it getting some good use. He was sure the wood had an Arthur shaped dent in it as he'd never seen anyone else sitting here looking over the array of headstones.

Pearl had insisted on being buried. It had been one of very few things they'd disagreed on. Arthur was adamant he would be cremated. He didn't want to take the risk of being buried alive. Pearl had teased him that it was only because he was a little claustrophobic. She might have had a point there. Although he disagreed with her choice, he had to admit that he was grateful he had somewhere to go and sit and feel closer to her. In some silly way the simple headstone inscribed with her name had brought him more comfort than he could admit. It gave him a sense of purpose, a task he didn't mind doing week in week out. Apart from his accidents, he'd only missed a Sunday visit once before and that was due to a heavy snowfall which brought most of the country to a halt. He didn't want to think about who would visit her once he was gone. He remembered his final word on the argument about burial versus cremation – the problem with gravestones was the unwanted legacy you left behind.

'Hello, love. Me again, I've missed you.' He rubbed a hand against the smooth cold stone of the headstone and collected his thoughts.

'I was out of action for a while, nothing for you to worry about,' he added quickly. 'Anyway, I thought you'd like to know that the neighbours opposite have finally decided to replace their fence. I know, I know, it was a complete eyesore. I hope that they pick one that's not as garish. I mean, really, who paints a fence blue? Although,' he chuckled, 'remember that time when we said we would fix up my mother's shed? What colour did she go for? Electric yellow or something? It was the seventies, I guess.'

The smile slipped. A lump rose to his throat every time

his dear mother popped into his head. It had been thirty-five years since he'd lost her but there were some people you never stopped loving. He roughly wiped his eyes and cleared his throat.

'Sorry! I don't know what's come over me. It must be all this pollen in the air.'

Arthur rarely cried. He could count on one hand the times when he'd really sobbed. When he'd lost Pearl, when he was told his mum had just days left to live, and when he was seven and his brother had given him such a good whack on the head with a toy car he had needed stitches. At the mere thought of Reg his sadness evaporated into anger. His hands curled into fists and an ugly burning sensation spread across him. If their poor mother could see how her two sons were now she'd be appalled.

'Actually, I'm not sure if pollen exists in February, perhaps it's the painkillers I'm on.' Arthur pulled his jacket tighter against the chilly wind that had picked up. 'I do have some news though and I'm not sure if you're going to like it but I feel the odds have been stacked against me.' He cleared his throat, his eyes watching a white-winged butterfly flutter past. 'I'm going to look around a retirement home with Jeremy. He says it's for the best.'

Arthur wasn't thrilled about the thought of tomorrow's tour but there was nothing he could do about it, apart from not make a scene. He knew that he had put his nephew in an unenviable position and that he should feel grateful he had someone so concerned about his welfare.

'Right. I'd best get on, my darling.' That lump had risen in his throat once more. He missed her terribly. 'Oh, I forgot to say, the vicar invited me to some OAP club. Can you think of anything worse? Next he'll be pushing for me to join the luncheon club at the day centre, now that really would tip me over the edge. Although if Jeremy had his way I'm sure he'd be putting my name down for God knows what activities at this care home. He was very excited about something called chair yoga. Can you even imagine? Well, to be fair, you were always the social butterfly out of us, you would have no problem holding your own.' He smiled sadly. 'I'll hopefully see you properly very soon. Take care and if you can't be good, be careful.'

He uttered the catchphrase they'd shared whenever one of them went out without the other. It had always made Pearl smile. It was that cheeky twinkle in her eye that was exactly why Arthur had fallen for her, that glimmer had never faded despite the passing of time. He bit down the pain from his throbbing ankle as he got to his feet, brushed off his trousers and hobbled ever so slowly out of the cemetery.

CHAPTER 9

Izzy

It had taken Izzy three attempts to get out of the house already this morning; every time she thought they were ready she was forced to deal with something else. She'd forgotten Evie's bunny comforter, she'd left the changing bag in the hall, and then needed to double-check she had locked the back door. The Izzy before having a child hadn't realised how much she had taken the freedom of simply stepping out and then closing the door behind her for granted. Now it was a mammoth palaver that involved tight schedules, to-do lists and gigantic change bags.

Izzy was about to get into her car, doing a final mental check that she had everything she needed, when she realised that the bin men had left her wheelie bin blocking her drive. She groaned, Evie was already strapped in her car seat and not going to take kindly to any more delays.

'Mummy won't be long.'

Izzy went to drag her bin out of the way so she could reverse. She still hadn't got round to sticking those butterfly stickers on the side yet. She glanced at her neighbours' bins to see if she was the only one who was letting the team down. You could barely see the original colour of Mrs Peterson's bin for the assortment of large dog face stickers, all different breeds. It might not be art but it was certainly *something*. Izzy smiled to herself. She was about to jump in her car when she saw Arthur's front door opening.

'You're back!' Izzy called out loudly, unable to contain her surprise at seeing him on his feet again so quickly.

He jumped back in fright and knocked his empty wheelie bin over at the surprise of hearing Izzy's voice.

'Oh God. Sorry! I didn't mean to startle you.' She jogged over to help him pick his bin up from where it had toppled to the pavement, flushed with embarrassment. 'I've been waiting for you to come home. I tried calling the hospital to see how you were doing but no one would tell me anything. Anyway, welcome home! I hope that you're OK?'

Arthur blinked quickly. Izzy clapped a hand to her warm cheeks.

'Sorry! You must be wondering who the hell I am! I'm Izzy, I live at number forty-five.' She glanced back at her car, it would only be a matter of time before Evie grew bored of waiting and let the world know about it. 'I think technically we already met when you delivered that parcel over to mine the other week. I'm the one who called the ambulance for you, I have to say it was quite a shock. I thought you'd just left the television on and well, my grandparents would be appalled to think of the electricity bill if they'd done the same and I was planning on coming over to investigate and—'

Arthur held a hand up. 'Please, take a breath, dear.'

'Sorry. I haven't spoken to another adult for a while. I'm

at home with my daughter, Evie, all the time and although she's adorable, she isn't the best conversationalist.' Izzy let out an awkward laugh at the same time as she heard the familiar shrieks from her car. Evie's patience had run out. Izzy's shoulders sank at the sound.

'That's my cue to make a move, I guess. But anyway, I just wanted to say hi and that it's good to see you back on your feet. If you ever need anything please let me know. So, yep...' She trailed off. She was expecting Arthur to jump in and say something but he didn't.

'OK, well, I'll let you get on... er... bye.' She turned and trudged back to her crying baby.

'We're so lucky with Indiana, she slept through the night pretty much straight after bringing her home from hospital,' a mum wearing a trendy coral cable-knit jumper said. The colour matched her shiny gel nails.

Izzy had decided that she would listen to Nina the health visitor's advice and give a mother and baby group a go. She hoped it was a chance to meet other new mums who she could connect with, maybe it would make her feel less alone. At the very least it would break up her day a bit. But she had almost called the whole thing off after an incredibly stressful twenty minutes trying to find somewhere to park. She'd finally spotted an elderly gentleman in a shiny Honda slowly reversing out of a space, as she waited for him to go she thought of Arthur. During his absence she had invented this fairy-tale reunion – he would embrace her with a single tear falling down his cheek, thanking her for saving his life, telling her she wasn't to blame for not acting sooner. He would invite her in for a cup of tea and a fig roll – her grandparents always had a stash of them in a battered biscuit tin – and coo over Evie. Perhaps even offer to step in as a sort of rent-a-grandad, maybe taking her to the park or feed the ducks. All the things that she had hoped from her dad or Andrew's parents. Except her dad was on a year-long secondment lecturing at a university in Vienna and Andrew's parents lived in Scotland and were a seven-hour car journey away. But what Izzy hadn't expected from Arthur was that lukewarm reception. She told herself that he was probably still on a lot of medication from the hospital but the Arthur-daydream had shattered.

'Same. It's nowhere near as life-changing as I imagined it to be,' a mum with incredibly shiny, brown curls said in agreement.

Izzy tried to focus and be present. Harder said than done being so uncomfortably sat cross-legged on the outside of the circle of padded baby mats, trying to join in and nod along with the other mums.

'I mean, don't get me wrong, it's life-changing but for all the right reasons. Artie has slotted in as if he's always been here.'

The woman took a sip out of her KeepCup and placed it on the parquet floor. Her trendy Tiba + Marl backpack changing bag was blocking Izzy from picking up a sensory toy to waft over Evie's face like the other mums were doing. She'd tried and failed to catch the attention of two younger mums opposite but they were taking selfies of their babies with dog-ear filters. The only other woman in the small stuffy room was a grandma who'd spent most of the session complaining about her daughter-in-law to Tina, the class leader.

'I was bracing myself for sheer hell but it's been pretty

plain sailing,' the third lady, wearing a chic Breton striped top, piped up.

'Same! See I blame these mummy bloggers who go on and on about needing gin to survive the day, who call their kids dickheads and moan the whole time. It's as if it's fashionable to make out how hard it is but really it's all about your attitude.'

Attitude. In Izzy's eyes, motherhood was more batten down the hatches and grip onto the side ropes than plain sailing. It was hard to keep a positive attitude when you were completely broken with exhaustion. Izzy didn't know how others did it. They didn't have crusts of sleep in the corner of their eyes – ironic given Izzy had only managed to get a solid three hours last night. They didn't smell of milky sick. They had even managed to match their outfits together with jewellery. Jewellery! And was that lip liner she saw? Her self-esteem took a battering. She thought she'd made an effort with the quick swipe of tinted moisturiser that she'd fished out of the pocket in the car door. The other mums all looked well rested with clean hair. Izzy had scraped hers back into an unwashed messy bun, again. How had they managed to get a shower without a background crescendo of tears? How had they survived another torturous night feed without dropping off to sleep and waking a microsecond later convinced they'd squashed the baby?

'Pfft,' Izzy snorted loudly without meaning to.

The sound made the three women turn to face her.

'How are you finding it all?' one of them asked, turning to Izzy, waiting for her to chip in with another glowing report on motherhood. Izzy shifted uncomfortably under their gazes. She wanted to scream that she was drowning. That reading those slummy mummy type blogs gave her a hint of hope that she wasn't alone. But maybe they were right, maybe it was all fabricated clickbait.

'Erm, yeah, it's challenging at times. But I wouldn't change it for the world,' she hastened to add.

The truth was that her nipples were sore, her willpower was defeated and her body was screaming for a decent chunk of undisturbed sleep. But she had clearly said the right thing as they nodded then turned back to their babies, each cooing in unison.

'Right, ladies.' Tina clapped her hands together to get the group's attention. 'If you all pick up two toilet roll tubes and gently tap them together, it creates a lovely sensory sound that's easy for you to replicate at home.'

Izzy had been handed a piece of silver foil to 'waft in her baby's face' as it was apparently very sensory but Evie had been fast asleep in her car seat since they had arrived. All the other mums began wafting and tapping the recycling as if this was a totally normal way to spend a Monday morning.

'I can't believe how fast time is going. I was saying to my husband, just last night, how soon maternity leave will be over,' Backpack Mum said, jutting her bottom lip out. 'It might sound crazy but I've already started thinking about schools. You know you need to get their name down as soon as possible if you want to get them in anywhere half decent.'

'So I've heard. It's the same with childcare, although we're looking at nannies to help us out...'

Izzy zoned out. Unlike the other women here, her time was dragging not speeding by. It felt like a lifetime ago since her office waved her off in a blur of good luck balloons and well wishes. She still felt incredibly anxious when she thought of Pauline and the pitying look she'd given Izzy in the supermarket car park. Thankfully, she must not have said anything to the team as no one had been in touch, not even Joanna.

Izzy forced herself to join back in with the conversation, which had moved on to the contentious topic of early weaning but she struggled to follow along with what was going on. Her backside was grumbling at being sat on the church hall's hard floor, she hadn't known the words to any of the nursery rhymes the other mums had sung along to and she had half-heartedly jingled some bells in her sleeping daughter's direction.

'How long has she been in that?' one of the mums asked Izzy a short while later. 'You know they say babies should only be in their car seats for thirty minutes at a time.'

'I heard it was twenty,' another piped up, looking at Izzy disdainfully.

A flush of heat rose to Izzy's cheeks as she fumbled with the car seat straps, hurrying to get Evie out. Damn it. She was so grateful that her daughter was finally asleep; she hadn't remembered the safety rules that had been drummed into her by the midwife. Immediately Evie began to cry. The noise was met with sympathetic glances from the women. Izzy began vigorously rocking Evie, her cheeks blazing, but the abrupt wake-up call had seriously pissed her off. Within seconds all the other babies began to cry too. Soon the room was an orchestra of solidarity sobbing and exasperated sighs.

'I think we might make a move. See you next week!' Izzy shouted across the noise. She grabbed her things without a backward glance and raced out.

Well that went well, she thought.

'Babe? What are you doing?' Andrew asked, walking into the kitchen, back from work.

Izzy looked up from the recycling box she was crouched over. She was rummaging for some shiny paper or cardboard tubes but there just seemed to be a lot of empty wine bottles. 'I'm trying to find some sensory toys.'

'Sorry? What?'

'I went to this mother and baby class today, apparently it's better for babies' development if all their toys are natural,' Izzy explained, wondering if a Pringles tube would suffice.

'Oh, that sounds… nice.'

'It wasn't. Every week they have different themes, this week was sensory i.e. chucking loads of silver foil in the baby's face. Next week is baby massage.'

'Yeah? Well you might learn some new techniques that maybe we could try?' Andrew winked.

'Not unless counting *this little piggy* on your toes is some weird fetish I didn't know about,' she said, ignoring the look of rejection on his face.

'So, did you enjoy it? The baby class thing?' he asked as he turned the tap on and filled a glass of water.

'Where do I start?' Izzy groaned. 'All the other mums may as well have been speaking in a foreign language. They know all these modern nursery rhymes, they talk about stuff I'd never heard of – Sleepyheads, Perfect Prep and baby-wearing—'

'Baby-wearing?'

'It's when you put the baby in a sling,' Izzy clarified. She'd hastily googled that one too. 'I never knew it had a name.'

'Babe, you need to see it as a challenge. You picked up Italian quickly enough, maybe this is similar,' Andrew offered, unhelpfully. That was a couple of weeks bingeing on Duolingo before their honeymoon so they could pick up the hire car without resorting to Google Translate. 'I'm sure it wasn't that bad.'

'Trust me. You weren't there.'

'They're probably just as inexperienced as you. You're all in the same boat, right?'

'It didn't bloody feel like it,' Izzy muttered. 'Oh, but some good news… I spoke to our neighbour earlier. Arthur?'

'The old guy whose life you saved.'

Izzy pulled a face. 'That's a bit over the top.' She was still racked with guilt that she hadn't acted earlier when she'd first spotted his television had been left on. 'He's back home and looks like he's recovering well.' She didn't go into the disappointment she felt at his lukewarm reaction.

'That's good to hear. Oh, there's something I forgot to mention…' Izzy didn't like the look he was giving her. 'My mum and dad are coming to stay for a few days.'

'When?'

He took a large gulp of his water before answering.

'Tomorrow.'

'What? Andrew! Why didn't you tell me sooner. Tomorrow?!'

'Yeah, I know sorry, it completely slipped my mind. They've been going on at me for ages about coming down. Mum said it's not fair they've only met Evie once.'

'That's because they live so far away. I don't mind them visiting but I need some prior warning, just look at the state of the house!'

'It's fine, honestly. They don't care about stuff like that. They just want to see us – well Evie mostly.'

Izzy was convinced he walked around with blinkers on, ignoring the dust, cobwebs and general grubbiness of their house that had settled since Evie had arrived.

'Well I'll just have to try and find some time to do a quick tidy then.' Another thing to add to her list. He took for granted how challenging it was to keep the house clean whilst in charge of a demanding newborn.

'You don't mind, do you? It's not like you've got anything on. I mean I can cancel if it's going to be a big deal.'

He was right, she did have zero plans but still, she gritted her teeth. 'No. It's fine.'

'Cool, thanks. I'm just going to get changed and go for a quick run. That OK?' He placed his empty glass in the sink.

Izzy nodded and turned back to the random assortment of plastic wrappers and empty milk cartons. There was no point getting into an argument about him inviting his parents to stay without checking with her first. As they lived so far away this would only be the second time they had seen Evie, and Izzy actually got on with them quite well, it was more the inconvenience than anything else.

With a deep sigh she decided to make a start on tidying up a bit before Evie's next feed. She suddenly remembered that there was a used nappy wrapped in a plastic bag currently festering in Evie's change bag. As she emptied out the contents into the bin, she caught sight of the leaflet that Nina the health visitor gave her. The one about postnatal depression. If she was honest the number of symptoms she could tick was worrying. Lack of energy, feeling tired all the time, problems concentrating, a low mood, Izzy could identify with all of these. Difficulty bonding with your baby – no, she definitely didn't agree with that one; despite all the hard work, Izzy knew she loved Evie unconditionally.

She carried on reading what the treatments were. Apart from therapy and antidepressants, self-help was a big one. 'Talk to your friends and family about how you are feeling, rest when you get the chance and make time for yourself to do the things you enjoy,' she read before putting the leaflet in the bin along with the nappy bag. Izzy wasn't depressed; she was just exhausted, just like every other new mum.

CHAPTER 10

Arthur

Arthur couldn't take his eyes off the dubious-looking stain that had seeped through the magnolia Artex ceiling. He looked back at Jeremy, who was deep in conversation with the retirement home manager, Miguel, a round barrel-shaped man who smelt faintly of onions. Was no one else seeing this? Arthur told himself not to make an issue out of it. The more he thought about it, the more he had to concede that Jeremy was right; he was vulnerable in his own home. The risk of falling whilst trying to keep the large house going all on his own was worrying. He couldn't bear the thought of another stay in hospital. This was exactly why he'd agreed to come here today. But RoseWood Lodge was even worse than he'd mentally prepared himself for.

For one, it looked nothing like the images from the brochure. He'd not see one resident smile, let alone flash dazzling grins like the fools on the front cover had done. Miguel had kept them waiting in the drab reception area for far too long. Then, when the 'tour' finally got started he'd seemed distracted, as if showing them around was a waste of his time. They'd pretty much speed-walked through the cold, dimly lit communal corridors that had the odour of overcooked cabbage. His ankle had twinged the whole way round but he refused to ask them to slow down.

'This is the day room.' Miguel jabbed his thumb at a large room filled with an assortment of wing-backed chairs and mismatched side tables. *This Morning* boomed from the television that was fixed to the far peach-coloured wall but not one resident was actually watching it. They were all lost in their own worlds. One lady was simply staring at a closed fire exit door. There was a man being helped from a wheelchair into an armchair by a slip of a girl in a blue tabard. Arthur feared he would no doubt be sat there for the rest of the day. Neither him nor his young helper spoke or even smiled at one another.

'Right now is... er... free time,' Miguel explained, taking in the look of horror on Arthur's face. 'You've just missed our weekly cooking class that the residents love. We also have bingo coming up this afternoon!' He plastered on a bright smile that didn't reach his red-rimmed eyes.

'Bingo... that would be fun, wouldn't it, Arthur?' Jeremy gave his uncle a gentle nudge. Arthur couldn't bear to look at him. 'I saw in your brochure that you also have a cinema room?'

Miguel coughed and shifted on his feet. 'Ah, it's er... going through a slight refurbishment at the moment. Any other questions?'

'Yes,' Arthur finally spoke. 'I thought the self-contained flats each had their own lounge? Not that we had to watch television together in one big room like the Waltons.'

'Yes, you're right sir. I'll show you the apartments in a second. Many residents simply prefer to spend time here instead of being locked away on their own like prisoners.' He let out a belly laugh at a joke that Arthur didn't get.

A woman with a severely curved spine shuffled past, bent in half over a metal Zimmer frame.

'Morning, Dot!' Miguel bellowed.

Dot ignored him and carried on shuffling. She reminded Arthur of the tortoise in 'The Tortoise and the Hare', a story he'd loved when he was younger. She looked full of intent to win some unknown race.

'Dot!' Miguel shouted even louder, making Jeremy jump. 'Morning!'

Dot turned to face them with a slow smile of recognition. 'Harold?'

'No, no, it's Miguel.' A flush of colour rose to Miguel's cheeks.

'What have you done with my Harold?' Dot barked, her hand tightening its grip on the Zimmer frame.

Miguel turned to Jeremy. 'She gets confused. Let's keep moving, yes?' He nodded and then waved to Dot. 'See you soon!'

They were hurriedly ushered out of the room back down another identical corridor.

'She's one of our longest-standing residents – lovely lady. Right, I'll show you the apartments!'

The visit had ended shortly after they'd been whisked round a typical 'apartment', which was no larger than a very cosy studio flat. The unmistakable smell of bleach stung Arthur's nose. He wondered who had last laid in that narrow single bed in the freshly made 'bedroom'. It explained why the residents preferred to spend time in that godawful day room when the alternative was to be cooped up like a battery hen.

'Where would all my things go?' Arthur asked, taking in the minuscule dimensions.

Jeremy cleared his throat. 'Well we did talk about the fact you may need to downsize…'

'Downsize yes, but this basically calls for me to pack a suitcase, a small one at that!'

'It might be good for you to declutter yours and Aunty Pearl's things,' Jeremy said brightly. 'It might be a nice way to help you with… moving on.'

Luckily, for Jeremy's sake, Miguel interrupted. 'We have some clever storage solutions in every apartment.'

It would need to be a spectacular magic trick if he was to bring even a quarter of his possessions here, Arthur thought glumly. He could probably stand in the centre of the room and touch each wall, it felt that claustrophobic.

'Behind here is a hidden drawer that offers double the space to store your belongings,' Miguel said, pointing to the low-level cupboards in the kitchenette, just above the scuff marks in the cheap wood. He went to demonstrate by pulling it open with a flourish but nothing happened. 'Ah. I might need to get the maintenance men to give it a lick of oil,' Miguel said between huffs as he tried to prise open the drawer that refused to budge.

Not long after, Miguel had shoved some paperwork in Jeremy's hands and half bundled them out of the building with a cheery wave. Arthur imagined it was probably to avoid them seeing anything else that may put them off signing on the dotted line. As they made their way to Jeremy's car, Arthur felt extremely grateful that he wasn't being left behind. His heart felt a little funny thinking of the people who were.

'Can you drop me at the cemetery please?' Arthur asked Jeremy a little while later, breaking the silence that had settled in the car.

Whenever Jeremy gave Arthur a lift anywhere he usually insisted on playing the radio too loud until a slight disagreement would break out about the rubbish they insist on calling music these days. This time, however, he'd not even bothered to turn it on. They both sat lost in their own thoughts, neither of them vocalising what Arthur's future now looked like.

'Oh, er, of course.' Jeremy flicked his indicators on. 'Would you like me to stay in the car? I can drop you home after.'

'No,' Arthur said firmly, then cleared his throat. 'I mean, no thank you. I could do with the walk. It will do me good, especially as I'm not on the crutches.'

'Oh yes, I had noticed they were gone. I hope you're not rushing your recovery. I'm sure the doctor said he expected you to use them for a couple of weeks.'

'He said to use them until I felt able to manage without them,' Arthur clarified.

Jeremy took his eyes off the road to look at him. 'Hmm. Well I still think you should be taking it easy. I don't mind waiting.'

'I'm fine. I need to stay active.'

'It looks like it might rain. Would you like an umbrella, just in case?'

It was one of those days where moody low clouds cast everything in a dull grey colour. Occasionally a shard of sunlight would burst through but it was a futile performance.

'OK. Thanks,' he grudgingly accepted the offer and glanced

out of the window. There was a mum pushing a navy blue pushchair at the pedestrian crossing.

Arthur thought about Izzy. Perhaps he had been a touch brusque with her yesterday when she'd sprung out of nowhere as he went to retrieve his bin. Izzy was the one who had sounded the alarm after all. Maybe he should have invited her and her crying baby in for a cup of tea? That was what Pearl would have done, she would have sat them both down and put the kettle on, probably magicked a fig roll from somewhere too. He decided that he would go over and properly thank her when he was feeling up to it.

'Oh Arthur,' Jeremy broke his thoughts. 'I meant to ask you the last time I saw you, but do you have a ladder I could borrow? Elaine is on at me to sort the guttering out.'

'You'll need a fully extendable ladder for a job like that, I've only got a smaller wooden one which would be no use.'

'Ah.' Jeremy smacked his lips together. 'No worries. But… er… perhaps I could still pop around in a few days? I can let you know how I got on clearing all the muck from the drainpipes. Originally she asked me to hire a tradesman to do it but I'm sure it's an easy job to do on my own.'

'Sure,' Arthur said distractedly.

Jeremy parked outside the entrance to the cemetery and rapped his fingers against his steering wheel as if he was about to say something else. An elderly couple, probably around Arthur's age, were slowly making their way past. The gentleman had a hand on his wife's lower back, guiding her as she stepped around a puddle. In an instant Arthur felt a painful longing for his own wife to look after. It took him a few moments to realise that Jeremy was talking to him.

'What did you think of that place? That Miguel seemed… er…' Jeremy couldn't finish his sentence.

'Two months.'

'Sorry?'

'I want two months until I have to move.'

'Oh, well actually for your own safety we really should be looking at a much sooner moving date. We can release some equity in the house. Miguel said they have a bed available right now—'

'I need two months, which takes us to the twenty-sixth of April. I want time to pack everything away myself.'

'I'm not sure you'll be able to manage it all on your own, Arthur. I mean, I can ask Elaine if she wouldn't mind helping and—'

Arthur raised a hand. 'I want to do this myself. Say goodbye in my own way.'

'That also means no carers, no home-safety evaluation, no supervision.'

'Arthur! I really think—'

'I'm serious. I want to spend the final two months in my home exactly the way it is. I promise you I will be extra careful but I do not wish to be treated like a baby. So, two months,' Arthur repeated, firmer.

'OK…' Jeremy let out a deep sigh. 'If you insist.'

Arthur imagined that Jeremy was probably amazed he had agreed to moving there at all.

'Thank you.'

'I'll get on to the estate agents about selling your house. Then we'll have to make a start on all the paperwork and get packing.' Jeremy absently wiped off some dust from the dashboard with his finger. 'I know it must be tough for you but let's try and make the best of things?'

Arthur didn't quite know what to say to that so he said nothing.

'That's a plan then.' Jeremy clapped his hands together. 'I don't want to keep you from... well, whatever it is you've got planned for the rest of the day! Just take it easy walking home.'

Arthur said goodbye and got out of the car. He plodded through the entrance, past the stone pillars without a backward glance. He finally heard the car's tyres crunch over the gravel and drive off. Arthur wandered down the path, past the old oak tree and the green metal litter bin which was full of dead roses and carnations that had been stuffed inside, their brown stalks trying to escape. He kept going until he reached her simple grave. Pearl hadn't wanted any fuss. When they'd had a brief chat just a few months before she'd died, on their way home from an old school friend's funeral, Pearl had insisted that if she went first he was not to spend lots of money on a headstone.

'I won't be around to see it, so use that money on something nice for you instead,' she'd instructed, before Arthur had changed the conversation. It was not a topic he wished to discuss. He always thought he would go first, it wasn't meant to be like this. He set his eyes on the simple black granite stone in amongst the sea of other headstones, like wonky teeth poking through the uneven earth. He realised he'd followed her wishes but not used the money on 'something nice' for him. He didn't need anything, what he needed was in a box six feet below.

'Hello, my love,' he said, swallowing the lump that still rose every time he came here. He placed a hand on the cold, solid stone then turned to sit on the nearby bench.

He'd heard people say that life is like a good book. Even though you know that at some point the story is going to end, you keep turning the pages wanting to see how it all works out. Well, for Arthur he could see the final chapter clearly enough. His short but horrible spell in hospital had been an insight into where he would spend his final days, either a bed on a ward of other old codgers grasping on to their last breath as some underpaid nurse did their rounds, or, if Jeremy got his way then in a personality-less 'apartment' that, within hours of his passing, would be cleaned out for some other poor fool to move into.

The other alternative was for him to have another accident at home, one that could be a lot more serious. He didn't much fancy his final days being dragged out. No, he wanted the end to be quick, simple and preferably painless and most certainly on *his* terms. A plan had begun to form in his mind as he'd wandered around the soulless corridors of RoseWood Lodge earlier, half listening to Miguel bleating on about deposits and upgrades.

After he'd lost Pearl, Arthur had felt at times that the rest of his story was not worth reading. He should have jumped ahead to the last chapter but he'd been too cowardly to actually do something about it. Before he knew it the painful lonely hours had turned into days, which had turned into weeks, which had turned into almost two years. But during that time of getting on with things his health was worsening as he grew older. His body was weaker and previously simple tasks now seemed a lot more challenging. He had kept going without stopping to question why. Now he knew what to do.

'So, my darling,' Arthur said to the headstone. 'I can't stay long as I've a lot to be getting on with, I hope you don't mind. I just wanted to pop by and tell you that I'm going to be OK. That I've got a plan. I hope you'll forgive me if I don't go into detail as I know you'll only worry that I'm taking too much on, but trust me that it's the right thing to do.'

Arthur had hidden the full truth from Jeremy. He had asked for two months as he needed to buy himself some time. The twenty-sixth of April. That date was serendipitous, it would take Arthur to the anniversary of Pearl's death – two years exactly. He was going to play along with Jeremy's plan. He was going to do everything Jeremy asked, except actually move into RoseWood Lodge. His self-imposed deadline was a chance to get his affairs in order, then he would check out – on his terms.

Arthur thought back to those long and terrifying hours following his fall, when he had been all alone in serious pain, uncertain if help would come. He remembered lying on the carpet, berating himself for not being braver and sorting through Pearl's things. Now he had been given a chance to put that right. It was exciting to see it as a final project: Operation Pearl. He would clear out their belongings. His house would be sold, all the necessary paperwork completed and any loose ends would be tied up. He vowed to himself that he would leave this world without any regrets.

He liked the idea that he was clearing the slate, leaving nothing for anyone to do once he was gone. He'd even get his funeral planned and paid for so that was also taken care of. In death, as in life, he didn't want to be a burden. He would leave this world when *he* was ready, not be shipped out of his lovely home and forced to spend his final days withering away, staring at a fire exit. Jeremy was right when he said they had a plan. The only thing was just one of them fully understood it. Arthur was going to be reunited with Pearl. The countdown was on.

CHAPTER 11

Izzy

Izzy's house had never been so clean. She had spent all day bleaching, mopping, tidying and spraying air freshener with wild abandon. It had taken longer than she'd planned, not difficult to understand why with a baby to entertain and feed and change, but it was done to a high enough standard for her mother-in-law, Christine, not to raise an eyebrow. At least, from the outside, it would appear that it was business as usual in the Carter household.

Izzy sank on to her bed; Evie had fallen asleep to the noise of the hoover. She allowed herself this moment of calm and focused on her breathing like she'd learnt in her overpriced hypnobirthing classes, smiling at her small peaceful baby. Evie was lying on her back with her arms up in a pose as if surrendering to sleep, her fists slightly clenched, ever so small flutters of movements danced across her eyelids. Her chest was slowly rising and falling under her soft pale grey baby-gro. Her plump skin free of imperfections, full cheeks that you just wanted to kiss, the unmistakable biscuity smell from her downy head. Her rosebud pale pink lips were slightly parted, suckling at the air. She was perfect. It was these moments that made Izzy's heart swell, she just wished she was able to have more of them.

No matter how tough life had become since Evie had been born, Izzy needed to embrace and make the most of these times with her beautiful baby girl. She slowly leaned in and deeply inhaled her daughter's smell, the toxic mix of pheromones and oxytocin dancing up her nostrils. She planted a kiss on Evie's soft peachy forehead. How did something so utterly perfect come from her and Andrew? She sighed. She longed to join Evie and take a nap herself, it was amazing how well she could function on such little sleep nowadays, but her visitors would be arriving any time.

Izzy was sure that Andrew had specifically roped his mum in to come and help them out, he was very sheepish about how last minute their impromptu visit was when he'd dropped the bombshell last night. Right on cue, Izzy heard a car pull up onto their drive. She closed her eyes and took a few deep breaths.

'Here we go.' She lolled to her feet, putting her game face on. Andrew wasn't due back from work for a few hours so she would have to play hostess until then. It wasn't that she didn't get on with her in-laws, she just felt like she had to be on show, as if she had to prove she was worthy of their precious son.

'Izzy, you're looking… well!' Christine sang, looking Izzy up and down as she opened the front door. Her eyes resting a second too long on the rolls around Izzy's stomach. She immediately wished she'd worn something less clingy; at least the navy jersey top was clean.

'Hi, Christine, lovely to see you again.'

'Now, where's my beautiful granddaughter?'

'She's asleep at the moment. Come on in. Do you need a hand getting things from the car?'

'Graham can bring it all in.' Christine clattered about the kitchen as if it were her own, barking orders to Graham to be gentle with the wheels of her suitcase. It was alarmingly larger than Izzy had expected. 'So, tell me…' She flicked on the kettle and leaned closer to Izzy. 'How are you finding things? Andrew said it's not been plain sailing.'

He did? 'Er yeah, it's—'

'But it's all worth it, isn't it?'

'Mmm. Something like that.' For the first time ever she longed for Evie to wake up early from her nap. Izzy picked up the screen of the baby monitor that was sitting on the worktop and held it to her eye hoping for the slightest flicker of movement so she could go and get her. Izzy wasn't in the mood for a heart-to-heart with her mother-in-law, who wouldn't be able to understand even if she could open up to her. Christine had willingly given up her career to raise her two boys with pleasure. Izzy had seen enough photographs of Andrew and his brother in matching hand-knitted jumpers on various educational 'adventures'. She was a natural mother. Izzy also knew that Graham had enjoyed a hot home-cooked meal every single evening when he returned from work. Christine would be horrified at her son's current diet of takeaways and freezer food.

'Tea or coffee?' Izzy asked, seeing a chance to change the subject.

'Tea, please. Milk, no sugar. Then I'll have to show you the photos of my girls' weekend away. Oh I had such a laugh!

You'd think a group of knitters would be tame but we had an absolute ball,' Christine giggled. 'And I haven't told you about the latest with the horticultural society.' She shook her head in a you-won't-believe-it kind of way. 'Oh and I must show you the place we'll be staying in Florence in June. We've been taking Italian lessons at the college as part of their evening classes. And we've been doing the language app every day, I've almost reached bronze level, whatever that means.'

Izzy felt exhausted just listening to her mother-in-law's hectic social calendar.

'Sounds like you're making the most of your retirement,' Izzy smiled.

Graham had only recently stopped working as an accountant and Christine, who had been working part-time in a local café, was relishing having him around to join her on all the hobbies and groups she filled her days with.

'Do you know what?' Graham said, joining them in the kitchen. 'I honestly don't know how I found the time to work.' Graham looked at Christine, who cleared her throat and leaned across the counter to look at Izzy.

'Izzy love, can I give you some advice?' Christine began hesitantly, placing a hand on her sleeve. Izzy wasn't sure she was going to take it but nodded politely.

'You make sure you keep a piece of *you*.'

'Sorry?'

'I loved being a stay at home mum, I don't regret a minute of it, but when they left to go to uni, well, I was ever so lost. They talk about having an empty nest and my lord it was true. It broke me. All their lives I had been needed and then,' she clapped her hands together, 'they were gone and I just felt like I didn't know what my purpose was.'

'I had no idea,' Izzy said softly. She had never seen this side of her mother-in-law before. 'You know your boys will always need you.'

'Oh, I know, love.' Christine patted her arm kindly. 'But not in the same way. Since the moment they were placed in my arms in the hospital I knew that I had to look after them and keep them safe and teach them the ways of the world. And then one day they would go off to discover it on their own. It's the way it should be. It's just my own fault, I suppose, as Andrew and Richard were my world, I had nothing else to define me. That's why I started going to all my groups, isn't it, Graham?'

'Yup. And now we have to schedule in the diary three years in advance as you have that much going on.' He rolled his eyes good-naturedly then slurped his tea.

'Three years is a bit dramatic, love,' Christine chided him. 'But that's my point, Izzy. It's so easy to lose yourself being a mum – and that's wonderful, it really is. But at the same time I wish someone had told me not to forget about my own future too, as they won't be babies forever. It goes in the blink of an eye.' She looked as if she might cry. Christine let out a loud sniff and fixed on a smile. 'But anyway, enough about me. What have you been up to?'

'Oh, you know, trying to enjoy every moment.'

'I was thinking on the drive here just how much easier you new mums have it nowadays. I mean with social media and whatnot. Back when my boys were very little if I wanted to connect with another mum I had to get out and start a conversation face to face. You can message anyone anywhere at the touch of a button now. Amazing really.' She shook her head incredulously. 'It must be hard for you though, you know, what with your mum and all.'

This was not a topic that Izzy was in the mood to dive into, especially not right now. Having Christine stay only highlighted the gap where Izzy's mum should be.

'Well, like I said, we're coping alright,' she said tightly. 'You know what? I think I've just heard Evie. I'll quickly nip upstairs and check on her.'

Izzy didn't wait a second longer to escape from the kitchen. She heard Christine call behind her as she flew past.

'Oh Izzy! You really must send me more photos. My neighbour is always showing off videos and selfies of her little grandsons. I feel terrible not having daily updates like the ones her daughter-in-law sends her.'

'Sure,' Izzy said through slightly clenched teeth, mentally adding it to her to-do list.

CHAPTER 12

Arthur

It had been a morning of frustrations. Arthur had burnt his toast, the last two slices of bread too. He'd propped open the windows to try and remove the acrid smell left behind. Secondly, he'd noticed what looked like tiny bite marks around the leaves of Pearl's potted petunias. He suspected a hungry caterpillar was to blame but he couldn't be sure it wasn't the pigeon with an apparent death wish. And finally, he'd had to put up with one of his neighbours playing country music at a few decibels higher than necessary as their car remained stationary, engine running. But for the first time in a long time, the day didn't loom long in front of Arthur. He felt like he had a purpose. Operation Pearl would fill the many hours until he could be back in his pyjamas. There were eight weeks left, so really no time like the present to get started.

He decided that he would tackle his bedroom first; namely his wardrobe and chest of drawers. Arthur wasn't a lover of fashion, never had been. He opted for practical and comfortable. He thought he only had a sparse collection of clothing, but, by emptying everything onto his bed he was shocked at what he owned. Who in their right mind needed thirty-seven handkerchiefs? He chose his favourite three and put the rest into a bin bag he had prepared for the occasion. Next, he pulled open the drawer that contained his summer clothes; in the bag went his tropical-print shorts he had worn once, after Pearl's encouragement, and two bright T-shirts that had come in a multipack from Tesco. He didn't know what he had been thinking.

Moving slowly and methodically, he cleared eighty per cent of what he owned. Gone were the decades-old polyester jackets, the unworn long-sleeved rugby shirts Jeremy had bought him over the years, and the novelty Christmas jumpers Pearl had unearthed at some charity shop. The few items of clothing that remained were well-worn loyal servants. For the next eight weeks he would have a rota of two pairs of pyjamas, two pairs of slacks, three shirts, a polo shirt, two identical jumpers and seven pairs of underpants and socks. That would surely be enough. He was a little embarrassed by how many holes he found in his socks and how saggy the elastic of his briefs had become. This was exactly why he was grateful to be doing this himself. No self-respecting gentleman should have another man (in this case, probably his nephew) rooting through his drawers, both literally and figuratively speaking.

He broke for lunch and a much-needed sit down. As he tucked into a cheese omelette with three cherry tomatoes on the side of his plate for good measure, he felt rather proud of how well it was going. It had taken him less time than he'd imagined, he felt lighter after shedding so many clothes he simply did not need. Perhaps he should have done this months ago. It really was rather satisfying to be so productive after so long being sedentary.

He padded up the stairs to his bedroom knowing that Pearl's clothing was next. This was a task he needed to steel himself for. He gripped the handle of her wardrobe door. Perhaps he could put it off till a later date, he still had time. Arthur pulled himself together. This unenviable task wouldn't become any easier if he waited. It had been almost two years since her wardrobe doors had last been opened, he simply could not stomach it before. He'd had no need to get rid of her things, it wasn't like he, or anybody else, would be using the space. Her blouses and dresses and jackets had stayed out of sight, hanging up neatly from when she'd placed them there for the final time. At the thought of her hands last touching the fabrics he felt his stomach clench slightly, he took a deep breath. Operation Pearl was happening one way or another. He needed to be brave.

He opened the door and pulled out a couple of long cardigans, smiling sorrowfully at the lilac one especially, something about the hue had made her pale blue eyes sparkle. It reminded him of a dress that she had once owned that was a similar lavender colour. She had sewn it herself on her mother's sewing machine from a pattern she'd picked up at the market. He remembered her self-consciously tugging at the sleeves, telling him they hadn't come out as neat as the one the model was wearing, but, in Arthur's eyes, she looked wonderful. It must have been at least sixty years since he'd seen her in that dress but he would have given anything to see her in it again. All he had left was the memory of her twirling around in front of him, asking him if she looked alright. He swallowed the lump in his throat and composed himself.

'Pull yourself together, you silly fool.'

He managed to work his way through the rest of the clothes hanging up without any other pointless emotion-filled pauses. He then moved onto the drawers inside the wardrobe. It had felt plain wrong bundling up her tights, socks and bras and placing them into a bin bag. A husband didn't have the right to go rummaging through his wife's knicker drawer, but it was best that it was him doing this unwanted task rather than their nephew or, heaven forbid, a stranger. Arthur continued to work quickly and efficiently, not stopping to get swallowed up in the memories that snapped at the edges of his tired mind. At the bottom of the wardrobe was a large shoebox. Arthur lifted the lid and smiled sadly at what was inside. It was from the church's shoebox appeal. Pearl loved filling them with toothpaste, deodorant, socks, knitted hats and any other odds and ends she'd picked up from jumble sales or car boots. Inside was a small pad of lined notepaper and a pen, there was a chocolate bar that had passed its sell-by date seven months earlier and a battered-looking crime novel with a 20p sticker on the front. Arthur emptied the contents of the box into the bin bag. A couple of hours and three bin bags later, he was almost done. Arthur felt worn out from the relentless waves of nostalgia. He longed for a sit-down and a cup of tea but he daren't break his momentum. He tied the handles of the full bin bags and readied himself to say goodbye.

The smell immediately hit Arthur as he stepped foot into the charity shop. It was slightly musty but familiar and comforting at the same time. Jazz music played from a battered radio with a 'not for sale' sticker sellotaped over one of the speakers. Arthur wasn't even sure what the charity was, he'd only chosen to come here as it was the closest one to the bus stop. It had been a bit of an adventure just getting Pearl's clothes here. Thank goodness Jeremy hadn't seen him struggle with the bin bags, Arthur thought, he would be so cross with him for not asking for a lift and some help. His nephew had offered to drive him whenever he needed it but Arthur hadn't wanted to wait in case he changed his mind. He hoped it was like ripping off a plaster – the quicker you were, the better.

In a way it had felt quite nice being on a bus with Pearl's clothing resting at his feet. It was like she was sat there with him. They used to travel this same route when they were both working, before they could afford a car. They would sit with their knees touching, a packed lunch on their laps and fingers interlaced, chatting about the things they had planned that day. Today, Arthur was subjected to coarse rap music booming from the phone of the man sat in front. The bus seats were grubby, stained with chewing gum, and it smelt of cigarette smoke. No one spoke to one other. He tightened his grip on the plastic bin bag, wanting to poke a hand through and grab hold of one of Pearl's soft jumpers or cardigans, to know she was there beside him once more. He longed to smell her perfume on the fabric currently bundled up next to his legs, a scent that had long faded. He forced himself to stare out of the steamed-up window and not let the tears fall.

'Hello there,' said a chirpy woman behind the counter. Arthur was the only customer in the brightly lit shop. 'May I help you?'

'I'd like to donate these items please,' Arthur said, his voice a little hoarse. He realised she was the first person he'd spoken to all day and it was almost two o'clock.

'My, that's a lot of stuff!' The shop assistant put down the sticker gun she was fiddling with on the counter. 'Here, let me help you.' A name badge that read 'Joan' was pinned to her plum-coloured blouse. She came out from behind the counter and kindly took the heavy bin bags from Arthur, his shoulders sank in relief. Joan was about the same height and build as Pearl had been. She wore a little more make-up than his wife used to, the grey stuff on her eyelids complemented her light blue eyes that were creased in a genuine smile.

'Clothes, is it?'

Arthur nodded. 'Yes… women's clothes mostly.'

She didn't appear to pick up on the slight waver in his voice as he said that.

'Great. We can always do with some new stock. You wouldn't believe how quickly we sell out of good quality items of clothing, especially in the ladieswear section.' She nodded her head to the single rail on the opposite side of the shop. 'Well, section is probably over-egging the pudding a little.' She laughed lightly. 'But what do they say about aiming high!'

Arthur wiped his brow with a handkerchief and smiled politely. He could do with a cold drink and a sit-down before he tackled the journey home. Thankfully he hadn't needed to pick the crutches up again as his ankle was much better, but he was suddenly very aware of it throbbing. He had pushed himself too far with this single trip.

A very tall teenager appeared out of nowhere. 'Thanks, Freddie, love,' Joan said as he picked the heavy bags up as easily as if they were filled with air and disappeared into the far end of the shop. 'Freddie's here for work experience. The poor lad's lumped with me! Right then, I just need to ask if this is the first time you've donated here?'

'Yes, it is.'

'Wonderful. And can I check that you're a gift aid donator?

'Sorry. A what?'

'Do you still have to pay income tax? If so it means that we can apply for extra help from the government and we can claim gift aid on your donation.'

'Oh, well, yes I do.'

'Lovely. Would it be OK if I take some details from you?'

Joan pulled out a chair for Arthur from behind the counter the moment he nodded. Arthur swallowed his pride and accepted the seat. His muscles rejoiced in relief.

'It's quiet enough in here. I'll join you, if you don't mind?'

'Be my guest,' Arthur said.

'I promise it won't take long.' Joan carefully sat down on a carved wooden stool that had a £5 price sticker now covered by her bottom. 'Saying that, they give us these tablets to use.' She waved an iPad and rolled her eyes. 'I can't seem to get my head around these things, so my apologies if I take a little longer than I should.'

'Not to worry.' Arthur didn't have anywhere he needed to be. 'Although I don't know what's wrong with a pen and paper.'

'That's exactly what I said to the bosses!' She smiled brightly. 'Ah, here we go.' She tapped on the screen. 'Right then, may I ask what's your name?'

'Arthur Winter.'

Joan stuck her tongue out in concentration and tapped a finger on the screen, silvery nail polish sparkling in the light.

'And your address?'

'Thirty-nine Birch Tree Way,'

'Oh, that's just by the common, isn't it? Lovely part of town.'
There was some more tapping.

'Would you like to subscribe to our newsletter?'

Arthur shook his head. 'No thank you.' He wouldn't be
here to read it.

'OK. And finally, would you please sign here.'

Arthur took the tiny stick she was offering him and scrawled
a funny-shaped squiggle on the screen. It looked nothing like
his actual signature but Joan didn't seem to mind.

'Thank you. There! All done. If you do bring in any other
donations in the future, then you just need to give us your
name and we can look you up on the system. Saves us having
to faff like this again.' Joan grinned.

'That's good to know,' Arthur replied, however, he hadn't
actually minded the unexpected questioning. 'Would you like
me to look at that for you?' He nodded to the sticker gun lying
flat on the counter, next to a neatly folded pile of T-shirts.
'I noticed you were having trouble with it.'

'Forget the iPad, *this* is the bane of my life. It keeps on
jamming, which means that everything is currently ninety-nine
pence as I can't work out how to fix it. I told you I wasn't
very good at technology and this isn't exactly a mod con! I've
asked head office for a new one but that'll take a few days to
arrive and stock is already piling up.'

Arthur took it from her and popped open the plastic casing.
He could see the problem straight away. 'There's a piece of
plastic that's bent out of place slightly. Have you got something
small that I could use to try and prod inside to remove it?'

Joan scanned around the counter. 'Erm… I've been trying to keep Freddie busy by asking him to tidy up but I fear he may have done too good a job. Will this do?' She unclasped her name badge.

'Perfect. Good thinking.'

Arthur used the sharp end of the pin to get into the small hole and remove the stubborn piece of plastic that was blocking the dial.

'There. I think that's worked.'

Joan took the sticker gun from him, within seconds small bright yellow stickers began flowing out across the surface of the counter. 'Arthur! Thank you. That's honestly saved me such a lot of hassle!'

Arthur could feel his cheeks heating up under the look she was giving him. It really was nothing. It had been a long time since he'd felt a sense of pride that comes from helping someone. He wasn't sure what to say.

'Oh… No problem. I—' He was interrupted from saying anything else by the ringing of a bell. The door to the shop opened and two middle-aged women walked in, laughing about something.

Joan got to her feet and tucked her stool away. Arthur followed, the moment over, briefly leaning his weight on the counter, hoping he would make it home on his painful ankle.

'I hope to see you soon, Arthur… and thank you once again!'

Arthur left the shop feeling Pearl would approve of her things going here. Sadly, this sense of satisfaction didn't last long. Arthur felt his resolve wobble the moment he sat, utterly exhausted, on the bus ride home. How on earth was he going to manage to clear out everything he owned if it took him all day to sort and donate some clothes from a single wardrobe?! The scale of his project suddenly overwhelmed him. This was going to take him forever. He had thought two months was more than enough time to get everything in order, especially as he didn't have anything else going on in his life, but perhaps he had bitten off more than he could chew. Perhaps he should call Jeremy and ask for an extension, an extra couple of weeks or months maybe. But he knew there was no way his nephew would agree without insisting Arthur hired a carer in the interim.

He glumly looked out of the window. If he was going to meet his deadline and make sure Operation Pearl was a success then, as much as it pained him, Arthur was going to have to ask for help.

CHAPTER 13

Izzy

Izzy's in-laws had made themselves at home with alarming speed. If looking after a newborn baby wasn't tiring enough Izzy now felt even more exhausted, from making them many cups of tea, to listening to their long-winded stories about their recent house extension, to the numerous times she had to politely stand her ground defending decisions on how she chose to parent Evie. Izzy felt like everything she did was being scrutinised. From the way she lay Evie down in her cot – 'we were always told to put babies to sleep on their front' – to changing her nappies – 'have you thought about using reusable ones, much better for the environment?' – to what she dressed Evie in – 'I'm sure she's too cold, hand me the knitted hat and booties I made for her. She likes them.'

Izzy also found herself getting unjustifiably annoyed at the way Christine flitted around the place like some housework fairy. All the jobs that she had struggled to get on top of since having Evie had suddenly been ticked off with efficient speed. During the short time she'd been here Christine had cleared the towering laundry pile, blitzed the bathroom and even scrubbed the oven. Izzy knew she should feel grateful but instead Christine's dynamic energy only highlighted how much her own standards had slipped recently.

She was currently feeling like a spare part. Andrew was at work. Graham was having a nap on the sofa, emitting low nasally rumbles every so often and her mother-in-law was playing with Evie on the rug, singing songs and tickling her toes.

'Why don't you go out and meet a friend for coffee or get your nails done or something?' Christine asked.

'Oh... er...' Izzy stalled. She had promised herself after leaving Evie at the supermarket that she would never leave her again.

'We'll be fine, love,' Christine smiled.

Evie clearly adored having her grandma stay, it was apparent by how easily she went to sleep for her, but it still felt like a huge moment for Izzy to *leave the house* without her baby girl.

Christine turned towards Izzy. 'You've just fed her, I know where her nappies and clean clothes are and there's enough toys here to keep her amused for hours.'

This was what you wanted, a voice in Izzy's head reminded her – *time to yourself*. She stumbled to her feet and cast a last look back at the calm scene on the living room floor, her heart constricted so much she wobbled.

'If you're sure you're OK?'

'Course! Go on, take your time, love.'

Izzy didn't really know what to do with this unexpected slice of freedom. Maybe she should call Joanna for a chat? But she would be at work, so would her dad, so would anyone else she knew. So, she did what any sane person would do, and put her coat on, headed outside and stuck giant colourful butterfly stickers onto the side of her wheelie bin. With a sad sigh she pressed on the final sticker, just as she spotted Arthur shuffling towards her. He was wrapped up in a thick, dark brown coat, the one with the missing button. His thin white hair moved in the chilly wind.

'Hello,' Izzy said politely and quietly, not wanting to make him jump. She expected him to walk straight past but to her surprise, Arthur stopped and came to stand near her. She saw he had a roll of bin bags in his hand.

'Hello. It's Izzy, isn't it?'

Izzy nodded.

He cleared his throat. 'I'm sorry for how short I was with you the other day. I wasn't quite feeling myself. The doctor gave me some heavy painkillers that made me a little groggy.'

'Oh. Don't worry, it's fine.' She really wasn't expecting an apology from him. 'I'm sorry for surprising you like I did. Probably the last thing you needed was me rabbiting on!'

Arthur nodded to the butterfly stickers. 'I see Mrs Peterson has roped you into this art project too?'

'Yep. They've been sat on the side for a while so I thought I should finally stick them on, I don't want to get into her bad books and let the neighbourhood down. I'm not sure if this is the look she was hoping for. I mean, personally, I think it's a bit of a mess...'

There was a pause as they both stared at the cluttered and bright bin.

'I think you might be right,' Arthur said with a wry smile. 'Where's your baby?'

'Evie? She's with my in-laws as they're staying with us at the moment, so I've been given a bit of a break, which is... nice.'

'Well, you make the most of it.'

'Mmm. Have you stuck your stickers on yet?' Izzy asked.

'No, not yet. I'm afraid my fingers don't work as well as they used to with fiddly things like this. Well that's my excuse anyway.'

'I can give you a hand if you like? I mean, I've got time.'

Arthur seemed surprised at the offer. 'Oh. Thank you, that would be helpful. I suppose it would save me a job and keep me in Mrs Peterson's good books.'

Moments later Arthur was back holding out enormous sunflower stickers.

'Let me,' Izzy said softly, taking the packet from him that he was struggling to open. 'Sunflowers huh? You got lucky.'

'Apparently the koi carps had sold out. At least they're not as garish as the ones number forty chose, and that's saying something!' Arthur said. They both turned to look at the primary-coloured racing cars plastered across the wheelie bin over the road. 'It makes sense he'd choose that style considering how he insists on keeping his engine running for so long in the mornings.'

'Yes! It drives me potty too! I've thought about bringing it up with him but I didn't want to come across as a bad neighbour.'

'Pfft. If I could move half as fast then I would be out there with you,' Arthur said in solidarity. 'It's not just the noise of the engine but the terribly loud music he insists on subjecting us to.'

'You're not a country and western fan then?' Izzy smiled at the look Arthur gave her.

'Heavens no. But please can you explain to me just what those racing car stickers bring to the close?' Arthur shook his head. 'Listen to us … bin art indeed! I almost told Mrs Peterson what I really thought about her scheme but luckily I stopped myself. In the grand scheme of things it doesn't matter if I have to look at decorated wheelie bins once a week. Soon it will be someone else's problem.'

Izzy finished sticking the sunflowers on then looked at him blankly.

'I won't be around much longer. I mean, I'm moving to a home.'

'Oh. Is this because of your accident?'

Arthur nodded. 'Yes. All systems go, as they say. I've already made a start on clearing my house, well, I *thought* I was making progress but I fear I've just made a big mess.'

'You're doing this on your own? Packing up your entire house?'

'Yes. I suppose my nephew will help when he can but he's very busy. The truth is I don't mind now having something to fill my days; it just feels like there is rather a lot to do. It's quite overwhelming.'

A thought suddenly popped into Izzy's head. Here was her chance to relieve her guilt for not checking up on him sooner. She was still disappointed in herself for ignoring her gut feeling that something was wrong.

'I'm free if you'd like me to help with anything? It would be no trouble,' she added.

'Really?! That would be most helpful.'

'In fact…' Izzy tapped her phone to check if there had been any missed calls or frantic messages from Christine. The screen remained blank. 'I can start right now.'

'Are you sure you don't mind?' Arthur repeated as he led Izzy into his house through the side gate. They followed the path around the edges of a garden that was much neater than hers. Similar in size but with a well cared for lawn, colourful established bushes and perfectly pruned borders.

'Nope, anyway it will be quicker with the two of us. I've even got a label maker I can bring over, which will change your life!'

'Just in here.' He held open the door to a makeshift conservatory that led into the kitchen. 'Well there's plenty to be labelled. I have to admit it's a little daunting how much there is to do. There's a lifetime worth of stuff to go through.'

Izzy was only half listening, she felt like she had stepped back in time to the 1970s. A Formica worktop sat on faded buttercup yellow cabinets, retro mustard patterned splashback tiles ran down the far wall. There was even a hatch that opened onto a very brown lounge, everything appeared to be coloured in swirls of caramel and chocolate. A rush of nostalgia surprised her, it was exactly the same decor her grandparents had chosen. Then she noticed the state of it.

'Oh,' Izzy gasped, swinging her head to take in the scene in front of her.

'Yes… It looks a bit of a mess…' Arthur trailed off, looking around sheepishly. 'Oh dear. I was out of bin bags so I nipped to the shops to get some but I'd forgotten how disorganised I'd left everything.'

It looked like he'd been burgled. Cutlery drawers were pulled open, cupboard doors revealing bare, sticky shelves. The entire work surface was covered in mismatched crockery, glasses, tins and packets of food. A bag of pasta had spilled onto the pale blue lino.

'Wow. This looks like a real deep clean.' Izzy was frozen to the spot.

'I guess I got a little carried away.'

'A little…' Izzy echoed. 'I can see why you feel overwhelmed. In my experience it's better to start with one cupboard at a time rather than the entire room. Break it down into manageable chunks.'

Something caught her eye, hung to a corkboard amongst scraps of papers with phone numbers for plumbers and a list of the bin collection dates was a large year-to-view calendar. The sort she had in her office at work. It had an image of forget-me-knots across the border but it was the thick crosses that caught her attention. A date had been circled in red biro.

'Is that when you're moving?'

The twenty-sixth of April. It was two months away.

Arthur nodded. 'It should be enough time for me to get everything in order.'

Izzy admired his confidence. This was a big house clearly filled with a lot of stuff, it would take forever to sort through every room by himself, especially considering he was still technically recovering from his accident.

'I would offer you a cup of tea but, well, I can't get to the kettle.'

'Oh. Don't worry, thanks. Maybe it's best if we clear some space so we know what we're working with?' Izzy suggested.

She began picking up ribbons of pasta from the floor. The last thing she wanted was Arthur slipping and having another fall. 'Then we can make piles of things to bin, donate to charity, and keep?'

'Good idea. I want the keep pile to be the smallest of them all. I don't need much, to be honest with you. I'm long overdue a good sort out. Operation Pearl, I'm calling it.'

'Operation Pearl?'

'That was my wife's name. She would be beside herself if she knew I had invited a guest into the house whilst it was in such a state.'

'Well we will soon have it looking back to normal! OK, perhaps it would be easier to tell me what needs to stay in here? Like the microwave, fridge and oven, obviously.'

'Well, if I'm honest the oven is slightly redundant. A lot of my meals are heated in the microwave. I also only need one dinner set. It's not like I have much call for a gravy bowl or a cheese board these days. All the other crockery can go. One spoon, knife, fork, plate, bowl and glass – perhaps two mugs for when I have visitors, well my nephew Jeremy – that's all that needs to remain.'

'Speaking of your nephew, should we make sure we create a pile of things to leave to him?'

Arthur shook his head. 'Jeremy doesn't need anything, he would probably only take it out of duty.' He pulled out a stack of dinner plates, some with chips on the edges and handed them to Izzy. 'Let's chuck the lot. I'm not sure even the charity shop would want them.'

'One man's rubbish is another man's treasure.' She glanced at the plates doubtfully. He was right, they were long past their best. 'Let's put the things for the charity shop over here, I can bubble wrap the fragile items later.'

They moved awkwardly around the other. Occasionally bumping elbows or going for the same cereal bowl then sharing an apologetic half smile. As she got to work Izzy wondered how Christine and Graham were getting on, if Evie missed her or had even noticed she'd left. There were no phone calls asking for her to come back, which was a good sign, and she was literally just over the road if they needed her.

'Why have I hung on to such pointless items?' Arthur said. He was holding up a pizza cutter that had a plastic red pepper as a handle. 'I don't even know where this came from!'

Soon pasta bowls, side plates and egg cups were added to the haul. A metal whisk, potato peeler, ice cream scoop and bread knife joined them. Plastic margarine tubs went in next, followed by empty ice cream cartons and Tupperware boxes of differing sizes and levels of opacity. They mostly worked in silence, passing things to one another to place in the bin bag or to put to one side for the charity shop. He was right, the keep pile was very small.

'There, all done.' Arthur stepped back, his knees creaking loudly; only dust and a small cobweb remained at the back of an empty cupboard. You could see the work surface once more, the floor was free of pasta ribbons and the room seemed to have doubled in size.

Izzy dragged his sunflower-covered wheelie bin to the side door and filled it with everything too damaged to donate to charity. The rest she put into neat piles ready for him to decide what to do with.

'Is that the time?' Izzy gasped as she caught sight of the

oven clock. It had been three hours since she'd left her house. Her boobs felt uncomfortable and full of milk, Evie was due a feed any time now. 'I should probably head back. But I can come over tomorrow and maybe bring some cardboard boxes to help us? I'll have Evie with me, if that's OK?'

'That would be wonderful, if you're sure it's no bother? Oh, actually I've got an estate agent coming over tomorrow so maybe the day after, if you're not too busy?'

'Sure. Right, well… I'd best be off.'

Izzy and Arthur did an awkward sort of dance to open the kitchen door. She gave him a cheery wave and let herself out.

'Evie is just a joy. She did the funniest thing earlier,' Christine said with this faraway look. 'Graham, what was it? I said I'd have to remember.'

Graham shrugged, passing her his plate at the dinner table.

'Nope, it's gone.' Christine shook her head. She dished out a generous helping of shepherd's pie. 'She is the spit of Andrew at this age. It takes me back. He was just *the* cutest baby.' She squeezed Andrew's cheeks before he gently swatted her away.

'Mum!'

'It doesn't matter how old you are, you'll always be my baby.' She winked at Izzy. 'You'll see, love. All mothers feel exactly the same!' The smile faltered. Izzy was sure she spotted a look between her mother-in-law and her husband. It was the same whenever Izzy's mum was brought up. It was as if any accidental mention of her mother would cause Izzy to have a spectacular breakdown.

'Has your dad been over much?' Graham asked, unaware

of any awkwardness as he tried to remove a stubborn cork from a bottle of red wine.

Izzy nodded. 'Briefly after Evie was born. He managed to organise a flying visit to come and meet her, which was amazing but just too short. He's planning to come back at the end of this term, if he can get the leave, but I'm hoping he'll stay for longer in the summer when his teaching is over.'

'I wished we lived closer too. I'd love to see you all every day,' Christine said. 'You know if you ever need us then all you have to do is call.'

'Very true. So, have you two got any plans for the summer?' Graham asked, offering the wine. Izzy decided against having any, she didn't want to risk a lecture on the implications of alcohol and breastfeeding.

'Not yet. Although we'll probably have to get Evie's passport sorted soon if we're going to take her away for our first family holiday,' Andrew said. They hadn't specifically spoken about where they would go but the thought of a holiday sounded pretty good to Izzy.

Christine tutted. 'There's plenty of time for that. You don't want to risk her getting poorly in some Third World country.'

'I think you mean developing nation and I was actually thinking of a week in Costa del Sol but…'

'Even so! There's all the logistics to think about. I mean, how are you going to take everything you need on the plane? Will they let you carry enough nappies? What will you do about sticking to a bedtime routine in a different time zone? That's before you factor in sun safety. I'm not even sure if they make super-strength baby sun cream that's sensitive enough for her delicate skin. We didn't take you and Richard abroad until you were in secondary school. I don't see the need for all the unnecessary expense and effort when you have some wonderful places on your doorstep! Have you thought about Cornwall?'

'That's not exactly on our doorstep, Mum!'

Izzy ate her food, suddenly overwhelmed at how this fictional holiday had turned into a logistical nightmare. According to Christine, Izzy was supposed to cherish every moment and soak up being a mum, but also still be the same person she was pre-kids, despite not having the time or energy to do the things she would do before Evie.

'I forgot to ask what you got up to today, love?' Christine asked Izzy, changing the subject. 'We watched Evie for a bit so she could have some time to herself this afternoon.'

'I actually went to help Arthur,' Izzy said, finishing a mouthful.

Evie didn't seem to notice Izzy had even left her. Clearly Grandma was just as good a replacement, if not better. Not only was Evie taken care of but the washing up had been done and Christine had even made a start on dinner – a gloriously comforting shepherd's pie. Izzy felt a bit silly for thinking her six-and-a-half-week-old baby would miss her.

'Arthur?' Andrew raised an eyebrow.

'Who's Arthur?' Christine asked.

'He's a neighbour, he had a fall recently.'

'Well, that's only half the story,' Andrew jumped in. 'Izzy's being very modest. She was actually the one who found him – he was in a really bad way – and called the ambulance. God knows how long he'd been lying there or what would have happened if she hadn't been there to help.'

'Oh gosh!' Christine clutched her chest dramatically. 'How terrifying for you.'

'It was nothing,' Izzy said quietly, she didn't like to be reminded of that horrible evening.

Andrew sipped his wine. 'I didn't know you had become friends though?'

'I wouldn't say *friends*. I just felt like he could do with some help, that's all. He's moving into a home soon. Speaking of which, do you know if we have any spare boxes in the loft from when we moved here?'

'Er... I think so.'

'Do you mind having a look for me at some point? I said I'd take some over for him to help with his packing.'

'Sure.'

'Well moving into a home is probably the best place for him. It sounds like he's not coping on his own,' Christine soothed.

'Poor sod,' Graham piped up. 'When I get to that stage just shoot me. It's not pretty, is it, dribbling into your soup without the faintest idea of what day it is.'

'I don't think it's going to be like that,' Izzy frowned. 'It's a big deal to move out and live somewhere new at his age.'

'Dad wasn't suggesting anything, babe.' Andrew placed a firm hand on Izzy's. 'I think he just meant that growing older is not exactly a walk in the park.'

'Sorry, love.' Graham's cheeks grew pink. 'I didn't mean to offend.'

'Has everyone finished? I've made an apple crumble for pudding. I know it's your favourite, Andrew.' Christine bustled about collecting the empty plates.

'I'll give you a hand, love.' Graham jumped to his feet to help.

'What was all that about?' Andrew asked Izzy when they were alone.

'What?'

'About Arthur? I felt like you were a bit short with my dad just now.'

'Was I? Sorry,' she sighed, pulling her hair from her bobble and running her hands through it. 'I'm tired, I didn't mean to be rude, I just felt like he was being quite negative, that's all.'

'Are you sure that's it… tiredness?'

'Yes. Why? What else would it be?'

'Well,' he quickly glanced to the closed kitchen door. 'Mum mentioned something to me earlier when we were giving Evie her bath…'

Izzy stopped playing with her hair, waiting to hear what he was going to say next.

'She said she'd heard you crying this morning.'

Izzy roughly scooped her hair into the bobble and piled it on her head.

'Iz? She's worried about you. She suggested that perhaps you should go and see someone, a doctor? She thinks it will help if you talked to someone – a professional – about how you're feeling? I mean, I guess with your own mum and—'

Izzy finally turned to face him. 'I'm fine, Andrew. I'm exhausted and no wonder since I can't remember when I had more than three hours sleep in one go! Nothing more than that, now please just drop it.'

Her in-laws were leaving tomorrow. As much as she had liked seeing them she would be glad to have her house back.

Andrew seemed to revert to some pre-pubescent child in his parents' presence. He basked in their praise of his fatherhood abilities but having them stay only made Izzy feel even more inferior. Andrew looked as if he was about to say something else but the kitchen door opened and out bustled Christine.

'Cream or homemade custard?'

CHAPTER 14

Arthur

'Alright? I'm Kevin from Trinity Estate Agents. Are you Mr Winner?' A tall man wearing a cheap burgundy-coloured suit offered Arthur a nicotine-stained hand, followed by a feeble handshake. His trousers didn't quite cover his hairy, sock free, pale ankles.

'Winter,' Arthur clarified.

'Sorry! I can't read my own handwriting half the time. Winter. Hey, like *winter is coming*!' He put on a low rumble of a voice.

'Pardon?'

Kevin licked his tongue against his teeth. 'Not a *Game of Thrones* fan, then?' Arthur had no idea what this man was saying. Was he drunk? 'Alright if I come in?'

He already had one shiny loafer wedged in the door. Arthur nodded and tried not to choke on this man's strong aftershave as he moved past.

Kevin sauntered into the lounge then perched on the arm of Pearl's chair. 'So, Mr Winner, your nephew booked me to take some photos of the place, size it up and then get you a valuation of how much dollar you can expect to walk away with.' He pulled out his mobile phone and tapped the screen. 'You lived here long?'

'Six decades.'

'Woah. What's the reason for the move? You downsizing?'

'Something like that.'

'I can tell you now that we sold a similar property on Barrow Lane, just round the corner, for at least five per cent higher than the asking price. You'll be pleased to hear that houses like this don't stay around for long.' Kevin began walking around the room pointing his phone at different angles, the camera shutter-click audible. 'We can do some awesome things with photo editing nowadays. You won't be able to recognise the place once I've played around on photoshop.'

'Isn't that a bit underhand?'

'Nah. Everyone does it. You just touch up the images, adjust the colours, make it less… brown.' He continued to snap away. 'These carpets are pretty trippy!'

Arthur bit his tongue. They had been the height of fashion at one time.

'Nowadays people like to have a project. Put their own mark on it, you know? This place is ideal for that.'

'Sorry?' Arthur frowned.

'Well, Arthur mate…'

Arthur clenched his jaw. He most certainly was not this man's mate.

'It's a little, how can I say it… dated. Now I don't mean any offence by that.' Arthur felt his blood pressure rise at the cheek of this youth coming in here talking to him like this. Him and Pearl had chosen every wallpaper, paint colour and piece of furniture to suit their tastes. 'But, in this day and age no one wants things like this.' Kevin nodded to the hatch in the wall between the lounge and the kitchen. That hatch had once been a focal feature. Pearl used to dramatically fling the wooden doors open and call that dinner was ready, then with a wink she'd declare the café was closed, it was a joke that never wore thin. 'People want open plan. I see you've got a south-facing garden. Nice. What I reckon will help is if we forget to mention the... extension.'

He was referring to the lean-to at the back of the kitchen. Once upon a time Pearl had had grand dreams about having a conservatory. She'd seen it on some telly programme back when a bloke with a ladies' haircut was adding cherubs to everything. Arthur had surprised her by building his own version by knocking together some MDF and a plastic roof. Pearl had been genuinely thrilled, as if it was the most wonderful thing she had ever seen. Neither of them mentioned the fact it leaked whenever there was a spot of rain or that she only used it to house her tomato plants.

'I built that with my bare hands.'

'Yeah, you can tell,' Kevin said, winking. 'I'll just nip upstairs and have a gander if that's OK?'

'Be my guest,' Arthur grumbled. *Careful not to trip on the carpet*, he thought as Kevin jogged up the stairs two at a time.

He had just settled in his chair to wait to hear what else this rude young man had to say about his home when there was a knock on the door. *Who was this now?* He had purposefully removed the welcome mat hoping that people would get the message, but it didn't seem to be working. He peered through the glass. It was Mrs Peterson from number forty-three, waiting patiently on his doorstep. He'd recognise those bright flowery tops she always wore anywhere. He wanted to sink lower into his chair but instead he sighed loudly and got to his feet.

'Arthur! How are you?' She was wearing what could only be described as an orange patterned tent. Arthur noticed her dog, the shaggy-haired border collie, was sniffing around at the pansies on his path. 'I've been meaning to pop over ever since I came back from my holiday. I had a lovely break gallivanting around the Big Apple. My daughter lives over there you see. I saw it all – Times Square, Staten Island, the Empire State Building, and I even caught a show on Broadway. I know, lucky me, right!'

It was only then that Arthur realised he hadn't seen his colourful neighbour around in a while, her dog walks were usually like clockwork. Arthur didn't know what to say to that. 'Er, lovely.'

'I just wanted to pop by and—' she gasped. 'Oh dear, have you had an accident?'

He followed her line of sight. Behind him, leaning against the bottom of the stairs were the two NHS prescribed crutches he'd stopped using. They had been fairly handy in removing cobwebs from above the doorframe.

'Oh, er, yes.'

'Are you OK? What happened?'

'I recently had a fall. I was a little clumsy, that's all.'

'Oh good heavens, what a shock it must have been for you.' She tilted her head. 'Well the reason for my visit, apart from to see how you're doing of course.' She let out a trill of a laugh and placed a chubby hand on his arm. A flash of glossy painted nails contrasted against the beige of his bobbled jumper. Arthur worried that she might give him a reassuring hug. He would not like that one bit. He moved his arm away in surprise. 'Is to ask – oh sorry, I didn't realise you had company!'

The irritating estate agent had jogged down the stairs and was grinning at them.

'I'm almost finished. Just need to take a quick look outside then I'll be on my way.' He wandered through to the kitchen. Arthur could hear the back door opening and closing behind him.

'Ooh. What's going on?' Mrs Peterson asked, straining her neck to peer inside.

'I'm getting the house valued.'

'Are you moving?'

'Yes.'

'Is this because of your accident?'

Arthur nodded. 'Something like that.'

'Oh. Well it'll be a shame to see you go. I had to put my own father into a care home,' A misty look crossed her eyes. 'It's never easy, is it?'

Arthur was about to say something when Kevin reappeared.

'All done! I'll head back to the office and get this worked up then I'll be in touch.'

He nodded goodbye to Arthur and Mrs Peterson, wafting offensive aftershave in their faces as he went. Arthur had hoped that she would follow him out too, he needed a sit-down, he'd had quite enough this morning and still hadn't done anything for Operation Pearl yet either. However, Mrs Peterson's feet remained planted to the ground.

'Sorry? What was it you came round for?' Arthur asked.

'Oh yes! I almost forgot. I've been thinking about joining

Neighbourhood Watch so we can all be more vigilant with what's going on in the close. I just wanted to ask if you would pop one of the yellow stickers in your window to help deter anything untoward? I'm waiting on the welcome pack but hopefully it should arrive before you move. Fingers crossed we may even get a visit from a PCSO to give us all tips on how to make our homes more secure!' she said with as much excitement as if she had planned afternoon tea with the Queen. 'I've noticed that you stuck your bin stickers on too, they look great. I think it'll make a real difference, especially if you now have prospective buyers coming round. What do they say? Kerb appeal sells houses!' She chuckled then clapped her hands together. 'I'd best be off, but if there's anything you need then you know where I am.'

Arthur breathed a sigh of relief as he shut the door behind her. Only two months until he would finally get some peace.

Arthur knew he shouldn't have chanced it when he stepped out of his house to ominous clouds this afternoon, and now it was getting dark. Despite the risk that the heavens would soon be opening he'd needed to get to the pharmacy before it closed. His pills had almost run out and he'd gotten quite used to relying on them to catch some decent sleep. The fine shower he'd left his house in was quickly growing heavier. Drizzle clung to the sleeves of his jumper. He was furious at himself for forgetting his coat. He decided to take the shortcut home before he got totally drenched. He winced as he picked up speed to cross the road. It took him across the empty car park of an industrial estate that had been built here around ten years ago. Before that it was terraced houses and winding back alleys he knew with his eyes closed. The passageways all led to the Engine Pub that had once stood here. A majestic Victorian building full of nooks and solid beams, the only food served were fist-sized bread rolls wrapped in clingfilm stuffed with a wedge of cheese and homemade pickles. A real pub.

Pearl had scolded him when he'd let slip after a few pints of the landlord's secret home brew with his workmates that he would take this quicker route home. Arthur's drinking days were long behind him. Back then it had never crossed his mind that he may unknowingly step into some sort of trouble. He hadn't been here in years, not since the pub closed down and the land had been snapped up by developers. Arthur sighed, everything was always changing. He slowly shuffled across the exposed car park. The street lamps hadn't flicked on yet despite the heavy grey sky hiding any last trace of sunlight.

Just then he heard a noise behind him. He thought he was all alone. He turned as quickly as he could and narrowed his eyes. The dim light made it difficult to see if anything, or anyone, was lurking in the wild bushes that bordered the car park edge.

'Stop being so ridiculous,' he scolded himself out loud but a shiver danced up his arms.

He picked up his pace, wincing at the pain that shot up his legs from the exertion. Why hadn't he just got wet and braved the longer route from the bus stop, at least that was on the main roads with adequate street lighting? The rain was really coming down now, his feet having to go slower around the puddles on the uneven path.

A discarded lager can bounced along in a gust of cold wind. The tinny sound made him jump. He was getting closer to the far end of the empty car park now. All he had to do was turn right down a short path, that thankfully had a working street lamp, and then he would be almost home. How he longed to be sat in his armchair with a cup of tea, resting his ankle.

Arthur heard music and smelt cigarette smoke coming from the path ahead. There was a cackle of female laughter and deep, throaty male grunts coming from the group of five or so teenagers congregating before him. He hesitated, perhaps he could turn around, but that would mean crossing the exposed car park again. He had come this far; he just had to pull himself taller and walk faster. By his reckoning there was only twenty yards to go to reach the home straight. The lone street light flickered above his head. Another smell hit him: paint fumes. They were spraying graffiti across the wooden fence that ran down one side of the narrow path. Arthur kept his head low and held his carrier bag from the chemist closer to his chest. Maybe they wouldn't notice him, or if they did they'd just ignore him.

'Alright, old man!'

Maybe not.

'You come to join us, mate?' a young man bellowed. He had downy fur above his top lip, curled up in a menacing sneer. He looked frankly ridiculous sitting on a low bicycle, with a spray can in one hand and his lanky legs jutting out. The fence behind him had been daubed in brilliant white paint, swirly bouncy letters that read 'FUCK DA POLICE'.

'Nikki, you invited your boyfriend?' another guy, with a shock of bleached blond hair sniggered.

Arthur could only just make out the glare that the teenage girl gave him in the dim light. Most of them had their hoods up. Arthur wasn't sure if it was to shield themselves from the rain or look more menacing.

The girl they were teasing stuck her middle finger up at them and brushed her hair from her face. She looked so familiar but Arthur's brain was too busy racing with *Daily Mail* headlines of elderly men who found themselves confronted by hooded youths to place her. He scuffed a large pebble with his shoe which sent it skittering, the movement threatening his balance.

'Piss off, Kian,' she replied, her young voice at odds with her adult language.

As Arthur grew closer, he saw that there was a bicycle dropped flat on the wet ground. There wasn't enough space on the pavement unless someone moved it. He couldn't step around it as spiky hawthorn bushes ran on the other side, barricading them all in. His escape was completely blocked.

He was going to have to find his voice and ask for help. 'Would you mind just—'

'Just what?' The leader of the pack dropped his own bike to the ground, pulling himself to his full height. A spray can clanged on the concrete.

Arthur coughed. 'If you could just move this bicycle then—'

'You want me to roll out a red carpet for ya too?'

'No. I just—'

The lad was baiting him to impress his friends. He was the gatekeeper and, judging by the smirk on his spotty cheeks, was thoroughly enjoying this power. Arthur debated trying to pull the bike up himself but he knew he didn't have the strength or dexterity to bend so far down and get up again without doing his back in.

They locked eyes for a second before the teen turned away.

Relief flooded Arthur, he thought this power struggle was over and he could be on his way home. But, instead, the hooded lad turned back, sucked his teeth and spat on the pavement, narrowly missing Arthur's shoes. Someone 'ooohed' and sniggered. Strings of spit glimmered in the light.

Don't rise to it, a voice in Arthur's head warned.

Arthur stared at his feet and then at the offender; he was so young, a boy not a man. His ankle throbbed and his hands trembled but all of that discomfort was overshadowed by a sudden realisation.

To hell with this! What have you got to lose? Why shouldn't he confront these hoodlums? It wasn't like he had Pearl waiting for him at home. What exactly did he have left?

'Don't you think you should all be at home? It's late and this is no place to be hanging out after dark,' Arthur said, ignoring the growing beat of his heart. He refused to let them see how intimidated he felt.

'You what?' Grasshopper legs loomed over him.

'I said, it's better if you all went home. You have got homes to be going to, haven't you?' Arthur wished he had the physical strength to stand up for himself but all he had were his words and they weren't making any difference.

The lad let out a sharp bolt of laughter. 'Who do you think you are, telling us what to do? Go on, piss off.'

Arthur forced his eyes to stay locked with the ringleader.

'I said… do one!' He spat again, like a snake spitting venom from its fangs. Fast and unapologetic. This time the stringy ball of spit hit Arthur's right trouser leg. Arthur could no longer feel the raindrops on his face, instead he burned with frustration at his cowardliness. He knew he was invisible.

It had started once he'd retired and he didn't have anything that defined who he was as a person. Pearl told him to stop complaining but Arthur hated it. He hated his body giving up on him, he hated that he could do nothing to stop the ageing process, he hated that he and Pearl were just faceless old people in a town full of old people. He hated that this was the attitude of the youth of today; ignorant and rude with zero respect for anyone else.

The two girls gasped in shock. The one who looked familiar flicked her heavily made-up wide eyes between the two men. 'Just move the bike, Kian. Stop being a dick.'

The other girl she was sharing a white headphone in her ear with simply pursed her lips, waiting for a fight to break out.

The boy laughed, it was forced and brittle. 'Shut up, Nikki. So, old man, I'll do you a deal. I can move the bike or you could simply turn around and go back the way you came.' He reached a hand to the front of his tracksuit bottoms, lifting his jacket to reveal the waistband.

Arthur swore he saw something that glinted. Blood rushed to his head. Was that the blade of a knife? Arthur was ready to meet Pearl again but not by bleeding to death in a graffitied ginnel that smelt of cheap aftershave and cigarette smoke. For a few seconds the only sound was the obnoxious rap music and Arthur's strangled breaths.

'I'll move the bloody bike,' Nikki shouted.

Arthur was sure his heart was going to burst out of his ribcage.

'Come on. This is boring AF.' The ringleader made a sucking noise with his teeth and put two fingers up at Arthur, who wasn't sure how he had remained standing throughout this ordeal.

No sooner had Nikki pushed the bike to one side than Arthur moved as fast as his trembling legs could take him. He didn't dare look back.

CHAPTER 15

Izzy

Izzy was lying propped up on her bed feeding Evie. She had given her a lovely warm bath, changed her into soft powder-pink pyjamas and had read her a bedtime story. Christine had sworn by this method, so Izzy had decided to give it a try. Except the peace and quiet was interrupted by Andrew on a mission.

'Have you seen my white shorts?' he asked, rushing in and rummaging through his chest of drawers. 'I can't find them and I'm running so bloody late.'

'Hello to you too,' Izzy muttered. Once upon a time he would have pounced on her if he had seen even a hint of nipple, nowadays it was a normal occurrence that she went around half dressed with a baby attached to one boob.

'Sorry, babe.' He planted a quick kiss on her cheek and gave Evie a gentle squeeze. 'It's just that I said I'd be there fifteen minutes ago.'

'Be where?' The question stopped in her mouth. Her heart sank. She remembered he was going out to play badminton with a few of his mates.

'I did tell you.'

'I know, I forgot. Have you not seen the weather though? It's really grim out there.'

'It's an indoor sports hall, it'll be fine. So... shorts? They were in the laundry pile.'

'Then they're probably still there,' she said. 'Just give them a spray with Febreze, I'm sure that should do it.'

She could hear him muttering under his breath as he thundered down the stairs to the kitchen where an overflowing pile of dirty clothes sat next to the washing machine. A few minutes later he was back in the bedroom, giving his shorts a generous spray of aftershave in the crotch region.

'Find them?'

'Yeah.'

'Have you had a good day?' She hadn't spoken to him since half past seven that morning, over twelve hours ago, when he'd raced out of the house for work after skipping breakfast and complaining they were out of coffee.

'Fine, yeah. You?' he asked, quickly taking off his suit trousers. Andrew shimmied into his shorts and looked around for a pair of clean socks.

'The usual. Changing nappies, cold tea and a heated debate on *Loose Women*. Oh, I had a phone call from the health visitor.' She had almost forgotten about that.

'Everything OK?' he asked absently. He pulled his T-shirt over his head and stood in front of the mirror, running his fingers through his hair.

'Yeah, well...' Izzy took a deep breath. 'She asked me a lot of questions about how I was doing and—'

Andrew glanced at his watch. 'Sorry, babe. I really need to

go. Can this wait till another time?' He leaned down to kiss Izzy's head. 'Don't wait up. I think we'll probably go for a pint after as it's Deano's birthday.'

'What about dinner?'

'I'll grab something later,' Andrew called, running down the stairs. 'See you!'

'I meant for me,' Izzy said under her breath as she heard the front door slam shut. She closed her eyes. Nothing had changed for Andrew, he still had his freedom, his social life, and even his body shape had stayed the same. Whereas she didn't recognise herself anymore.

She gently put Evie down in her cot but had barely made it to the kitchen when the baby monitor sprang to life. Evie was having a meltdown. Izzy could have cried with frustration. So much for a relaxed evening on her own. She had done everything Christine had done to settle her, she didn't know where she had gone wrong. As she thumped up the stairs she remembered reading something about taking an unsettled baby for a drive, apparently the noise of the engine soothed them to sleep.

'Right, come on. Let's get your coat and Mummy can find her car keys, sweetheart.'

Izzy had been driving around aimlessly for the past twenty minutes. Miraculously Evie had fallen asleep but she didn't want to risk returning home and waking her yet. It wasn't the evening Izzy had planned but just being in the car was allowing her time to think, mostly about how distant she felt with Andrew. She could feel her throat clogging with unshed tears. Having a baby was supposed to bring them closer together but she had never felt so alone.

Rain thrummed on the roof and fogged up the windscreen. Her stomach rumbled, reminding her that the last thing she had eaten was a slice of cold toast six hours ago. She decided to treat herself to a drive-through, she craved a hot meal that she hadn't had to cook for herself. If she kept the engine running hopefully Evie would stay asleep long enough for her to eat it in peace. Sod the diet. Izzy pulled up to a set of temporary traffic lights, she was too busy thinking what she was going to order that she almost didn't register what her headlights illuminated.

'What the?' She peered forward, flicking the windscreen wipers up a level to clear the persistent drizzle.

Wait… was that?

'Arthur?' she yelled, winding down her window, shivering at the gust of cold air that rushed in.

'Izzy?' Arthur turned, shielding his eyes from the bright headlights.

'What on earth are you doing out in this weather? Where's your coat! Can I give you a lift?'

He blindly shuffled around to the passenger door and sank to the seat. He placed a soggy carrier bag by his feet, Izzy noticed his hands were trembling.

'What are you doing out on a night like this?' Izzy asked as he fumbled with his seatbelt.

'I went to the chemist but I took a wrong turn.' He glanced behind him out of the fogged-up window. 'What are you doing here?'

'I was trying to get Evie to sleep. But forget about me, are you OK?'

Arthur nodded, his eyes still trained out of the window as if he was looking for something.

'I was actually heading to the drive-through but there were some roadworks so I took a diversion and I'm glad I did! Do you mind if we stop quickly? I've not had any dinner and it looks like you could do with warming up.'

Arthur pulled his eyes away from the window and told her that was fine. The colour had drained from his face, his white hair was slicked to the top of his pale head and his glasses were wet with raindrops. They drove in silence to McDonald's, the yellow arches glowing in the gloomy evening light.

'Hey, what can I get for you?' a robotic voice called through the machine.

'I've never been to a drive-through,' Arthur said, staring at the large lit-up screen in front of them.

'Shall I order for us both?' Izzy asked him. Arthur nodded. 'Two large chips, a strawberry milkshake, a coke, and an apple pie please.'

Izzy found a space in the car park. She ever so gently turned the engine off, her eyes trained in her rear-view mirror. Thankfully, Evie stayed fast asleep. Izzy sighed in happy relief and handed Arthur a packet of chips and a small pot of ketchup.

'We should be OK to eat this if we're quiet. I thought I'd just get all my favourite things for you to try. Here, give this a go,' she handed him an apple pie. 'Careful. It's hot!'

'Thank you,' Arthur said, cautiously nibbling the edge.

Colour had returned to his cheeks and his hands had stopped shaking. They ate in silence, watching raindrops race one another down the windscreen.

'I'm surprised you noticed me,' Arthur said eventually. His voice was low and fragile.

'Well my headlights were on and—'

'I didn't mean that.'

Izzy finished chewing a chip. 'Oh. So what *were* you doing out here? It's a long walk from home.'

'I thought I'd take a shortcut from the chemists but I got a little lost. Well, a lot lost. Thank you for stopping.'

'Honestly it's fine. It's nice to see you again actually. I've been worried about you.'

Arthur scrunched up his napkin in his large wrinkled hands. 'I've been worried about you too.'

'Me?' Izzy turned to face him but his eyes remained fixed ahead.

'The day I delivered that parcel to you, I thought you seemed a little overwhelmed. I'd been meaning to stop by, but then I had that fall. However, if I'm honest, I don't know what I would have said to you that may have helped.'

Rain was falling softly on the roof. The air was warm and smelt of salt and cinnamon. Evie was gently snoring. Despite being total strangers it felt like a safe space to talk. There was none of the awkwardness that had been there in the mess of his kitchen just yesterday.

Izzy swallowed. 'Let's just say the reality of being a mum has been different from my expectations. Very, very different.' Her voice was wobbly and as thin as glass. She knew she couldn't say any more without crying.

'Sleep deprivation is a form of torture, you know?' Arthur said. 'In the sixteenth century they used it as a method to hunt witches. Apparently they would keep those accused awake for days and days until they hallucinated so much they confessed.'

Izzy nodded. 'I can understand why! It sure does send you

148

loopy. It's not just the sleep thing. I feel like I'm failing at everything.'

'Oh. I'm sure you're not,' Arthur said softly. 'Everything just seems a lot harder when you've not slept.'

Izzy nodded, she was frustrated with herself for getting so teary. *God damn hormones!* 'I never expected to be this tired all the time.'

'I remember back in the day they said liver was the best cure for tiredness, something to do with the lack of iron.' He shrugged. 'I'm no expert, far from it, but I think you probably need to hang on in there. Don't they say that it's all a phase?'

'Well I hope the best is yet to come,' Izzy said with a small smile.

'I may be speaking out of turn but I'm sure you're almost certainly not giving yourself enough credit for how well you're doing.'

'Thanks.' Izzy sniffed. 'Do you have any children?'

Arthur shook his head. 'I always thought that Pearl and I would have our own brood one day but it just wasn't to be. Jeremy is the only family I have now. How about you? Where do your family live?'

'My dad is currently in Vienna, he's a teacher out there so I don't get to see him that often, sadly. He's got a whole new life and, well, let's just say he's not the best at keeping in touch.'

'What about your mother?'

Izzy felt that familiar lump rise in her throat. She hesitated. 'Um… My mum died when I was little.' She stopped suddenly as if the words got trapped in her mouth, surprising herself.

'Ah.' Arthur nodded slowly. 'I'm sorry to hear that. I imagine it's made being a mother yourself even harder without her?'

Izzy could feel that lump expanding. 'It's fine. Well, it's not *fine*, you know, but it is what it is.'

'*It is what it is*,' Arthur repeated. 'You learn to create a life with a hole where they should be, I suppose.'

Izzy blinked the unwanted tears away. 'Sorry, I don't know what's come over me. Probably hormones, they're usually to blame!' She slapped on a tight smile.

'No need to apologise. You're quite right, losing someone you love is the hardest thing you'll ever experience. You can't imagine making it through the next hour, let alone the next day, but somehow you do and before you know it the days add up to become years and then you're sat thinking how the hell have I survived without them for this long?'

Izzy nodded to the empty chip packet in his hands, wanting to change the conversation. 'Have you finished?'

'Yes. Thank you. It was delicious.'

'You're welcome, I can't believe you've never been to a drive-through before! Next time I'll treat you to a Big Mac.' She shoved the empty wrappers away and turned on the engine. They drove home in a surprisingly companionable silence. It was only when Izzy pulled up on to Arthur's drive that he spoke again.

'Please don't tell Jeremy about picking me up in a strange place. He'd only worry that I'm losing it and will rush to move me into a home sooner.'

'I won't, but I think you should probably be taking it easier. After your fall you should be resting, not going off on epic adventures!'

'I know. I'll make sure to plan my visits to the pharmacy better,' Arthur said.

'Well how about I do that for you in the future? I'm more than happy to run a few errands for you. I'm at home all day with Evie and it would be nice to feel useful. To be honest it would give me something to do.' Izzy rummaged in the pocket of the driver's side door, searching for a pen. She tore off a large strip of the fast-food paper bag and wrote her mobile number down.

'If you ever need anything then please call me. I can be over within minutes.'

'Thank you.' Arthur took the piece of paper and cleared his throat. 'Actually, I wondered if...' Another pause. 'Well, if perhaps... you might be able to help me take a few boxes to the charity shop or the tip? If you had the time?'

She thought by the way he was building up to ask for a favour it would be a lot more demanding than just a quick run into town.

'Of course! I had already planned to pop over tomorrow anyway with some cardboard boxes. I can also take a look at what needs to go and try and get it in my boot?'

'That would be great. Thank you.'

Clearly asking for help didn't come natural to Arthur but then again, as Izzy only knew too well, sometimes it's the things we don't say that we need others to hear the loudest.

CHAPTER 16

Arthur

'Good morning, dear,' Arthur said with a smile as he opened his front door to Izzy and a pram the following morning. 'I didn't expect you here so early.'

Izzy's own smile faltered. 'Oh sorry! We've been up for hours. I forget that everyone else hasn't.' Her brown hair was piled messily on the very top of her head like an elaborate hat. She was wearing a jumper with a stain on the shoulder, Arthur wasn't sure whether to mention it or not.

'Honestly, it's fine. I'm an early riser myself. One of the frustrating consequences of getting older.'

The truth was he was grateful for the early start. His disturbed dreams had been full of spitting youths threatening him with knives, he was keen to have something to take his tired mind away from his lucky escape last night. He had been utterly relieved when Izzy had turned up out of nowhere, like a knight in a shining Renault.

Today had every chance of being a black cloud kind of day but Izzy's bright smile was the ray of sunshine he didn't realise he needed. If he'd learnt anything in that alley it was that he was doing the right thing. Any doubts about his self-imposed exit from this world vanished after coming face to face with that menacing teenager. There wasn't much Arthur could control any longer but ending his own story was one of them. The best thing was to keep busy and push forward with his plan. There was plenty of work to be done and having an enthusiastic volunteer to help was a huge bonus.

'So I've brought some things I thought you might need.' Izzy stepped to one side to reveal flattened cardboard boxes by her feet, rolls of masking tape and bin bags in each hand. 'The countdown is on after all.'

Arthur gave her an odd look. 'Sorry?'

'Till your big move. Operation Pearl?'

He bumbled. 'Yes *that* countdown. Indeed! Er... please come in.'

They awkwardly bustled around each other so she could push the pram into the hallway, wiggling it tightly against the wall. Arthur peered into the bassinet at Evie wrapped up inside.

'Someone looks very comfy,' he said with a smile. 'How old is she?'

'Seven weeks already. Amazingly, she seems pretty chilled this morning. I just hope she stays that way. Right. Shall we carry on where we left off? In the kitchen? There were the bottom cupboards that we didn't have time to sort through?' Izzy asked, billowing open a bin bag.

Arthur led the way.

She bent down and opened a cupboard. It was full of baking equipment. An array of chunky oatmeal-coloured mixing bowls, piping bags and metal tart cutters stared back at them.

153

Arthur cleared his throat, which had unexpectedly become thick with emotion. 'Pearl liked to bake. She could give that Mary Berry a run for her money.'

If he closed his eyes he could picture puffs of flour carried in the warm air, hear the radio on low, and imagine Pearl's apron fastened in a double knot around her waist. She would dance around the kitchen in her slippers, padding effortlessly across the lino following the recipes she held in her head. God, how he missed hearing her off-tune singing between the heavy rumbles of the electric mixer.

'Are you OK? Do you want to come back to this one later?'

'No. I'm fine. It's just the dust,' he coughed. He had to pull himself together. 'If you wouldn't mind just putting everything in a box? It all has to go. I've never been much of a cook and I'm not going to start baking now.'

Arthur moved on to the next cupboard. 'Fifteen glass ramekins! Whoever needed so many pointless things!' he exclaimed as he took them out and lined them on the kitchen counter, turning his back on the baking equipment that Izzy was packing away.

'There's something else at the back here,' Izzy said, contorting herself to reach the far corner. She carefully pulled out a thick-bottomed casserole dish and wiped away the smear of dust from the deep blue lid.

Arthur shook his head with a smile. 'Well, well, well. I've not seen this for years. It was a wedding present from Pearl's parents. It may not look like much but it was the first *new* thing we ever owned. We were so poor when we tied the knot, we had to do everything on a shoestring and call in as many favours as we could. We certainly didn't expect gifts, especially not something as smart as a brand-new casserole dish. It might sound like nothing nowadays but this was Pearl's prized possession. I remember my mother gave us a toaster – secondhand, my aunt donated a bed that also doubled up as our sofa and Pearl's sister – Jeremy's mother – made us a quilt from some old fabric she'd nabbed from her factory job. It was all very generous but there was nothing like the feeling of opening up a box containing something brand new. It was... well I can't put it into words.'

'When did you get married?'

'1955. I was twenty, Pearl was nineteen. We were so young, just playing adults, but of course we thought we knew it all. We moved in with a friend of Pearl's aunt after our honeymoon to Blackpool, but she was a bit of a battleaxe so we ended up sharing a freezing cold two-up two-down with another couple. I lost count of the amount of times I unwittingly walked in on someone using the outside toilet. Eventually we saved up enough to buy this place.' His smile faltered. 'I never could have imagined still being here after all these years. It's funny to think I'll soon be saying goodbye.' He handed the casserole dish to Izzy. 'Perhaps Jeremy might like to keep this?'

'I'm sure he would,' Izzy smiled before letting out a deep yawn. 'Oh, excuse me!'

'That's probably listening to my stories,' Arthur chuckled.

'No! I love hearing things like that. I just had another rough night with Evie.'

'Let me make you a cup of coffee.' Arthur placed his hands on his hips and looked around. 'It's probably time we took a break.'

'If you don't mind, that would be lovely, thank you.'

*

Evie began crying the second Arthur placed the steaming mug on the coffee table.

'That's sod's law.'

Izzy glanced at her watch and let out an exasperated sigh. 'She can't be due another feed yet. No! I followed the rules in the baby book to the letter this morning.'

'You may have read the rules but Evie didn't. She's a baby, she won't understand.'

'Other babies do.'

Arthur raised an eyebrow. 'Really?'

'OK well the ones at the baby group I went to do.'

'Here, let me jig her about in her pram and you drink your coffee. Perhaps she might fall back to sleep?' Arthur got to his feet and was pushing Evie's pram from the hall and into the kitchen before Izzy could stop him.

'Thanks, that's kind but I should probably take her home. I'm still getting to grips with feeding her in front of others. Do you mind if I nip to your loo and then I'll be off?'

As Izzy escaped to the toilet, Arthur had an idea. He had a vague memory of Pearl doing this for Jeremy when he was a baby. He turned on the washing machine and parked Evie's pram in front of the doors. Within moments her crying quietened.

'Oh my God. You're a genius! Why have I never thought to do that?' Izzy said, her eyes wide as she tiptoed into the kitchen.

'Shhh.' Arthur raised a finger to his lips. 'I think she might actually fall back to sleep.'

They both stood and watched as Evie's eyelids fluttered and grew heavy to the rhythmic noise of the laundry spinning in the drum.

'There.' Arthur was taken aback by how satisfying that felt.

Izzy shook her head in amazement. She looked as if she had tears in her eyes. 'Now I've discovered that you're a secret baby whisperer, you'll never be able to get rid of us!' she grinned.

'My pleasure. Now, how about we have that cup of coffee.' Arthur plodded out of the kitchen with a satisfied smile.

CHAPTER 17

Izzy

A week later and Izzy was back at Arthur's house. The truth be told she was actually finding it hard to stay away. It wasn't just an excuse to get away from her own four walls, or to help him finish clearing his kitchen; she liked being here. There was a nice feel to the place. It reminded her of her grandparents' house, the flood of nostalgia wrapped her like a warm hug, it made her feel happy. Maybe this was *exactly* what she needed.

'Shall we start with this today?' Izzy asked Arthur, pointing to the large display cabinet in the corner of Arthur's lounge. The glass shelves were filled with all sorts of bric-a-brac-stall ornaments. She had been dying to rummage inside since she'd first stepped foot in this room.

Arthur nodded from his armchair and waved one of the rattles Izzy had brought with her over Evie who was lying happily on a playmat near his slippers.

'You can probably put it all straight into a bin bag. There's nothing sentimental in there just a lot of other people's unwanted junk. It's full of random things that Pearl bought from jumble sales, car boots, and holiday souvenir shops.

I never understood why she became so attached to half the stuff in there. She would polish the ornaments and regularly rearrange the shelves as if she were a proud girl with a dollhouse. It made her happy, so I never questioned it, but there's certainly nothing of any value in there.'

'Hmm. I agree with Pearl on this one. Just think, everything in here has a story to tell,' Izzy said, catching Arthur roll his eyes. She knelt down to pull open the polished walnut doors under the glass shelves but they were locked.

'Do you have a key to open this?'

'Probably somewhere.' Arthur scratched his head. 'I'll have a look upstairs later. The other doors, the glass ones, shouldn't be locked.'

Izzy gave them a good tug to open them. 'I know you said it can all go in the bin but we should still try to do this right. Charity, keep or bin.'

'Yes, boss,' Arthur smiled.

Izzy held up a cream teapot. 'This?'

'Bin?'

'It's part of a Lady Diana Spencer and Prince Charles wedding commemorative tea set,' she read with a frown. 'I don't think you can just chuck it.'

'Oh. Er, do you want it?'

'Well… no.' Izzy inspected it. 'But someone might. I'll add it to the charity shop pile. OK, how about this?' She picked up a miniature Blackpool Tower, no taller than a can of cola.

'Charity shop.'

Izzy carefully picked up a paperweight, feeling the smooth glass heavy in her hands. She remembered her own grandma had a collection of them sitting on the bureau in her small office. As a child Izzy loved to bring them close up to her eye and gaze at the kaleidoscope of colours trapped inside. Arthur instructed her to place them in the charity shop box.

'Actually, can I keep this one?'

'Of course, dear. Take anything you like.'

Next up was a decorative punch ladle, Arthur let out a chuckle at the mere sight of it.

'What's so funny?'

'That's got me into trouble before! I'd use it to stir my famous fruity punch cocktail that we served at our summer BBQ parties. There was a phase when we would have an annual shindig on summer solstice, it was a seventies thing,' he explained. 'I'd always add an extra glug of brandy behind Pearl's back, it used to get the party off to a great start. At one party I remember an old colleague, Bill, got a bit carried away and was drinking it like it was water. He ended up doing the conga down the street with one of Pearl's sisters, much to her and her husband's dismay.'

The laughter quietened down and in its place was a wistful sort of smile.

'Do you ever get lonely, Arthur?'

'Sorry?'

'I mean by the sounds of it you were quite the social butterfly.'

'Oh no, not me. That was always Pearl. I would just take drinks orders and man the barbecue, she was the one flitting between couples making conversation like the perfect hostess. I suppose I've always preferred my own company. I just didn't expect to have so much of it!'

'You don't fancy looking for some companionship or even giving online dating a go then?'

'Hah!' Arthur let out such a bark of laughter it made Izzy jump. 'No, there's not a woman out there who could fill Pearl's shoes. Right then, I think it's time I put the kettle on,' he said hurriedly. Izzy sensed he wanted to change the subject.

'Good idea. I need a caffeine hit before I tackle the other shelves, but I'll go and do it.'

'No, no. You should rest. Evie is more than happy on this play mat thingy for a bit, you should be making the most of it!'

'I won't argue with that. She's never as calm at home as she is here.' Izzy wasn't sure if it was the crazy patterned carpet that was the ultimate sensory toy or perhaps it was the fact that she herself felt happier here than at home surrounded by mess and unfinished chores. Whatever the reason, she wasn't complaining.

Izzy was having the best dream about trekking in the rainforests, helped by the fact that her jungle leader was Tom Hardy. She could have stayed in this tropical paradise much longer if only her bladder hadn't forced her to wake from this glorious nap. She had no idea how long she'd fallen asleep for but everything didn't feel as painful as it had before. Her limbs felt loose and relaxed, her head a lot less fuzzy and her chest wasn't as tight. She stretched and ran through the things left to do before Andrew came home from work. As she slowly opened her eyes she frowned. She didn't recognise the Artex ceiling. That's because she wasn't on her sofa taking forty winks like she thought she'd accidentally done, she was still at Arthur's. She must have dropped off when he went to make them both a drink. Her dribble was on his cushion. *Oh my God, how embarrassing!* She glanced around the empty lounge. *Where were Evie and Arthur?* She wobbled to her feet, still foggy from the deep sleep. As she opened the door to the kitchen she could hear Arthur's voice coming from the back garden, he was speaking softly. *Wait – was he singing a lullaby?*

Izzy couldn't help but smile at what she could see from the kitchen window. Arthur had wheeled Evie's pram out into his garden. He must have picked her up and placed her into her carrycot whilst Izzy slept, and he was slowly wandering along the grass pointing things out to her. Evie was lying on her back, staring up with big peaceful eyes at the twinkly shadows passing from the trees over her head. Suddenly Izzy's eyes filled with tears. She felt her heart clench at the sight of the pair of them on this impromptu stroll. She was taken aback by an overwhelming sense of longing for something which she could never have. She desperately missed her own family. Arthur caught sight of her at the window and waved. Izzy sniffed, shaking away the fleeting cloud of grief and enthusiastically waved back.

'I didn't want to wake you!' Arthur said as Izzy crossed over his lawn to them. 'I hope you don't mind? I was very careful picking her up and I made sure that it's not too chilly out here. I just thought you could do with some rest and Evie might like to have a look at the flowers. We often get butterflies flitting around that buddleia bush.'

'Mind? I feel like a new woman,' Izzy said, with a sudden urge to hug him. 'Thank you. If anything, I'm a little embarrassed! I've never dropped off like that before.'

'Don't be. You must have needed it.'

'Has she been any trouble?'

'Not one bit. I was just giving her the royal tour, I think

she's going to be a horticulturist when she grows up. Do you know much about plants?'

Izzy shook her head. 'Nope. Not a clue. In fact, that was one of the things I was worried about before having Evie, I used to lie awake panicking that if I couldn't even keep a fern alive then how would I manage with a human!'

'Well I think you're doing a splendid job.'

'Thank you.' Izzy had to quickly turn away so he wouldn't set her off again. 'Shall we head back inside and carry on with that cabinet?'

'What's this?' Izzy pulled out a heavy trophy from the back of the glass cabinet.

'Where did you find that?'

'It was hidden a bit behind some records.' Izzy moved her thumb to wipe off the thick smear of grime to read what was inscribed on the plaque, missing the dazed look on Arthur's face. 'International Swimming Championships February 1953, First Place – Arthur Winter.' She read out loud then whistled. 'This was yours? You were a swimmer?'

'Well you'd hardly know it now.' Arthur glanced down at himself. 'But back then I was a bit of a water baby, yes.'

'A bit?' Izzy laughed. 'You swam for our country! I'd say you were practically a merman.'

'I'll never forget that race. As soon as the klaxon rang, I shot into the water. I was neck and neck with Roger Lloyd on the outside lane. This ginger-haired, freckle-covered young lad had been my toughest rival. At the last lap I thrashed the poor Welsh boy, the place erupted and I felt like I was in a dream. Smiling for the flashing cameras as I emerged from the water. When that trophy was passed to me, well, I felt like a celebrity!'

'Do you swim much nowadays?'

'No, no that's all in the past,' he said quickly. 'What about you? I bet Evie likes to have a splash around?'

Izzy shook her head. 'She's never been. Andrew's always working. I mean, she'll probably go to lessons when she's older.'

'Why don't you take her?'

'Me? On my own?' Izzy put the trophy to one side. She wouldn't have a clue where to begin with taking a baby swimming. It was hard enough just getting out of the house let alone trying to achieve anything else.

'Well why not?'

'I don't know. That would also mean trying to squeeze back into a swimming costume.' The thought of trying to do just that filled her with dread. Her postpartum body was soft, her stomach rippled with stretch marks. She foolishly had expected to snap back after having Evie, like all the celebs in the *Daily Mail* sidebar seemed to do, but it had changed completely. She had barely looked at herself naked since having Evie. In the mornings she jumped from the shower into her stretchy maternity clothes avoiding as many reflections as possible. 'I need to lose a bit of baby weight first.'

'Pfft. If your clothes don't fit then buy bigger ones, that's what I used to say to Pearl. Life's too short to eat like a rabbit. Oh and the trophy can go in that pile there.'

'No!' Izzy gasped. 'It can't just be chucked away. For one it's made of silver so might be worth something and two you won it for ENGLAND!' she emphasised as if Arthur had forgotten.

'It should be on display for all to see. If you don't want it in your new home then maybe you could donate it to the local leisure centre? I'm sure they'd love to know that they have a champion in their midst.'

'I don't swim. Not anymore.' Arthur shook his head; Izzy couldn't quite read the expression on his face. 'Like I said, it's a long time ago.'

'Swimming is like riding a bike! Once you know how to do it, and you clearly knew how to do it, then it never leaves you. You should get back in the water, Arthur. It's really good for you. Have you been to the new pool in town? It's really lovely and modern. There's even a coffee shop and a juice bar.'

'I don't think that's for me.' Arthur gave a slight roll of his eyes. 'Like I said, the trophy can go in the bin or to the charity shop but please can we move on?'

Izzy was a little taken back by how quickly he had changed his tone. She nodded and pulled out a box of cross-stitch patterns, relieved to have something else to deal with. But as she continued to sort through the rest of the glass shelves she found herself growing more confused. If he was such a water baby back in the day then why was he so reluctant to get his trunks on now? Izzy felt like she wasn't able to pry any further, despite the many questions building in her mind from the snapshots of Arthur's life.

CHAPTER 18

Arthur

'I spent most of the weekend trying to find the key for that thing,' Arthur said, nodding to the display cabinet. 'I had a quick look. I'm afraid it's a bit of a jumbled mess inside.'

'Oh.' Izzy couldn't help but let out a gasp as she opened the cabinet doors.

There were three shelves bursting with thick photo albums piled on top of one another, empty ice cream tubs that had papers and photographs crammed inside, and stacks of files and torn envelopes.

He felt a little embarrassed. 'Pearl used to tell me that there was a method to the madness. This was very much her domain.'

Izzy took a deep breath. 'Let's just do a shelf at a time? You don't want to feel too overwhelmed and Evie's due a feed soon.'

She started trying to carefully prise the photo albums without toppling everything else out. 'I'll just move these here and— whoops!' Individual photographs fluttered around her like confetti. 'Sorry, I'm not sure which album they fell out of!' Izzy scooped them up and passed them to Arthur.

'I must have only been five or six here. I used to carry that tin car everywhere with me.' Arthur smiled nostalgically at the faded black-and-white photo in his hand, his gap-toothed childhood grin almost as wide as his mother's. Her bright beaming smile and neat pin curls was how he always remembered her.

'She's beautiful.'

Izzy picked up the loose photographs and came to sit on the sofa near Arthur. Evie was sucking her fingers and lying happily on a mat near the window.

'She was, all my friends had a bit of a crush on her. People said she reminded them of a silver-screen actress. Deeply embarrassing when you were growing up,' Arthur laughed lightly. 'She was always exceptionally turned out, even during the war she would sleep with rags in her hair so it was perfectly curled the following day and ration her lipstick to make it last. I remember her rubbing beetroot juice on her lips at one point.' He shook his head, baffled by the concept.

'Who's this in the snazzy jumper?' Izzy held up a faded colour photograph of a young boy holding a green frog-shaped kite.

'That must be Jeremy.' Arthur squinted. 'He had a bit of an obsession with frogs, if I remember rightly. Everything he owned had an amphibian of some sort on them.'

'When I was younger I went through a phase when I would only wear something with a picture of a dolphin on. My dad worried that I'd never grow out of it, he envisioned walking me down the aisle in a wedding dress covered in dolphins.' She laughed. 'Ooh. Is this one you?'

Izzy picked up another photo; it was of a handsome man

with thick gelled-back hair, standing with a cocktail glass raised in a toast next to a tastefully decorated Christmas tree. It could have been a retro vinyl cover for a Christmas album. His patterned woollen jumper and pearly white teeth were nostalgically cheesy. 'You were quite the catch!'

'That's not me.'

Izzy's smile faltered as she caught the tight grimace on Arthur's face.

'That's my brother, Reg.'

'I'm sorry. What happened to him?'

Arthur turned the photograph face down on the coffee table. 'I don't know.'

'You don't know?' she repeated.

'He might still be alive. We haven't spoken in quite a few years.'

'Oh. What happened? If you don't mind me asking?'

Arthur let out a long, slow sigh. 'Let's just say he was a one-off, there really was no one quite like Reg. He could be very difficult, I honestly don't know how his wives all put up with him.'

'Wives?'

'Yes, he was married a few times, being the Lothario that he was. Winnie was my favourite, she had the patience of a saint, but even she struggled to deal with him. That was his second, or was it his third wife? I'm not so sure. Pearl used to hate it when I'd call him the next Henry the Eighth.'

'Hang on, her name would have been Winnie Winter?'

Arthur looked as if he didn't get the joke.

'So did you and Reg just lose touch with each other?'

'Hmm. Something like that.'

'You really don't know where he is?'

Arthur shook his head.

'Do you not fancying trying to find him?'

Arthur coughed, he looked annoyed that she was firing so many questions his way. 'It's a long story but let's just say that ship has definitely sailed.'

Just then the doorbell rang. 'Would you mind getting that please? Arthur asked, his tone brighter at the unexpected distraction. 'It might take me a while to get up.'

Izzy placed the photo albums on the sofa where they landed with a thump and went to open his front door.

'Oh, er, hello,' the man on the other side stuttered, taking a half step back.

'Jeremy, we're in here!' Arthur called from the lounge.

'You're Jeremy? Hi, I've just been hearing all about your love of frogs! It's nice to finally properly meet you,' Izzy smiled warmly, stepping aside to let him in.

Jeremy frowned in confusion. 'Sorry... who are you?'

'I'm Izzy, Arthur's neighbour. We're just in the middle of sorting through some old photos.'

'Right, er...' Jeremy followed Izzy into the lounge, his eyes widened as he saw Arthur surrounded by opened photo albums and scattered prints. 'What the... there's a baby!' he exclaimed.

'This is Evie,' Arthur chuckled. 'Izzy's daughter. Izzy has been a great help with starting to get things ready for the move.'

'It looks like it's going... well.' Jeremy gawped at the messy lounge.

'It's my fault. We got a little caught up having a walk down memory lane,' Izzy explained; she looked as if she suddenly didn't know where to put herself.

Jeremy smiled tightly then placed his hands on his hips. 'Where's everything gone from in here?'

'The things that were in the cabinet have been bubble-wrapped and put it into boxes by the kitchen door,' Izzy explained as Jeremy walked straight into the kitchen to have a look.

'I told you I was going to start packing up,' Arthur called behind him.

'Wow… I am impressed,' Jeremy stuttered, returning to the lounge. 'What's this?' He was holding the swimming trophy Izzy had placed to one side. Arthur's smile dropped.

'Didn't you know that Arthur was a champion swimmer?' Izzy asked Jeremy, who was inspecting the silverware.

'I thought I said that was to be thrown out?' Arthur said curtly.

'Throw it out?' Jeremy spoke loudly. 'Why ever would you do that? It's probably worth something! A decent jeweller can melt the silver down at the very least. What else have you thrown away? I hope you're being sensible!'

'Of course I am,' Arthur said.

Jeremy pulled a face that said he didn't believe him. 'Hmm. it's a good job I've come over. It seems like you need someone to make sure that you're making sensible decisions. I really think it would be a good idea if I had a look through everything. You know, Aunty Pearl would want me to just double-check…'

The atmosphere in the lounge suddenly tightened.

'And this is why I've not asked *you* to help me pack up,' Arthur said through clenched teeth. 'I'm more than capable of deciding what to do with *my* things. You saw for yourself the boxes in the kitchen that are waiting to be donated to the charity shop, Izzy has been making sure I don't just bin the lot. Anything of value will be put to one side, you don't need to worry. You won't be short-changed on your inheritance.' He locked eyes with Jeremy who quickly looked away, his cheeks flushing pink. Izzy didn't say a word, she was crouched down by Evie avoiding making eye contact with the men. 'Anyway, to what do we owe this unexpected visit?'

Jeremy placed the trophy in the empty display cabinet. 'I thought we should probably have a catch-up as I've not seen you since the visit with the estate agent. How did it go?'

Jeremy had been so attentive, a little too much for Arthur's liking, whilst he was convalescing but since he was released home he had only telephoned him for updates. Arthur didn't want to appear needy by bringing this fact up.

'Fine. Fine…'

'You have a lot to discuss so we'll leave you to it!' Izzy said hurriedly. She bent down to pick Evie up from the playmat, who cried out at having to move from her sunny spot.

'Don't go on my account,' Jeremy said, a little sheepish after Arthur's dressing down.

'No, no. It's fine. I'm sure you two have lots to sort out.' Izzy flashed a polite smile. 'Arthur, do you still want me to take you to drop some things at the charity shop tomorrow? I was thinking about ten o'clock, as that ties in with Evie's nap.'

'Yes please. If you don't mind?'

'Of course not. I'll see you then. Nice to meet you, Jeremy.'

Izzy waved and let herself out, clearly grateful to be making an escape from the family tensions.

Arthur felt embarrassed that she had witnessed all of that. He wasn't in the mood to hear what his nephew had to say; if anything, he wanted to ask Jeremy to go and Izzy to stay but he knew that there were a lot of things that still needed to be ironed out if he was to meet his deadline.

'Right. Let's get down to business,' he sighed and turned to Jeremy.

CHAPTER 19

Izzy

'I'm sorry about Jeremy yesterday,' Arthur said as Izzy drove to the charity shop. 'I think he was caught off guard. I mean, the last thing he expected was to see me with visitors, let alone a young woman and a baby! The look on his face was something else,' he chuckled.

'The poor man. I bet he wondered what the hell was going on. But don't worry, I understand, I'd be the same if I saw a strange woman in my uncle's house going through his things.'

'Well, after you left I told him in no uncertain terms that he had nothing to worry about. I really was rather cross at how he had behaved. You've been a big help and I didn't like what he was insinuating.'

'Oh, well, thank you, and you know that I'm happy to help. To be honest it's been good for me getting out of the house and having a purpose again.'

'And you're sure you don't mind ferrying me around like this?'

'Arthur, it's no bother. I could do with picking up a few bits for tea whilst we're in town too.'

'Well let me at least pay for parking.'

'Deal,' Izzy smiled.

Izzy pushed open the door to the charity shop and manoeuvred Evie's pram past rails of ladies' coats and a spinning stand with reduced-price birthday cards on. Arthur had gone to pick up a prescription.

'Excuse me, are you accepting donations?' Izzy asked a lady with a sleek grey bob, who was neatly arranging paperbacks. She had a name badge pinned to her flowery blouse.

'We sure are,' Joan replied, giving Evie a big over-the-top smile.

'Great. I've got quite a few boxes in the boot of my car,' Izzy said. 'I wondered if someone may be able to help me with them? I'm parked right outside.'

'No problem, I'll ask Freddie to help.' Joan called through to the back of the shop. Moments later a gangly teenager wearing a T-shirt with the name of a band Izzy had never heard of appeared.

'Would you mind helping this lady please, Fred?'

He nodded and followed Izzy to her car.

Izzy popped open the boot. She had managed to fill it with quite a few of the cardboard boxes which had been in Arthur's kitchen; she was getting worried they were becoming a trip hazard. She hadn't asked him if Jeremy had had a rummage through or not, she thought it was best not to bring that up again. Arthur was right, these were his things so he could do what he wanted with them.' Who were they to argue with his wishes.

'Just those, please. Are you OK to carry them all? They might be a bit heavy.'

Freddie gave a grunt of a reply and stacked three boxes on top of one another. Soon he was wobbling precariously to the door of the shop. Izzy managed to catch the top box that was sliding downwards just in time.

'Oops!'

Freddie gently placed the other boxes on the floor and wiped the sweat from his forehead. 'Anything else?'

'Nope, that's all. Thank you.'

'Thanks, Freddie, love,' Joan smiled brightly as the teenager sloped back into the back of the shop, she then took some details from Izzy as she was a first-time donor.

'Oh. Would you like to buy a raffle ticket whilst you're here?' Joan asked when she had finished. 'It's three pounds for a strip and we've got some lovely prizes to be won.'

'Sure, why not,' Izzy said, opening her purse. The bell to the shop chimed as the door opened behind her the second Joan had torn her off a strip of numbers.

'Oh hello again,' Joan smiled shyly.

Izzy took her change then turned round, surprised to see Arthur walk into the shop.

'Hello,' he greeted Joan with a polite nod of the head.

Izzy noticed Arthur's cheeks had also turned a little pink. She waited, expecting him to do the introductions, but he just stood there jingling the loose change in his trouser pockets awkwardly glancing around the empty shop.

'Lovely weather we're having,' Joan said. 'I'm glad things are finally brightening up out there. I feel like it's been so gloomy and grey for such a long time.' She brushed back a strand of silvery hair.

'Mmm,' Arthur responded.

There was another long pause. Izzy felt like a spare part, perhaps she should give these two some time alone. 'Arthur, do you want to meet us somewhere... or?'

'No, no.' He pulled himself together. 'I suppose we had better get on. Well, Joan, it was lovely to see you again.'

'You too, dear.' She blinked quickly then smiled at Izzy. 'Thank you for the donations!'

Arthur held the door open for Izzy as he said goodbye to Joan. They wandered down the street, past a guy playing a guitar and murdering a Taylor Swift song. Izzy was brimming with questions.

'So... ?' she asked when they were far enough away from the noisy musician.

'Sorry?' Arthur seemed like he was in his own little world as they manoeuvred past a couple in matching cagoules.

'The woman in the charity shop? I just wondered how you knew the shop assistant. Joan...'

'Joan? Oh, I don't, well, not really. I've just donated some of Pearl's things there before.'

'Well you certainly made an impression on her,' Izzy said with a wink. If she didn't know better she would have bet good money that Joan had the hots for her man Arthur.

Arthur frowned in confusion. His naivety was quite touching.

'Do you fancy grabbing a coffee before we head back? I could do with finding somewhere to change Evie's nappy.'

Arthur seemed a little surprise by the question. 'I suppose we could. If you'd like? *Grabbing a coffee* isn't something I've ever really done.'

'Well then this one is on me. The café on the corner does the best flat whites around.'

'Flat white?'

'It's a type of coffee, strong but milky. A lifesaver in a cup when you've had no sleep.' Izzy led them both across the square of shops. She stopped abruptly seeing who was walking towards them, giving her a cheerful wave and calling her name.

'Who's that?' Arthur leant in and asked.

'That's the health visitor.' Izzy replied, smiling tightly. 'Hi.'

'Hello, Izzy, lovely to see you again!' Nina looked like the type of person never to have a bad day. 'Oh hello,' she smiled at Arthur. 'Is this Evie's grandad? You must be very proud!'

'Oh no, I'm not,' Arthur bumbled. 'You see—'

'This is my neighbour, Arthur,' Izzy jumped in.

'Oh, it's nice to meet you. Izzy, I had hoped to see you at the drop-in clinic this week?'

'Sorry, I've been quite busy.'

'That's probably my fault,' Arthur said, raising a hand.

Nina nodded politely. 'Well I'm glad to hear that you're finding things to do. Have you thought any more about the mother and baby group I recommended?'

Izzy couldn't bear the thought of going back to that hot stuffy room, bunched together with other women she had nothing in common with, suffering the tedious conversations and being made to feel like a worse mum than she already did. There was nothing to gain from putting herself through that ordeal. It only highlighted how badly she was coping compared to those other Insta-perfect mums.

'Mmm. It's not really for me,' Izzy replied.

'Oh that's a shame. But don't give up! There are plenty of other classes out there for new mums. That leaflet I gave you has a list of local resources you can access. The library also has a noticeboard with details of popular community groups that you might want to check out. Maybe you just need to be like Goldilocks and try a couple until you find one that's just right?'

Izzy gave an non-committal sort of nod. 'Maybe.'

'Speaking of which, have you had a chance to look at the leaflet I gave you?'

'Yeah, I err had a quick read.' Izzy really didn't want to get into this right now, not in front of Arthur.

'Good. Well I'd love to have a proper chat with you, and see how little Evie is doing, of course. Will you please try and come to the clinic soon?'

Izzy nodded and said goodbye, watching Nina walk away.

'It sounds like you're not keen on the mother's meeting thing she mentioned,' Arthur said as they made their way to the café.

Izzy let out a small groan. 'I went once and hated it. It was Nina who wanted me to get out more and make some mum friends.'

'Oh. Right.'

'I feel bad but I mean it's not like Evie even gets anything out of it, she was asleep most of the time, leaving me to suffer awkward conversations with other mums who I have nothing in common with.'

'You're all in the same boat, aren't you?'

'You sound like Andrew.' Izzy shook her head. 'Just because we happened to have a baby at around the same time doesn't mean we're going to be lifelong friends. I much prefer the chats *we* have.'

'Me too, love,' Arthur said as he held open the door to the coffee shop. 'But I won't be around for much longer.'

'You're only moving to the other side of town!' Izzy said, navigating pushing the pram around a cluster of low tables. Smells of coffee beans and warm pastries filled her nose. She spotted a couple of empty sofas at the back of the shop where they could sit.

'Yes, well, no, well I mean…' he stuttered awkwardly. Izzy gave him a quick look. He quickly cleared his throat. 'What I mean is that you should find some friends your own age, ones with a baby so when Evie gets older and more interactive, you have someone to share this all with. It's not just that you should have friends yourself but little Evie will need some playmates of her own. I think you should try again. It's probably one of those things you have to stick with?'

'Hmm, I guess…' Izzy said, taking her eyes off Arthur and onto the large board behind the counter. 'Right, you grab those seats and I'll get the drinks in. This one is on me!'

CHAPTER 20

Arthur

Arthur wasn't quite ready to leave his warm bed just yet. He lay there listening to the rest of the cul-de-sac coming to life around him. Car engines were running and doors slamming as people got ready to go to work or school. He heard the teenage girl from number forty-one moaning that she couldn't find her PE kit. Her father, the man who had an obsession with gaudy Christmas decorations, arguing back that she needed to get more organised. Arthur had been restrained by Pearl on numerous occasions when he'd threatened to go and cut the nodding reindeer's head off or break the fuse to the flashing lights glaring into their lounge. Pearl had called him a scrooge and simply closed the curtains. It suddenly dawned on Arthur that those pesky bright lights wouldn't be an issue again. He wasn't going to be here by Christmas. He wasn't going to be spending the festive season at RoseWood Lodge either.

The only flaw in his plan was Izzy. He had avoided any offers of well-meaning help for so long but he had surprised himself at how much he enjoyed her company. It was nice to have someone to talk to and the baby had been no trouble at all, she didn't seem to cry half as much as Arthur had braced himself for. They would have a cup of tea together and a little chat before starting to sort out another box or drawer. Izzy was so patient with him, listening to him share stories on the objects she'd uncovered, she seemed genuinely interested. For his part, Arthur was enjoying hearing her own tales. She was a lot brighter than the woman he had first met all those weeks ago on her doorstep.

A funny sort of feeling rose in his stomach when he thought of her. He felt terribly guilty that she was giving up so much of her time without knowing the full story, exactly why Arthur was so keen to get his affairs in order. But he could see no other way. Another pair of hands was invaluable. She had said herself how helping him made her feel a little better; he tried to focus on this and not think about what would happen when she learnt the truth: that Operation Pearl was not just about downsizing. Arthur swallowed, he would have to cross that bridge if it ever came to it.

Speaking of Izzy, Arthur had no time to be dawdling as she would be over soon. He hoped that some of her magic would rub off on him today. He was going to need it. There was still his office, two bedrooms, the loft and the garden shed to clear, not to mention paperwork to sort out and loose ends to tie up. He'd agreed with Izzy that the more sentimental tasks were to be completed by him alone. And right now that's what he needed to be getting on with. It was time to get out of bed and finish going through the rest of Pearl's belongings.

He started with her collection of handbags. He had never understood why she had needed so many. He winced as he creaked to his knees to dig them out from the bottom of the wardrobe. He started with the smaller ones. The type that you would carry in your hand or under an arm on special occasions – a clutch bag he seemed to remember she called them. The powder blue satin one looked like it had never even been used, the same went for a near identical pale pink one. He vaguely remembered her carrying the black one covered in sequins to his mother's funeral; she had worried endlessly that it had been far too jazzy for the occasion. He told her kindly that he doubted anyone would even notice.

He opened each one and checked inside. A few bobby pins, an old Tesco receipt, boiled sweet wrappers and a tiny sample of perfume in one. He fished out three snapped emery boards, picked up some loose Tic Tacs and had to wash ink from a leaky ballpoint pen that had stained the lining of another of the bags. Arthur placed them with the rest of the things waiting to go to the charity shop. But something niggled at him, he couldn't quite put his finger on it.

There was one more, he remembered, picking up his pace. He'd walked past it every single day since she'd died, it had blended into the rest of the house. It was the bag she'd used most often. She'd left it hanging up on the coat rack near the front door, ready for when she needed it next. It broke his heart knowing it would never be picked up by her again. He'd only opened it once since she'd passed away, needing to take the ID from her purse for all the legal death-related paperwork, a simple task that had felt mammoth in that deep abyss of grief.

He was amazed he'd been able to even forget it was there, until now. The soft slouchy grey leather was worn and loved. It wasn't in the best of nick but someone might benefit from it. He couldn't bear to just put it in the rubbish bin. This one was the hardest of all. Pearl had rarely been without it, but what was the point of holding on to it, especially with his deadline looming? He took a deep breath as he unzipped it and told himself off for getting so nostalgic over a silly handbag. There were half a packet of mints, a scrunched-up tissue, a tube of lipstick and a train ticket stub inside. Arthur frowned. He couldn't remember the last time he and his wife had got the train anywhere. He drew the ticket closer to his eyes, removing his glasses to peer at the tiny printed letters. A return to Blackpool. Dated two weeks before she died. *Why on earth would she have a ticket to Blackpool in her handbag?* It had to be almost three hours away and was not a place either of them had visited or had any connection to. What was in Blackpool that would interest Pearl?

The sound of the doorbell made Arthur jump. He scrunched up the train ticket along with the mints and threw them in the bin. He shook the unusual item out of his mind as he went to open the front door.

'Morning!' Izzy looked very bright and perky standing on his doorstep this morning. She was wearing a pretty navy sweater and had tied her hair in a long loose plait. Arthur thought it suited her like that. 'How are you doing? I've got supplies! I popped to the corner shop as I'd run out of milk. I also got you a few bits. You might not want or need any of this but...'

She handed him a plastic bag as he held the door wide for her to push the pram into the hall. She was over almost every day now. Sometimes they worked efficiently packing, sorting and talking; other days they drank tea and watched a quiz show on Channel 4 and tried to answer the questions quicker than the contestants. Arthur wasn't sure which days he preferred the most.

'That's very kind of you, dear,' Arthur said. Inside the care package was a tin of tomato soup, a carton of orange juice, a bag of chocolate buttons and a crossword puzzle book. He couldn't remember the last time someone had thought of him like this. He coughed away the sudden emotion that had risen to his throat. 'Shall I put the kettle on?'

'I'll do it. Do you mind just watching Evie? And then I'll make a start with getting a box from upstairs.'

'I've been thinking,' Arthur said, later that afternoon. He was standing with his hands on his hips looking at the growing stack of charity shop boxes and bin bags multiplying by his back door.

'Hmm?' Izzy replied, a little distracted as she finished breastfeeding Evie.

'This is all taking too long. I think we might need a new strategy.'

'What do you mean?'

'A more efficient way to get rid of my things. Catching the bus with a bin bag for the charity shop is going to take me a long time and I don't want to have to keep relying on you for trips to town.'

Last week Arthur had managed to take a few lighter bags to the charity shop, once with Izzy's help and once on his own. Joan was always there to greet him and have a lengthy chat about the weather, parking charges going up and rumours that a Waitrose was going to be opening in the town. None of these subjects he found particularly interesting but he nodded along and made the right noises whenever she paused to take a breath. He got the sense that she didn't have that many people to talk to either.

'I don't mind!'

'I know, and thank you. But I still feel like it's taking us too long.'

They were getting close to the halfway point.

'I know what you mean.' Izzy thought for a second. 'We could give Facebook Marketplace or eBay a go?'

Arthur looked at her blankly.

'They're online selling sites,' she explained. 'You just need to take a photo, add a description and either send whatever you've sold in the post or ask people to come here and collect it themselves.'

'But I'm not doing this to make money. I just want everything to go.'

'I guess you could give it away for free but it's a bit time consuming.' Izzy chewed her bottom lip. 'I know! You could have a yard sale? People can come and take what they want in one fell swoop. We can put up posters advertising a time and date and then I'll lay what you want gone on your front lawn with a notice for people to help themselves? Anything that doesn't go I'll ask Andrew to take it to the tip?'

Arthur thought about this suggestion for a moment. 'I think that seems like a rather sensible idea.'

'Great! I'll knock up some posters and ask Andrew to print them off at work. I'm sure he won't mind.'

Izzy walked over to the box nearest the door.

'Oh, are you getting rid of this?' Izzy asked, holding up a canvas painting that had been hanging in Arthur's hall. It was a scene of a summer meadow, the brushstrokes picking up the wisps of cloud in the pale cornflower blue sky. Colourful wildflowers were clustered in the foreground.

He glanced up. 'That? Yes, Pearl picked it up from some jumble sale, I was never so keen on it. Why?'

'I just wondered if maybe I could keep it? It reminds me of the field near where I used to live when I was a kid.'

'Of course, take it. It all has to go!'

Izzy admired the painting once more before putting it to one side. 'Thank you.'

'So, what's on the agenda for today?' Arthur asked, clapping his hands together.

'Paperwork day!' Izzy said with genuine enthusiasm. 'I've got Andrew's shredder to help us out. I'll go and grab it in a sec, it's just under Evie's pram.' Izzy glanced at the four large cardboard boxes that Arthur had been using as a sort of filing system. There were years' worth of receipts, bills, birthday cards, newspaper cuttings and correspondence to plough through. 'I guess I'll need to follow your lead.'

'I've tried to make a start but Pearl was a receptionist so paperwork was always her domain,' Arthur explained.

'OK, well for starters, I doubt you need to keep the warranty for a slow cooker you bought from Woolworths in 1996.' Izzy grinned, holding up a yellow slip of paper.

It wasn't long before Arthur got the hang of using the shredder. 'I should have done this years ago!' he chuckled to himself, watching it churn out neat ribbons.

'Have you come across anything interesting yet?' Izzy looked up from the piles of paperwork dotted around her on the lounge floor.

'No, just a lot of things that Pearl had held onto for far too long. I can't say there's anything out of the ordinary, oh… apart from a train ticket. I found it when I was sorting through her handbags,' Arthur replied. For some reason he had struggled to get this from his mind. As soon as he said it out loud he realised how silly it sounded.

'A train ticket…?' Izzy frowned.

'Yes, it might sound like nothing – and I'm sure it probably is – but well, Pearl never took the train anywhere. She had no need to. It was to Blackpool, of all places.' Arthur bumbled. Izzy was giving him a strange look. He wished he'd not mentioned it now.

'Blackpool? Hmm. Did she go on a trip with friends? A girls' break, that sort of thing?'

Arthur shook his head. 'I would have remembered that, it wasn't something she did.'

'Did she keep a diary? Maybe she wrote it down there?'

'I don't remember ever seeing her write a journal.'

'I thought you said she did a lot with the church, could it be linked to that?'

'Do you know what, I think you're right! That would make sense. She must have had one of her weekend worship groups.' He gave a satisfied nod.

'Weekend worship?' Izzy repeated.

'Yes, some of the congregation would visit another church around the country, so they could join up in praise or something,' Arthur explained. 'It was something she did alone – never my cup of tea, all those hymns and psalms and such like.'

'Well there you go. Case closed.' Izzy grinned and moved on. She began telling him about Andrew's job, she was annoyed he was working late again. Arthur tried but failed to follow the conversation. If Izzy was right and Pearl had been away with the church then he presumed they would have travelled in the church minibus. Pearl had never mentioned getting a train, it was such a rare occurrence that he was positive she would have brought it up. Something still didn't feel right. He and his wife didn't have secrets, they shared everything, they knew each other inside and out. But something about this niggled him and he wasn't exactly sure why.

CHAPTER 21

Izzy

Izzy took a deep breath and turned to the woman she didn't recognise sitting on the mat next to her. *She's just like you,* she told herself. Izzy had left her house super early to make it here on time. She had taken Arthur's advice on board and had vowed to make an effort with her and Evie's social life. Yes, he was only moving to the other side of town but perhaps he was right that it would be good for Izzy to build a relationship with someone her own age, someone in the same boat as her – if that person existed. She needed to change her mindset and make more of an effort with the mums at the baby group, if not for her then for Evie's sake, she needed baby friends to hang out with. She didn't want her daughter's development to suffer as a result of her mother's stubbornness.

'Would you like a drink? I'm just going to grab one before we start,' Izzy asked the mum, who was trying to take off her baby boy's jacket.

'Oh, er, yes please.' She smiled gratefully. 'It's my first time here. We haven't been able to get our act together before now.' She brushed her fringe from her tired eyes and shook her head.

'Babies, hey. Oh God, I've just realised I forgot to pack any baby wipes! He's managed to get it over himself and over me.' She pointed to the wet stain on her black leggings.

'Here' – Izzy handed a pack from her own changing bag – 'I've learnt the hard way to have spares, and even spares of spares on me at all times. I'm Izzy, by the way.'

'Thank you! I'm Lorna and this is Charlie,' Lorna said, wiping the mess from her thigh. 'What's your little girl's name?'

'This is Evie.'

'I'm loving her leggings, they're so cute!' Lorna scrunched her nose up at Evie.

'Thanks, it's our second outfit of the day too. Isn't it ridiculous the amount of washing someone so small can produce? Would you like tea or coffee? They have these special reusable mugs with lids so at least you can have a hot drink whilst you're winding the bobbin up.' Izzy tried not to roll her eyes.

'Coffee please. Milk, no sugar and definitely not decaf,' Lorna said with a grateful smile.

'Coming up. Are you OK to keep an eye on her?'

'Sure. Hello, Evie, look this is Charlie!' Lorna began waving a hoop with multi-coloured ribbons over both of the babies' heads, instantly mesmerising them.

Izzy got to her feet, saying a quick hello to the other mums who were slowly filing in. As she poured out two mugs of coffee, she smiled to herself. She never thought she would be the one handing out baby wipes to other mums in their time of need. Arthur would be pleased.

'Right, ladies, good morning all!' Tina, the class organiser, chimed over the chatter. 'Just a quick announcement that later on we've got a special visit from Bubble Babies who're here to tell you all about their fabulous baby swimming sessions!'

'Don't you hate it when you feel like you're being guilt-tripped into signing up to things?' Lorna turned to Izzy, gratefully taking the mug of coffee. 'The first – and last – baby group I went to I managed to leave with Charlie's name on the waiting list of an overpriced baby yoga class and three expensive decorative plates with his handprints on. It's like they prey on your tiredness to get your hand in your purse. As soon as I got home I cancelled the class but I'm still not sure what to do with the plates. They were really naff as well.'

'A present for the in-laws, perhaps?' Izzy suggested. 'My mother-in-law would love something like that.'

'Oooh. Good idea. My husband just told me I had to be firmer and say no as soon as any company approached me. But I find stuff like that so hard. I mean, part of me doesn't care if Charlie can't speak Mandarin before the age of two and another worries that I'm damaging his development if I don't sign him up!' She quickly threw a hand to her mouth. 'Oh God, don't tell me that you've signed up to do Mandarin classes!'

'Ha, no, don't be silly. I've barely found the motivation to come here, let alone anything else.'

'Phew. Have you taken Evie swimming yet?' Lorna nodded to the two women in matching royal blue polo shirts with the Bubble Babies logo printed across their chests. They were struggling to put up a pop-up banner of a baby swimming underwater, a cheesy replica of the Nirvana album cover.

'No, not yet.'

Lorna looked at least two sizes smaller than Izzy, so wouldn't have to worry about what she looked like in a cozzie,

Izzy thought. She caught herself. Remember what Arthur had said – *if your clothes don't fit then buy bigger ones* – if she put off going swimming until she lost enough weight then she'd be putting it off forever. Perhaps she shouldn't be anything other than who she was right now; a new mum who was doing her best. Maybe life was too short to stress about how she looked in Lycra.

'We've been to the local pool a few times with Charlie. They have quieter sessions on a weekday morning that are good. The baby pool is lovely and warm too.'

'Oh really? Did he like it?'

Lorna tipped her head to the side. 'I think so. I mean, he didn't cry, which is always a win, but to be honest he just seemed a little underwhelmed by the whole thing. I think we can easily make a big deal of all these firsts, you know, the first swim, the first time they clap, the first time they sleep the whole night through – well, I'm still waiting on that one. When actually it's more for us than them, the baby doesn't have a clue what's going on!'

Tina clapped for the group's attention, interrupting Izzy from replying. She welcomed the two women from Bubble Babies. They looked like hyper-active children's TV presenters in their matching T-shirts, trendy headbands and painted-on smiles.

'I bet they can see the pound signs in this captive audience,' Lorna whispered, making Izzy laugh before she was flashed a please-be-quiet look by Tina.

'Hello there! I'm Faye and this is Zara. We're here today to tell you all about our local Bubble Babies sessions that we know you and your baby will love!' She spoke with a high-pitched frenetic voice. 'You're never too young to start your splashing journey!'

'*Journey*,' Izzy mouthed, pretending to stick her fingers down her throat, making Lorna giggle.

Zara stepped forward and nodded dramatically. 'Exactly right! Babies as young as two weeks old have benefitted from taking a dip with us. They immediately feel at ease in the warm water of our specially heated pools, reminding them of the safety of the womb. In our classes we guarantee that both you and your babies can connect, develop and have fun! We offer small guided sessions with certified instructors to help you and baby get the best start in life by gaining confidence in the water. It can even help with their sleep,' she said with a knowing wink.

'Sold!' Faye called out, laughing at her own joke. 'What else do I need to know?'

'Well, I'm so excited to share with you that we have a new class starting on a Monday morning. We also are about to launch our brand-new weekly Splashing Grannies sessions, aimed at grandparents!'

'Oh Jesus. Both my mum and mother-in-law would freak if they knew about that,' Lorna whispered, rolling her eyes. 'They'd squabble over whose turn it was to get in the pool. I'd never be able to get them out of the water.'

Izzy smiled tightly. She didn't have that 'problem'.

'These sessions are a great way for grandparents to spend quality time with their grandchildren, as well as being beneficial for both young and old! Classes start at just…'

Izzy zoned out of the rest of the sales pitch. She thought back to Arthur's swimming trophy, how odd it was that even his nephew had no idea about his uncle's talents. What a waste it was that he had clearly once been so passionate about swimming but now seemed so disinterested in his achievements. Izzy politely took a Bubble Babies leaflet being passed around the circle of mums. She looked at the glamorous older model advertising the Splashing Grannies session and felt the spark of an idea.

'Well that was a bit of a cheese-fest. You going to sign up?' Lorna asked as normal chatter resumed in the group. She had already scrunched up the leaflet she was given.

'No. Well, not exactly,' Izzy replied vaguely. The over-the-top sales pitch had inspired her to do something, she just needed to see if she was able to bring it to life.

CHAPTER 22

Arthur

They had reached the halfway point. The last week had flown, in part due to Arthur discovering how much fun you could have shredding. Nothing was safe with this new toy around. Whilst he gleefully tore up a ten-year-old bill, Izzy was carefully going through the drawers in the sideboard that contained stacks of cards. She wanted to make sure there weren't any important documents that had been wedged in the hefty pile. Arthur had told her he would happily shred the whole lot but she'd insisted that they should be thorough – just in case.

'This is adorable!' Izzy held up a faded Christmas card. It was a wintery scene of an ice rink with rosy-cheeked snowmen watching on the sidelines. 'I mean, I've tried not to pry but I couldn't help but take a look at this one.'

Arthur glanced up from the reams of ribbons around him. 'Ah, you've found my card.' He chuckled. 'Pearl always acted surprised when I'd give it to her on Christmas Day morning, pretending not to know what the envelope contained.'

'Merry Christmas to my wonderful wife' was written in

wispy clouds in the inky blue sky. The years 1975, 1976, 1977 and so on until 2017 were written in biro on the back.

He shook his head, smiling at the memory. 'If anything, I was environmentally aware before my time. Any old fool can go and buy a new card but it takes effort and thought to keep the same one going for so long.'

'It's brilliant. Did you say you were married for over sixty years?'

'Yes. Sixty-two happy years.'

'What was she like? Your Pearl?'

'Where do I start?' Arthur sighed happily. 'She was just wonderful. She would do anything for anyone. She made you feel like you were the only person that mattered. I wasn't the only one who thought so either. Lots of people came up to me at her funeral telling me how special she made them feel.'

'She sounds lovely.' Izzy smiled at the card once more. 'What happened? I mean, how did she die?'

'It was like any other day really,' Arthur said. 'We'd just finished lunch and I went for a snooze on the sofa. Pearl was going to do a spot of gardening, she wanted to prune her rose bushes that she had been singing to each day hoping they would grow. I'm happy enough to do a spot of weeding or mowing the lawn, but she was the green-fingered one of us. Everything in our garden is thanks to her. Anyway, I woke from my nap and realised she was still out there. I read my paper for a bit then went outside to see if she wanted a cup of tea and that's when I saw her.' Arthur paused. 'I thought she was sunbathing at first. She was lying on the grass, her face tilted to the sun with a sort of peaceful expression. The trowel I'd bought her for her birthday was in her right hand, a smear of soil on her cheeks.' His voice wobbled ever so slightly. 'She didn't move when I called her. The closer I got I realised she wasn't sunbathing or taking a nap, she'd passed away.'

'Oh, Arthur,' Izzy's eyes widened. 'That must have been terrifying for you.'

Arthur swallowed. 'I called an ambulance but it was too late. She was here one minute then gone the next.' He clicked his fingers. 'Just like that.'

'God, I am so sorry.'

'Thank you, dear.' He cleared his throat. 'Pearl and I, we were among the lucky few. We found one other so very young. You couldn't have believed that two people could have been as happy as we were. So when she passed, it felt like I'd lost half of myself. I try to take comfort in the fact that she was surrounded by her beloved roses, at peace in the sunlight. I'm so glad that she didn't suffer. If I close my eyes she is exactly the same person as she was the day I last saw her. Of course I wish I'd had the chance to say goodbye but it wasn't to be,' he shrugged sadly. 'My last words with the love of my life was me thanking her for a delicious cheese omelette and telling her I was going to have forty winks. No profound declarations.' He tried to fix on a smile. 'Not that I ever did grand gestures of romance. In fact, if I had been about to tell her just how wonderful she was then she would probably have told me off for being uncharacteristically soppy.'

'I'm sure she knew without you telling her,' Izzy said softly. 'But, wow. Sixty-two years, what's the key to such a long happy marriage?'

'Surprises,' Arthur said after a moment. 'Well, that worked for us.'

'The surprise of getting the same Christmas card each year?' Izzy laughed.

'It would have been a surprise if she hadn't!'

Arthur gave one last long look at the card, let out a sad sigh and prepared to feed it into the mouth of the shredder.

'Wait! You can't do that!' Izzy leapt to her feet.

'What am I supposed to do with it? Everything has to go, remember?'

'No. Not this, it's too precious. I bet it could have a place in the record books or something.' She took the Christmas card from him and clutched it to her chest.

A smile lit up Arthur's face. 'Fine, just this one.'

Izzy and Evie had gone home hours ago but Arthur was still sat feeding old bills and receipts into the mouth of the shredder. In went takeaway menus, a supermarket coupon that expired three years ago, and a flyer for somewhere called Golden Sands who were having an open day back in 2016. Why on earth Pearl had kept all of this was beyond him. In it all went, making a rhythmic whirring as colourful ribbons flowed out. He sifted through the now much emptier box to see what he could shred next. There were a handful of faded postcards bunched together with an elastic band. One from Venice, another from Sydney and the others with generic palm trees on a deserted beach.

Arthur turned them over to see who had sent them. Immediately he clenched his jaw at the sight of that familiar handwriting. 'A waste of a stamp', he remembered muttering as Pearl had shown him the exotic images on one side and his brother's messy scrawl on the back. Reg had loved to show off, to rub Arthur's face in his exciting jet-set lifestyle. A lifestyle that Arthur knew was all for show and achieved in the most unscrupulous fashion. The purpose of these pointless holiday messages was not that 'he wished they were here' but to highlight how boring Arthur's life was compared to his. The white sandy beaches of Mexico or the azure waters of the Italian Riviera triumphed over Arthur and Pearl's week in Benidorm or chilly trips to the coast with a flask and a tartan blanket. Arthur could feel his blood pressure rising. It had been thirty-five years since he had last seen his brother yet he still had the ability to infuriate him. He tried to remove a paper jam from the shredder, grumbling at the sudden bad mood this had put him in.

'Come on, you stupid thing!' he shouted in frustration.

After a heavy thump with a clenched fist the shredder came back to life. He realised that he only breathed a sigh of relief once all the cards had been forced through the metal mouth and destroyed.

Arthur should have felt a sense of satisfaction now his paperwork was down to a single lever arch file, but he struggled to shift those postcards from his mind. As much as he told himself to forget them, he couldn't understand why they were still in his house in the first place. Had Pearl saved them on purpose or had she simply forgotten about them?

The 'For Sale' sign had gone up outside his house, marking him out from the other houses in the cul-de-sac. There had been two viewings already, both of which he'd made sure he was either sat with Pearl at the cemetery or on a lengthy trip to the charity shop listening to Joan give him an update on her day. He couldn't face being at home as strangers wandered through his rooms, loudly declaring the things they would do to 'put their stamp on it'.

He mentally ticked off how many days he had left – thirty and counting.

He was slowly but surely emptying his house and Izzy's yard sale was set to take place at the weekend. The contents of his loft overflowed to his landing, boxes of junk and unwanted clutter lined his hallway, but he didn't mind as he was looking forward to watching so much go in one fell swoop. Hopefully. Arthur felt like he was on track with that side of things. Only in the quiet of the night did he try and form an actual plan of action for when his time was up and he had got all his affairs in order. The countdown was fast approaching. He had been too preoccupied with packing and paperwork to think about what he was going to do about his exit strategy. The *how* part of the plan. Arthur decided he needed to do some more research into the matter. Hence, he was at the library, hoping for inspiration to strike.

As he flicked through the newspaper, his eye was drawn to a story of a young man who had recently jumped from a bridge. That seemed like a nasty way to go. This poor fella's death had been reported as suicide. That word didn't fit comfortably with Arthur. Suicide was for the very depressed, those with greater life problems than he. What he was planning to do was more 'checking out'. He was tired and he was ready to go, that's how he saw it. It felt perfectly rational to him but he knew others wouldn't see it this way, Izzy and Jeremy especially, which was why he knew he still had to keep Operation Pearl a secret.

There was another story about the rise of people addicted to painkillers in the UK. Perhaps he could overdose on sleeping pills? That had to be one of the most painless ways to go, but slipping into a silent slumber was not going to work as he didn't have access to that many tablets. It would surely ring alarm bells if he were to ask his GP to prescribe him the amount required. He wasn't sure he could buy them over the counter, not ones that would be strong enough for the job. He remembered that, back in the day, if you wanted to be done with this world then sticking your head in the oven seemed to be a popular choice. Sylvia Plath had a lot to answer for. But that wasn't for him, he doubted his knees would support him long enough for one thing.

The next page was an advert to visit Switzerland. That was where that Dignitas clinic was, he mused. He pondered for a second looking into consenting to assisted suicide, to die with dignity, but then he remembered that he hated flying and foreign food didn't agree with him. No. He wanted to be at home, his home.

Arthur glanced at the six public computers on the other side of the quiet room. Everything was on the web nowadays, there was probably a website that listed every comprehensible way of dying, perhaps that would help Arthur make his mind up. A teenage boy with messy curls tucked under a baseball hat had been sat at the screen nearest to the counter but he'd left after a librarian had told him to turn down the volume on whatever computer game he was playing. It had been hard for Arthur to concentrate on what he was here for. Thinking about ways to die whilst hearing zombies being slaughtered was quite off-putting. If only he could surf the net with headphones on and look for solutions himself, but Arthur wasn't computer literate; in fact, he was embarrassed by how little he could do on the web. It had simply passed him by, the whole technology craze. By the time Arthur realised it was clearly here to stay it had been much too late to teach this old dog any new tricks. Arthur sighed. He hoped that the perfect idea would come to him soon. In the meantime he would take out the latest Ian Rankin book he'd not read yet. Soon the television would have to go, so he would need something to fill his time.

There was a handwritten note waiting for him on the door-mat on his return from town. Arthur tore open the envelope, immediately smiling at the neat swirly writing.

'Hi Arthur, I thought we should have a break from packing and do something fun! I'll pick you up tomorrow at ten o'clock. Love, Izzy and Evie x'

He was growing rather fond of the pair of them. He was about to put the note to the side when he realised there was another line at the bottom of the paper.

'P.S. Pack your trunks and a towel!'

Swimming. They must be going swimming. His smile faltered and his mouth grew dry. The previous spark of excitement at a nice trip out somewhere was quickly replaced with a rush of jumbled memories and emotions.

He should cancel. He could quickly head over to Izzy's house and thank her but give some made-up apology of why he wasn't able to go. She would never understand the truth. He shrugged his jacket back on. As kind as her invitation was, it wasn't just a case of going for a quick dip, no, it was so much more than that for him. There was a reason he hadn't got back into the water and he was in no hurry to have to explain himself. It was easier if he made her forget the whole thing.

He patted his pockets for his house keys. He would bet money on it that this idea was because of that stupid trophy she had found. He remembered how her eyes had lit up, the surprise on her face that he had once been a swimming champion. Pfft. He shook his head. So much wasted talent all because of *him*. Arthur clenched his jaw, telling himself not to get worked up. He couldn't afford to have a setback.

Arthur glanced at the note again. Izzy certainly had changed since he'd first met her, handing over that misdelivered parcel to a woman who had the weight of the world on her shoulders. The girl who had been bringing his bins in, delivering his paper and helping pack up his house – without knowing the full story – was a world away from that hollow-eyed woman. He stalled. He didn't want to upset her. In fact, she was the reason he had been given this chance to get all his affairs in order. He shuddered to think of how things might have been, following that fateful encounter when she'd found him after his fall. Arthur was grateful to her for giving him the opportunity to say goodbye and check out on his terms. Not that she knew any of this.

He paused, one hand on the door.

Now he thought about it, perhaps he had also done some changing himself. He wasn't one for letting others in, especially not someone who was fifty years his junior. If you'd told him just six months ago he would have found a new friend in a thirty-something young mother, he would never have believed you. They had built up something of an unusual but warm friendship. He genuinely enjoyed her company and that little Evie was a delight. Since they had come into his life he felt a lot less alone. It was nice to feel needed.

'What's the worst that can happen?' He sighed deeply. It had been sixty-six years. Perhaps he should try and dip his toe back in the water. He took his jacket off and hung it up on his coat rack. As hard as this would be, he owed it to Izzy to give it a go.

CHAPTER 23

Izzy

Despite this being her idea, Izzy had been tempted to call the whole thing off. She'd had a crisis of confidence standing in front of her bedroom mirror earlier, trying on her swimming costume to check it still fit. She felt like a seal with extra blubber in the plain black maternity one-piece, all she could see was unwanted jiggly bits and ghostly white legs. It wasn't just about how she looked; she'd been nervous about the logistics too. Panicked thoughts had raced through her mind all morning as she'd packed her swimming bag, making sure to cram in two of everything just in case.

You're doing this for Arthur, she reminded herself, as she went to pick him up. The demo from the grinning Bubble Babies duo had inspired Izzy to encourage him back into the water. Clearly he had been a keen swimmer when he was younger; she wished she knew why he gave it up. She sensed there was more to the story than he had told her. Perhaps if he reconnected with the swimming pool it might give him a new lease of life.

'What did Andrew say about us coming here today?' Arthur asked as they slowly made their way across the car park.

He hadn't said much on the drive to the leisure centre. Izzy thought it was because they were heading away from their usual territory and branching out into the unknown, or maybe it was because Evie had been sick just as she'd strapped her into her car seat; the smell was quite off-putting. Whatever the reason was, she was sure that once they were in the pool it would all be fine. She hoped.

'Weren't you saving Evie's first swim for when you could go as a family?'

'I guess I realised that I was being silly putting pressure on myself that it needed to be so perfect. I'm sure he won't mind, especially if he knew that his daughter's first ever swim was with a national champion. Oh, hang on, that reminds me.' Izzy rummaged in her pocket and pulled out her mobile phone. 'I need to take a photo of this moment!' She lifted Evie from her pram and carefully passed her to Arthur. The swimming pool sign was in the background, a giant steel wave that glinted in the sunlight.

'Oh, er…' Arthur ever so gently cradled Evie and gazed down at her with a look of admiration on his face. It made Izzy's heart bloom.

'You're a natural!' She winked, taken aback by the sudden rush of emotion. 'Say cheese!'

'Izzy?' a woman called out as Arthur carefully handed Evie back.

Izzy turned to see Lorna, the fun mum from the baby class, wandering towards them. Her towel-dried hair was swept up in a messy ponytail, mascara smudged under her eyes and a bright smile on her bare face.

'Hi! So you decided to come for a dip? Inspired by that

cringe-worthy Bubble Babies demo? Oh, hello.' She smiled politely to Arthur.

'Arthur – this is Lorna, we met at a baby class recently.'

'Oh, I remember you telling me about this mother's meeting, I didn't know that you'd given it another go,' Arthur said to Izzy before turning to Lorna. 'Hello.'

'We bonded over a packet of wet wipes. You must be Evie's grandad! I bet she's the apple of your eye? She's such a gorgeous baby!'

'Oh, er,' Arthur chuckled, blush spread to his cheeks.

Izzy laughed. 'No, this is—'

'You're spot on, I am very proud. She is a little bobby dazzler.'

Izzy looked at Arthur and was about to say something when Charlie began to cry. 'Whoops,' Lorna said. 'I've totally outstayed my welcome. The boss has spoken! I'll hopefully see you next week, Izzy? Have a lovely swim.'

'Your friend seems nice,' Arthur said as Charlie's cries faded away.

'She is.' Izzy felt oddly shy about admitting making new friends in her thirties. It just felt a little sad. 'I remember now what I meant to ask you – how come Jeremy didn't know that his uncle was a champion swimmer?'

Arthur looked away. 'It's not something that has ever come up.'

'How can I help?' the receptionist interrupted, preventing Izzy from asking him any more about it.

'Two adults for swimming, please?' Izzy hoisted her large gym bag onto her shoulder. She turned to Arthur. 'Oh, wait, you'll probably get a senior citizens rate?'

'Over sixty-fives get reduced entry,' the receptionist said, without glancing up from her computer screen.

'One adult and one over sixty-five then, please?'

'Sure.' The receptionist nodded to the card reader machine. Arthur jangled the loose change in his pocket.

'I'll get this. My treat,' Izzy said, opening her purse. 'You can get the next one.' She tapped her card on the screen. 'Arthur here swam for his country. When was it? The forties?'

The receptionist raised an eyebrow in that polite but disinterested manner people did.

Arthur's cheeks grew red as both women turned to look at him. 'The fifties,' he coughed.

'Nice. Would you like to sign up to our membership whilst you're here? You get a free towel if you join today, and if you sign up for the year then your first month is free.'

'I won't be needing that,' Arthur said, before hurriedly adding. 'I mean, with moving and all.'

'Are you sure? We could join together, it might be fun. I could meet you here once a week. It would help me to get fit. I mean, you're only going to the other side of town and—'

'No. Let's see how we get on today first. Come on, we had better get a move on,' Arthur said, heading for the changing rooms.

Before long they were all ready to swim. Arthur was wearing a tight navy blue swimming cap that made his long, large ears appear even longer and larger. His green trunks were pulled up so high over his stomach that Simon Cowell would be jealous. A smattering of curly bright white hairs on his chest looked like frosting.

'I thought this was just a leisurely dip.' Izzy nodded to the goggles in his hand and a nose-piece he was clipping on. Next he'd be pulling out flippers and a snorkel.

'I thought I'd dress for the occasion. After all, Evie's first swim deserves it.'

Evie was wearing a tiny pink glittery costume that stretched over rolls of baby chub. Izzy tried to fasten the plastic key fob bracelet onto her wrist, remembering just how vulnerable public swimming made you feel. She'd put on two stone of 'baby' weight thanks to spending the whole of the pregnancy pretty much 'eating for two'. Jagged mauve stretch marks wove across her saggy stomach and her upper thighs certainly had an extra jiggle in them. They reminded her of the skin on a rice pudding. She took a deep breath. Her body had performed a miracle. You didn't push out a nine-pound human and walk away unscathed. Arthur's loud grumblings pulled her back to the present, he was trying to work out how to get the communal showers to work before they entered the pool.

'You just push that silver button.'

'Silly me.' He rotated his head under the warm jets.

'You're not nervous, are you?' she asked.

'Nervous?' he scoffed, shaking droplets off his nose. 'Don't be ridiculous. Come on. I've got a lot to be getting on with, you know. We can't dawdle here all day.'

Izzy and Arthur made their way around two yellow cones warning of wet floors. Blue, red and white bunting was strung along the rafters from a recent swimming gala. The odd stray hair lay in small puddles of water on the floor tiles. Shrieks of excited youngsters echoed off the high glass roof. A lifeguard in his late teens sat high on an aluminium framed chair observing a gaggle of giggling teenage girls in matching bikinis. The young lad had been playing with his shirtsleeves to draw attention to his flexed biceps.

Izzy desperately wanted to get into the pool and hide her body under the cover of water. She had to remind herself to take it slow across the slippery tiles for both Arthur and Evie. Eventually she gently eased her daughter into the warm water of the baby pool. There was a man and woman throwing a blue plastic ball to their young son who was diving to retrieve it.

'I think she likes it!' Arthur chuckled, watching Evie gurgle away contentedly to herself. 'Thank you for inviting me. I feel very honoured to be here with you both.'

Izzy had catastrophised that Evie would erupt into an uncontrollable meltdown the moment they stepped foot in here but Arthur was right, she was enjoying it. Izzy let out the breath she didn't realise she was holding and watched Evie's eyes light up, mesmerised by the patterns bouncing off the roof.

'Thank you for coming. Anyway we're not just here for Evie. Why don't you go and have a proper dip?' Izzy nodded her head towards the Olympic-sized swimming pool.

'Hmm. Maybe in a bit.' He began playing peekaboo behind his large hands, making Evie chuckle, the sound was like a warm hug. 'Oh, I meant to ask, do you need me to help with any preparations for the yard sale?'

'Nope. I think everything is under control. Andrew has taken some flyers into his office and I'll stick some on lampposts later this week. I've also emailed the local paper to see if they'll add it to their "what's on" section. Let's just hope it doesn't rain.'

'And that people turn up.'

'People *will* show up,' Izzy said confidently. 'Right, don't put it off any longer, you go and have a proper swim.'

Arthur rubbed his nose. 'Maybe I should stay and help you with Evie.'

'She's fine. I'm fine. Go on. We came here to see a champion in action.'

Arthur nervously glanced at the large pool where a couple of older women were doing breaststroke down one of the lanes. The furthest one was empty.

'I really don't think—'

'Go on.'

If she could get undressed and squeeze herself into unforgiving Lycra in public, then he could relive his youth. She was sure he would soon get over whatever trepidation was holding him back. Arthur paused for a moment then gave Evie a wave and carefully pulled himself up the low steps and out of the baby pool. Izzy watched as he took care crossing the damp tiles. He gently eased himself into the bright blue water. She could practically feel the sigh of relief as he slipped in. Soon he was off, propelling himself forward, barely making ripples as he glided through the water, a contented smile on his face.

Izzy felt a swell of happiness watching him effortlessly make his way up and down the empty lane. He clearly was a natural. She looked down at her daughter splashing a chubby hand in the water and chuckling at the beads of water going everywhere. This was so much better than she had ever imagined. The idea to come for a quick dip was to encourage Arthur to get back in the water, but, as she grinned at her darling baby, proud for forcing herself out of her comfort zone, she didn't know if she was doing this for her or him.

This fuzzy feeling came to an abrupt end five minutes later. Arthur's shaky voice at the side of the pool startled her. Izzy looked up to see him shivering on the edge, his face was ashen and his hands were trembling.

'Arthur! What's happened? Are you OK?'

'I'd like to go home now.' He had gone alarmingly pale.

She hurriedly hoisted Evie from the water and collected their towels from near the poolside edge. 'Arthur, are you OK? Has something happened?'

She glanced behind him to see if there had been some sort of commotion that she'd missed. The two older women were still doing breaststroke and having a natter, the bored lifeguard was slumped in his chair, and the family were still playing happily.

'No. I'm fine,' he said, without conviction. 'I'm suddenly just very tired.'

Izzy kept her eyes on him, waiting for him to expand but he stayed silent. Evie was squirming in her arms, protesting that her swim had been cut short so rapidly.

'You've gone very pale. Is it your ankle? Is it hurting you?'

'Yes… That's it.'

They began to carefully make their way to the changing rooms, watching their footing on the slippery floor.

'Do you want me to call someone? The doctor? Jeremy?'

'No, no. I'm not ill, there's honestly nothing to worry about. I've just overdone it.'

'If you're sure? How about we get you a coffee in the café and you can have a sit-down—' She didn't know what else to suggest. What had happened in the brief moment she was alone with Evie? What had brought on this sudden change in him?

Arthur shook his head. 'I'd just like to go home.'

Izzy paused. 'We can always try again another day?'

He didn't say anything.

'Arthur? I said maybe we could come back once your ankle is fully healed. You probably need to build up your strength a bit.'

'Mmm.' He hesitated. 'Yes. Maybe... I'm just going to get changed. I'll meet you outside shortly.'

Arthur headed straight to the showers without giving her another look. Izzy stood there shivering, feeling he was hiding something from her; she just didn't know what.

CHAPTER 24

Arthur

'Did I miss any customers when I was inside?' Arthur asked Izzy as he joined her in his front garden.

'Nope, we've not had anyone pop by yet. But I'm sure people will be here soon enough!' she said with a bright optimistic smile. 'Now, you promise to tell me if you get too tired or want to head in for a proper rest.'

Izzy had made sure he hadn't carried anything too heavy when they'd been setting up, even taking an empty coat stand from his hands, which he thought was a little excessive but he appreciated her concern. Thankfully, as there had been lots to do to get ready for the yard sale, his 'episode' at the swimming baths the other day hadn't been bought up by either of them. He'd lied when he'd told Izzy he needed to leave because he was tired. The truth was he'd been transported back to the summer of 1953. The day of the London Swimming Meet. The exact day he'd been hoping to never think of again. It was this memory that had almost threatened to drag Arthur under. He had spluttered and kicked his legs to the side of the pool, wanting to get out and go home immediately. The panic on Izzy's face had mirrored his own but he couldn't begin to tell her just what that innocent swimming trip had reminded him of and all he had lost. He knew he would never step foot back in there again. He'd made up the excuse that he'd overdone it but what he didn't tell Izzy was that Arthur had seen himself as a young lad, standing in line for the next race. Instantly he was back there, preparing to take his position on the diving board.

He never should have accepted Izzy's invitation in the first place, the memories brought to the surface had knocked him for six. He scolded himself for going along with her foolish plan, annoyed that she'd found the trophy, annoyed that Pearl had kept it for all these years without him knowing. He needed to keep busy, to stop himself reflecting on the past and his lost opportunities. As soon as Arthur had returned home and washed the chlorine from his skin, he'd thrown all his swimming gear in the bin. Where it belonged. *What a waste of money*, he thought.

'I'll be fine. Thank you.' Arthur had his hands on his hips surveying his front garden. 'Are Andrew and Evie coming along at some point?'

'Nope, they've gone to the park instead for some much overdue daddy and daughter time.'

'Are you certain you want to stay? I mean, if you're missing out on family time then—'

'I'm happy to have a break! Honestly, Arthur, it's about time Andrew had a taste of what I do every day, even if it's just for a few hours. I've been looking forward to today,' she grinned, 'It's nice to do something different.'

Arthur noticed that she was wearing a bit of make-up for

a change. Her usually pale cheeks had a touch of colour and her eyes looked framed by black mascara. He glanced at his watch. They both stared at the empty road. It looked very unsightly seeing everything laid out on the front lawn like this. He hoped that Pearl wouldn't mind airing their dirty laundry in public. There was less than a month until his deadline. He needed this to go well to help him reach it.

'I'm not lugging it all back inside,' Izzy said, as if reading his thoughts, wiping sweat from her forehead. 'It'll all go. There's so many bargains here.'

Arthur had planned to give everything away for free but Izzy had suggested they at least had a collection box for charity, that way people could give a small donation. Arthur had said that he'd like the church to have whatever they raised. He thought Pearl would have agreed with that. But he knew that Pearl wouldn't agree with how Arthur was deceiving Izzy. His wife had hated liars, she would be most upset to think of him using Izzy's hospitality like this, without her knowing the full story of exactly *why* everything needed to go. The closer they got to deadline day, the more the guilt crept in. Wasn't he just as bad as Reg for lying? Deep down Arthur knew that he should confess the real reason for Operation Pearl. But he honestly didn't know how to word it so she would understand. He watched as she rearranged the bric-a-brac table she'd set up, so oblivious to her part in his fictional plan, and told himself to be brave.

Arthur cleared his throat. He took a deep breath. 'Izzy love, before we start—'

'What's going on?' their balding neighbour from number forty-one called out from his driveway, immediately interrupting Arthur.

'Arthur's having a clear-out,' Izzy explained, relieved to have someone show some interest. 'If there's anything you fancy, please feel free to take it away!'

Arthur promised himself that he would try and speak to Izzy another time, this clearly wasn't the right moment. The man wandered over to have a look at the assortment of household items currently sunbathing on Arthur's front lawn. He put his hand out for Izzy to shake. 'I don't think we've met, I'm Gary, by the way.'

'Hi, nice to meet you. I'm Izzy from number forty-five and this is Arthur.'

Gary nodded hello to Arthur. 'What's the point of all this? Ahead of the big move is it?' he shouted, gesturing at the For Sale sign. Arthur noted that Gary didn't raise his voice quite so unnecessarily when speaking to Izzy.

'You don't have to shout, I can hear perfectly well.' Arthur couldn't warm to the man who chose such obnoxious Christmas lights.

Gary ignored this and picked up Arthur's garden spade, giving it a once-over. 'How much do you want for this? I'm after some new tools. Lisa, that's my missus, she's been going on at me to sort our garden out for ages.'

'It's all free but we're collecting donations for St Augustine's church.'

'Nice one.' Gary nodded, fishing in his pocket for some loose change. 'Where are you moving to, by the way? Anywhere nice?'

'RoseWood Lodge.'

'Ah. My old man was looking to go there but he passed away before we could reserve him a spot.'

'Lucky bugger,' Arthur mumbled under his breath.

'You sure you don't need any of this stuff for your new place?'

'No, it's all got to go.'

Gary gave Arthur a funny look. 'All of it? When I went to have a look around with my dad we were given a list of stuff he could bring with him.'

'Oh?' Izzy glanced at Arthur. 'Have you got a list?'

'Erm, well…'

'How much you want for this, love?' a woman with an unflattering eighties-style haircut shouted. She was waving one of Pearl's vases in the air, trying to catch Arthur's attention. Since talking with Gary four different cars had pulled up alongside the kerb. Books, lamps and one of the rugs that had been in the spare room were all being picked up by total strangers.

'It's all free!' Arthur called from his perch, relieved at the distraction. Gary had wandered away with his spade. Arthur knew that Izzy would mention this list later, he'd need to lie and tell her his room at RoseWood Lodge was fully furnished or something. Yet another lie to keep track of, not an easy task with his memory, he thought glumly.

'What? It's all free?'

Arthur nodded.

'All of it?' the lady repeated.

Perhaps they should have made a large sign.

'But donations are welcome!' Izzy called, rattling a washed-out baked beans tin in the lady's face. 'We're raising cash for St Augustine's church.'

'Free?' Another man asked. 'Barb, you hear that? We can

just take what we like. Quick – grab that food blender. My mum will have that.' He turned to Arthur. 'Does it work? Do you know if it's been PAT tested?'

Arthur blinked. He had no idea when it had last been used, it wasn't like this guy was going to come back demanding a refund. Arthur wouldn't be here to deal with it if he did.

'Yes, all in good working order.' He crossed his fingers.

'What about this?' A DVD player was being brandished in the air by a man with long sideburns.

'Everything electrical works. It's all free and has to go!'

To his astonishment even more things started to get picked up off his lawn. Other cars were arriving and soon there was a slight traffic jam as people wanted to make their way into the cul-de-sac to see what was going on. For a minute or two he worried he'd have to break up a fight between a stocky man in a football shirt and a woman wearing a tight tracksuit who were arguing over who had their hand on his silver bread bin first.

'See! I told you this was a good idea!' Izzy beamed at Arthur as she shook her money tin in another customer's face. The football fan conceded defeat and picked up the coat stand instead.

Izzy was right. Things were going quicker than Arthur had imagined. This was, dare he say it, actually quite fun. The large pile of Pearl's sewing patterns went to a girl with a nose piercing, wearing a denim jacket covered in pin-badges. He imagined her pulling out the paper patterns and crafting something herself. He liked this idea immensely.

'I didn't know you were planning this!' A familiar voice caught his attention. It was Mrs Peterson out walking her three dogs. 'What a good idea. Although, you should have said! I could have called on the whole street to get involved. No doubt everyone has unwanted clutter they could have donated.'

'Thank you but I think we have enough.' He needed to get rid of his own things, not take on someone else's.

Mrs Peterson perused the bric-a-brac table. 'I haven't had a good clear-out since Pete left. There's all sorts of things stuffed in my loft and garage that could go to a good home. Oh this is lovely!'

Arthur was struggling to keep up with what Mrs Peterson was saying, wittering about a ceramic ornament she'd picked up. Gary's family had returned home, his wife and two daughters had walked over to see what was going on. The older girl looked familiar. Arthur tried to peer past Mrs Peterson's larger frame to get a better glimpse of her. The girl caught Arthur's eye, said something to her father and ran back to her house. *How very strange,* Arthur thought.

'Are you there, love?' Mrs Peterson asked, waving a hand in front of Arthur's eyes. 'Wherever you went then, I'd love to join you!' She laughed heartily.

'Sorry.' Arthur shook his head. His brain was whirring, he knew that girl from somewhere.

'I know I'm meant to be de-cluttering but I'll take this please?' Mrs Peterson waved the ceramic figure around.

'Fine, fine, take it.' *No, it couldn't have been?*

'Oh, no! Stop that!' She chided one of her dogs who was having a poo on the grass, close to a stack of *Reader's Digest*. 'Have you got a bag I can use to clear it up?'

This brought Arthur back to the present. As he grudgingly

handed over a plastic bag, grumbling that was five pence to scoop up some dog poo, all thoughts of the young neighbour vanished from his mind.

The next few hours passed by in a blur. So much had gone Arthur could see his lawn again. This had certainly saved them weeks of trips to and from the charity shop.

'Wow. Well that went better than I expected,' Izzy said, handing him a bottle of water. 'Andrew will be pleased. I think he was worried that he'd come home and our house would be full of your things!' She laughed. 'I've hung that painting you gave me up in my kitchen. Oh, that reminds me, did you know that it was done by a prisoner?'

'Pardon?'

'The wildflowers painting, the one that I think you had in your hall. It has a stamp on the back from Moorfield prison,' Izzy said, taking a gulp then putting the lid back on the bottle.

Arthur was grateful he was sitting down.

'Erm, I had no idea.' He tried to calm his quickening heart. He never expected to hear the name of that place again. 'Pearl picked it up from a jumble sale a few years ago.'

This had to be a huge coincidence, surely?

Izzy looked as if she was about to say something but was cut off by the sound of a car pulling up. 'Oh, here's another punter! Let's hope they pick up the last few things.' She stood to attention. 'Are you sure you're OK?' She frowned. 'You've gone a little pale.'

'Have I?' Arthur clasped a hand to his cheeks.

'Why don't you go inside and rest for a bit? I can manage on my own. I'll call you if I need some help?'

Arthur nodded. He took this opportunity to make his way inside; she was right, he needed five minutes to collect his thoughts. He couldn't fathom what was happening. But he suddenly felt like his past wasn't done with him yet.

CHAPTER 25

Izzy

Izzy scurried around picking up the toys strewn around the floor, moved a couple of dirty glasses and plumped up the cushions on her sofa. She was spending so much time at Arthur's nowadays she couldn't understand how her own home still got so messy at the end of every day and why it was always her that was expected to keep on top of it. There was certainly an unspoken gender divide over the chores. She promised herself that she would have a chat with Andrew at some point about him squeezing into a pair of Marigolds but right now she was too busy to risk a row erupting. It was bad enough that she barely saw him; she didn't want to spend the time they did have together arguing, especially not tonight.

'Wow, you look nice!' Andrew whistled as he walked in, loosening his tie and dumping his work bag on the floor where she had just tidied. 'Everything set for our special guest?'

'Almost.'

Her first reaction was to snap at him for being late, again, on the one night when they actually had plans. She really could have done with him being home on time. It was hard enough doing the bedtime routine on her own, let alone try and get everything ready for dinner at the same time. She'd had to wrestle Evie to get her in the bath, she'd screamed having her hair washed and whined when Izzy had put her in her cot. That was before she'd got herself changed and swiftly applied a touch of make-up to her tired face. Thankfully the flowers Andrew had sent her earlier softened her from going nuclear. She had been so touched when the doorbell rang this morning with a florist delivering an enormous bunch of spring flowers.

To say thank you. I don't tell you enough how much I appreciate all you have done, A.

She'd put them into a vase, her spirits lifted by how thoughtful he could be. All her nagging and muttering under her breath must be going in somewhere. She would have to ask him later what had prompted this out-of-character romantic gesture.

'Should I be jealous that you're going to all this effort for another man?' Andrew laughed, trying to nuzzle her neck and wrap an arm around her waist.

Izzy's smart black and gold top was a little tighter around her stomach than she would have liked and she was still in her maternity jeans, but she'd wanted to make an effort for herself, she wanted to feel more like the old Izzy. She had pinned her hair back into a neat low bun, dabbed on her favourite perfume and even applied some lipstick. Arthur was used to seeing her at her worst but she felt like tonight was an excuse to do something different and something special. It had been a long time coming that the two men in her life got to properly meet for the first time.

'Stop it,' Izzy batted his roaming hands away. 'He'll be here any minute, so hurry and get changed.'

Andrew tried his luck one more time.

'Go!' She playfully whacked him on the arm with *The Very Hungry Caterpillar* book she'd picked up off the floor.

'I'm going!' he laughed.

Izzy had just finished lighting the tealights in the centre of the dining table when she heard a tentative knock at the front door.

'Arthur! Please, come in.'

He slowly stepped inside. 'I didn't want to wake Evie by ringing the bell.'

He was head to toe in his trademark biscuit-brown shades, wearing a smart, slightly creased, chocolate-coloured shirt under his coat. His thin white hair had been neatly combed to one side and he smelt of honest, clean soap. He looked lovely.

'The nice chap at the off licence recommended this,' he said, handing over a bottle of red wine.

'Thank you! You didn't need to bring a gift, that's very thoughtful of you. Come on in. I hope you're hungry?'

Izzy whirled around him, offering him a drink, taking his jacket and telling him to sit down and make himself comfortable.

'Red or white? Or beer? Or a soft drink? Sorry! That was presumptuous of me! I've got some squash or orange juice if you'd like?'

'A glass of whatever wine you've got open would be fine, thank you.'

'Arthur! The famous Arthur!' Andrew walked in with his

hand outstretched. 'Great to properly meet you. I feel like I already know you, thanks to the amount that Izzy goes on about you. Any other husband would be jealous!' He winked.

'Shush. Don't listen to him, Arthur.' Izzy handed Arthur a glass.

Arthur smiled bashfully. 'Well, thank you for having me. It's very kind of you to invite me for dinner.'

'You're welcome.'

'Little Evie in bed, is she?' Arthur looked around hopefully.

'Yes! And I'm hoping she stays that way.' Izzy had everything crossed that Evie would behave, she didn't want her to wake and interrupt this rare adult-only time. 'If you'll excuse me, I just need to make sure it's not going to burn.'

Izzy left the two men to it and hurried to the kitchen, closing the door behind her in case she set off the smoke alarm. As she dished up she felt this strange sense of calm wash over her, she suddenly felt like herself again. She used to love having people over. Here she was cooking dinner, no, *hosting a dinner party*, dressed up and looking forward to some actual adult conversation. Usually she'd be slumped in her pyjamas on the sofa, dribbling onto a cushion, fighting to stay awake long enough to make it through a whole episode of *EastEnders*. She felt rather proud of herself. She couldn't have imagined doing this even just a few weeks ago. Yes, she would pay for this late night tomorrow but for the first time in a long time she felt like the old Izzy.

'Right, come and take a seat!' she called to the two men, as she waltzed through to the dining room with a plate in each hand.

'It smells good – oh,' Andrew frowned as Izzy set his plate down. 'What are we having?'

'It's liver.'

'Liver?' Andrew echoed.

'Yeah, I heard that it was full of iron, good for tiredness apparently.' Izzy smiled at Arthur, who gave her a wink. 'It's also a superfood.' She looked down at her own plate. She had to admit that, whilst it looked like the online recipe, it still wasn't the most appetising of dishes. Two fat slabs of pale meat covered in slightly burnt onions, sat next to a mound of stodgy yellow mashed potato.

'Ah! This takes me back. This was one of my mother's favourite dishes to cook. I've not had it for years.'

'I hope it tastes OK. *Bon appétit!*'

There was silence as they all picked up their cutlery and tried to cut through the meat. It was ridiculously tough.

'Mmm. Delicious,' Andrew said, finally swallowing a mouthful. 'So have you got up to much today, Arthur?'

'Oh well, the usual really. I went to the cemetery for a short while this morning. I like to pop in to sit with Pearl when I can, and then I've been sorting out things at home this afternoon. Since our very successful yard sale it's been a lot easier seeing what's left to go through.'

He was right, the sale last weekend went so much better than they could have hoped for. Once his front lawn was back to its normal state, Izzy had emptied her baked beans tins in Arthur's lounge and counted the coins. The total amount they had raised for the church came to almost £250, incredible considering Arthur had been prepared to give it all away for free. She had invited him to come for dinner to celebrate.

'I can't imagine what we'd have done if it had been

a washout!' Izzy smiled. 'Is that why you chose St Augustine's? Is that where Pearl is buried?'

'Yes. Speaking of which, I must take the donations over at some point soon.' He tapped the side of his wrinkled temple. 'How about you both? Have you had a nice day?'

'Well I had a lovely surprise earlier when I opened the door to this enormous bouquet.' Izzy pointed to the flowers artfully arranged in a vase on the side table. 'Andrew can be quite the romantic when he wants to be.'

Andrew coughed loudly. 'Sorry. A piece just went down the wrong way.'

'He must have taken a leaf out of your book, Arthur, with this kind surprise.'

'They're lovely,' Arthur said politely.

'Arthur was telling me about how the key to a successful marriage lies in surprises,' Izzy explained to Andrew, who hungrily finished his glass of tap water. He kept his eyes on the jug as he replenished his glass.

'I'm… er… glad you like them,' Andrew said. 'So tell me a bit about yourself, Arthur. Have you always lived around here?'

'Yes. For most of my life actually. I was born on Victoria Street and haven't ever left the area. There was talk at one point of emigrating to Australia with Pearl when every man and his wife signed up to be Ten Pound Poms, but I could never leave my mother on her own. It was never something we spoke of again, even after she passed away.'

'Did you not travel during the war?'

'I was only a lad then. I was four when war broke out.'

'Oh, sorry.'

'I was evacuated and sent to live with a family near Torquay, so I suppose that's the only other place I've lived. I was there for eighteen months in total.'

'On your own?'

'No, with my brother, Reg.'

Izzy remembered the photo of the suave man in the Christmas jumper. She still couldn't believe that Arthur had a brother out there but knew nothing about him. What must have happened to have caused such a rift between the two of them? She was curious and promised to try and bring it up with Arthur when the moment was right.

'I can't imagine how your mum was able to send her two babies off.' Izzy shivered at the thought of being parted from Evie for such a long time.

'Two boisterous boys, more like,' Arthur corrected her. 'And yes, it was unbelievably tough but it was for the best to keep us all safe. I don't ever remember being scared, in fact, some of my happiest memories were from that place.'

'Does Reg live nearby?' Andrew asked. Izzy spotted a fleeting look on Arthur's face. She hadn't told Andrew about Arthur's estranged brother.

'I'm not sure where he is. We lost touch.' He took a large gulp of wine. 'Jeremy is the only family I have left.'

'Ah. The one who drives a Skoda?'

Arthur nodded.

'I was thinking of getting one of them when I next trade mine in. They seem decent.'

'Jeremy is the one to ask about all of that. He knows an awful lot about cars. And cricket.'

'Well tell him to head over here the next time he visits you.

You've lived over the road for a long time haven't you? Izzy said it was something like fifty years or so?' Andrew asked, putting down his fork. 'I bet it'll be hard to leave?'

'Sixty-two years.' Arthur thought about this for a second before answering. 'My time has come.'

'Well I think you're dealing with it really well, Arthur,' Izzy said, proudly. 'It's a big change but you're certainly approaching it in the right way.'

Arthur gave a simple smile then looked down at his plate. They all picked up their cutlery and carried on eating.

The meat was tough, the vegetables too soft and the mashed potato too lumpy but Arthur finished every single scrap on his plate, which was more than could be said for Izzy and Andrew.

'Anyone fancy dessert?' Izzy asked, collecting the plates.

There was a moment of hesitation.

'It's apple pie, shop bought,' Izzy added, getting to her feet.

'Lovely!' both men replied in unison.

'That went well. He seems like a nice guy,' Andrew said as he waved Arthur off. Izzy was sure she saw him wobble a little as he walked over to his front door. Andrew had introduced him to his favourite apple brandy as a nightcap. It was strong stuff. She kept her eye on him through the window to make sure he got in safely.

'He really is. That's why I want to do something nice for him.'

'Like pack his house for him...'

'I know I'm doing that but I feel like I should still do something more.' Izzy took a deep breath and prepared to share what had been running through her mind. 'I think I'd like to try and find his long-lost brother, Reg. I mean, I don't really know how to go about it – not without enlisting the help of Davina McCall and her *Long Lost Family* programme. But in this day and age it shouldn't be too difficult to track someone down on your own? Surely?'

'Has Arthur ever said that he *wants* to find his brother?'

'Well, no. Not in so many words. I just think it's desperately sad that he's got a brother out there, someone who has played such a key part in his life, but, for whatever reason, they now don't have any sort of relationship.'

'I guess, but all families are complicated, Iz. He might not want you to find him. There must be a reason they're not in touch.'

Izzy wafted a hand in the air. 'Perhaps they just lost contact, people move and change phone numbers. It could easily happen.' She ignored the look Andrew was giving her. She knew herself how optimistic this sounded but it wasn't totally unthinkable. 'The first part of the plan is to track Reg down then, once I know where he is, I'll go from there.'

'Let's pretend you're right,' Andrew said slowly as he poured himself a final glass of Calvados. 'Where do we begin? I guess social media is the best place to start?'

'I've already done that,' Izzy admitted. She'd searched online the first time Arthur had mentioned his brother, curiosity getting the better of her, but then she'd forgotten all about it until this evening. 'I've not found anything.'

'OK. So what *do* you know about this mysterious man? Where does he live? How old is he? Is he married?'

'I don't know,' Izzy groaned.

'Well why don't you just ask Arthur?'

'Because then it won't be a surprise!'

Andrew sighed and ran a hand through his hair. He was looking a bit squiffy. She liked seeing him relax like this. 'Is there anyone else you could ask, apart from Arthur, who might be able to help?'

'I don't have Jeremy's details,' Izzy said. 'I don't think Arthur's ever mentioned anyone else that I could ask...'

There was a moment of silence. Suddenly something came back to her.

'Apart from Reg's ex-wife!' Izzy sat up. 'Why didn't I think of that before.'

She picked up her phone and went straight to Google. It was a long shot, especially as neither Reg nor Arthur had any presence on social media, but it was still a possibility.

'I've just remembered Arthur telling me that Reg had been married a few times. One wife that he mentioned was called Winnie Winter. There can't be too many of them, so that could be a start!'

'Winnie Winter?' Andrew laughed. 'Genius.'

Three names popped up on Facebook. The first Winnie Winter was a nurse in her late forties from Kampala, Uganda. Izzy tapped on the second name. A twenty-something student with rave-style face paint. One last chance. Izzy crossed everything and clicked on the final Winnie Winter. The photo was of a West Highland white terrier running across a lush green field. Could this be her? There was no more information on her age, location or interests other than the button to add as a friend or send her a message.

'Go on, message her,' Andrew encouraged from over her shoulder, his breath smelling of apples.

Izzy's fingers flew across the keyboard. She asked Winnie if she knew a man named Reg Winter.

'It's worth a try,' Izzy said, crossing everything. Arthur had said all along how he wanted to tie up any loose ends before his move, and deep down she had a feeling that never speaking to his brother again would be something he would regret.

CHAPTER 26

Arthur

Arthur was stood on his doorstep waiting for Jeremy. The fresh air was a welcome relief to soothe his slightly fuggy head. He wouldn't say he was hungover exactly, but he wasn't as sharp as he usually felt either. Much to his surprise he had really enjoyed himself last night. He was glad he had accepted Izzy's kind invitation, especially as he'd been in two minds about going. He still felt so guilty hiding the truth about Operation Pearl from her. Every time he tried to come clean it was never the right moment. He really didn't want to hurt anyone with what he was planning on doing, least of all Izzy. He feared that, by spending more and more time with her, when the truth presented itself she would be furious he hadn't confessed earlier. However, if he declined going for dinner then she would only ask more questions. The easiest thing, he decided, was to accept her kind invitation and continue keeping up appearances.

In all his time of living on Birch Tree Way, Arthur had never been inside another house on the cul-de-sac. Izzy's front room was the exact same dimensions as his but it felt a lot cosier.

Perhaps it was the pile of plastic baby-related paraphernalia in the corner, or the many large fluffed-up cushions on the sofa, or the potted plants and candles dotted around that made it look so inviting.

At first Arthur had been a little surprised that Izzy hadn't mentioned the bouquet he'd sent as a thank you for her help with the yard sale. But perhaps he hadn't been clear enough on the note, as Andrew had taken all the credit. Not that Arthur blamed him. A happy wife meant a happy life, after all. Actually, the more Arthur thought about it, it was probably an unexpected coincidence that may improve their relationship. He was used to Izzy muttering under her breath about her husband's downsides so it was lovely to see her looking so genuinely touched that he had been thoughtful for a change. Arthur didn't want to upset her by revealing the truth.

Yes, it was a very pleasant evening, Arthur thought. Pearl would never have believed that he was the one holding his own at social functions without her; he couldn't believe it himself, it really was quite something. He glanced at his watch. Jeremy would be here in ten minutes, he was driving him into town to sign some papers or something, Arthur hadn't paid much attention when he'd called him earlier. He figured he was best to continue to do and say as he was told. Arthur's only request was that they stop at St Augustine's church as he wanted to pass on the donations from his yard sale to the vicar. He had made Izzy do a recount after she'd told him how much they'd raised. The verified total had given him a nice warm feeling that had taken him aback. Arthur checked his watch once more, he had just enough time to run a quick errand. There was something he wanted to do.

'Hi! It's Arthur, right?' Gary checked. It was the first time his elderly neighbour had been stood at his doorstep so his look of surprise was somewhat justified.

'Yes… er…'

'Gary!' Gary filled in the blanks that Arthur was on the tip of remembering, jabbing a thumb to his chest.

'Gary, yes. Sorry to bother you but I wondered if your eldest daughter might be interested in this?' Arthur stepped back to reveal a carrier bag at his feet. Inside was a large box of acrylic paints, two unused canvases and a pack of paintbrushes. Pearl had gone through a phase thinking she would become the next Picasso but soon got bored, complaining that it was easier to paint her nails than the jug of sunflowers she'd carefully positioned on their dining room table. 'I found them after the yard sale, we must have forgotten to put them outside.'

'Oh right, lovely. Let me get her for you, she's probably messing about on her phone upstairs. Nikki!' Gary turned and bellowed up the stairs.

'WHAT?' the young girl shouted back a few seconds later.

'Come here, please.' Gary rolled his eyes. 'She's always locked away in that room glued to her phone. I swear that thing is fused to her skin.'

Arthur was cut off from replying by the thundering of clumpy boots pounding down the stairs. She was dressed entirely in black.

'What—' Nikki stopped as she saw Arthur.

'Hello,' Arthur said politely, noticing that all her swagger puddled out at seeing him.

She knew who he was and he, in turn, had finally figured out why the young girl had looked so familiar. She'd been with that group of kids graffitiing in the alleyway that evening.

'Arthur here has come round to see if you want these paint... things.' Gary said, turning the large box over in his hands, whistling in the way that people do when they're faced with something that looks expensive. He was oblivious to the atmosphere between Nikki and Arthur.

'I noticed that you have a budding interest in the art world. So I thought you might be able to make use of these?' Arthur coughed. 'Or you could share them with your friends... perhaps they might be able to make more use out of them?'

Nikki shot her eyes to the carpet, refusing to meet Arthur's knowing smile. Her cheeks flushed deep crimson. Her phone was grasped tightly in her right hand, buried between chipped black nail varnish and stacks of silver rings.

Gary looked between the pair of them, lost in confusion.

'I've seen her walk past carrying a large art portfolio bag for school,' Arthur clarified quickly.

'Oh. I must say she's never shown us any of her work. What do you say, Nik Nak?'

Nikki mumbled something under her breath, still refusing to make eye contact with Arthur.

'You can do better than that. It's really kind of Arthur to bring this over for you.'

Nikki looked as if she wanted the ground to swallow her up. She tilted her face, finally meeting Arthur's eyes. 'Thank you.' Her voice was so small.

'You're welcome. Do you think your friends would be able to make some use out of them?'

Gary let out a chortle of laughter. 'Arthur, you clearly haven't seen the types that Nikki hangs around with. I doubt they're particularly creative.'

'Oh, I don't know about that. I'm sure every child has hidden depths and talents. It just takes the right person to bring this out of them, isn't that right, Nikki?'

Nikki gave a half shrug with her bunched-up shoulders, her eyes trained at her feet.

'Sorry, Arthur, forgive me! I should have invited you in, instead of leaving you hanging on the doorstep!'

Arthur paused for a moment. He could see Nikki bristling at the thought of him coming in and telling her dad exactly what her and her friends had been up to.

'No, no thank you,' he said after a moment's pause. 'I'd best be off, lots to be getting on with.'

Nikki mumbled something under her breath, glancing at her phone screen that had lit up.

'What was that?' Gary asked her.

'I said – can I go now?'

Gary rolled his eyes and flashed a what-are-you-like-smile, which Nikki took as her cue to bolt back up the stairs, taking the steps two at a time.

'This is really kind of you and I'm sure she's grateful, even if she didn't show it.'

'Oh, I'm sure she is,' Arthur smiled innocently. A car horn beeped. Jeremy was waving from his car window. Arthur could hear the radio playing from a few yards away. 'Take care now.'

'Yeah, you too.'

Arthur plodded over to his drive just as Jeremy pulled up.

'Hello! All ready to go?'

'As ready as I'll ever be.' Arthur carefully got in the passenger side.

'You know, Arthur, you're taking this move much better

than I expected. I mean, I know it will be a big change for you, but you're coping with this upheaval really well. I guess I just want to say thanks and, well, I hope you now appreciate why it's necessary,' Jeremy said, eventually turning down the radio as they joined the main road. 'I think once you've unpacked and got settled you're going to have a really lovely time!' Without realising it he was doing that irritating thing when he raised his tone at the end of each sentence, as if talking to a child.

'Hmm.' Arthur looked out of the window.

'So the estate agent called me earlier. They've already had two offers, which is fantastic news.'

'Oh, right.'

'I knew your place would get snapped up quickly.'

Arthur cleared his throat. 'So what were the offers?'

'One from a couple, around my age, who are chain free with a large deposit. They've offered the asking price.'

'And the other?'

'A couple who've got a young toddler and a baby on the way. So on the plus side they're looking to move fast although they are in a chain. They've offered three grand less than the asking price.'

Instantly Arthur thought of Izzy with baby Evie. It would be wonderful for the children to grow up together and for Izzy to have someone like her as a neighbour. It would mean new life to the cul-de-sac.

'Sell it to them.'

'But—'

'I want the young family to have it.'

It was Arthur's house and Arthur's money. His decision was final.

'If you insist.' Jeremy paused. 'You do know that, regardless, we'll still be on for the date you insisted – the twenty-sixth of April – to move you into RoseWood? That's three weeks tomorrow. This doesn't change that.'

'I understand.'

'Great. Well, I'll call them back and let them know your decision.'

Arthur looked out of the window, suddenly feeling a little funny. *This is it, Pearl.* He raised his eyes heavenward. The house was going to be sold and it was all becoming very real.

Five days later and Arthur had decided that enough was enough. Today was going to be the day he came clean to Izzy, if only he could pluck up the courage. There just hadn't been the ideal moment since her and Evie had arrived earlier this afternoon. Right now she was wrestling with his heavy bookcase in the lounge, quickly growing frustrated at the fact it was taking all her might to wiggle it away from the wall.

'Are you sure this needs to go? Can't the new owners inherit it? I mean, it weighs an absolute ton,' she wheezed.

'I doubt it's to the buyer's tastes. Plus, Joan mentioned she was after larger items of furniture for the shop, the last time I was there and…'

'Oh, did she?' Izzy raised an eyebrow. 'Or is it just a ploy to see you again?'

Arthur shook his head at such a silly suggestion. 'Let me give you a hand with it.'

'I think you'll do your back in. Seriously, what's inside this wood? I thought once all the books were gone it would be much lighter.'

'It belonged to Pearl's parents. It must be almost two hundred years old. They made things to last in those days.'

'You're not kidding. This could survive a nuclear war,' Izzy wiped sweat off her forehead. 'How did you even get it in here in the first place?'

'With difficulty.' That wasn't entirely true, back when they'd moved in he'd barely noticed the bookcase being so cumbersome. It hadn't moved from this spot for over sixty-two years. Ornate decorative designs were carved into the top beam. Arthur ran a palm across the dark mahogany grain. The metal platelets that held the chunky panels of wood in place had rusted a little. It was never to his taste but as a family heirloom he couldn't say anything in case it offended Pearl.

'Remember to bend at the knees,' Izzy ordered. But even with both of their strength it refused to move.

'Try again?'

A puff of air and reddened cheeks, this time they managed to shift it a few inches.

'It's too heavy for us to get any further with it,' Izzy spluttered. 'I don't want either of us to do ourselves an injury. Maybe we should leave this for Jeremy and the removal men?'

Arthur agreed. 'Good idea, I'll go and put the kettle on, shall I?'

'Oh yes please. Evie should be getting up from her nap soon so I need to make the most of it!'

Arthur plodded to the kitchen and boiled the kettle. He had grown used to the space in here, the clean lines of the work surfaces and the lack of haphazard piles of crockery filling his cupboards. Only having one of everything – and two mugs – suited him fine. He should have tried this minimalist living thing sooner. He had been so scared to erase any part of Pearl from the house he hadn't realised just how long he had put up with all the meaningless clutter. He had become stuck in a rut, when actually, tidying up had been unexpectedly refreshing.

'I didn't know if you fancied a biscuit?' Arthur walked back in with a mug in each hand, preparing to tell Izzy about the young family buying his house. 'I think we deserve one after trying to move that thing.'

He froze. Izzy was on her knees, scrabbling a hand in the small gap they'd created behind the bookcase.

'Arthur?' She leapt to her feet to take the steaming drinks from his trembling hands. 'Arthur, are you OK? Here, sit down.' She carefully walked him over to his armchair. 'What is it?'

'Wh-wh-where did you find that?' He couldn't take his eyes off what she had unearthed and placed on the top of the bookcase. Lying next to a paperclip, a frayed red leather bookmark and a small bit of plastic, was a gold bracelet.

'Here, have a sip of your tea.'

He stared at the simple chain. It was unbelievable to see it after all these years.

'I'm guessing there's some story behind this?'

Arthur nodded. He had never expected to see it again. 'This changes a lot of things.'

'What do you mean?'

Thankfully his heart had stopped hammering so violently in his chest to allow him to put words together to explain.

'That bracelet was the last thing Reg and I argued about. Our last conversation in fact.' He felt hot and sick and overwhelmed with a sudden rush of exhaustion all at the same time.

'Why?' Izzy pressed, her voice soft but focused. 'What happened?'

Arthur had been purposely vague about his brother with Izzy. It wasn't a topic he liked to dwell on particularly. But now the truth was staring them in the face, he needed to be a little clearer about what had gone on. He sighed deeply.

'It was the day of my mother's funeral, thirty-five years ago. We held the wake here. Pearl had been fussing about for days before making sure she had enough sandwiches, pots of overly brewed tea and homemade cakes neatly laid out. She had been baking non-stop since we lost my mum. I don't know why, it wasn't like we were expecting hundreds to turn up and eat all of this food she'd prepared but I guess that was her way of coping with things.

'She had also been putting vases of freshly cut flowers from the garden out everywhere to lift the mood or something.' Arthur shook his head. 'It was a wake, I'm not sure how cheerful some bunches of gladioli made things.'

Izzy's small smile boosted him on.

'It was the first time Reg had visited our house. For reasons I won't go into, our relationship was already somewhat strained. We barely shared three words at the funeral but Pearl invited him back along with a handful of other guests who knew my mother. And to give him his due, I remember him being polite enough.'

Instantly Arthur was taken back to that day.

'Can I give you a hand with anything, Pearl?' Reg asked, tugging at the too-tight shirt collar. Arthur was grateful he had at least covered the many tattoos that snaked up his arms.

'No, I'm fine thank you, Reg. You just sit down and make sure you have something to eat,' Pearl said kindly.

Soon the last mourner left, with a slice of cake wrapped in silver foil that Pearl had insisted they take. It was only Arthur, Reg and Pearl remaining.

'Well that went well,' Pearl said, clapping her hands together, breaking the awkward silence. 'Anyone for another cup of tea?'

Arthur knew she was just trying to say something to break the tension. He had been polite to Reg but now he wanted him gone so he could change out of his sombre suit and be alone with his thoughts. It had been a long, tough day.

'No thank you. I'm sure Reg has somewhere to be getting to.'

'Oh, er, yes. Thanks though…' Reg mercifully took the hint. He got to his feet and said a stilted farewell.

'I do wish you two would sort it out. Your mother wouldn't want you to bicker anymore,' Pearl said with a heavy sigh, watching Reg leave.

'When he apologises then we can think about it,' Arthur muttered, too exhausted for another lecture.

'You haven't seen my bracelet, have you?' Pearl asked the following day, wringing her hand over her bare wrist. 'I'm certain I had it on yesterday.'

'We searched the house high and low looking for this thing but it never showed up. The only explanation was one that was staring us in the face. Reg must have taken it.'

'Did you ask him about it?'

'Of course I did! I hit the roof. I'm not proud of the telephone conversation we had. He denied it all completely, saying he wouldn't betray our hospitality, that he'd changed. But clearly, the man was not to be trusted. I finally had proof for Pearl to see that, despite her best efforts, our relationship was irretrievably broken beyond repair. Once a crook, always a crook. The stolen bracelet was the last straw. I knew then that my brother would never change. Even Pearl, who had always been a lot more soft-hearted, insisting that everyone makes mistakes, couldn't argue with the truth. She never mentioned him again.'

'But... he didn't take it.' Izzy ran the thin chain between her thumb and forefinger.

'Clearly not. It must have fallen off Pearl's wrist and behind the bookcase when she was putting the vase of flowers there.' Arthur swallowed. 'Reg was telling the truth.'

The painful words hung in the air.

'I must have missed something, I don't get why you jumped to the conclusion that he'd stolen it from you?' Izzy blinked.

'He was a troublemaker. One who chose a life of crime over doing the decent thing. For all those years I believed he'd never changed but... I guess I was wrong.'

'So you never saw him again after that day?'

'I told him in no uncertain terms that we were done. With our mother passing our last link had been severed. The stolen bracelet was the final nail in the coffin. I told him if he ever tried to contact us again I would go to the police. The solicitor dealt with Mum's affairs separately. I never heard from him again.'

Izzy's eyes widened. 'Not even when Pearl died?'

'He probably doesn't even know,' Arthur admitted.

'And you really don't know where he is?'

'No.' Arthur felt utterly exhausted. He was struggling to continue answering her questions when his own head was in such a spin.

'But what if, say in theory, you did have the chance to find where he is… would you want that?' Izzy asked after a pause.

'Is there something going on?' Arthur narrowed his eyes.

Izzy studied her nails, avoiding his eye. 'Like you said yourself, this changes everything. I just think that you might want to think about finding him and making amends, especially as now you know the truth?'

Arthur stayed silent, trying to process what she was getting at.

'You also said this house clear-out isn't just about getting rid of possessions. It's about coming to terms with any loose ends you need to tie up. I'd say this was a loose end.'

'I was talking about cancelling my gas and electricity.'

'But what if—'

'I haven't got time! OK?' he snapped, sharper than he meant.

'What do you mean? Oh, a break from your busy schedule of packing or reading the paper? Of course you have time,' she scoffed.

'I'm not going to be here in a couple of weeks.' Why wasn't she listening to him?

'You can still find Reg from your new place. I'll help—'

'No! I can't find him because I won't be alive,' Arthur shouted, the sound making Evie cry from the pram in the hallway where she had been peacefully napping. Izzy's mouth dropped and her eyes shot wide. 'What?!'

'I have fifteen days left. The twenty-sixth of April wasn't

a real date. Well it was, I mean, it is. But, it's not the date I was planning on moving.' He took a deep breath, he felt very wobbly and couldn't look at her in the eye. 'I was planning on checking out.'

'Checking out?' she echoed.

'Taking my own life,' he said in little more than a whisper. He hadn't said it aloud before.

'What! The two-month deadline wasn't a countdown to your move? It was a countdown to you *killing* yourself? You weren't packing up to go to a home. You were packing up for good?' She shook her head in disbelief. 'Wait... and I was helping you?' She spat this last part. Evie's crying intensified.

'I couldn't tell you! I couldn't tell anyone.' Arthur felt as if he was watching this conversation from a distance. His tone was coming out all wrong – too haughtily, as if he was scolding her.

'So what? What are you going to do? Kill yourself one day in between our visits? How the hell do you think I'd cope with that?' Her voice was high-pitched and jumpy. Her hands were trembling. 'I can't believe this!'

Evie's crying was giving Arthur a headache. He didn't know what to say to make this right, to make Izzy understand.

'I tried to tell you. I—'

'Bullshit you did.'

Arthur had never heard her swear before. He felt like he'd been slapped.

'What the hell do you think Pearl would say about this?'

Suddenly Arthur wanted her out of his house. This was his life, it was his decision and he didn't need to be made to feel guilty for choosing to end it as he wanted. It didn't concern anyone else, especially not someone he hadn't even known six months ago. Evie's cries were increasing in volume.

'Don't you dare mention Pearl. You don't know anything about me.'

'I thought I did! But clearly I was wrong. I thought we were friends but you're right… I don't know you at all.'

'Get out.'

'What?'

'I said, get out!' he shouted. Spittle had formed at the side of his open mouth.

'Fine.' Izzy jostled the pram down the hallway, gently shushing Evie.

She didn't look back as she slammed the door shut behind her. Arthur tried to calm his raggedy breathing down and unclench his fists. His knuckles had turned white. That girl didn't have a clue. If she had experienced loneliness like he had then she would understand, but she knew nothing.

CHAPTER 27

Izzy

Izzy had tossed and turned all night, eventually falling into a deep, dreamless slumber at some godforsaken hour after feeding Evie. She was beyond grateful when Andrew had taken Evie downstairs telling her to stay in bed this morning. But, as lovely as this unprecedented lie-in was, she couldn't help herself replaying her fight with Arthur. A whole range of emotions swirled in her tired mind. She had been betrayed by a close friend and it hurt more than she ever could have imagined it would. Nausea washed over her as she tried to process what he'd admitted. Her body craved more sleep but her head was swimming. She had been an unwitting accomplice in helping him tick things off his final to-do list. How little he thought of her and their friendship for him to lie to her like this. How foolish she had been not to see the signs – this wasn't downsizing to move into a retirement home, this had been an epic clear-out getting rid of almost everything he owned. He was tidying up one final time. It seemed so utterly obvious now.

Izzy flung off the warm duvet. Even though Arthur had lied to her, she was worried about him, he shouldn't be left on his own. He had told her in no uncertain terms to leave him alone but she couldn't do that, what if he actually went through with it? She needed to call someone but she didn't have Jeremy's number. Perhaps she should alert the police that she was concerned about her neighbour's mental health? Except, well, if he was so serious about taking his own life then why hadn't he done it already? Why go through with this circus? This performance? Izzy shook her head. No, there was something holding him back.

The shock cleared for a second as a thought sprang to her overwhelmed mind. If she could find his brother, maybe *he* could convince Arthur that life was still worth living. Despite Arthur's reservations at confronting his past, she was convinced that finding Reg was the right thing to do. Blood was thicker than water, after all. Izzy scrambled to find her phone. The search for Reg had suddenly intensified. She groaned loudly, she had forgotten to put it on charge overnight so the battery was dangerously low. Praying it would last, she opened Facebook to see if the potential Winnie Winter had been in touch. But Izzy's message remained unread. Just then she heard Andrew race up the stairs.

'Ah, you're up!' He looked the exact opposite of how Izzy felt. 'I've just put Evie down for a nap.'

Izzy stared at him. 'Is everything OK? Why are you not dressed for work. Where's your suit? I mean, thank you, I—'

'She's fine! Don't give me that look. I think I can manage to get her down to sleep, well, I FaceTimed my mum to help,' he admitted with a proud smile. 'But, I did it because I have some news for you...'

'Oh?'

'I need you to hurry up and get ready because we're going away! I've booked today off, in fact I've booked Monday off too so we can have a nice long weekend together.' His face lit up even more. 'Surprise!'

'What?' Izzy blinked in confusion.

'I've packed mine and Evie's things – again my mum helped by giving me a list of what we would need to take. Jeez, that kid might be small but she comes with a lot of stuff. I don't know how you do it when you leave the house with her! Anyway, all you need to do is jump in the shower and pack a bag for yourself for a few nights away.'

Izzy froze. She couldn't just go away, not now. Not leaving Arthur like this.

'But—'

'I know what you're going to say but I've taken care of everything. I've booked us in at this amazing log cabin resort, where we can just go and hang out as a family. Oh and there's even a spa.'

She felt completely thrown off balance. His words were not computing in her mind.

'We're… we're having a long weekend away? Now? This weekend?' she stuttered.

'Yep! Surprise!' His broad smile faltered at her lukewarm reaction. 'I wanted to do something nice for all of us, as a family, so I secretly booked a couple of days off work. You don't need to lift a finger just sit back and relax.'

Izzy continued to gawp at him. Who was this man and what had he done with her husband?

'But what about Evie? Her cot, routine, naps… I've not packed and sorted her stuff. There's so much to organise!'

'It's all taken care of, like I said. My mum has been a big help, she agreed that it would do you good to get away for a bit. That I need to pull my weight a little more.' He coughed and glanced at his watch. 'But we really need to get a move on babe. Your new mum pamper package is booked for midday. I've even scheduled in stops so Evie isn't in her car seat for too long. Come on, tick tock!' He spun out of the room, leaving Izzy feeling as if she was in some parallel universe.

Andrew was a man on a mission. He had packed the car and bundled Izzy and Evie in before she could protest. As he locked the front door, checking he had got everything, Izzy glanced over at Arthur's house. Jeremy's car was parked on the drive. Izzy breathed out – that was a small relief. If he was there then he could make sure his uncle wasn't going to do anything silly.

Part of her wanted to leap out of the passenger seat and run over to check on him, perhaps this was all some sick joke – not that Arthur was one for sick jokes – the other part of her was too hurt to even be in the same room as him. The way he had spoken to her, the lies he had told her and the fact that their friendship was all a sham had been a painful pill to swallow. Perhaps this spontaneous trip away had come at the best time, maybe they both needed to have a bit of space and to take a few days to let the dust settle. Izzy hoped that he would soon come to his senses and see how stupid he was being.

'Right, next stop – holiday!' Andrew chimed as he tapped the car's inbuilt satnav.

The fact Andrew had gone to all this effort was a huge step forward for them both. It was time to put her family and their needs first.

'Great,' she said, clocking Andrew's smile as she turned up the radio.

Izzy should be on top of the world. She had spent the past hour being smothered in essential oils and posh face creams. Andrew had booked for them to stay for three nights in a deluxe woodland log cabin in the Peak District. It was only an hour and a half away from Birch Tree Way but, right now, that felt like a world away from their problems. There were forty of these cabins dotted around a sprawling forest site so it really felt like they were in their own little bubble. There was a small soft play, a traditional country pub and even a swanky fitness suite with a spa. Andrew really had thought of everything. It was the ideal place to come and get away from it all, except Izzy was struggling to do just that.

No matter how hard she tried she couldn't switch off from worrying about Arthur. She sighed deeply, aware of the constant knot of tension that had been in the pit of her stomach since discovering the truth. She clung on to the fact that he hadn't completed Operation Pearl before now. She prayed that whatever was stopping him would still be the case by the time she returned home.

Izzy stood outside the doors to the lavender-smelling haven of the spa and pulled her phone out. She had five minutes before Andrew was joining her to use the onsite pool. They were going for their first official family swim. It wasn't lost on Izzy that the last time she had visited a pool had been with Arthur. She couldn't escape him. Half of her was back in Birch Tree Way. If she could speak to him and make sure he wasn't going to do anything stupid then she would feel a whole lot better, then she could actually be present with her family instead of mentally agonising over the incomprehensible plans of an old man back home.

There was zero phone signal in the log cabin, even the Wi-Fi was patchy at best, but out here she managed to just find the right spot so quickly dialled Arthur's number. Yes she was angry and didn't really want to talk to him but there was no way she'd be able to enjoy this break without getting that peace of mind.

However, his phone rang out. There wasn't the option to leave a voicemail. She frowned at her screen, unsure what to do next, annoyed at herself for not having Jeremy's number, when she heard Andrew call her name.

She couldn't help but smile at the sight of her husband steering the pram towards her, it made her tummy do a little flip. He'd slung a towel over his shoulder and inflated the giant yellow baby float which was precariously balanced on top of the pram hood. 'Hey, was your pamper package nice?'

'Amazing. Thank you,' Izzy said, leaning in to give Evie a little squeeze. She was growing much better at spending time apart from her and not being racked with guilt. 'She looks very happy with her daddy. Did you have fun?'

'Yeah, all fine. She mostly watched me get everything together for our swim. We'll have to have words about her pulling her weight a bit more,' he joked.

'Have you packed the swim nappy?'

'Check.'

'And a towel for Evie? She has one with a hood.'

'Check.'

'And some cream in case the chlorine dries her skin out?'

'Yep. I even brought some baby shampoo.'

'Wow.'

'And I didn't even need to call my mum for help,' he said with a wink.

'Sorry. I shouldn't interrogate you like that.'

'It's fine. You're the pro at this, I'm merely your willing apprentice.' He pulled a face and made Izzy laugh. 'I know I've not exactly been hands-on but I'm ready to try and change that. If you'll help me?'

She nodded. These were the words she'd been hoping to hear for a long time.

'Right, I think we're ready for our dip...'

The smell of chlorine, the whirr of the hairdryers and the humid heat of the changing rooms transported her back to their local leisure centre. Her mind raced with unanswered questions. Why hadn't she brought up what had caused Arthur's speedy exit? Had that been some sort of warning sign? Did something happen that tipped him over the edge?

'What's going on, Izzy? You're half here and half somewhere else.' Andrew waved a hand in front of her face.

'Sorry, babe.'

'Do you want to tell me what's going on? You're not annoyed that I sprung this holiday on you? I thought I was doing the right thing, I—'

'No! No, it's not that. Yes, it was a complete surprise but I'm—'

'I knew I should have told you about it. I just thought it would be an adventure, like the ones we used to have when we'd jump in the car and go off to random places at a weekend.'

'It's lovely, it really is.' Izzy gently stroked his arm. 'My head is just a bit full, sorry.'

'Do you want to talk about it?'

She slowly shook her head. 'Maybe later. Come on, let's get this one in the pool.'

In all honesty, Izzy wasn't sure where to begin.

CHAPTER 28

Arthur

Arthur felt even more exhausted than when he'd gone to bed. He had struggled to get to sleep and then when he had drifted off vivid dreams of his mother had jolted him awake. The heated disagreement with Izzy had been playing on a loop through his mind since he'd forced himself to get up and start the day. His opinion hadn't changed. It really was none of Izzy's business. Who was she to tell him what to do? She had no idea of the years of pain and hurt Reg had caused him. And to bring Pearl into it? How dare she! He was angry at himself for letting Izzy into his home and his heart. All that woman had done was interfere. Before she waltzed in here Arthur had barely thought about Reg. But since Izzy had been in his life it was as if she had opened some imaginary box full of painful memories. Photographs, postcards and even innocent trips to the swimming baths: Reg was everywhere.

He nicked himself shaving and slightly scalded his hand making himself a cup of tea. Today was clearly going to be one of those days. He tried to keep himself busy. There was Pearl's make-up and jewellery box to sort through but everything felt like one huge chore. The wind had been knocked out of his sails.

Just as he summoned the energy to make a start, there was a knock on the door. Arthur suspected it would be Izzy and Evie coming to apologise. Then again perhaps she was waiting for him to do the same thing, he thought. There was a small part of him that wondered if his reaction had been too over the top. He may have said some things he regretted. However, a larger, more stubborn part of him wanted to see if she would back down first. But, to his surprise, it wasn't Izzy standing at the door. It was young Nikki waiting on the other side instead.

'Oh, hello.'

'Hi.'

'Is everything OK?' Arthur scratched his head.

'Yeah. I just wanted to come and say sorry about what happened with my mate. OK, he's not my mate but anyway, the thing is that I know I should have, like, properly helped you that night.' The jumble of words spilled out of her mouth. 'He was bang out of order speaking to you like that. I s'pose I should have come over here earlier but I thought you'd go mental at me.' She scuffed her black boots on the path.

'Thank you,' Arthur said, trying to follow what she was saying. 'You seem like a nice girl, can I ask why you want to spend your time with people like that?'

Nikki shrugged. 'Dunno. I don't really know the lads. Kian was sort of seeing my mate but she realised what a di—, sorry, idiot he is.'

Arthur could think of a few choice words to describe the boy's threatening behaviour but none of them were suitable for this young girl's ears.

'He was out of order. He just wanted to scare you, he never had a knife on him or nothin' like that.'

Arthur was sure he had seen a glint of something silver in the lad's waistband.

'He carries around a spatula, the sort you use for cakes,' she said as if reading his mind. 'He just wants to look hard as loads of the other lads in the year above have knives on them. But it wasn't like he'd ever hurt anyone with it. Anyway, we've stopped hanging around with them lot now.'

'I'm glad to hear it.'

'But yeah, er, thanks for the art stuff. That was really nice of you.'

'You're welcome. I was being honest when I said to your dad that I'd seen you with the large portfolio, you are talented. Just please don't waste your talents on graffitiing other people's property.'

Nikki bobbed her head. She looked so very young.

'Listen, please don't tell my dad about what happened. He'd kill me if he knew…'

'I won't.'

'Thanks. So, err, you moving soon?' She nodded to the sold sign at the edge of his front lawn.

'I am.'

'Shame. You used to have the best sweets for Halloween back when me and my sister did trick or treatin'. We'd always make sure to come to you first.'

Neither of them mentioned that this tradition hadn't been honoured since Pearl had passed away. Instead, Arthur had sat in the dark, ignored the doorbell and spent the evening muttering to himself about it being a ridiculous concept in the first place.

Despite this being the first time they had had a proper conversation, Arthur felt like he knew Nikki and her sister. He had silently encouraged them when they'd wobbled up and down the pavement outside his house on bikes with stabilisers. He thought how smart they looked as they stood posing in their uniforms on their very first day of school. He had purposefully ignored the noise they'd made during lively birthday parties held in their back garden. Snapshots of their lives. That's the thing with neighbours, Arthur thought, you see so many glimpses into their world but you never really know what's going on.

'I remember she sponsored me when I did some silly spelling bee thing at school once, she believed I could be at the top of the class. She was right,' Nikki said bashfully. 'She was nice.'

'She was.'

He was about to say something else when Jeremy's car turned the corner into the cul-de-sac.

'That's my nephew.' Arthur frowned. He couldn't remember them having made plans today.

'I'd better go anyway. Thanks for, you know, and er… sorry again.' Nikki gave a small awkward wave and jogged away as Jeremy pulled up onto Arthur's drive.

He got out of the car puzzled at the teenager running away from his uncle's front door.

'Everything OK?'

'Fine, fine. Hello. I didn't know we had plans today?'

'Ah, well I just thought I'd pop over as we have quite a lot of things to discuss with your move now fast approaching. And to help us I've brought cake!'

Arthur's heart fell hearing that Elaine had been baking

again, he had learnt the hard way not to trust Elaine's culinary skills. He wasn't sure how Jeremy had managed to stay alive for so long living with a woman who used salt with such wild abandon.

'Come on in then.'

Arthur held the door wide for his nephew. He really was not in the mood but it would distract him from stewing over Izzy at least.

'Arthur?' Jeremy gasped as he wandered into the lounge.

'Yes?'

'What's happened in here?'

'What do you mean?

Jeremy was standing next to the sofa scratching his head. 'Where's all your stuff?'

'Gone. Well, most of it,' Arthur said, easing himself into his armchair.

Jeremy was gawping at the empty bookcase, the pictureless walls and the dusty spaces where all the trinkets used to live in the display cabinet. At first Arthur had found his lounge a little cold and bare but now he quite enjoyed the extra space. He had never realised just how big the room was.

'Where has it all gone? How have you managed it, you know, with your ankle and all?'

'I've had help from my neighbour.'

'Lizzie?'

'Izzy. Now will you please sit down? You're making my neck ache looking up at you.'

'Sorry. I'm just in shock. The last time I popped over it was looking a bit more bare but this is … something else.'

Arthur shrugged. 'I wanted to save you a job having to do it on my behalf.'

'Well, I have to say I'm very impressed, even if you should have been taking it easy.' Jeremy sat down, roaming his eyes across the sparse room in disbelief.

'So,' Arthur cleared his throat.

'So, let's get down to business. I've had a call from the estate agent,' Jeremy said with a firm nod of his head.

'Oh right. Is everything OK?'

'They've heard from the family who are buying this house.'

'Has their chain fallen through? I've heard that's very common.'

'No, in fact, the opposite.' Jeremy looked up from the fairy cake he was tucking into. He'd arrived with a full Tupperware of them. 'Do you want one of these by the way?'

'No, thank you. I've just eaten.' Arthur lied. 'So, as you were saying…'

'Yes. They've been able to move everything forward. Someone's come into some inheritance or something, so it's actually sped the process up. It means that you're moving earlier than planned!' Jeremy grinned, giving Arthur a thumbs up.

'How much earlier?' Arthur felt this funny sinking feeling in his stomach, he couldn't even blame Elaine's cooking. 'I thought we had agreed the twenty-sixth of April. We've still got two weeks to go.'

'Well, yes but that was before. The estate agent imagines you'll be able to exchange and complete this time next week,' he said with his mouth full, a blob of icing on the tip of his nose.

This time next week! Although that was only a week ahead of his deadline he wasn't sure he was ready for Operation Pearl to be done so soon. It would mean he would miss Pearl's anniversary. Arthur needed to remember to breathe. He wasn't speaking to Izzy, he hadn't completely cleared his house and he hadn't finalised exactly how he was going to die. His plans were already a mess and now this too.

'But we originally agreed two months. I picked the twenty-sixth as it was an important date for me. I chose it for a reason.' he tried to say as firmly as he could.

'I know but there's not just your needs to think of I'm afraid. It's only a week earlier, surely that's not a big deal?' Jeremy must have picked up on the panic on his uncle's face. 'Now don't worry, I've already spoken to RoseWood Lodge. They have your room waiting for you so all you need to do is enjoy your last weekend here then get yourself ready. It must be fate as you've cleared out so much stuff already! This neighbour of yours is some sort of superhero helping you to pack all of this away.'

'I don't know about that,' Arthur said quietly.

'Well you'll have to start to say your goodbyes in the next week as I'm sure everything is going to go quite fast now.' Jeremy brushed some crumbs to the carpet. 'I'd better be off. I'll speak to Elaine about coming over maybe Thursday next week. I'm afraid I'm working the other days so I won't be able to visit before then. But, in the meantime I'll have a look at getting some quotes from removal firms. It won't be a lot considering there's not much left to move!'

'I don't think that will be necessary.'

'You're right, maybe I can get it all in the boot of my car.'

He got to his feet and tucked the Tupperware box under one arm. 'Oh. Maybe don't pack up everything. I thought you might like to take some pictures to brighten your new place up? Not that it needs brightening up, it looked homely as it was.' He added hurriedly. 'Right, is there anything you need from me before I go?'

Arthur shook his head. He had done quite enough already.

CHAPTER 29

Izzy

Smells of garlic and aromatic spices wafted from the small kitchen of the log cabin, making Izzy's stomach growl. Andrew had been to the onsite shop and bought a bottle of red and all the ingredients needed to make his signature curry. Their family swim had clearly worn Evie out as she had gone to sleep without a fight, it was like she could sense that her parents needed some alone time. Andrew had also lit the log-burner casting the cabin in a gorgeous amber glow and synced his phone to the inbuilt speakers so Coldplay were serenading them in the background.

'Can I help with anything?' Izzy asked.

'Nope. Dinner is almost ready,' Andrew said, pouring a second glass of wine for them both. The first had slipped down too easily for Izzy's liking. 'Cheers.' He clinked his glass to hers. 'Then I thought maybe you might like to have a bath?'

Izzy stared at him. 'OK, should I be getting worried now?'

'What do you mean?'

'I mean, this.' She waved her arms wide to take in the romantic setting. All it was missing was a fake-fur throw, some tealights and scattered rose petals. 'Coming here, booking me a spa treatment, cooking dinner, offering to run me a bath?'

Andrew got up to stir the sauce. 'I just wanted to treat you.'

Izzy furrowed her eyebrows. 'Have you done something wrong? You're not having an affair, are you?'

Andrew threw his head back and let out a bark of laughter. 'An affair? You think I have the energy for that! Stop being so worried, Iz. I promise you now there's no one else and never will be. I just wanted us to spend some quality time together. I've been caught up in work and haven't been able to put the family first as much as I wanted.'

'Oh OK…'

'You're doing an amazing job with Evie, I probably should tell you that more.'

'I'm sorry for moaning a lot.'

'You don't moan that much…'

'Liar.' Izzy grinned.

Andrew raised his glass. 'I'd like to say a toast to my beautiful wife and the most brilliant mother to our child.'

'Are you drunk?' Izzy laughed.

'I'm not drunk, I'm just happy!' His face then grew serious. 'Actually, there is something I want to get off my chest.'

'Oh?'

'Yes. I want to apologise for not being there as much as I should have been. Having Evie has been a whirlwind and I guess I wasn't prepared for how much everything would change, but I promise you right here and now that I'm going to be a better husband to support you more.'

'I'll drink to that,' Izzy smiled, clinking her glass to his. 'You're right, the past few months have been a rollercoaster.'

'But you make it look so easy. Seriously, you do. Why are you shaking your head?'

She suddenly wanted to tell him how much she had been struggling. She wanted him to understand that, despite how it might appear from the outside, the reality was very different. 'I didn't realise just how hard it would be. Motherhood, I mean. Babe, these past few months have almost killed me. I don't know how others do it but it certainly hasn't come easy to me. I thought I was giving out clear signals that I needed some help – and by help, I don't mean your mum coming to stay.'

Andrew smiled bashfully. 'Iz, you've never actually told me this before. I knew you were exhausted but I had no idea you were hating it.' He looked genuinely upset.

'I don't hate it,' Izzy sighed. 'I really don't. I mean Evie is wonderful, we're so lucky to have her but, well, motherhood is just not how I imagined it would be. That's all.'

She thought back to how many times in those early days she had imagined striding into his work and dropping the baby off then escaping to sit alone in a dark room. It was true that she hadn't actually spelt it out to him, but that's because she had never found the right moment to open up about how she was feeling.

'Everything's changed for me too,' Andrew said. 'I have this strange sense of duty that wasn't there before. I feel like I have to work twice as hard now Evie's here. I want to be able to give us the life we dream of but, well, I guess working all the time isn't the way to do it.'

Izzy shook her head. 'We would rather hang out with *you*. I don't want you to miss out on this part of her life either.'

Of course she would love to spend more time with Andrew and Evie as a family but Izzy had to admit that things had seemed a bit easier recently. Perhaps it was the fact they had a sort of routine nowadays or perhaps Evie was just a little older or perhaps it was Arthur's influence, but recently Izzy didn't feel like she was drowning all the time.

'You're right. I'll make more of an effort to be there for you both.'

Just then all the stress, the bickering rows, the late nights working and the swear words muttered under her breath when she thought he couldn't hear didn't seem to matter as much.

'You're a brilliant mum, Izzy, and I should tell you that more often.' He topped up their wine glasses. 'As we are sharing things.' He took a deep breath. 'There's something I should probably come clean about.'

'Jesus. What now?'

'It wasn't me who sent you those flowers last week. I took the credit but they were from Arthur.'

Izzy blinked. 'Arthur?'

'Yeah.' Andrew rubbed the back of his neck. 'I guess there was some confusion on the note. Both of our names start with the same letter and all. You just looked so happy that I went along with it…'

That bubble of happiness popped.

'What? So you lied to me.'

'It was a small white lie, more of a misunderstanding, one that I didn't correct if anything!'

'Do you realise how bad that makes me look?' she groaned. 'I never thanked him.'

'I'm sorry. I didn't think it would be a big deal. I guess

I really have been failing you.' His eyes shot to the floor. 'Clearly he knows you better than I do. The funny thing is that Arthur was the one who suggested we come away. He said he thought you could do with a break.'

Izzy raised her eyebrows. 'He did? What else did he say?'

'That I was lucky to have such a wonderful wife, that you'd been a really good friend to him and you deserved to be looked after more. He told me about how he'd surprise Pearl with little things to make her happy and I wanted to do the same for you. Shit! The dinner's burning!' Andrew leapt to his feet to turn off the pan of rice that had boiled over. He quickly thrust open a window and wafted a tea towel at the steam.

'He was a better friend than I realised,' Izzy admitted quietly.

CHAPTER 30

Arthur

Arthur glanced out of the window for the seventh time that morning. He clenched his jaw and tried to avoid looking at Izzy's empty drive. He had been thinking about her a lot. Since Jeremy's visit yesterday and his new, tighter deadline, Arthur had decided that he needed everything gone as soon as possible, even the bigger pieces of furniture he'd earmarked for Joan at the charity shop. He simply did not have the time to waste. He knew Jeremy had said he would sort it but the whole point of Operation Pearl was that others wouldn't be clearing up behind him. So, instead, he had spotted an advert for a local removal firm on a leaflet which was posted through his front door and wasted no time in calling them. It was serendipitous that they had just had a cancellation so could fit him in. He needed the slate to be completely clean before he could do the deed. But the men he had hired were currently running twenty minutes late.

His house phone sprang to life in the far corner of the room, jarring him from his thoughts. The house phone never rang these days, not since all the well-meaning 'how are you getting on' phone calls from Pearl's friends after she passed away. Arthur's reluctance to spend hours passing meaningless chitchat meant they had dried up quickly. Only Jeremy had this number and even then he rarely used it. Arthur slowly made his way over to the phone when he remembered there was one other person who had this number: Izzy.

'Hello?' He felt his heart quicken as he picked up the receiver.

'Hello. Is that Arthur?' a female voice asked at the other end. It didn't sound like Izzy.

'Yes. Who's this?'

'Arthur! It's Joan!' He could practically hear the woman's smile down the line. 'From the charity shop?'

'Oh, hello.' *Why was Joan from the charity shop calling?*

'I haven't caught you at a bad time, have I?'

'Actually... I...'

Joan must have misheard him. 'Great. Well I wanted to call you myself to let you know that...' she paused for effect. 'You've won!'

'Won?'

'Yes! You've won the top prize in our raffle!' She laughed gently.

Arthur had never won anything in his life.

'Sorry?'

'I know. It's great news, isn't it!'

'I haven't entered any raffle.'

'A lady called Izzy Carter entered you. It must have been a few weeks ago now.'

'Izzy?'

Joan carried on talking. 'Are you able to pop by the shop

to pick up your prize? It would be lovely to see you again, we've not seen your face in here for a while now.' She paused. 'I wanted to check that everything was OK with you?'

Silence filled the space between them.

'Arthur? You still there?'

Arthur swallowed back the unexpected lump that had risen to his throat. He felt rather foolish.

'Yes, yes. I'm very much still here.' He was about to say something else when his doorbell chimed. 'Sorry, I... er... I need to go.'

Arthur replaced the receiver with a bewildered shake of his head. He didn't have time to let the unexpected news sink in and wonder what it was he'd won, or the fact that Izzy was behind it all as his doorbell rang again.

'Coming!'

'Arthur Winter?' asked a stocky man with angel wings inked around his wide throat, and hands the size of rugby balls. Arthur felt a little trepidatious opening the door to this hulk of a man. A neat name badge was pinned to his tight black polo shirt. *Tony: Happy to Help*. Behind him was a small white lorry with the back shutter pulled up, exposing the empty space inside. Space that was soon to be filled with Arthur's bigger, heavier items of furniture.

'Yes, that's me. Come on in.'

Arthur led the man into his lounge and stood awkwardly beside him.

'Right. What needs shiftin' and where's it goin'?' *Tony: Happy to Help* asked. His voice was deep and throaty.

Two younger and leaner guys emerged from behind Tony. They each had a rolled-up cigarette behind one ear and matching severe haircuts that exposed their pale necks. They too glanced around the room, taking it all in.

Arthur cleared his throat. 'Ah, well, I've put a Post-it note on the things that need going.'

He had been particularly pleased with himself for this stroke of inspiration.

'There's two rather heavy wardrobes upstairs and a desk in the spare room that has seen better days,' Arthur explained. 'I'm not able to move them myself.'

Arthur had chuckled to himself that perhaps he should stick a Post-it on his chest for when he'd done the deed, but he wasn't sure whoever found him would have the same sense of humour.

Tony nodded. 'And where we moving them to?'

'The tip. I think they're long past their best.'

Tony gave a nod to the younger guys who strode purposefully up the stairs. 'It's gonna get a little dusty in here. You might want to leave us to it?'

'Oh, right. Of course. I've got some errands to run.' Arthur shrugged on his jacket, he may as well go and pick up his prize from Joan at the charity shop, whatever it may be. 'Oh, how much do I owe you?'

Tony slapped a meaty hand on Arthur's back. 'We'll sort all that when you get back.'

'Arthur!' Joan smiled as the bell chimed his arrival. 'I didn't expect you to come over so quickly.'

Arthur wasn't sure what to say. Maybe it did look a bit overly keen but he was on a tight schedule.

'I was just passing,' he lied.

'Well it's great to see you. Let me just nip out to the back to get your prize.' Joan hadn't mentioned what it was that Arthur had actually won. He hoped it wasn't some ridiculous stuffed teddy bear that he'd have to sit with on the bus all the way home in order to avoid hurting her feelings.

'Here we go!' Joan had returned and thankfully there were no stuffed animals in sight. She was holding out a thick envelope to him. 'Congratulations!'

Arthur took it and tore open the seal, mumbling a thank you. He felt a little embarrassed with Joan, and the work experience boy, and now a lady who was hovering by the counter after having just paid for a Stephen King novel, all looking on expectantly.

'You've won brunch for two at Belvedere Bites,' he read aloud to his captive audience. 'Brunch?'

'It's a mix of breakfast and lunch,' Joan explained.

'They do like *the* best halloumi fries in there,' the work experience boy said.

Arthur had never had brunch before. His mealtimes were like clockwork. No one had ever mentioned brunch being an option before. Judging by the look on the faces before him it was a wonderful prize to win.

'Oh, how lovely! Who are you going to take?' the Stephen King fan asked. She had quite strong coffee breath.

Arthur's first thought was to ask Izzy but that was swiftly replaced with the memory of their last conversation. Jeremy would be with Elaine. He didn't have anyone else he could invite.

'You've got time to think about it,' Joan said with a tinkle of a laugh. 'I don't think it expires for another few months.'

But Arthur didn't have a few months, he only had a week

until a brand-new family were moving in. If he was going to check out on his terms then he literally had days left to do it.

'W-w-would you like to go with me?' The words were out of his mouth before he could stop and think about them.

'Me? Are you sure?' Joan looked surprised. 'Oh Arthur, I wasn't suggesting that—'

Arthur raised a hand to stop her protesting. 'I know you weren't. But if you're free, maybe tomorrow, then you're more than welcome to join me.'

'Tomorrow?' She laughed again. 'You don't like to let the grass grow under you, do you?'

Arthur shook his head. She had no idea.

'I'm actually working tomorrow. We still have the shop open on a Sunday, you see.'

'Oh.'

'I can swap my shift and come in earlier, if you like?' the work experience lad piped up. 'Didn't Debbie say she was around to help too?'

Suddenly Joan seemed a little coy. She nodded her head. 'I'll give her a call. That would be lovely, thank you Arthur. How about I meet you there at ten?'

'Great.' Arthur tucked the gift voucher in his jacket pocket. 'See you then.'

If nothing else, it would be a lovely last supper.

The second he turned his key in the lock, Arthur knew something was wrong.

'Hello? Tony?' he called as he plodded down the hall. There was no reply. He walked into his lounge and thought he was going to topple over.

Everything had gone.

Everything.

The heavy antique bookcase, including Pearl's recently rediscovered bracelet that he'd placed on the top in a small glass dish, was nowhere to be seen. The display cabinet, the coffee table and the television had disappeared. The heavy feet of the sofa had left a ghostly imprint on the grubby carpet of where it once stood. They had even taken his much-loved, battered armchair.

Arthur stumbled into the kitchen in utter disbelief. His heart was racing dangerously fast as he tried to take it all in.

His cooker had been jimmied out of the tight spot, leaving decades-old undisturbed dust and crumbs behind. The microwave had gone. The kettle and the toaster and the knife set too. Bizarrely, they had spared his fridge.

'What on earth!' Arthur needed to steady himself, clasping a trembling hand on the empty worktop.

He rubbed at his eyes as if his furniture would magically materialise in front of him. It was no good. Tony and his pals had cleaned him out of everything. It was easier to work out what they hadn't taken rather than what they had. The same sinking feeling hung heavy in his stomach as he gingerly climbed to the top of the stairs. The door to the spare room was open. Just dust, fluff and ghostly furniture imprints on the carpet remained.

He swallowed and opened the door to his bedroom. The wardrobe had gone like he'd originally requested but so had everything else including Pearl's mother's antique chest, containing his wife's wedding dress. Luckily his bed was still there, the mattress sad and unloved in this stark space. They'd left him a bed and a fridge. That was it. Trembling, he made his way downstairs, trying to think clearly.

He needed to find the leaflet with Tony's number on it. Perhaps it was just a misunderstanding. Maybe they thought Arthur was ready to completely move out. It could be an easy mistake to make, given the Sold sign outside, Arthur thought, trying to stay positive. He must not have been clear enough with Tony. Perhaps the Post-it Notes had slipped off. Wires had been crossed. Arthur would call and explain that they had been too efficient, he would probably laugh about it later.

Except Arthur couldn't see the leaflet with Tony's details on it anywhere and there wasn't anywhere for it to hide. He was about to redial the last phone number he'd called but his telephone was gone too.

An awful thought entered his mind. This wasn't a mix-up. You don't just pack all this furniture up by accident. How could he have been so naive? He suddenly felt very old and very foolish. He was one of those people he'd read stories about in the paper. Naive pensioners taken for a ride by scam artists. Tony had stolen from him and there was nothing that Arthur could do about it. He couldn't even call the police to report the crime.

He felt like his legs might give way. Thankfully he remembered he had a deckchair in the shed, this was one spot where nothing had been touched. He blew off the cobwebs and erected the uncomfortable chair in the centre of his empty lounge. It was almost farcical. He awkwardly inched his bottom onto the striped, sun-bleached fabric. He needed to think. Should he go to the police station? But what would he say? In any case, he didn't want everything back. He had less than a week before the new family moved in. It would mean his final few days would be highly uncomfortable but he would manage.

Arthur shifted on the creaking chair. His knees were unnaturally close to his shoulders. Perhaps he should see this as a good thing. It had saved him, well Jeremy, a job in getting rid of the heavy items once Arthur had gone. It wasn't ideal that a bunch of crooks were driving around town with his belongings but they had to go somewhere eventually. After all, he was preparing to leave nothing behind once he was gone. All he could do now was figure out exactly when that would be.

CHAPTER 31

Izzy

It was the perfect lazy Saturday morning. Izzy was feeding Evie in bed and Andrew had just got back in with a fresh cup of coffee for them both. She couldn't remember the last time this had happened so was enjoying every second of it.

'What do you fancy doing today?' he asked, flicking through a visitor guide book he'd found in the cabin. 'There's some cool caves nearby.'

'Mmm, I'm not sure that's going to be pram friendly.'

'Yeah, good thinking. How about taking a ride on Britain's first alpine style cable car? Sounds pretty cool, no?'

Izzy glanced at the page he was showing her. She suddenly had a funny sense of déjà vu. 'I think I've already done that. It looks weirdly familiar.' She lay Evie in her cot and then took another, closer look at the photos. 'Do you know what... I remember going somewhere like that with my mum. I've got this memory of her telling my dad off for rocking the cable car. She didn't tell us how scared of heights she was as she didn't want us to be afraid but she was literally terrified for the whole ride. We took it in turns to sing silly songs to take her mind off how high up we were.'

Izzy shook her head in amazement at this long-buried memory coming to light. The shock of discovering the truth about Arthur and his unfathomable scheme had brought to the surface a lot of emotions Izzy thought she had locked away. When she lost her mum she was too young to process what it all meant. She was upset, of course, but she wasn't able to truly realise the magnitude of growing up without a mother until she was a little older. Trying to navigate motherhood without her own mum beside her has been harder than she could ever admit to herself.

'I miss my mum so much, Andrew,' she said, her voice full of sadness.

Andrew turned to face her. He looked like he didn't know how to deal with her sudden outburst.

'I mean, I *really, really* miss her.' She swiped away tears that had sprang from nowhere with her palm. 'I know I don't talk about her but that's because I don't always know what to say.'

'I can't imagine what you went through. Iz, it's only natural that you're going to wish she was still here, that she could meet Evie and see what an amazing mum you are.' He pulled her close and gently kissed her forehead. 'I had wondered if having Evie would bring up all these memories for you. I guess I was too scared to mention your mum for fear of upsetting you, but I'd honestly love to hear more about her.'

'Thank you.' Izzy sniffed. 'Did I ever tell you when she came first in the dads' race at my year one sports day?'

'Sorry – your mum came first in the dads' race?'

'Yeah! My dad was working but Mum didn't want me to

miss out as all the other kids had both their parents there taking part. So she stepped up and only went and won it! There was a lot of damaged male pride that day.'

Izzy smiled, remembering going to bed wearing the silver medal her mum had won, every night for a week. 'Or did I tell you that once she promised me the tooth fairy would visit but blatantly forgot so ended up making up this whole charade about how she must have got lost and that I had to draw her a map to find my room, all the while distracting me so she could leave fifty pence under my pillow.'

'No, you never told me that,' Andrew said, stroking Izzy's hair. 'OK, this is going to sound cheesy but your mum lives on in you and the way you mother Evie. I mean she's got her name after all! I think it's important that she hears these stories about her. I guess she's probably too young right now but when she's older she'll understand that she has a grandma who isn't with us anymore, one who would have loved her unconditionally.'

Izzy nodded. She felt better for that little cry. There were so many layers to loss but Andrew was right, just because her mum was no longer here it didn't mean she didn't influence the way Izzy brought up her own daughter.

'I know it's hard to pin down your dad but maybe you should try and tell him how you're feeling? I bet he misses her just as much but doesn't want to tell you in case he upsets you. You should cut yourself some slack though, babe. The fact you've held it together since becoming a mum yourself is bloody amazing.'

'Well I haven't always held it together. I'm not as perfect as you think I am.' Izzy took a deep breath. 'A good mum wouldn't leave their baby behind at the supermarket.' She winced, waiting for Andrew to hit the roof. 'I was too scared to tell you because you'd think I was a terrible person. *I am* a terrible person. But it was an accident! I swear she was only on her own for a few minutes and—'

'Babe. It's fine.' He looked as if he was trying not to laugh at how flustered Izzy was getting retelling this story. 'We're both going to do loads of silly things in her lifetime. This poor kid is going to be the experiment, that's what you get for being the first child. I mean, when we have our second then we might have to be on the ball a bit more...' He winked.

'You're not mad?'

'Mad? No! It was clearly an accident. She's fine. You're the one who'll remember this more than she ever will. I'm sure the shock of it means you'll never do it again.'

'Never.' Izzy shook her head then paused. 'Wait... what did you mean when you said *have our second*?'

'I meant one day!' he laughed. 'Do you not fancy doing this all over again in the future? No matter what you think you *are* a great mother and Evie would love a little brother or sister to one day boss around. Everything is bound to be easier the second time round too, I mean, we have all the gear and know what to expect, plus I'm sure that Arthur would love to be on hand to help you out with childcare.'

Izzy shook her head. 'Not any more he wouldn't.'

'Why not? He loves Evie and—'

'We had a fight.'

'What? When?'

'On Thursday. Just before we came here.'

'A fight? About what?'

'About the fact that he has been lying to me.' Izzy took a deep breath, preparing to tell him all about Operation Pearl; the truth, not the version she had been going along with. 'Instead of helping him pack up to move to a retirement home I have actually been helping him tick off jobs on his final to-do list.'

Andrew looked at her blankly.

'He's not planning to move. He's planning on taking his own life, to end things on his terms rather than be shipped off into a home.'

'Shit!'

'I know.'

For a moment neither of them spoke, the only sound in the room was the repetitive lullaby playing from the stuffed sheep in Evie's cot.

'That's a lot to take in,' Andrew said eventually. 'I knew you had something on your mind, I had no idea it would be something as mad as this. Babe, why didn't you tell me?'

'Because you've gone to so much trouble with all of this.' She spread her hands around the cabin bedroom. 'Plus, Arthur is a grown man. If he wants to kill himself there isn't much I can do to stop him. His nephew was at his house when we left to come here so I knew he was safe then. He's not gone through with it yet so there must be something holding him back. I just haven't figured out what it is.' She chewed her lip. 'I'm sure that if I can show Arthur how much he has to live for, how much people love him then he'll rethink the whole stupid plan.'

'Do you know what? I think that you need to find Reg. He might be the key to this. Did you hear back from his ex-wife?'

Izzy shook her head. 'Nope. My messages haven't been read. I don't even know if that was the right Winnie Winter.'

'Hmm. It might be time to give Davina a bell and get in

touch with the *Long Lost Family* team,' Andrew suggested. 'Or how about you hire a private investigator to help you out?'

'I suppose I could look into it but that all takes time and time is something that I'm worried Arthur's not got much of.'

'Right have we got everything?' Izzy did a final scan of the cabin. Somehow they had managed to make this just as messy as their front room in very little time. They were heading out as Andrew had read about a nearby tea room where they served the best Bakewell tart in the world, apparently. Evie was fighting a nap so Izzy hoped that she would nap in the car on the way there.

'Baby. Changing bag. Car keys. Phone,' Andrew listed things off.

'Ah, I've not got my phone.' Izzy stopped him. 'Oh, it's charging by the TV. Can you grab it for me, please?'

Andrew strode over and picked it up. 'You've got a message.'

'From who? I thought I couldn't get a signal here?'

'Dunno, you must have 4G on. It's from...' His eyes widened. 'Winnie Winter.'

Izzy leapt across the room, almost twisting her ankle on a squeaky soft flamingo strewn across the floor. *She'd replied!* She quickly tapped open Facebook Messenger, her heart beating with anticipation.

Yes. I know a man named Reg Winter.

That was it. But that was enough. That short and sweet message gave Izzy more to go on than any of her other attempts to track Reg down. She couldn't move her fingers fast enough to reply.

Hello! Thank you so much for replying! I don't know if Reg
ever mentioned his brother Arthur? I'm Arthur's neighbour
and well, I'm trying to reunite the two men. Do you have any
details for Reg so that I can get in touch with him please?
Thank you so much. Izzy x

'What did she say? Iz?' Andrew asked, rocking a whingeing
Evie at the same time.

Izzy felt giddy with excitement. She was convinced that if
she could find Reg and get the siblings to patch things up then
Arthur would realise what he had left to live for and stop his
senseless Operation Pearl plan. The estranged brothers had
a lifetime of catching up to do for one thing! She couldn't take
her eyes off her phone screen as it flashed 'Winnie is typing.'
A reply came back after a few tense seconds.

I do but I'm not going to share this sort of information over
the internet.

'Iz?' Andrew was staring at her, waiting for a response.

Perhaps I can come and meet you? I can explain a little
more and tell you why I'm doing this? I'm sorry to rush you
but I fear that time is running out.

Izzy typed then pressed send.

'I'm dying here! What did she say?!' Andrew asked louder.

'She knows where he is! Hang on, she's typing.'

It wasn't long before her phone vibrated once more.

You can find me at Willoughby Community Centre, Barrow-Upon-Avon. I'll be there tomorrow between 3 p.m. and 5 p.m.

'You should go,' Andrew said, coming across and reading over her shoulder.

'I don't even know where this place is...'

Izzy waited for Google Maps to load. She shook her head in amazement, it was only forty-five minutes away from where they were.

'Tell her that you'll meet her tomorrow.' Andrew nodded at Izzy's phone. 'It's important.'

Izzy's fingers hovered for a second on the keypad. She was suddenly consumed with apprehension. Perhaps Arthur hadn't found Reg for a reason or there was something more that he'd never told her.

'I know you feel hurt by what he did but I really think you can save him Iz. You've been so much happier since he's been in your life,' Andrew broke her spiralling thoughts. 'Going to meet Winnie could change everything for Arthur. It could encourage him to live again.'

'You're right.' Izzy took a deep breath. Of course she wasn't going to give up now. She replied to Winnie, telling her she'd see her tomorrow.

'Hang on – what will you and Evie do?'

'We'll have a daddy and daughter day,' Andrew shrugged with a smile. 'We'll be fine.'

Izzy leaned over and kissed him.

CHAPTER 32

Arthur

Today was going to be the day Arthur died. Granted, his current circumstances were far from ideal but he would have to make the best out of the bad situation. He couldn't fully blame Tony and his men for having stolen all his furniture, Arthur had made his house unliveable long before they turned up. He had removed the love and soul from the four walls. He thought about Izzy and what she would say if she knew he'd slept under a towel and had swapped his beloved armchair for a faded deckchair. He could picture the look of horror on her face that he had let things get this far. But, then again, perhaps she would have little sympathy – he had brought it on himself. Arthur didn't want to imagine Jeremy's reaction. He only had himself to blame for these dire circumstances.

A heavy sadness had set in like rot. He was ready to sleep for a hundred years. If he needed a sign that it was time for Operation Pearl to reach its conclusion then this was it. However, he had plans for today. If he had a telephone he would have called Joan at the charity shop and given his apologies. He was not in the mood to socialise but he had no way of cancelling brunch and he didn't want to stand her up, so he would suffer it.

Just a few hours more, a voice chimed in his mind. He could be reunited with Pearl by supper time. This brief delay would also allow him to resolve exactly *how* he was planning to depart this life. He had been toying with a certain idea he hoped would work. He pulled himself together once he thought of it like that. Today would be his final day.

Joan looked very relaxed. Her smart light grey trousers stopped just above her slim ankles. A chic navy sweater was draped over her shoulders. She had let down her shoulder-length silver hair that Arthur had only ever seen pinned back. Sunglasses were perched pointlessly on her head. She had also put some lipstick on, a berry sort of colour. Arthur didn't want to tell her it was bleeding into the lines around her thin lips.

'What can I get you to drink?' the waitress asked, pulling out a notepad to take their order. Arthur couldn't remember the last time he'd dined in a restaurant, he'd grown used to hearing the lonely rattling of his own cutlery at home. Eating out wasn't something that he and Pearl had done much of either. It was all overpriced and involved complicated unspoken rules.

'Just a coffee. Black, no sugar please,' Arthur asked. This place was somewhere in-between a French bistro and a yuppy wine bar. Small neat tables huddled under distressed wooden wall signs and chrome light fittings. It wasn't to his taste but it was rather charming in its own way.

Joan held up a hand. Her collection of gold bracelets jangled as she did.

'Oh Arthur, let your hair down.' She turned to the waitress. 'We'll both have a Bucks Fizz.'

'It's… ten o'clock,' Arthur spluttered.

'And?' Joan asked, sitting back in her seat. They had been tucked in a booth table away from the speakers. He was grateful not to have to strain to follow the conversation – another of the reasons he and Pearl had given up on eating out.

'Arthur. When you get to our age every day is a blessing. Why wouldn't you want to celebrate it with a little glass of fizz every now and again?' She had a twinkle in her eye.

'Here you go.' The waitress was back with two champagne flutes. 'Are you ready to order?'

'Arthur here has won brunch for two.'

Arthur rummaged in his jacket pocket for the piece of card to show the young girl.

'Cool, what can I get you?'

'Er…' Arthur squinted at the menu. The font was difficult to read and the pound sign was missing for some unknown reason. He also hadn't heard of half of the things on there. What was a jackfruit, when it was at home?

'Shall I order for us both?' Joan suggested. Arthur nodded, relieved. 'In that case, may we please get the smashed avocado on sourdough? One of those granola bowls – they're delicious. Oh, and how about a full English?'

That was one thing Arthur did recognise. 'No tomato for me please.'

'Cheers!' Joan said, raising her glass, once they were alone again.

Arthur raised his too, feeling strangely guilty for such an indulgence.

Joan smiled affectionately at the way he tucked the napkin into his shirt collar. It was the same look that Pearl had given him whenever they ate spaghetti Bolognese at home. Pearl hadn't been far from his mind since he'd sat down. Of course, there was nothing illicit in sharing the company of another woman. They were just two people having a quiet brunch, except, and Arthur may be a little rusty, Joan had been twiddling with her necklace quite a lot. Back when he was courting that had been a green light to make the first move. She also giggled at a lot of things that Arthur didn't realise were at all amusing. He shook the obscene thought from his mind.

'So, tell me about yourself, Arthur,' Joan asked, cutting open a poached egg that oozed out across what looked like mushy peas on toast.

'Well,' Arthur finished chewing his mouthful of sausage. The table was heaving under the different dishes Joan had chosen, he had never shared food like this before. Usually he would order what he wanted and Pearl would have done the same. He blushed as his fork clanged with Joan's as they both went for a sweet potato hash brown.

'You have it.'

Joan chuckled. 'Thank you. So, you were saying?'

'Oh well, there's not much to tell really.'

'Everyone has a story. Let's start with the clothes you brought to the shop, they belonged to your wife?'

'Yes, Pearl. She passed away almost two years ago now. It's taken me a while to get round to going through her things.'

Joan nodded. 'It's not an easy task. I lost my Harry seven years ago.' The bright smile that had been on her face since arriving faltered. 'Emphysema. Smoked like a chimney, of course they all did back then, but it got him in the end.'

'I'm sorry.' Arthur cleared his throat. If her pain had been anything like what he'd felt since Pearl had gone, well he wouldn't wish that on his worst enemy.

Joan gave a small shrug. 'We're the lucky ones, I guess. We're still here, living and breathing and enjoying the small delights that this world has to offer.'

'The ones left behind, more like.' Arthur couldn't help but grumble under his breath.

'I'm sure we'll join them soon enough, but,' Joan raised her glass, 'in the meantime, we should appreciate the things we get to experience. Whether it's a glass of bubbles with new friends.' She nodded to Arthur. 'Or waking up to a new day hearing birdsong from your window. We all have such little time on this planet. It really is just a blink of the eye in the grand scheme of the universe.' Joan sipped her drink. She laughed at the look Arthur was giving her. 'What? You don't get to my age without trying to figure out what the point of it all is.'

'And? What did you decide?'

'Good wine, good company and a good night's sleep,' She laughed. Arthur thought she had a nice laugh. Not too loud or dominating. A sort of laugh that made you want to join in with the joke. 'Seriously though, it's all about the little things. The things that many take for granted. It's also about raising a hand in the air to let people know you're still here and still useful. Age is just a number after all.'

'Is that why you started volunteering at the charity shop?'

Arthur thought that Joan and Pearl would have got on

pretty well, they were both similar in their charitable ways. They put him to shame with how little he did for anyone else.

'I suppose so. I was lost without Harry. I needed to feel like I still had a purpose. You know what it's like when you retire, your days just don't have the same feeling about them as they once did. You get so used to being on the go but when that stops it can be quite alarming how difficult it is to get started again. Use it or lose it, they say.' She put down her cutlery. 'You should try it, volunteering I mean, it's quite a lot of fun!'

'I think you do a marvellous job but, well, it's not for me, thank you.'

'So what have you been up to since you lost Pearl?'

Arthur struggled to think of an answer. He wanted to say: existing but felt like it might kill the mood.

'This and that.'

'I really got into gardening after Harry died. We used to grow vegetables together, you would never meet a man as proud of his tomatoes as my Harry,' Joan said with a sad smile. 'I felt I owed it to him to keep his hard work going, not that I ever produced such bumper crops as he did.'

'I'm a bit like that with my rose bushes,' Arthur admitted. 'Pearl loved them so I decided I needed to keep them alive with as much care as she did. However, there's this pigeon who's seemingly determined to stop me.'

'A pigeon?'

'Yes, we've been locked in an ongoing battle for almost two years. I'm convinced it's the same one too.' Arthur laughed at how silly this sounded. 'I've been trying to chase him away by banging a baking tray. My neighbours must think I've lost the plot.'

Joan was laughing along. 'Well, it certainly sounds like a unique method. Do you have any other hobbies? Apart from pigeon-chasing, of course!'

'Erm... no...' Arthur blushed. 'Do you?'

'Oh I love to keep busy. I swim, do Pilates, meditate...'

'That sounds very tiring.'

'Not really, not when you enjoy it. I've always been an early bird than a night owl. Because I'm learning new things every day I can barely stay awake to make it to the ten o'clock news! You have to keep busy as a widow or else you can get trapped in a pretty dark place. It's tough going from sharing your life with someone to finding yourself all alone. Everyone needs companionship and a healthy body and mind. I also read voraciously, at least two books a week, mainly so I can legitimately attend the local book club where they serve terrific wine.' She winked.

Just then a baby began crying, sharp angry bursts that reminded Arthur of Evie. The cry of a newborn. He glanced over to see a young mum patting her baby's back and swaying to the side as she quickly slurped her coffee.

'You've got a granddaughter, haven't you?' Joan asked, following where he was looking.

'Sorry?'

'The woman and the adorable baby I met in the shop that one time. The one who bought you a raffle ticket? I forgot her name. I presumed she was your grown-up granddaughter. I bet she's the apple of your eye, that one.'

'Oh, actually...' Arthur paused, he doted on both Izzy and Evie like any proud grandad would. His chest tightened at the thought of never seeing her little face again. He pulled himself together. It was best this way.

'No. That was just my neighbour and her daughter, she was helping me run some errands,' he said tightly. 'Do you have any grandchildren?'

'I've got two teenage grandsons. Alfie and Louis. They live in London and are little mischief-makers but I love them dearly.'

Arthur was grateful to the waitress who had appeared to clear away their plates.

'Thank you. It was delicious.'

'Can I get you anything else?' she asked.

Arthur watched Joan play with her necklace again. 'I wouldn't mind a coffee. Arthur? Would you like one or do you have somewhere you need to be?'

He thought of what was waiting for him. A funny sort of uncertainty washed over him. It wasn't just his cold barren house that beckoned him once brunch was over, but the task in hand. As soon as he was finished here he was going to check out and be reunited with Pearl. He knew he should feel at ease with his decision, content and happy about what lay in store, so then why was he finding excuses to put the moment off?

'A coffee sounds good to me,' he said, watching Joan's face light up.

Arthur rang Izzy's doorbell for the second time. He had eventually said goodbye to Joan and made his way home. It was a shame. In a parallel universe they would have become quite good friends, he thought. He'd ended up enjoying himself – who knew brunch could be such fun? And afterwards the first thing he'd wanted to do was tell Izzy all about it. In fact, there was lots he wanted to tell Izzy but most importantly it was time to apologise. He couldn't leave without making things right between them. However there was no answer when he knocked on her front door. He peered through the glass of her lounge window but couldn't see the TV on or any activity inside.

'Arthur?' a familiar voice called. He turned around to see Mrs Peterson walking her dogs towards him. 'Everything OK? I think she's gone away. The car's not been there for a couple of days and they had some luggage with them. Quite a lot actually, from what I could see from my window.'

'Oh. Right.' Arthur felt his spirits fall.

'Was it anything important?'

'No.'

'You sure? You look a bit peaky, if you don't mind me saying.'

'Well ...'

'Hang on! I'm sure I've got her phone number somewhere. She gave it to me when I was thinking of starting a cul-de-sac WhatsApp group. Do you want to come over to mine for a minute whilst I look for it?'

Arthur didn't have the foggiest what she was going on about but he followed her over to her house nonetheless.

'Come in, come in!' Mrs Peterson bustled to the side, closing the front door behind them. A shaggy-haired dog jumped up on its hind legs as Arthur shuffled into the hallway. 'Down, boy!'

The dog obediently scampered away to a back room.

'Please, come and take a seat. Let me get you a glass of water, you do look a little pale, love.'

Arthur didn't have the energy to decline. He simply did as

he was told and took a seat on one of the two brown leather sofas. The lounge was the same size as his, and Izzy's, but all three were completely different. His was stark and empty, Izzy's was warm and strewn with baby toys, Mrs Peterson's was a shrine to her canine companions. It was cluttered and a little bit smelly. Everywhere he looked there were ornaments of dogs, framed photos of different dogs and even cushions and a dog-print patterned throw over her sofas. A mustard-coloured rug, covered in dog hair, took up most of the floor space.

'Here we go.' She placed two glasses of water carefully on a wooden side table, putting each one on top of a coaster shaped like a pug's face.

'Right, where's her number?' Mrs Peterson opened the case of her phone and peered at the screen, poking her tongue out in concentration.

'Ah, here you go. Do you want me to write it down for you?'

'Would it be at all possible to call her from your phone?'

'Course. Hang on.' She pressed a green call button and handed it to him.

They both smiled awkwardly at one another as he waited for it to connect. He wasn't sure exactly what he was going to say to Izzy, especially not in front of Mrs Peterson. Arthur suddenly wished he'd had time to rehearse his apology.

'Hi, you've reached Izzy!' It went straight to voicemail.

'Do you want to leave her a message?'

Arthur shook his head and handed the phone back to Mrs Peterson. He had never been good with automated answering machines, always bumbling and tripping on his words before the beeps cut him off.

'Well, that's that then.' Arthur sighed deeply. Maybe it was better this way.

'She might call back or return from wherever she's gone soon,' Mrs Peterson said positively, unaware of how important it was that Arthur got to say goodbye to her. 'Was it anything urgent?'

'Yes, well, no,' he stuttered then took a breath. 'It's fine. Thank you for your help.'

They both sat in silence as if trying to think of something to say next.

'Lovely place you have here, Mrs Peterson,' Arthur said finally. He would finish his glass of water, so as not to look rude, then head back home.

'Oh, call me Sue! And thank you, it's my little haven.' She looked around the cluttered room, smiling. 'I think we have the same bathroom floor tiles.'

'We do?'

Sue blushed. 'I noticed the sold sign outside your house, so I had a little look on Rightmove. I have to say I'll be sad to see you go. The cul-de-sac won't feel the same without you. I just hope that the next lot who move in are just as nice as you and Pearl.'

Arthur had barely bothered to give the woman the time of day since Pearl had died, or even whilst she was still alive.

'I hope they agree to your bin art.'

Sue laughed. 'Oh that, yes! Me too. That was just a silly thing I wanted to do to bring the neighbours closer together. I mean we all live in spitting distance but we're so focused on our own daily business, it's hard to connect. I guess that was why I warmed to Pearl so much. She was so kind to me when Pete left.'

'Pete?'

'My ex.'

'Oh. Sorry.'

'Thanks. It was a horrible time, especially as Lucy was going through those difficult teenage years. I mean, it's never easy when your parents separate and we tried to keep it as civil as we could in front of her but, well,' Sue let out a sigh. Her eyes had gone a little glassy. 'You can't shield children from everything. I know she took it badly. I think, in a way, that's why she moved so far away for university.'

Arthur noticed a framed graduation photo above the fireplace. It was next to a charcoal drawing of a Labrador.

'Does she visit much?'

'Lucy? No, sadly.' Sue shook her head, staring at the beaming young lady in a gown and mortar board. 'She never really came back. After uni she got a job in sales working for this big fancy company in New York. She's busy with her own life now.'

'Oh yes,' A faint memory popped into his head. 'Didn't you go and visit her there?'

'Yes!' Sue seemed surprised that he'd remembered.

'Well that must have been nice for you to spend time together.'

'Mmm,' Sue nodded, then suddenly shook her head. 'Actually, Arthur, it was awful. Lucy was working all the time so I just traipsed round on my own getting very lost. And it rained almost every day too!' Her voice had gone a little wobbly. 'I missed the dogs ever so much. Silly really, I know they're no match for people but, well, I guess that was why I got them in the first place. You'll know yourself what it's like coming back to an empty house. Once Lucy and Pete left, I hated returning home.' Sue sniffed. 'With dogs around you've no chance of silence. They're not called man's best friend for nothing!' She laughed softly.

It made sense now. The woman who Arthur had always seen as a busybody was actually someone who was very lonely and just desperate to connect with others. The relief on her face when she was reunited with Fluffy her cat was understandable now. Her pets were her life since others had left her.

'I guess you've been in a similar position, adjusting to life without Pearl? Did I tell you I found one of her shoebox appeals not so long ago? I don't know why I'd held onto it for all this time. I must have put it in a cupboard and, well you know how it is, you forget what you own half the time! She really was a wonderful woman, wasn't she? Always helping others.'

Arthur shifted on his seat. She was an angel. He couldn't imagine anyone saying such lovely things about him when he'd gone.

'There was only a couple of tins of food and some tooth-paste in there so I took it to the local food bank.'

'That's nice of you,' he said politely, tapping his thumbs together.

He wanted to go home now. Izzy hadn't returned his call and he was growing increasingly tired. The past few days were catching up with him.

'Well someone should benefit, it was the least I could do. I was thinking the other day about that poor man she was helping. Awfully sad story, wasn't it? Just tragic that in this day and age it takes the charity of others when they should be being cared for by professionals.'

Arthur was half listening, he gulped the last of his water and eased himself up. He tried to surreptitiously brush off the dog hairs stuck to his trouser legs.

'Hmm. Right well, I've taken up too much of your time. Thank you again for letting me use your phone.'

'Of course!' Mrs Peterson pulled herself together. 'If she rings back I'll come and let you know right away. Take care now, Arthur.'

CHAPTER 33

Izzy

Izzy hovered uncertainly in the doorway of Willoughby Community Centre, taking in the scene in front of her. A group of octogenarians wearing chunky, black headphones, danced around without a care in the world to music that only they could hear. Wrinkled arms waved in the air, two bald men high-fived one another and a group of women with identical blue rinses shimmied around a handbag that was placed in the centre of the parquet floor.

'Izzy Carter?' A very short but sprightly woman wearing a floral tracksuit glided over to her.

'Winnie?'

'The one and only!' Winnie shouted. 'Oops, sorry!' she said, flicking a switch on her headphones. 'Marvellous, isn't it? We have a silent disco every Sunday. The songs change every time of course but, boy, it certainly feels good to let your hair down! Well, for those of us who still have some.'

Izzy nodded bemusedly. She felt like she was being filmed for some candid camera show.

Winnie took off her headphones and offered them to Izzy.

'Would you like a go? Michael Bublé's on now. Now that's a man who knows how to get your hips moving,' she said, with a cheeky glint in her eyes.

'Er, I'm OK thanks…'

Izzy had anticipated a sedate coffee morning or perhaps a quiet game of bingo, not to stumble into a pensioner rave-up.

'He's not going to do himself an injury, is he?' Izzy nodded to a gentleman sat on a chair in front of them, waving a walking stick in the air wildly. Had he just tapped that woman beside him on her bottom?

'We all know our limits,' Winnie said. 'Growing old disgracefully, that's what we call it. Right then, Izzy. Shall we go and have a chat? I don't want to miss the last dance.'

Izzy followed Winnie to one of the free tables, a little out of the way of the crowded dance floor. She shook her head, she needed to focus on why she was here and not get sidetracked with gyrating bottoms.

'So, I think it's probably easier if you start?' Winnie said, slowly easing into the chair opposite. 'I have to say that you mentioning the Winter brothers was a bit of a blast from the past!'

'I thought me getting in touch with you might be a little out of the blue.' Izzy cleared her throat. Her palms were clammy, not helped by the temperature in this stuffy room. She had already taken off her jacket but still felt too warm. She wished she'd brought a bottle of water to sip, something to help her dry mouth. 'So, the reason why I got in touch is that I want to do something nice for Arthur, he's my neighbour and we've become friends.' That word felt sticky in her throat. 'I've recently had a baby and having Arthur around has made everything a little easier to deal with.' Her chest tightened as she thought of it like that. She had a sudden urge to cry but she bit down on her bottom lip and forced herself together. 'A long story short but I'm worried that time is running out to reunite the two brothers, which is where you come in. Reg is a tricky man to track down and I hope that you might be able to point me in the right direction.'

'Tricky should be his middle name,' Winnie chuckled. 'He's a troublemaker, that's for sure. If I'm honest, that was what attracted me to him. No one can resist a bad boy, isn't that right? I heard someone say that on *Love Island*. It was true then and is still true now. He was in prison, you know.'

'Oh? What for?'

Winnie sighed and shook her head. 'This and that. It was like trouble always found him. He promised me that he would change and, foolishly, I listened.'

As she spoke a memory flashed in Izzy's mind. 'Which prison was he at? Do you remember?'

'Moorfields,' Winnie said, distracted by a couple who were almost gyrating on one another.

'Really? Are you sure?' Izzy knew this rang a bell. Wasn't the stamp on the back of the painting from Arthur's hallway, the one he had believed Pearl had picked up from a jumble sale, from HMP Moorfields?

'I'm sure.'

'Sorry, it's just a lot to take in,' Izzy rubbed her temples. 'Do *you* know what went on between them? The brothers, I mean. I know there was a falling out over a bracelet but I get the feeling there was something more that caused such a rift between them.'

Winnie shook her head sadly. 'You know what, I don't think I ever found out. They were never particularly close, much to their mother's disappointment. She was a wonderful woman, by the way. She deserved all the happiness in the world but unfortunately she appeared to be one of life's unlucky ones. Her husband died young and she was left to raise two wilful boys. Reg wasn't one to talk about his feelings. All the men weren't back then, boys don't cry and all that.'

'How long were you married for?'

'Four short but wild years. We eloped.' Winnie tilted her head, a dreamy faraway look on her face. 'It was so romantic but got us both into a world of trouble, well with my parents especially. I got the feeling that Reg's mother was just upset that she didn't get to be part of our big day. We didn't stay long in England after we married. Reg was always travelling for work you see.'

'What did he do?'

'This and that,' Winnie said vaguely, with a shake of her hand. 'None of it entirely legal but we had a wonderful time gallivanting around the world just the two of us.' She sighed again.

'And then what happened?'

'Well then I realised that although that lifestyle was exciting and glamorous it was also not compatible with having children. I desperately wanted to have a family of my own but Reg wouldn't give up his ways for a stable, boring "routine",' she said in air quotations.

'I see.'

'So, we came back to England where I got a job and found us a nice little place to live but it wasn't long before Reg got into trouble. In hindsight, I think he was rebelling against me and our plans for the future. The traditional life was never for him and, naively, I thought I could tame him.'

'So you got divorced?'

'Eventually. It wasn't the done thing back then of course,' Winnie flashed a sad shrug. 'We remained married in name for a lot longer than we were actually married. I kept the surname Winter, as my maiden name never suited me. Oh! Excuse me a minute.' She got to her feet and waved her arms to catch the attention of a lady who was veering a little too close to the cups and saucers laid out on a trestle table. 'Sorry, I just need to make sure Blanche is OK.'

Izzy shifted and jiggled her knees, waiting for Winnie to come back, it was time to ask the big questions. She needed to leave here with answers and Winnie was her only chance to help.

'Where were we?' Winnie asked, sitting down once more.

Izzy cleared her throat. 'Do you know where I can find him? Reg?'

'I have a question for you first,' Winnie said, cryptically.

'Sure! Fire away.'

'Does Arthur know you're doing this?'

'No,' Izzy met her eyes. 'I wanted to surprise him.'

Winnie nodded slowly, waiting for her to expand.

'He's having a hard time at the moment.' *That's putting it mildly.* 'There are a lot of changes happening, and well,' Izzy paused. 'I had hoped that this big gesture would show him just how appreciated and loved he is. That there are people out there who care for him and his happiness.'

'You must be very good friends to go to all this trouble.'

Winnie turned to face her fully and held Izzy's eye. 'But you're sure he doesn't know where his brother is?'

'I'm sure. He said that he hadn't seen Reg in years, they lost touch after their mum died. He didn't even know if Reg was still alive.'

'Oh, right,' Winnie said, her face pinched into an expression that Izzy couldn't quite read.

Izzy was about to say something more when she heard a ringing sound from her bag. She immediately panicked that it was Andrew calling to say something had happened to Evie but as she looked at the screen she saw it was a mobile number she didn't recognise. She muted it, whoever it was would leave a message or call back if it was urgent. This was more important.

'Sorry. Er, right, where were we?'

'I was about to tell you where you can find Reg.'

Izzy sat up straighter.

'I lost touch with him until about eighteen months ago when I got a call completely out of the blue from Reg's care home. For some reason I was still listed as his next of kin. His health had rapidly declined. Cancer,' Winnie mouthed with a shudder. 'I think they were worried he wouldn't hold on much longer.'

Izzy felt a wave of dread rise.

'I went to see him. Oh, it was awful. It wasn't just the shock at seeing him after such a long time, I mean there was that of course, I suppose I hadn't prepared myself for what state he would be in. However, it wasn't just his physical condition that was alarming but the place he called home. This awful dirty care home with nurses who couldn't give two hoots about him.'

She visibly shuddered at the memory. 'It was heartbreaking to see how much he'd changed, how he had possibly ended up in such a place. Do you know he had only had one single other visitor in all the time he was there?' Winnie shook her head. 'He should have been inundated with people by his bedside but as soon as all his money had vanished then so had these so-called friends. If anything it gave me a kick to sort my own plans out. That's why I come here, I'm determined to stay as physically fit and healthy for as long as possible.'

'And then?'

'And then what?'

'I mean, what happened to him?' Izzy couldn't take the suspense any more.

'Sadly I wasn't able to make the journey to visit him again. I did call him from time to time but it was very challenging and tiring for him. He struggled with finding enough breath to make conversation, you see.' That misty-eyed look had returned. 'I wrote him letters but never got one in response. It's just so sad.'

Izzy felt like she was about to leap out of her seat. 'Is he still alive?' she blurted out.

'Alive – yes, living – no.'

Winnie rummaged in her floral bumbag and pulled out a slim navy address book with gold embossed lettering on the front. She stuck out her tongue and flicked through the pages, Izzy noticed that many of the entries had been crossed off.

'Well now that I've met you and I'm confident you're not some scam artist, I can give you his contact details. You can never be too careful, not at my age. Tragically, Reg doesn't have anything left to be scammed out of. All his wealth clearly vanished if that home was his only option. Ah, here we go.'

Winnie turned the book to Izzy who pulled out her phone and took a photo of the page.

Reg Winter. Golden Sands Care Home,
Millverton Street, Blackpool.

There was a telephone number too, a landline written in a shaky hand.

'Thank you!' Izzy got to her feet and pulled on her jacket. Now she had his address she needed to be on her way. She couldn't shake the awful feeling that she was running on borrowed time for both Reg and Arthur's sakes.

'I have to say I am surprised that you're doing this,' Winnie said, zipping her address book back in her bum bag. 'It seems like you've gone to an awful lot of trouble.'

'What do you mean?'

'Well, Arthur should have known where Reg was all along.'

'Why do you say that?' Izzy turned back to face her.

Winnie frowned. 'Because of who Reg's other visitor was. The name that I saw again and again in his guest book was Arthur's wife… Pearl.'

CHAPTER 34

Arthur

With no dining table, Arthur ate two Ryvita crackers he'd found at the back of a cupboard standing up and looking out across the garden. It wasn't the ideal last supper but it was rather amusing just hovering with his dinner in his hand, he'd seen people do this on TV shows. He had always wondered why they didn't just sit down and be civilised. Now he was doing it, he could see the fun in it. Something caught his eye as he looked out of the kitchen window.

What the?!

The pigeon was back, this time it was pecking around the row of peonies. The pale pink pillowy heads had blossomed without Arthur noticing. His heart contracted as he thought of Pearl planting the flowers, she never got to see them bloom so magnificently. Arthur stalled. He didn't have a baking tray to bang so he rammed his hand against the glass. The bird twitched its head to stare at him for a second then flew off. Arthur debated about going outside to say goodbye to the garden, it was Pearl's love and joy after all, but he shook off the silly sentimentality. He hoped that the new homeowners would treat it with as much care as his wife had.

Instead of feeling weighed down under the silence of his house, Arthur sat peacefully with it. He realised there wasn't anything to fear in solitude. For the first time in a long time the minutes on the clock ticked forward without them being watched. He closed his curtains and set out the piece of crisp notepaper, smoothing out the edges as he placed it on the carpet near his slippered feet. A suicide note was too strong a word. He liked to think of it as his goodbye message.

I am not sure exactly what to say so I will be brief. If you are reading this then I have been successful with my plan. Jeremy, I know it might be a shock but I assure you that it is for the best. I fear I am the tiresome party guest who outstays their welcome. I never wanted to be a burden and for the past couple of years I know that I have been. The solicitor will go through everything with you but I have made sure that my will is all up to date. I've jotted down my wishes for my funeral and have paid for this in advance with the Phillip Street funeral home (information supplied on the following page). As you can see there is little left in the house that requires you to sort through. The spare key is beside this letter which should save the next lot of homeowners the hassle of getting one cut. The electricity meter is under the stairs and

the main stopcock is under the kitchen sink.
I hope I haven't forgotten anything. I wish you
and Elaine a lifetime of happiness. Please don't
be too angry. None of this was your fault.

Arthur

P.s. Izzy, if you see this note then please
know that I am sorry. You and Evie brought
me so much joy in these final months and
I want to thank you for everything you did
for me. I'm sorry I had to hide the truth from
you, I hope you understand that it was for the
best. I truly never meant to hurt you. Please
promise me one thing – you will give yourself
more credit in all you do, you are an excellent mother and Evie is lucky to have you.

There, no one could miss that there, Arthur thought flattening
it with his palm, moving it just so. He'd kept things brief
and to the point. No one liked wafflers, after all. He was
grateful that he had already placed his valuables – Pearl's
wedding ring, the framed photos from his mantelpiece, some
loose change, and the spare house key – in a large resealable
sandwich bag before that burly lot of removal men had turned
up. He had hidden it under the sink in an old empty tin of
washing powder, the same place he'd always kept their pass-
ports, knowing it was a spot no burglar would ever discover.
Thankfully Tony and his men hadn't found it. Arthur placed

the sandwich bag on the right-hand side of his goodbye note. He had everything ready.

He unsteadily lowered himself into the deckchair, his bottom gracelessly sinking to the floor. It wasn't exactly his beloved armchair but it would do. This is where he wanted to go, in his own home, on his own terms. Arthur hoped that once his nephew had read his note then he would understand, and, if necessary, he had Elaine to comfort him. He thought of Izzy, wherever she was. His gut twisted when he remembered the look of horror on her face when she had discovered the truth. Her driveway remained empty and there was no news from Sue that she'd returned his call. Arthur tried to ignore the emptiness in the pit of his stomach when he pictured them all congregating in the crematorium in his honour. They may be sad for a day but it was best this way, he told himself. Izzy had her own life to focus on, she had Andrew and Evie, she didn't need him bringing her down. If anything, he was doing her a favour. She had been nothing but a good friend and he had repaid her kindness with deceit. What sort of person did that make him?

He sat in his deckchair, listening to the rhythmic tapping of rain against his window pane, soaking up the last time he would hear the relaxing pitter patter fill the room. He was satisfied there were no more loose ends, everything was ticked off his to-do list.

He glanced at the carrier bag he had found under the sink. It was one of the quality ones from Sainsbury's. He'd spent ten pence on the bag for life, now he hoped it could at least deliver on its promise. Death by asphyxiation seemed like it was within his reach, unlike the other methods he had debated. With a deep breath he summoned the courage to pick the bag up, noticing just how thin his skin had become. He almost didn't recognise his own hands; the hands of an old man.

He wasn't really sure if there was a particular technique he needed to follow other than to put it over his head and tighten it around his neck. He stalled. Perhaps he should say something to mark the occasion? There was no one around to hear it but the moment felt right.

'Well, er. Goodbye, world.' His voice sounded different. The pitch a little higher than normal in the silence of the room.

He fumbled with the plastic handles and put the bag over his head as if slipping into the neckline of a tight pullover. The plastic sucked to his mouth as he breathed in. It smelt funny. He remembered he'd used the bag to carry a bottle of milk, which had leaked slightly. The cheese smell was terribly disagreeable. He whipped the bag off and filled his lungs with fresh air. His heart was beating a little quicker than usual.

He was about to put the bag over his head again when he hesitated. Something niggled him. It wasn't just the smell from the inside of the bag that was putting him off. He felt as if there was something he'd forgotten, some task he'd not yet completed. He ran through his final to-do list in his mind but nothing sprang forward. It was odd that he was hesitating so much. He should feel at peace that very soon he would be reunited with his darling Pearl. This was the final hurrah. The past eight weeks since his fall had been leading up to this moment. That was probably why his heart was racing and he was having a slight wobble, he told himself, he was simply feeling a little overwhelmed. Yes, that was it. After a couple of deep breaths he pulled himself together and focused. He had nothing to fear. He needed to be brave. For the final time, he slipped the bag over his head, closed his eyes and pulled it tighter around his face.

CHAPTER 35

Izzy

'So what does it mean?' Andrew repeated as they drove home.

They had not stopped talking about what it could possibly all mean since Izzy had returned to the cabin after meeting Winnie. Her mind had been all over the place. She wished they could pack up their things and cut the holiday short there and then. Arthur had until the twenty-sixth to complete Operation Pearl but her gut told her something else. She wanted to get home to see him with her own eyes. But Andrew had already ordered a takeaway for their final night and made a start on Evie's bath by the time Izzy joined them. So she vowed that they would leave bright and early the following morning. Despite all her good intentions; it had taken them longer than she would have liked to pack up the car and get Evie ready for the drive home. The journey was taking forever.

'I don't know, I'm still trying to piece it all together myself.'

Pearl's regular and mysterious visits with Arthur's estranged brother was too confusing to get her head around.

'And you're sure that Arthur had no idea about this?'

'I'm positive. The argument we had escalated because I was encouraging him to find Reg. He would have told me if he had known where he was! It's weird but now I know, there are other things that suddenly make more sense.'

'Like?'

'There was this train ticket to Blackpool that he'd found in Pearl's things. He thought it was to do with some church get-together she loved but the fact he even mentioned it to me proves that he found it odd. Then there's the painting he gave me.'

She thought of the watercolour of the wildflowers that had been hanging in Arthur's hall. Had the truth been there the whole time?

'The painting? That one you've put in the kitchen with the flowers on?'

'Yeah! Well it was painted by a prisoner. A prisoner from the same prison that Winnie told me Reg was banged up in. Arthur was led to believe that Pearl had picked it up from a jumble sale. But perhaps the answer has been staring us in the face. Reg must have given it to Pearl. They must have been in contact for years without Arthur knowing.' She stared out of the window and chewed her thumbnail. 'The question is why?'

'Do you think she was having an affair?' Andrew suggested before being shot a look from Izzy.

'No. I don't.' The truth was that she honestly didn't. 'But there has to be an explanation.'

She silently willed him to break the speed limit to get them home as quickly as possible. Izzy had had nightmares that Arthur had brought forward his plan and she'd be too late. She shook her head and tried to remain positive. He hadn't gone through with it yet and he still had eleven days until his self-imposed deadline. Perhaps, in her absence, he would even have come to his senses! It would all be some silly misunderstanding that they would one day laugh about. But, the closer she got to Birch Tree Way she knew she was kidding herself.

The moment they finally pulled up into their cul-de-sac Izzy felt her heart stop at the sight of a police car parked outside Arthur's house.

'What the...' Andrew breathed.

'Stop the car! Stop the car!' Izzy yelled. Her seatbelt was off before he'd come to a complete stop. *Had something happened? Was she too late?* She couldn't breathe. She raced over to Arthur's house and banged a fist against his front door. Her heartbeat thrumming in her ears. She pounded the door again, jabbing a trembling finger to his doorbell, but there was no sign of life inside. She stumbled to the lounge window, hoping to peer through like she had all those months ago when she'd first discovered him. But, despite banging a fist on the glass there was no sign of life. The heavy curtains were drawn but there was a slight gap allowing her to squint through the fussy net curtains. Izzy gasped at what she saw. Instead of a crumpled body lying on the patterned carpet like the last time she'd been peering through his windows, she couldn't see a thing. Arthur's lounge was completely bare. Was that a deckchair in the centre of the room? What the hell was going on?

'Iz?' Andrew called from their driveway, worry etched on his face.

'There's no sign of him,' Izzy said, feeling dizzy with nausea.

'There's no sign of anything, in fact. He's gone and so has all his furniture! I don't understand why there's a police car here? Oh God, Andrew, I'm scared!'

'Calm down. Someone must know something. Listen, leave Evie with me, you go and try some of the neighbours.'

'OK, good idea.' Izzy flew across to the only other house on the street with a parked car on the drive. She rang the bell and also hammered on the white PVC door for good measure. A cacophony of dogs began barking at her presence.

'Alright, calm down,' she heard Mrs Peterson say. 'Just coming! Now which of these keys is it?'

There was a jangle and scratch from the other side of the door. Every second felt like a lifetime to Izzy. Eventually the door opened.

'Oh hello dear!' Mrs Peterson's bright, welcoming smile dropped at the panic on Izzy's face. 'Everything OK?'

'Have you seen Arthur?'

'Arthur?'

'There's a police car outside his house. He's not answering his door and—'

Izzy stopped suddenly when she caught sight of a police officer sitting on the sofa in the lounge.

'Brian saw him go out this morning, love,' Mrs Peterson explained gently. 'Are you OK? I think you should come in and take a seat. You've gone very pale.'

'He's gone out? W-w-what are you doing here?' Izzy said to the policeman as she stumbled into the lounge.

'Hello, I'm Brian.' He flashed a kind smile and put down his cup of tea.

'Brian here is a PCSO, he's been helping me with the

318

Neighbourhood Watch scheme.' Mrs Peterson explained, keeping a worried eye on Izzy as she took a seat.

Brian held up some bright yellow stickers and leaflets to prove it. 'I spoke to Arthur myself actually.'

'You did?'

'We had a quick chat about the steps we should all be taking to secure our properties. He told me he couldn't talk for long as he was off out.'

'So he's not... dead?' Izzy could have fainted with relief.

Mrs Peterson laughed as if this was the most absurd thing she had ever heard. 'Why ever would you say that dear?!'

'Hang on. Did he say *where* he was going?' The relief was short-lived. Another thought entered her mind.

Brian shook his head, 'No, he didn't say.'

'How did he seem? Did he look OK?' *Not like he was about to head out and kill himself,* Izzy wanted to add.

'What's going on, Izzy?' Mrs Peterson asked, her tone more serious, finally picking up on the fact that this wasn't a social call.

'We need to find him. I'm really worried about him. I think he might be about to do something stupid,' Izzy said, blinking back the tears.

The following few hours were a whirl of activity. As soon as Izzy had shared the full story and once the words 'suicidal' and 'mental health problems' were mentioned it was a flurry of questions, phone calls and serious faces. A more senior policewoman had arrived after Brian the PCSO put in a call explaining the situation and asking for assistance in tracking down Arthur.

'Has he shown any signs of hurting himself before? Are there any relatives we could contact? Do you have any idea where he might be? Any places he likes to go?' The questions were coming thick and fast. It was all Izzy could do to keep up and hold back her rising fear.

'I had no idea. I mean, he was only here yesterday!' Mrs Peterson kept repeating. She had gone alarmingly pale. 'I feel just terrible!'

'It's no one's fault. People only show us what they want us to see,' Brian said, trying to comfort her. It was clear to see the level of excitement this routine house call had caused for him.

'He came here?' Izzy frowned.

'Yes. He was trying to find you, actually. He used my phone to call you.' Izzy remembered the call she'd ignored as she had been with Winnie. Maybe if she had picked up then Arthur wouldn't be missing now.

'Did he say anything or do anything out of character?' the policewoman asked.

'No, well, I mean it was out of character for him to come here in the first place. He's never been inside my house before. But, as I said, he needed to use my phone.' She suddenly let out a choked cry.

'It's alright,' Brian was patting her hand gently. 'I'm sure he'll be fine.'

Izzy spotted a look that the policewoman threw him. She was trying to locate Jeremy to see if he knew where his uncle was. Brian saw it too. He straightened up and cleared his throat, putting on a more professional tone of voice. 'We're doing all we can.'

'Did he leave here in good spirits?'

'Well, he looked a bit tired, I guess. To be honest I was initially concerned at how pale he had gone when he was outside your house, Izzy. But he perked up after a sit-down and a drink. Like Brian said when he spoke to him earlier today, Arthur's behaviour didn't set off any alarm bells. But I keep replaying the last conversation we had. I told him about my holiday and he told me about selling his house. I swear I never picked up on anything out of the ordinary!'

'Was there anything else you spoke about when he was here yesterday that you can remember?' the policewoman pressed.

'Um. I told him that I'd found one of Pearl's charity collections for a man she was helping. I took it to the food bank. You don't think that would have upset him, do you? I mean, it was just tins and toiletries, nothing of any value.'

'What man?' Izzy's ears pricked up.

'I never caught a name. Pearl used to ask me to keep things to one side, stuff I didn't need anymore, then she would fill a shoebox for him. I thought it was so awful that Pearl felt she had to help him out, as he clearly wasn't getting looked after right. The state of some of these care homes is really unbelievable.'

'Do you remember which care home?'

Mrs Peterson looked heavenward. 'Something to do with a beach…'

'Golden Sands? In Blackpool?'

'Yes! Do you know how he's getting on then?'

Izzy blinked rapidly. 'The man you're talking about is Arthur's brother.'

'Pearl never said, Arthur didn't either!'

'He doesn't know.'

The policewoman spoke over them. 'His nephew hasn't heard from him but he said he would go and check the cemetery as perhaps he went to visit his late wife's grave.'

'Of course!' Izzy jumped to her feet, kicking herself for not thinking of this sooner.

'Izzy? Izzy?' Mrs Peterson called over the sound of barking dogs, as Izzy raced out of the front door.

CHAPTER 36

Arthur

Last night certainly hadn't panned out like Arthur had planned. Things had started to go wrong when he'd chosen his mode of departure. The bag for life was not as trustworthy as one might expect. He'd had it over his head for a solid thirty seconds or so before realising that he was still able to breathe quite normally. It wasn't just the plastic bag that had let him down. His own mind was against him too, no matter how hard he tried he couldn't ignore the growing sense of unease that he'd missed something. His brain was whirring with last-minute thoughts and memories, flapping around like startled moths with every fruitless second that passed.

The train ticket he'd found in Pearl's handbag was particularly unforgettable. He'd never discovered why his wife had it in the first place. The church definitely had a minibus. He'd stood like a spare part at an unseasonably warm village fete, jangling a tin in his hand to raise funds for it as Pearl manned the cake stall. So why would Pearl take the train to a weekend worship trip?

The many times his brother's name had popped up in the

past couple of months, from the postcards to the discovery of the missing bracelet, was also a cause for concern. He'd shrugged off the coincidence of the prison stamp on the painting from his hallway but he knew he had been lying to himself. What were the odds that Pearl had found a painting at a jumble sale that had been created by an inmate at the exact same prison where Reg had been incarcerated. What were the chances?

Arthur had tried to shake these thoughts away and focus on the job in hand. None of those things, coincidences or not, mattered now. He pulled the bag tighter. But it was no good, other doubts and worries, each competing for his attention flooded his mind.

What if Izzy was right? Should he have tried to find Reg? Especially now he knew the truth about the bracelet. What's more, how could he even contemplate checking out without saying a proper goodbye to her and Jeremy instead of this cowardly exit?

'Bugger this,' Arthur said out loud, a few seconds later.

He tugged the bag from over his head and breathed in clean air. The limp carrier bag looked sad and deflated next to the side of his deckchair. The moment had passed. Arthur clearly needed answers. He had traipsed off to bed in a foul mood for another night under a towel in his desolate bedroom.

After an unexpected but very brief chat on his doorstep with a ruddy-cheeked policeman wittering on about house alarms, he had plodded all the way to St Augustine's church in the direction of his wife's grave this morning to hopefully find some sort of clarity.

'Arthur?' a familiar voice called to him as he made his way

past a row of lavender bushes, the bees humming determinedly. He turned to see the vicar jogging across the small patch of green grass separating them. Arthur's stomach sank. He wasn't in the mood for making small talk. His head was a noisy jumble of unresolved queries.

'How lovely to see you! We missed your face at the service yesterday.' He looked different without his dog collar and robes. He was wearing a green, chunky knit jumper, a checked shirt collar poking out of the top, dark recently pressed jeans and beige walking boots. 'I'm just about to head to the war memorial to meet the others for the Monday Walkers session. Start the week off on the best foot and all that! Are you able to join us?' he asked expectantly.

Arthur shook his head.

'That's a shame.' A look, Arthur wasn't sure how to describe it – concern perhaps, grew on the vicar's kind face as he walked nearer. 'Is everything OK?'

Arthur was about to say a hurried goodbye when he hesitated. He realised that the vicar might be the one person who could shed some light on what had been going on.

Arthur cleared his throat. 'Vicar, there was actually something that I wanted to speak to you about.'

'Oh?' He quickly glanced at his wristwatch. 'I'm afraid I don't have long but please fire away…'

Arthur spotted a robin that had landed on an unruly hawthorn bush. He took a deep breath. 'I have some questions about these church trips you organised, the ones that Pearl went on.'

The vicar scratched his head. 'Sorry?'

'The Weekend Worship trips.'

'I'm not sure what you mean, Arthur?'

A wave of confusion rolled across Arthur; why the secrecy?

'I'm talking about the weekend breaks that you organised to help other churches around the country. I just had some questions about them. Well, about the last one Pearl took with you to Blackpool. I know it was two years ago but I—'

'I'm afraid I have to stop you there. I honestly have no idea what you're talking about. *Weekend Worship,* you say? I've never heard of a Weekend Worship group, although it sounds like a jolly good idea! I certainly haven't been to Blackpool either, well the last time was probably when I was a youngster.'

Arthur blinked. He wasn't expecting that. He had hoped the vicar would clear things up, and tell him that perhaps the minibus had been in for repairs which is why they took the train that day.

'Wh-wh-what about the charity shoebox appeal? Pearl was in charge of putting odds and sods together for some poor bloke who—'

'I must stop you again there, Arthur. It's not something we have done as a church. Not since I've been here anyway. I'm sorry I can't be of more help.' He had the same tone and sympathetic head tilt that Jeremy was fond of using.

'Oh.'

A chirpy alarm began sounding from the vicar's jeans pocket.

'Ooops! That's my cue to leave I'm afraid. Are you sure you don't fancy coming for a little walk? I'm sure you'd really get on with the rest of the gang!'

Arthur shook his head. He had never felt so confused in all his life.

'OK, well you're very welcome to join us next week?'

The vicar gave a sprightly wave then dashed off towards the car park. Arthur felt a familiar wobble in his legs, he needed to take a seat and process what he'd just learnt. He blindly made his way over to Kenneth Black's bench next to Pearl's headstone. As usual he was the only soul in the cemetery. He sat down with a pained sigh, hopefully the peace and quiet of this place would allow him to try and clear his cluttered mind.

He sat there in confused disbelief for quite some time. The only sound was the birdsong and the rustle of wind through the leaves of the elm trees around him. The sun was warming his cheeks and the smell of cut grass wafted in his nostrils. He should have felt rather tranquil but given the circumstances he barely acknowledged any of this. Instead, he replayed the vicar's words. Weekend Worship had never existed. There was no church charity shoebox appeal. Pearl had lied to him. His darling wife, his soulmate, the person with whom he kept no secrets from had clearly been hiding the truth – whatever *this* was – from him.

'Hello, dear.' He took a deep breath and looked at her polished headstone. 'I think we need to have a little chat, don't you?'

If Pearl hadn't gone away all those times with the church, then where had she gone? Was it always to Blackpool? If so, what was there that had led her to deceive him like this?

Deep down, Arthur thought, he must have known that something was off. This was why he had hesitated, why he hadn't gone through with the final act. Right now he wasn't sure if he was grateful for that or not. He was very much alive but with a huge question mark over his wife's honesty.

Pearl Gweneth Winter. A beloved wife, aunt, sister and friend. Until we meet again. He had agonised on the right headstone inscription that could even begin to sum up his darling Pearl. Right now he felt he had a few choice words that he could add to that list. He clenched his jaw. No, she wouldn't lie to him. He had to get to the bottom of this and until he did he wouldn't sully her good name without giving her the benefit of the doubt. There had to be an explanation for all of this.

'You know that I would give anything to see you again. In fact, I was this close to making that come true.' He pressed his thumb and index finger together. 'But I'm afraid that some things have come to light that I'm, well, I'm a little hurt by, if I'm honest.'

Arthur rubbed his palms against his cheeks.

'Why didn't you tell me where you were going all those many times when you said you were away with church? What was so important that you felt you had to keep it from me? I thought we shared everything.'

He hadn't shared with her how terribly depressed he had been since she'd left him. Every time he came here to chat to her, he would concentrate on light-hearted topics of conversation such as the weather or the goings-on in the cul-de-sac, or even what he'd had to eat for breakfast, he would skim over the truth of how he spent his long lonely days. Without Pearl he had been merely existing. He had been so wrapped up in the negatives, the loneliness, the old age health complaints and the unjustness of Pearl being taken from him. When, in actual fact, he was a lot luckier than many people his age. He still had his independence, the use of his limbs, and his brain was as sharp as it had always been. But instead of making the most of this he had trudged around under a dark cloud feeling hard done by, angry and irritated. He felt as if he had been slapped around the face. This was the wake-up call he needed.

'I know you. You would never deceive me without a good reason.' He tried to push the swell of anger away. There was no point being consumed with rage, it wouldn't get him anywhere. 'I just need to find out what that reason is.'

He paused, watching that little robin hop on her headstone for a few seconds. Its tiny matchstick legs danced across the stone before flying away. He knew that Pearl wasn't going to answer him back but he had hoped for some sort of sign.

He let out a weary sigh, 'I know I said that I would do all I could to be reunited with you once more but I think I might need to take a rain check. I need to find out what has really been going on but also, well, the thing is... I've now got people who need me...'

He was taken aback by the sudden rush of emotion that clogged his throat. He thought of Izzy and Evie. Now the dust had settled on their argument he felt embarrassed for flying off the handle like he had done. She deserved better than that. He thought of Jeremy and how upbeat he had remained, always with Arthur's best interests at heart. He thought of Joan. Her dedication to squeezing every last drop out of life was commendable. Arthur had felt rather bone idle in comparison. He could do well to be a little more like Joan. Then again, perhaps he hadn't given himself enough credit since Pearl had died. Without his wife around, he had been forced to learn new skills like mastering the laundry, keeping the house running, cooking for himself and managing his finances. Of course none of this was anywhere near Pearl's standard but he probably should pat himself on the back for trying. In essence, without really meaning to, he'd kept himself alive during the toughest heartbreak he'd ever experienced and that was quite an accomplishment.

'When you care about someone you want them to be happy and I don't think that by going through with my plan to be with you they would be very happy. In fact, my love, I'm not sure I'm ready to leave them behind after all.'

CHAPTER 37

Izzy

Izzy raced towards St Augustine's church. She had no idea where Pearl's grave was or even if Arthur was here in the first place. She had driven on autopilot. The bizarre scene of Arthur's lounge running over and over in her mind. What on earth was a deckchair doing in the same spot where his much-loved armchair had been? What had he done with the rest of his things? Had he put two and two together and worked out that Pearl had been helping Reg? No matter which way you looked at it, that was a betrayal of some proportion. Had this discovery tipped him over the edge? He was already extremely vulnerable, perhaps this had been too much for him to take. Her brain was whirring with horrific premonitions at what she might find.

She wildly scanned the wonky rows of headstones, past clusters of trees and winding paths between the graves. Where was he? If he wasn't here then she had no idea where else he would be.

There was a man putting a bunch of dead flowers in a bin. For a split second she thought it was Arthur, he was around the same height and age, but he turned to face her, offering a sad smile. He walked off in the opposite direction, down another path she hadn't seen before that was blocked by a hedgerow. She followed him, rushing past him so quickly he made a noise of surprise. At the end of the path was another section of the graveyard. There was someone sitting on a bench with their back to her. Shoulders hunched over, head dropped low.

'Arthur!' She yelled. The world stood still.

'Izzy?' He turned slowly. It looked like he hadn't slept for a week. Coarse grey stubble covered his pale sallow cheeks. She had only ever seen him clean-shaven, she almost didn't recognise him. She flew down the gravel path over to the bench and almost made him topple over with the force of the hug.

'Are you OK?'

'Are you OK more like? What on earth was that for?' He let go of the soggy handkerchief clenched in his fingers to readjust his glasses.

She wiped the tears from her eyes with the base of her palm. 'I'm sorry, I'm just so happy to see you. I thought—'

'You thought that I'd checked out already?'

Izzy nodded, trying to catch her breath.

'Sit down,' Arthur patted the space beside him. 'You'll set me off in a minute. I don't know what to say. I certainly didn't expect this! I mean, I wasn't sure if you were speaking to me. We had that silly falling out and then you left.'

'Andrew took me on a surprise trip away. It was the worst timing ever! And when I came back there was a police car outside your house, you were missing, and well, I thought the worse!'

Arthur blinked. 'Oh, Izzy.'

'What are you doing here?'

'I came to think. I needed to get some answers from Pearl,' he said, his voice shaking. 'The date for my move to RoseWood has been brought forward. I'm moving this weekend.'

'So you're not completing Operation Pearl then?' she asked tentatively. She couldn't bring herself to use the words 'kill yourself'.

'No,' Arthur said firmly.

Izzy could have hugged him once more but Arthur took a deep breath to say something before she had the chance.

'I need to say I'm sorry, love. I... I... well, I was an old fool. I should never have spoken to you the way that I did. I'm not going to make any excuses for my behaviour. I am very sorry.' Arthur looked up at her with wide, red-rimmed eyes. 'It's been horrible not seeing you both every day. I'd gotten so used to having you around so not being able to talk to you has been unimaginable. I was too damn stubborn to apologise to you sooner and then when I came to my senses you weren't there.'

'But you were right, it wasn't my place to stick my nose in.'

Arthur shook his head. 'For so long I've thought that I didn't need anyone else. There was no point getting new friends at my late stage in life, so I stupidly pushed you away. But now I understand that I would be mad to throw away what we have. I've really missed you.'

'We missed you too,' she said quietly, watching him swipe at his wet eyes with his thumb. Her heart felt like it could burst.

'I'm sorry for how I reacted too. I was so hurt that you thought so little of our friendship not to confide in me how you were feeling, but that was hypocritical of me as there have been things that I've kept to myself when I should have opened up.'

'It sounds like we've both been foolish.' Arthur patted her hand. 'It's so good to see you again, dear.'

Izzy jumped as her phone rang in her pocket. 'Yes, I've found him! He's safe and fine. I'll bring him back now.' She hung up and turned to Arthur. 'Come on, let's get you home. There're a lot of people worried about you.'

Izzy had given Arthur her phone so he could call Jeremy. She overheard him say it was all a fuss over nothing but Izzy sensed how touched he was that so many people cared. He even shed a tear when he saw Evie again. Izzy was crying herself as she saw her daughter stare at Arthur with her big eyes in recognition, unaware of the rollercoaster he had been on. Evie wrapped a tiny hand around one of his fingers and Arthur kissed the top of her downy head. It was a beautiful moment.

The police had sat him down in Izzy's lounge for a lengthy chat and left pamphlets on mental health charities. Mrs Peterson had hung around for as long as possible, making cups of tea and small talk with Brian, who also lingered for longer than necessary.

Finally, Izzy was left alone with Arthur for the first time since she'd found him by Pearl's grave. Andrew was putting Evie to bed then they were all going to have a takeaway. Arthur would be staying in their spare room. She brought them both a steaming mug of coffee then sat on the sofa opposite and curled her bare feet underneath herself. She had debated pouring a slug of brandy into her cup to calm her nerves.

'What did Jeremy say?' Izzy asked as Arthur passed her phone back.

'He wanted me to thank you for letting me stay.'

'There's no way I'd let you go back to your house in that state. I still can't believe you didn't tell me about the removal men! I wish you'd let me call the police.'

Izzy had burst into tears when she'd seen what had happened to his house. She couldn't believe he had actually been living there. The sight of a lonely deckchair and a crumpled carrier bag would be a difficult image for both of them to shake off. He tried to hide the piece of paper lying on the floor by stuffing it into his pocket but Izzy had seen enough of it to know what it was. She had been so close to losing him, the thought made her feel sick.

'I think you may have involved the police enough recently.'

They both sat in silence and drank their coffee.

'I really have been an old fool,' Arthur said eventually. He was looking out of the window, across at his house, shaking his head gently. 'I shouldn't even be here now.'

Izzy put down her mug and took his hand in hers. 'Well thank God you are.'

They sat in a comfortable silence, still clasping hands. She slowly took a deep breath. In the spirit of their new complete honesty with one another she needed to come clean about everything she had discovered.

'There's something else you should know.'

Arthur looked at her.

'I don't want you to be mad but there's something I haven't told you. I've sort of been working on a thing.'

'A thing?'

Izzy nodded. She wasn't sure how he would take this. It had been a full-on day for him already without this bombshell she was about to drop. She sat up straighter. There could be no more secrets between the two of them.

'I know where Reg is,' she said quietly.

'Reg?' Arthur blinked.

She nodded. 'I've been trying to track him down for you, I thought it would be a nice thing to do, a way to thank you.'

'Thank me? For what?'

'For making me feel like me again, for helping me through the past few crazy months as I adjusted to motherhood.'

'I don't think I did anything.'

'You did more than you know.' Izzy shook her head at the look he was giving her. 'Anyway, what started off as a way to thank you then turned into something more. I met Winnie. I found her on Facebook – what a character! She's told me where we can find Reg.'

'Winnie? Sorry, what?'

'I know it's a lot to take in. I've found where your brother is.' Izzy lowered her voice. 'But I don't think he's in the best state.'

Arthur took off his glasses and gave them a polish with the hem of his jumper, blinking the whole time, processing what Izzy had just said.

'He's very poorly, Arthur. He's living in a care home in Blackpool.'

'So that's who Pearl was visiting…'

Izzy sat back. 'You knew?'

'No. Not exactly,' Arthur said. The colour that had finally returned to his face had now drained once more. 'I bumped into the vicar earlier who told me that those Weekend Worship trips Pearl took had nothing to do with the church. But I had no idea that it was Reg that she was seeing.'

'Don't you see? It all makes sense. The train ticket, the

ornament, the painting from a prisoner... So when she told you she was off on one of these trips she was actually seeing your brother.'

Arthur nodded, you could almost see his brain whirring at this deluge of information. Izzy paused for a moment to let some of it sink in. Arthur was the one to speak next.

'You said you spoke to Winnie?'

'Yes. I met her for a chat. From what she said, Pearl has been visiting Reg for a while. It sounded like he had no one else and well, since she died...' Izzy trailed off and rubbed her face. Her eyes felt gritty with tiredness. 'Arthur, this really is your last chance to make amends.'

There was an awkward moment of silence.

'Please tell me that you're going to go and visit him?'

'I swore over my dead body that I'd never speak to him again,' he said quietly.

'That was when you thought he'd stolen from you,' Izzy bit her lip. 'When you didn't know just how dire his circumstances were. You have a chance to put this right, to apologise for mistrusting him.'

'I'm sorry but the bracelet was just a small part of it. Izzy, you don't know the half of what this man has put me through my entire life.'

'You're right, I don't know so tell me. Did he have something to do with your swimming trophy? You never revealed what happened when we went to the pool together.'

'He cost me my whole career.' Arthur took a deep breath and put his glasses back on. He turned to face Izzy. 'That day we went to the baths, it was as if I was back in the summer of 1953. If I closed my eyes I could imagine the lines of benches full of excited bodies, jostling to get the best view, munching on popcorn as if at the movies, waving and singing and cheering the competitors on. If I focused really hard I could see my mother sat in a smart orange dress she'd sewn herself, telling all who would listen that it was her son out there in lane three. Memories of that glorious but bittersweet time flooded back and it just overwhelmed me.'

'Was that why you wanted to leave so quickly?'

'I only told you half the story when you found my trophy – the final one I ever won. It was the following competition I entered – The Great Britain squad qualifier – the one I would never forget, for all the wrong reasons.'

'I'd swam at my local lido to get out of my mum's hair since I could remember, but it was when I was fifteen and scouted by a man with a pencil-thin moustache and a love of Brylcreem in his jet black hair that everything changed; Ronnie O'Shea. He looked like he should be a film star, not a swimming coach. Ronnie encouraged me to meet him at the baths as soon as my shift at the factory was done. My mother was beside herself with excitement at what I could go on to achieve, there was even talk of the Olympics at one point! My father had been less keen, repeating that it was a hobby that had to come after everything else. He died before I ever got to lift a trophy.

'Reg would normally skulk next to our mother on the sidelines complaining that he was too hot or hungry or whatever he decided to moan about over the years. Intent on making sure everyone knew that he had been dragged there against his will. Coming to support me only interrupted time spent flirting with girls, or getting up to no good with that new gang he had been hanging around with. But on this particular day he wasn't there. I was on a high from the previous win, the trophy you would later unearth was still fresh in my mind but I had my sights set on a bigger, shinier one. I'd taken my place at the water's edge and glanced up to check my mother was watching, expecting to be met with her wide smile of encouragement. But she was talking to someone in an official-looking uniform. Her face changed to one of horror then she rushed away.

'I stumbled forward as a man with a whistle called for the competitors to take their places, my heart hammering, trying to work out what I'd just seen. My mother hadn't been talking to just anyone in the crowd, it had been a policeman. The klaxon rang out. Everyone dived into the water. Everyone except me. Ronnie O'Shea was screaming for me to wake up. I flung myself off the board and thrashed in the pool to try and catch up. But it was too late. The distraction had cost important seconds. I emerged from the water ashamed, confused and embarrassed. The irate shouts of Ronnie fading into the background. The policeman I'd seen lead my mother out was standing by the door to the changing rooms. It was Reg. He had been arrested for the attempted robbery of a jewellers and assaulting a police officer.'

'Wow,' Izzy breathed.

'I was convinced he did it to steal back some of my limelight, everyone was so excited that the Olympics beckoned. After that my training schedule became non-existent. The hard-earned money that had been saved to allow me to pursue my dream was now being spent on legal fees. Reg was found guilty and he never once apologised. Weekends were about prison visits instead of training days spent at the pool. Ronnie O'Shea abandoned me and I never competed again.'

'I'm not sure what to say, Arthur.' Izzy shook her head, she noticed that his hands were trembling retelling that tale. 'I can't believe that you never swam again.'

'Things were different back then. People talked, spread lies and gossip. The shame killed my mother, quite literally, she was never the same again after that. Reg was in and out of prison for years, unable to shake off the lure that came with living his fast and loose lifestyle.'

'And you never forgave him for stealing your dream...'

Arthur shook his head. 'I tried to be civil but then when he stole Pearl's bracelet it was the straw that broke the camel's back.'

They sat in silence for a while.

It was Izzy who spoke next, her tone softer. 'You're talking about something that happened a long, long time ago. The past should stay in the past, especially when you don't know how much of a future he has left.'

Arthur shifted in his seat. 'Well... it's a long way to Blackpool. Plus, I'm moving soon, so—'

'Arthur!' Izzy raised her voice. 'Stop trying to come up with excuses. Do you not want to know why Pearl was visiting him all this time? Why she never told you? I mean—'

'I'm scared, OK!' Arthur blurted out. The truth hanging in the air between them.

Izzy lowered her voice and spoke more gently. 'What are you scared of? You already know the truth with the bracelet, he wasn't the man you thought he was. You just have to go there and speak to him, man to man, admit you both made mistakes and bury the hatchet. You need to find out why Pearl had been caring for him... and hiding this from you.'

'It's not that easy, Izzy.'

'Why not?'

'Because,' Arthur pinched the bridge of his nose. 'Because what if he doesn't want to see me?'

'There's only one way you're going to find out,' she said resolutely, picking up her mobile phone. 'Let's call the home and see if we can go and meet him soon?'

She had dialled the number and lifted the phone to her ear before Arthur had the chance to stop her.

'Oh hello, I was wondering if you might be able to help?' Izzy put on a polite, higher pitched phone voice. 'I'm calling because I'd like to arrange a visit with one of your residents. His name is Reg Winter. I'm calling with this request on behalf of my neighbour, Arthur. He's Reg's long-lost brother.'

CHAPTER 38

Arthur

There he was. Reginald William Winter was sat hunched in a chair near the far window. The bright blue eyes that had once charmed hundreds of women were now drooped, buried deep into his skull under two thick, wiry white eyebrows. His skin was the same texture of a ripe nectarine, stretched over the prominent bones that jutted from his cheeks and chest. A patterned short-sleeved shirt hung off him displaying wrinkled, bluey-green faded tattoos that looked like smudges. Where had his baby brother gone? The handsome devil had vanished.

'Don't expect much from him, he's not our chattiest guest,' Pamela, the lady who signed Arthur in, said. 'I'm sorry to hear of your wife's passing. Her visits here really seemed to help lift his mood.'

'I'm sure they did,' Arthur mumbled. He felt as if he was having an out of body experience.

Pamela led him down the narrow corridors. This place made RoseWood seem like a palace. Every dark room he was led through smelt of urine and broccoli soup. The air was musty and heavy, as if it could settle on his skin and seep into his pores. He breathed through his mouth. Clearly no one had thought to open a window recently.

'Reg. There's someone here to see you!' Pamela shouted, giving him a shove on the arm to try and stir him. 'He says he's your brother. Pearl's husband! That's nice of him to come for a little chat with you, isn't it?' She turned to Arthur. 'I'll leave you both to it.'

Reg hadn't moved an inch since she'd wandered off. His eyes appeared to be focused on something that Arthur couldn't see, his mouth lax and shoulders drooped. He looked old. More than that, he looked like he'd given up. He reminded Arthur of someone he knew but he couldn't put his finger on exactly who.

'Reg. It's Arthur. I think we need to talk,' Arthur said, his face set tight. His heart was racing ten to the dozen.

Still nothing from Reg. Arthur's leg was starting to ache from standing waiting for a response. He decided to drag over an empty wing-backed chair, in an identical puddle brown colour to the one Reg was sat on, and sat down letting out an involuntary deep sigh as he did, his knees trembling slightly.

'Reg. Can you hear me?' Arthur said louder, leaning into his brother's peripheral vision.

Ever so slowly Reg's eyes shifted from the grubby window to Arthur's face. They widened in recognition.

'Arthur?' he rasped. Years of smoking had stolen much of his vocal cords but Arthur's heart leapt that he was at least able to identify him.

'Yes.'

What looked like tears glistened from Reg's cloudy eyes. 'I can't believe it! What are you doing here?' He fell into

343

a coughing fit. Arthur handed him a plastic cup of water from a side table. He lifted it with a trembling hand and stopped coughing, temporarily relieved.

'I'm sorry if this is a shock. You probably didn't expect to see me again but there are some things I need to say and I'd appreciate it if you would just listen and let me finish.'

Reg nodded and stayed silent. Arthur had tossed and turned for most of the night in Izzy's comfortable spare bedroom preparing this speech in his mind. He now wished he'd written it down. He cleared his throat.

'I always blamed you for Mum's death. Exhausted by the shame, the doctors said. We both know she was never the same again after you went to jail. However, even in her final days, she still spoke about you as her cheeky boy. Despite all the heartache and worry you had caused her, she still loved you and forgave you.' Arthur shook his head. 'But I could never be as forgiving. Not only did your selfish life choices kill our mother but you also lost me the chance at my dream career,' Arthur felt his voice breaking. 'And then you proved that I was right not to trust you when you stole from me.'

'I never stole a thing from you,' Reg spluttered, coughing once more.

Arthur gave him a look.

'Sorry, please continue,' Reg rasped.

'Ever since Mum's funeral, I vowed that I didn't have a brother. I'd lost her *and* you that day. We had exactly the same chances growing up, the same opportunities, but you chose the wrong path. The one that's led you here.' Arthur glanced around the room. He almost felt guilty for being so against the move to RoseWood, when it could have been so

344

much worse. He pitied anyone who was forced to spend their last numbered days in a place like this. Arthur took a deep breath. He was getting to the hard part now. He had to swallow his pride and admit what he now knew to be the truth.

'I know my visit here is completely out of the blue. I cut you out of my life believing that it was for the best. I wanted nothing more to do with you.'

Reg looked as if he wanted to say something.

Arthur held up a hand gently. 'Please, wait. Let me finish. I wanted nothing more to do with you but things have changed a little. I recently came across something that I'd not seen for a long, long time. It was hidden down the back of a bookcase.'

'The bracelet,' Reg said, finishing Arthur's sentence for him.

'Yes.' Arthur took a deep breath. 'I got it wrong. I shouldn't have accused you and, for that… I'm sorry.'

Reg didn't say anything.

'You don't seem surprised?'

'I knew I never took it, like I told you. I'm not the criminal you make me out to be, Arthur.'

'The spell inside, the tattoos, the unsuitable girlfriends and dubious jobs…' Arthur ticked things off his fingers.

'So you thought *once a crook, always a crook*. I get it.' He paused to launch into a bone-shaking coughing fit. Spluttering into a tissue. Arthur saw the specks of blood but pretended to look out of the window, waiting for Reg to get his breath back.

'Why didn't you try and prove me wrong? Why didn't you fight to save our relationship, well, what was left of it?' Arthur asked.

'What could I have done? You had your mind made up from the moment I was arrested all those years ago. But Arthur,

I wasn't the one who stole your dream career from you. I never stopped you competing. *You* chose not to do that.'

Arthur was shocked. 'How could I swim professionally when the Winter name had been dragged through the mud like that? Do you think any coaches wanted to take me on? Any sponsors wanted to work with me? The papers were filled with only one of us – you and your trial.' Arthur tried his best to keep his cool but he was finding it hard. 'Not to mention the savings that were supposed to be for my training that all went on you and your legal aid. There was nothing left in the pot for me. It would have taken me years and years to ever save enough again and by then it would have been too late.'

There was a moment's silence between the two brothers. Arthur glanced around the drab room at the staff huddled in the corner, engrossed with their mobile phones. He steeled himself. 'Of course, there's another reason for my visit...'

'Pearl.'

Arthur nodded, he suddenly felt too hot. The smell in here was making his head swim.

Reg's lower lip wobbled ever so slightly. 'They told me she'd passed away. I guessed as much when her visits stopped.'

'Yes. She died almost two years ago now. It was very sudden.'

'I'm sorry. She was one in a million.' Reg coughed. 'I wish I could have had a woman like that in my life.'

'You hardly did badly,' Arthur scoffed. He remembered the string of dolly birds that his brother would parade on his arm walking through town, each a near clone of the last.

'From the outside it might have looked like I had it all, the big house, the fast cars, the pretty women, when really *you* had everything I was searching for all along. And now look at me.' Reg slowly moved a frail arm across the room. Arthur thought back to those exotic postcards bragging of this envious lifestyle. 'Look where I've ended up. I'm going to die here, Arthur, having never experienced what you did… true love.'

Arthur and Pearl's life together may not have been as glamorous or exotic as Reg's once was, but it had been *their* life together. He wouldn't have traded that for all the tea in China.

Arthur glanced at his shoes, they needed a good polish. He lowered his voice a little. 'Pearl never told me about coming to visit you or the little care packages she sent you.' Arthur understood now that the shoebox appeal wasn't for charity but for Reg. He was the charity case.

'Please don't blame Pearl. I swore her to secrecy.'

'But why?' Arthur met Reg's watery eyes.

'I needed help. I lost everything, Arthur.'

'You used to brag about the many friends you had, not to mention all the women on the go too. Surely you had someone else to turn to other than my wife?'

Reg shook his head. 'As soon as the money dried up so did the women, and the people I thought were my friends. I had no one, but I had too much pride to ask *you* for help. You made it clear that you never wanted to hear from me again. Perhaps it was karma, I eventually got what I deserved.'

Karma, Arthur mused.

'I contacted Pearl when I truly hit rock bottom. I was being evicted, I had bills coming out of my ears and, with my health failing, I needed to be cared for. I had no choice but move in here and well, look at the place. You wouldn't house a dog in here.'

For the first time in a long time, Arthur agreed with him about something. Golden Sands was as bleak as they came.

'Thankfully Pearl started to visit me, I think she needed to see with her own eyes just how dire my circumstances were. She couldn't help with my financial situation but she could help to make things more comfortable for me by sending small care packages. She made the effort to come down and sit with me, keep me company for a while. Her regular visits kept me sane, a temporary respite.' A tear came to Reg's cloudy eyes. His voice broke slightly. 'Your wife did more for me than anyone and I never got to thank her. When she stopped coming, stopped sending those packages I feared the worst had happened. I had sworn her to secrecy to avoid hurting you, so I couldn't call you and see how you were coping without her. She used to keep me updated with what you were up to, the comings and goings of where you lived, the church events she was helping out with and so on. I felt like I had a lifeline to you.'

'She lied to me, Reg.'

'Because she knew it would hurt you! If you found out, you would have insisted she stopped coming.'

'Well... yes...'

Pearl had been a glimmer of hope to this man who had nothing left. If Arthur had known about the secret visits he would have been incandescent with anger and, like Reg said, ordered her not to come again.

'So many times she told me that it would be the last but I think she was overcome with worry that I would be left to rot here. Her good heart won over.'

It dawned on Arthur that Pearl had stopped nagging him to

make amends with his brother. She had stopped mentioning Reg because she had begun helping him herself.

'Did you give her a painting?'

Reg nodded. 'I was encouraged to take up the prison art classes, rehabilitation or whatever you want to call it. I showed it to her during one of her visits and she said she liked it, reminded her of somewhere you two went on holiday? It was a small token of my appreciation, a way to let her know how grateful I was. I supposed I hoped that you might ask about the prison stamp, put two and two together and make contact yourself.'

'I had no idea. She told me it was from a jumble sale. It has been hanging in my hall for years.'

'Don't you realise, Arthur?' Reg sighed. 'She's led you to me. Pearl was a good woman. Please, don't forget that. You really did have it all, Arthur.'

Arthur had been so focused on what he was missing that he had ignored what he had been blessed with. Tears were falling down Arthur's cheeks. Big, fat ones that he didn't care to hide or wipe away. So many years he'd held back and refused to cry but now he sobbed for the life the brothers could have had together, the lost chances and the years wasted. How foolish they had both been. Reg was right. Pearl had succeeded in what she'd hoped Arthur would have done a long time ago, she had finally reunited them.

Arthur made his way back to Izzy, who was patiently waiting with Evie in reception. He couldn't believe that Pearl's breadcrumbs had led him back to Reg. It all seemed so obvious now. However, he may never have followed the clues if it wasn't for Izzy encouraging him. Arthur passed a man in a wheelchair being pushed down a corridor. He thought about how close he was to going through with Operation Pearl. How he had prepared to die alone in his carcass of a house, in his depressing empty lounge. What sort of ending was that?

In a few days, Jeremy would pick him up and deliver him to RoseWood Lodge and that was where he would stay until his final journey out in a wooden box. He didn't have any energy left to fight this. Perhaps it would be quite nice to be looked after, to have his meals cooked and someone to do his washing. It would at least be warm and he could sit in a proper armchair once again. It was no palace but it was no Golden Sands either. He turned a corner, trying to find his bearings, when an idea came to him. It seemed so obvious now, it was almost laughable. He picked up his pace, time was running out to put it into action.

'Sorry, I didn't mean to sleep for so long,' Arthur said, blinking awake as they pulled onto Izzy's drive.

He knew Izzy probably had a hundred questions for him but now was not the time, so he had said he wanted to shut his eyes and get some rest. He had been asleep for much of the journey home.

'Evie's flat out too.' Izzy glanced in her rear-view mirror. 'I don't want to wake her and move her into the house just yet.'

'Well I'm in no hurry.'

She turned the engine off and they both remained in their seats, looking out at the familiar houses.

'Do you remember the first time we were next to one

another in this car? Back when I picked you up that miserable night?' she said quietly.

'When I was lost.'

'I think we were both lost back then,' she mused, surprising herself. 'God, so much has changed since then. Those hazy, early months of newborn life seem like a lifetime ago now.'

Arthur gave her a small smile, himself thinking back to the events that had led them to find one another. He could feel a lump jump to his throat so he coughed and tried to change the subject. 'I suppose I should call Jeremy and tell him how I got on.'

'How did you get on?'

'I feel like I've left a part of myself back in Blackpool. Silly really. I mean it's been so long since I had any sort of relationship with Reg but, seeing him like that, it just made all the arguments and misunderstandings seem so... insignificant I guess.' He sighed deeply. 'Thank you for driving me and well, for encouraging me to go in the first place.'

'You're welcome. I wonder what Pearl would say about it all,' Izzy mused softly. 'I imagine she would be pleased that you've made amends. You did a big thing going there today, Arthur, lots of people wouldn't have had the courage to do what you did.'

Arthur stared down at his thumbs. 'I suppose. I just feel like I need to do more, I'm just not sure what. Well, I have made one decision. When I call Jeremy I need to tell him I'm not going to be moving to RoseWood.'

Izzy turned to face him, her eyes widening.

'What? B-b-but... they're expecting you. Your house is due to be completed any day now. Please don't tell me you're—'

'I'm not moving to RoseWood, because it's a dump.' Arthur cleared his throat. 'I'd like to go and look at Cedar Lodge. The retirement home, sorry, village, near Waitrose. I know it comes with a price tag but surely at my time of life I deserve to be comfortable.'

'Wow. Arthur, I think that sounds like a great idea! I hate that we'll no longer be neighbours so I can't just pop in when I want or need to, however, hearing you talk positively about your future for the first time, especially after the past couple of days, is wonderful! As much as I am going to miss seeing you so often I'm excited at what your new life is going to be like.' She grinned. 'Let's go inside. You can call Jeremy and I'll make us both a nice cup of tea.'

Arthur smiled. 'Now that is something that I know Pearl would approve of.'

CHAPTER 39

Arthur

Arthur had surprised himself at how much he was looking forward to today's tour of Cedar Lodge, even though he would miss being Izzy and Andrew's house guest of course. Izzy in particular hadn't let Arthur lift a finger for the past few days. He relished coming down in the mornings to be greeted by Evie gurgling happily to herself on a brightly patterned play mat in the centre of the living room floor. He enjoyed the smell of coffee and the fabric softener coming from clothes draped on a clothes horse. He was growing used to noises surrounding him again, from the gentle whirr of the washing machine to the soft melody of one of Evie's toys she managed to kick to life. It felt like home. This sense of warmth and love and little luxuries made his decision even easier.

'I'm sorry Elaine hasn't been able to join us today,' Jeremy said, bobbing his knees, as they sat on a bench outside Cedar Lodge, waiting for Izzy to arrive. He had been very helpful sorting things out and cancelling his place at RoseWood.

'Her allergies, I suspect,' Arthur finished for him. He noticed Jeremy's cheeks flush a lovely shade of red.

Jeremy coughed. 'Well, er, no. I actually made that up. She doesn't have allergies.'

Arthur sat back, 'Oh?'

'Yes, well,' his nephew stuttered. 'The, er truth is... she finds you a bit difficult.'

'Me?!'

'She was a little intimidated by a comment you made about her baking skills, something about the rock cakes she gave you not long after Aunty Pearl had died. I think she just thought it was better if I saw you without her.'

Arthur thought about this. OK, so he was a little grumpy at times and it was likely that perhaps he had unknowingly hurt her feelings, but he didn't like the idea of someone actively avoiding him. He had to admit that that hurt.

'Can you please tell Elaine that I am sorry if I ever upset her. That was never my intention.'

'I will. Oh, I still have those things I borrowed from you. The electric drill and the ladder.'

'Keep them. I don't need them now.'

'Thank you.' Jeremy looked a little sheepish. 'You know, it's silly but I didn't even need them in the first place.'

'Sorry?' Arthur coughed. This was becoming a very revelatory chat indeed.

Jeremy shifted on the bench. 'I only borrowed them because I felt like I needed a reason to come round and visit you so often. I didn't want you to think I was checking up on you, so I thought if I asked for help then you wouldn't mind me popping in.'

Arthur tried not to laugh at the absurdity of it all.

'I honestly had no idea that you felt so low, Uncle Arthur.

I'm still trying to get my head round everything that's happened to you. If anything, I feel like I'm to blame.'

'What? Why ever would you say that?'

'If it wasn't for me pushing you to move then you would still be in Birch Tree Way and everything would be exactly the same.'

'Jeremy, I'm lucky to have someone like you looking out for me. I don't think I've ever told you that before. I know that, despite all my grumblings, you have my best interests at heart.'

'It's nothing.' He saw his nephew blush and shoot his eyes to the blue sky. 'I'm just trying to get my head around the fact that you've got a brother! I vaguely remember his name but I honestly thought that he'd died when I was younger. It must be brilliant news to rediscover him after all this time. I would have given anything to have a brother or a sister. Just think of all you've got to catch up on! I'd love to come and meet him.'

'I'd like that and I'm sure he would too…'

'I'm here! So sorry I'm late!' Izzy called out, jogging over from the car park. 'Andrew has taken Evie out and was struggling with the pram, the back wheel locks if you push it too hard and, anyway, I'm here now.'

Arthur smiled. 'You're just on time.'

They all padded in through the double doors to be greeted by a woman in her mid-forties who looked like an optimistic weather presenter, with a tight ponytail and dangling baubles clipped to her ears.

'Hello and welcome to Cedar Lodge. I'm Michelle, we spoke on the phone?' she said. 'Welcome, Arthur. I'll start by giving you a quick tour of the facilities, then we can go and have a nice cup of tea and I'll happily answer any questions you may have. Sound good? Right, let's go!'

Izzy gave him a wink and linked his arm as the four of them made their way around the bright and airy rooms.

'We have an active social calendar that you can partake in as much, or as little, as you like.' Michelle smiled, holding a door open to the gardens leading off from the wide entrance hall. 'We've got twenty-five acres of landscaped grounds, perfect if you want to get away from it all. I think of it as a little oasis.'

'It really is very pretty,' Izzy agreed, her eyes widening at the sight before them.

'We take pride in our gardens, and have a separate allotment for those green-fingered folk who are keen to keep up their hobby. I know that some people move here because they feel lonely,' Jeremy coughed loudly at this but Arthur was too busy taking in the immaculate lawns to notice. There were boules and croquet set up on the lush grass. He could picture Evie toddling around out there one day when Izzy came to visit. 'By living with a like-minded community of people it means that you can choose how you spend your time. I promise you will never be lonely here!'

Arthur cleared his throat. It was the first time he'd spoken since arriving. 'I've got some rose bushes in my garden. They are very special to me. I... I wondered if I could replant them here?'

'Of course!' Michelle grinned. 'We have one lady who moved her entire vegetable garden because her late husband helped plant it. We want this to feel like home, Arthur. Ah, speak of the devil,' Michelle laughed. 'That's the lady I was talking about!'

A woman was kneeling on a padded cushion with her back to the group, half behind a flowering bush. She was bent over, tending to the patch of soil in front of her. A small portable radio was playing classical music on the grass next to her.

'Cooee! Joan!' Michelle called.

Arthur couldn't hide the smile that broke out on his face as the lady turned and waved a garden glove in the air. He began to laugh and shook his head.

'Arthur!' Joan gasped.

'Wait – you two know each other?' Jeremy asked. Confusion etched on his face. Izzy simply laughed and murmured something about fate under her breath, loud enough for Arthur to hear.

'We do,' he nodded.

Joan got to her feet and jogged over. 'I had no idea you were thinking of moving here?'

'I had no idea that you lived here!' Arthur smiled at the coincidence.

'This has been my home for the past five years.'

'Joan is one of our star residents,' Michelle winked as Joan brushed the compliment away with her hand.

Jeremy coughed pointedly.

'Sorry,' Arthur remembered himself. 'Joan works at the charity shop. We've become... friends. This is Jeremy, my nephew. And Izzy.'

'Yes I remember!' Joan smiled. 'You have the adorable baby.'

'Evie, yes,' Arthur said as Izzy waved hello.

Jeremy stretched out his arm. 'It's lovely to meet you, Joan.'

'So nice to meet you too. I'll let you carry on with your tour. If you have time before you go you must check out the table tennis room, I'd love to challenge you to a game one time Arthur,' she winked. 'Hopefully see you soon.'

'Y-y-yes, you too,' Arthur stuttered, feeling warm under everybody's interested gaze.

'Right onwards we go,' Michelle said. 'If you're OK with stairs I can show you our snooker room and hairdressing salon? We've also got a heated swimming pool that is a firm favourite with residents.'

Izzy gently nudged Arthur as they walked past the shiny gymnasium and pool area. It wasn't as large as the local baths but it was clean and perfectly adequate. No podium seating just a handful of sun loungers next to potted palm trees at the water's edge. He had to admit it looked very inviting.

He was waiting for Izzy to tell Michelle that he was a champion swimmer, but to his surprise she just smiled and nodded along. That was his story to tell. Perhaps it was time for Arthur to get back in the water. He'd held a grudge that Reg had stolen his swimming glory for too long. In a way, Reg was right. Arthur had been the one too embarrassed to compete, too scared to fail, too nervous at putting himself out there. He had blamed his brother, when in fact, it had been Arthur who had been his own worst enemy.

Before long, Izzy and Arthur walked out of the automatic doors and into the car park that was edged with neatly tended shrubs and borders. Another car had pulled up to the entrance and a young black man with a logoed polo shirt was helping a frail lady from the back seat into a wheelchair.

'Do you want to wait here on this bench? Jeremy said he'd be along in a minute. I think he just wanted to have another look at their food hygiene certificates,' Izzy said, with a playful roll of her eyes. 'He certainly is thorough!'

Arthur watched the member of staff push the older woman away, they were both laughing at something.

'How about, once he's finished, we all go for a spot of lunch? My treat. We could even ask Joan to join us, I think you two would get on.'

'Sounds like a great idea,' Izzy smiled. 'I'm intrigued to know more about this *friendship*.'

'I don't know what you're trying to say.' Arthur felt his cheeks warming.

'I'm just teasing you. So, I've been thinking about what I'm going to do now your house is all packed up and you don't need me anymore,' Izzy said, pulling a pathetic face that made Arthur laugh. 'I've realised that I need to carve more time out for myself. Just a few hours once a week or so, but I think it would be good for me to hand Evie to Andrew so I can have some "Izzy time".'

'And what will you do with this newfound freedom?'

'I might join a book club or there's a Zumba class in the village hall that looks fun. Actually, I had a long overdue FaceTime with Joanna, a woman I work with, the person I would call my closest friend, I guess. Well, apart from you.' She nudged him gently. 'Anyway, we're going out for cocktails at the weekend. But, in answer to your question, I'll probably just be here pestering you!'

'You know you are both always welcome! What does Andrew think of all this?'

'He's been really supportive. He's happy to have the old me back. Well, not the old me, but the new version of me.'

They both sat in a comfortable silence looking at a white butterfly fluttering past.

'So, what do you think? Of this place, I mean?' Izzy asked. 'Michelle said they have availability for you to move early next week, if you're ready? Not that you're not welcome to stay in our spare room for a little longer whilst you decide,' she added hurriedly.

The sun broke through the clouds warming Arthur's face. He smiled at the rose bushes that lined the neatly tended borders.

'I'm ready,' Arthur said, tilting his face to the sun.

No, it wasn't home… but it could be, Arthur thought. It certainly could be.

CHAPTER 40

Izzy

Izzy felt like a new woman after six glorious hours of undisturbed sleep, the most since Evie had been born. She realised, in part, that her inability to switch off was also down to her worries over Arthur. Now she knew he was safe and was going to be looked after it was as if her mind could finally get some proper rest. It was amazing just how much energy she had, how much more 'with it' she felt.

It wasn't just the rare night of good sleep that had helped, in general she was starting to feel on top of things once more. The enormous mountain she once had to climb at the start of every day full of housework and nappies and feeding had become easier. Arthur had given her a purpose, Evie had become less demanding and Izzy had learnt how to cope better. Of course, there would be tough days. Evie would soon be teething and she heard on the grapevine that that was an utter joy, but instead of feeling paralysed with anxiety and apprehension, she felt optimistic that she was strong enough to cope with the next phase. That was all it was – a phase.

In fact, Izzy enjoyed going at a slower pace. She could

now see what a luxury it was to have the chance to binge-watch Netflix in her pyjamas in the middle of the day. To have nothing to achieve apart from making sure Evie was OK. No bosses to please, no stressing out over looming deadlines, no one barking orders. She had been too focused on all the things she had lost instead of looking at what she had gained. Suddenly she felt grateful to have a whole day with Evie to do whatever she wanted and now Arthur didn't need her help anymore she had all the time in the world to put herself and her daughter first.

'Morning!' Izzy chimed as she walked into the mother and baby group. For once she was one of the first ones here.

'Someone's feeling perky this morning,' Tina, the class organiser, said cooing over Evie as Izzy chose her spot. Today she would be on the inside of the circle. She carefully laid Evie onto a padded mat and found a rattle for her to play with.

Andrew had left for work a little later, giving her time to take a long shower, put on a swipe of coloured lipbalm and plait her freshly washed hair. If that wasn't enough of a treat, Arthur had also made her beans on toast for breakfast and held Evie as she ate it. For the first time in a long time she felt like she had her shit together.

'It's amazing what a decent shower and some concealer can do!' Izzy smiled at Tina, who was welcoming the other mums.

Izzy spotted Lorna rushing through the doors just as the class was about to start. Today there was a demo from a group of mum-entrepreneurs who had designed a range of breastfeeding cover-ups they were trying to flog. Izzy and Lorna had swapped numbers and added one another on WhatsApp after the last class. They had been sharing funny parenting memes and links to interesting baby-related articles ever since. They also spoke about other important topics like what naff reality TV show they were currently bingeing. It had been nice not to feel alone during the middle of the night feeds. Knowing there was another mum out there doing the exact same thing, struggling to stay awake and just do her very best, was unbelievably reassuring.

'Hey, please excuse the state of me. I couldn't find my hair brush and—' Lorna stopped still in front of Izzy. 'Woah. Someone looks nice.' She sniffed. 'Wait. Are you wearing perfume?'

'Will you still be my friend if I say yes?'

'Only if you tell me what your secret is.' Lorna gently placed Charlie on the mat next to Evie. 'If you've got yourself a live-in nanny then I'm never speaking to you again. I can't be the only one slumming it on my own.'

'Hah. Well I guess you could say I've got temporary help.' Izzy thought of Arthur. She'd almost not come to the group as she didn't want to leave him on his own. Whenever he was out of her line of sight she still felt a wave of panic that he would do something stupid. But he had insisted he would be fine, all she could do was hope and trust that he had seen how much he had to lose.

Lorna pulled a face. 'Oh?'

'It's a long story. Let me get you a coffee and I'll fill you in.'

'Well this sounds exciting. Oh, I also wondered if you had time to grab a proper coffee after this. A real one where we sit on squishy sofas instead of the floor? Let's treat ourselves! You know, if you wanted to…' Izzy could have sworn that Lorna suddenly seemed a bit embarrassed at putting herself out there and asking her to hang out away from the class.

'I'd love to but I can't today.'

She had to dash at the end of the class to get back to help Arthur. The exchange of his house was happening at midday. She saw Lorna's nervous smile falter. 'But how about tomorrow?'

CHAPTER 41

Arthur

Arthur turned the key in the lock and opened his front door. Izzy had been reluctant to let him leave her sight as she ummed and ahhed about going to the mothers meeting thing this morning. But he had promised her he would be fine and shooed her out the door. He wouldn't be long. The contracts had been signed and the new homeowners were due to arrive in a few hours. He just wanted to bid farewell to his home of sixty-two years for the very last time.

It smelt different in here. The familiar scent he used to be greeted with had faded. It wasn't the belongings that made a house a home. It was those who lived there that made the difference. If he was honest, the place hadn't been the same since Pearl had died. She had made this home. Whether it was doing the most mundane chores, baking, or singing to herself; her energy had brought the place to life. Her presence. The feeling of her being in another room had vanished on that sad, sunny day two years ago.

He plodded into the lounge, overwhelmed by the single deck-chair and a crumpled plastic bag. It looked such a depressing sight. He picked up the bag and headed towards the bin where it belonged. What had he been thinking? Since losing Pearl, he had thought of himself as an invisible solitary being, muddling through as best he could. It turns out that all he had to do was ask for help and let others in. He strode as quickly as he could to the bin, catching sight of something in his garden.

'What are you doing here?' He thumped a hand on the glass. 'Gerroff with you!'

The pigeon stopped pecking at the grass and twitched, turning its head to face him, their eyes locked for a split second. Arthur smiled, realising that he would actually miss his familiar foe. The bird's visits had been an almost daily reassuring presence that he hadn't truly appreciated. There was a tentative knock on the kitchen door, pulling him back from this moment. Izzy was waiting on the other side, chewing her lip. When he looked back, the pigeon was gone.

'Hey, I just let myself in. Are you ready?' she asked, her voice higher than normal, Arthur knew she was trying to sound as positive as she could.

'Do you know what... I think I am.'

He gently shut the front door behind him and pushed his keys through the letterbox. Jeremy had given his set to the estate agent for the new family to let themselves in and begin making this place their home. The house would once again breathe life and love and the thought of it made Arthur happier than he had expected. It was time to let others make their own wonderful memories here, and in turn, it was time for him to look forward instead of backwards.

'Any final words?' Izzy asked, standing back and looking up at the house.

Arthur shook his head and swallowed the unexpected lump in his throat. 'I don't think there's anything left to say.'

'Come on then, we probably have time for a cup of tea before Jeremy arrives. Andrew has put Evie down for a nap, so we can enjoy some peace. I bet you'll be glad to have your own space again!' she laughed.

Arthur turned to face her. It was so nice to hear her laugh again. 'Not at all. In fact, I'm not sure how I can thank you for all you've done. You're the reason I'm still here, Izzy.'

'Well thank God for that!' Izzy quickly blinked. 'Come on, we can't stand here sobbing on the doorstep, what will the new owners think!'

'I wondered if we could have another trip to Blackpool soon?' Arthur said as she gently linked arms with him and walked over to her house.

He thought of his brother, locked away, waiting to die in such a depressing care home. Reg would give anything to spend his last numbered days in a place like Cedar Lodge, being looked after by those who genuinely cared. He didn't know how much longer his brother had left but he knew that he needed to make up for lost time.

'Of course. We can go whenever you want Arthur. Just because you've got a new postcode doesn't mean everything has to change.'

Izzy had her front door open when there was a shout behind them.

'S'cuse me! Arthur?' A young voice called out.

Arthur turned to see Nikki running towards them with an arm stretched in the air.

'You go in, love, and put the kettle on. I won't be long.'

Izzy nodded and headed inside.

'Hello, dear,' Arthur said as Nikki jogged over.

'Hey. I wasn't sure if you'd left.' She had taken off her large backpack and put it on the ground between them. She crouched to her knees, trying to get the zip to open.

'I'm actually going later today.'

'Well before you go I wanted to give you this…'

She handed Arthur an A4-sized canvas. His breath got caught in his throat as he stared at it.

'I thought you could put it up at your new place,' she said, still crouching by her bag, now trying to close it. 'I used the paints you gave me, it's not perfect like, but…'

Arthur was speechless. He was holding a painting of Birch Tree Way. A tiny perfect replica of the familiar bricks, tiled roofs and neat windows in the cul-de-sac. Standing by the miniature front door of his house, in the exact same colour as his actual door, was an old man with tufty white hair, wearing glasses, a biscuit-brown cardigan and pressed brown trousers. Small blossoming rose bushes lined the neat path and the sky was a brilliant blue. Izzy's house had a tiny red pram near the door. A mini Mrs Peterson was holding onto a bright blue dog leash, looking as if she was being pulled along past Gary's house. Nikki had drawn herself, her sister and her parents in the individual windows.

'Do you like it?' she asked, her voice small and hopeful.

It took him a moment to take it all in. 'Very much.' Arthur nodded and patted in his trouser pocket for a handkerchief to dab at his eyes.

A look of relief fell across Nikki's bare face. 'Like I said, it's not perfect but—'

'It's perfect to me. Thank you.' He swallowed as she straightened up and shrugged her backpack back on.

'It's nothing,' she scuffed a boot into the tufts of grass. 'Good luck and all that.' She jogged away before Arthur could say any more.

Before long it was time to go. The journey to Cedar Lodge had been full of noise. Izzy and Jeremy were making polite small talk, commenting on what a lovely day it was, pointing out the nearby shops and the small park around the corner. Arthur nodded along, half listening to them, Nikki's painting tucked into a carrier bag by his feet.

Michelle had welcomed them with the same genuine warmth she'd shown the last time they'd met. It felt like he was moving into a lovely four-star hotel. His flat consisted of an open-plan lounge diner, a spacious bedroom with an en suite shower room, and a small plot of land through the double doors opposite the comfortable sofa. It was clean, light and very tastefully decorated. Impersonal enough for him to put his own stamp on it, like Kevin the estate agent would say, but cosy enough that it felt inviting. Jeremy followed her out to look over the final paperwork Arthur needed to sign, leaving Izzy and Arthur standing alone.

'How are you doing?' Izzy asked, shifting on her feet as if unsure where to put herself.

'Fine. A little overwhelmed,' he replied, 'but fine.'

'Well that's natural. It'll take you a day or two to find your feet and get to know where everything is I guess. Before you know it you'll have your own routine, I'm sure.'

Arthur nodded. He stared out of the large double-glazed window that looked onto a patch of freshly mowed grass, neat rows of lavender bushes and a bird bath where a small blue tit was ruffling its feathers.

'I got you a little moving-in present.' She handed him a neatly wrapped box.

'You didn't need to do that,' Arthur tutted good-naturedly, tearing open the colourful paper. 'Well now, would you look at that!' He smiled, lifting out a copper-coloured photo frame containing a snapshot of him and Evie, taken on their swimming trip. He remembered feeling taken aback by how light she was, how precious it had been for Izzy to trust him holding her.

'Just so you don't forget us.'

'Thank you. You know there's no chance of that.' Arthur gently rubbed a thumb over the baby's gummy smile.

'Would you like me to help you unpack?' Izzy asked, pointing to the small suitcase he had brought with him. As soon as Jeremy had learnt what had happened with *Tony*: *Happy to Help*, he had taken Arthur shopping and before he knew it he had a brand-new suitcase full of clothes with tags on, fancy toiletries and a very smart mobile telephone. His nephew had already shown him how to use it twice, instructing him to have it on him at all times, but Arthur had insisted he wouldn't need to call for help again.

'No thank you, dear. If you don't mind I'd rather do it myself in a little while.'

'Sure! Of course,' Izzy said, closing the large empty wardrobe doors. 'Oh, well, there is one thing I wondered if I could help you with…Where do you want this?'

Arthur saw a flash of polished silver as she lifted his swimming trophy from her own bag.

Izzy spoke before Arthur could. 'I've had it properly cleaned, it's got a real shine to it now! And before you tell me off for not

370

getting rid of it like you asked,' she bit her lip, 'I couldn't bear for you to do that. This belongs to be on show, for all to see.'

She gently placed the gleaming trophy next to Nikki's painting and the framed photo of Evie that Arthur had propped up on top of the empty bookcase. Izzy had her hands on her hips and a wry smile on her face. 'There! It looks great. Don't you agree?'

'There's something missing...' Arthur said, unzipping his suitcase that was resting on his bed. He pulled out the plastic bag of valuables that lay on top of his fresh new clothes. Inside were the collection of framed photographs that had lived on his mantelpiece. He swallowed the lump that had risen at the sight of Pearl's face. The anniversary of her death was tomorrow. He was planning on spending the day getting to know his new surroundings with Joan as his enthusiastic tour guide. Of course he would also make sure there was time for a moment of quiet contemplation of his wonderful wife. A woman who had kept him on his toes and surprised him in death, as in life. But he had lots to keep himself busy to try and teach this old dog some new tricks.

'There,' he said, placing each one along the shelf, stepping back to admire it all. His past, his love, his future. For the first time, in a long time, he had things to look forward to and people that he enjoyed spending time with. Yes, he thought, this really felt like home.

Author's Note

If you have been affected by any of the issues in this story then please don't think you have to cope on your own. Whether you're concerned about yourself or a loved one, these charities, organisations and support groups can offer expert advice:

The Samaritans offer confidential support for people experiencing feelings of distress or despair.
Helpline: 116 123 (free 24-hour helpline)
Website: samaritans.org

The National Childbirth Trust understands that becoming a parent is a life-enhancing experience, but it can also be challenging.
Helpline: 0300 330 0700
Website: nct.org.uk

Mind provides advice and support to empower anyone experiencing a mental health problem.
Helpline: 0300 123 3393 (Mon–Fri 9–6pm)
Website: mind.org.uk

The Pandas Foundation covers all mental health problems associated with pregnancy, birth and beyond.
Helpline: 0808 1961 776 (daily 11am–10pm)
Website: www.pandasfoundation.org.uk

Age UK is a service for older people, their families, friends, carers and professionals.
Helpline: 0800 678 1602 (daily 8am–7pm)
Website: ageuk.org.uk

Acknowledgements

To my children and my husband, thank you for everything. I don't take this life of ours for granted. It's not always easy but it is always worth it.

Thanks and gratitude to my editor Katie Seaman for her invaluable 'pushing' and unshakeable belief in Izzy and Arthur, to Clio Cornish for her advice in the early drafts and all at HQ for their tireless hard work backstage.

To Juliet and Liza at Mushens Entertainment, you are a powerhouse of wonderfulness, there's no other team I'd rather be on.

Thank you to my gorgeous family and friends for their never-ending encouragement and support. You know who you are. Big love to the Bookcamp crew. A special shoutout in particular to Matthew and Zuzanna Henshaw. And to Laura Hughes for brainstorming with me in Zizzi's – what must the other tables have thought!

Thank you also to the dedicated book bloggers, book sellers and book worms out there. Keep shouting loud and proud about brilliant books!

And finally a huge thank you to you – the reader. By buying my books you allow me to live my dreams and for that I am eternally grateful. Please consider leaving a review as they make a big difference. Please tag me in on social media (@ notwedordead). I would love to hear from you.

If you enjoyed *The Best Is Yet to Come*,
make sure you've read the emotional and
uplifting *How to Say Goodbye*

No one is ever happy to see Grace Salmon.

As a funeral arranger, she's responsible for steering strangers through the hardest day of their lives. It's not a task many would want – but, for Grace, giving people the chance to say a proper goodbye to the ones they love is the most important job in the world.

From the flowers in the church to the drinks served at the wake, Grace knows it's the personal touches that count – and it's amazing what you can find out about someone from their grieving relatives... or their Facebook page. But when she accidentally finds out too much about someone who's died, Grace is finally forced to step out of the shadows... and start living.